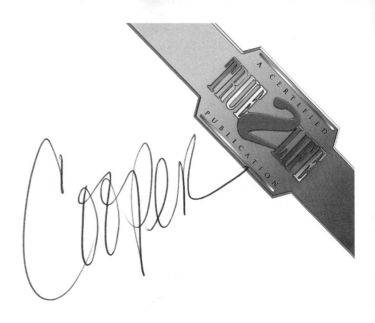

BACK 2 BIZNESS
THE RETURN OF THE MAYOR

by

Al-Saadiq Banks

BACK 2 BIZNESS
THE RETURN OF THE MAYOR

by
Al-Saadiq Banks

For information contact:
True 2 Life Publications
P.O. Box 8722
Newark, N.J. 07108

Website: www.True2LifeProductions.com
Author's E-mail: Alsaadiqbanks@aol.com

ISBN: 0-974-0610-7-7

"Don't look at me when I'm down…watch how I get up!"

–*Boulder from Orange St.*

May 31, 2009

Extreme silence fills the courtroom. Every single person sits with anticipation, awaiting the judge's verdict. Most have hopes of hearing a not guilty verdict but there are a few who are hoping for the total opposite.

It appears as if the judge's mouth is opening in slow motion. He drops his head low, before turning away from the spectators. "Not guilty," he whispers with disgust as he stares at the jurors who have all voted in favor of the defendant. The judge's ice cold look rips through the jurors' eyes one by one.

Loud cheering and applauding fills the courtroom. Attorney Angelique Reed loses her cool demeanor as she jumps out of her seat, damn near hitting the ceiling. "Yes," she blurts out loudly. As she locks eyes with the judge, she quickly regains control of herself. She ruffles the collar on her blazer as she looks over to her client, who sits there cool and calm. "I did it," she whispers as she grabs hold of his hand. "Yes!" This is the highest profile case that she has ever had to deal with in all of her ten year career. She realizes that winning this case will place her on another plateau. She believes there is no way left for her career to go but up after this victory. "I fucking did it!"

"Why wouldn't you?" the Mayor asks as he rises up from his seat slowly.

"A free man you are," she says with a bright smile. "Let's blow this joint," she says as she escorts him from behind the mahogany desk.

Nervousness quickly fills the Mayor's heart. He peeks back at the judge, awaiting some type of response but there is none. Signs of agitation are all over his face though. The quivering of his lips lets everyone know how furious he is.

A tapping on the Mayor's shoulder snatches his attention away from the judge. "Congratulations," says the beautiful woman.

"Thank you," he replies as he continues on his way. The people who are standing in the aisle are just happy to lay their hands on him. He looks around at all the Free the Mayor t-shirts that are being worn by many of the people who are in the courtroom. He arrogantly accepts the praise like the ghetto celebrity that he is. He peeks around discreetly, looking for his least favorite people in the entire world. Blended right into the crowd in the far right corner of the room there he finds the Federal Agent that's known to him as Dumber. The Mayor and the agent lock eyes momentarily before the agent's lips utter softly, the words, 'dumb ass nigga.' The Mayor winks arrogantly in reply.

He steps casually through the doorway. He can't help but wonder where the agent's partner is. Never has he seen them apart so that sets off his curiosity.

Minutes Later

After signing his John Hancock on a few documents, the Mayor is about to go on his quest for freedom. As he approaches the last door his heart thumps in his chest. He can't actually believe that his freedom is only a few steps away. He never actually believed this day would ever come. He's dreamed about it hundreds of times and now it's actually here.

He owes all the thanks to his main man and attorney, Tony Austin. He bears witness that it would not have been possible without him. The Mayor hasn't seen or heard from Tony in close to three years now. Even after being fired, Tony remained on the case. He couldn't represent him but he coached Angelique into victory.

The Mayor holds the door open for Angelique to exit. "No," you go first," she insists. "Freedom is new to you. What has it been ten or eleven years? It's my pleasure," she says as she snatches the door from him.

He steps through the doorway and takes two giant steps before standing still and inhaling a deep breath of the polluted air that he has grown to appreciate after breathing in central air year round for so many years now. He exhales slowly.

A dark tinted Cadillac truck pulls smoothly up to the curb. The Mayor pays close attention to the Maryland commercial license plates. Angelique takes the lead by stepping toward the backseat of the truck. She snatches the back door open before opening up the passenger's door as well. "Come on," she whispers as she nods her head toward the backseat. "Get in," she says as she gets into the truck and slams the door shut.

The Mayor slides into the backseat of the truck. At his entrance the pungent odor of cigar smoke snatches his breath away.

He coughs violently as he looks to his left. In no way is he surprised to see who is sitting behind the thick clouds of smoke.

Attorney Tony Austin blows a few smoke rings into the air before speaking. "Welcome home," he whispers as he extends his hand for a handshake.

The Mayor slowly extends his hand. He tries to retain his cool demeanor but deep inside he's extremely happy to see his main man. "What's the deal?" he asks as he looks into Tony's eyes. For the first time ever he sees a look in them that he's never seen before. The look of defeat he has in his eyes is the same look that was present on the day he fired him in court. Bags lie underneath Tony's eyes, looking as if he hasn't slept in weeks. The Mayor can't help but wonder what's going on with him. "You ok? How is life treating you?" he asks with a look of major concern on his face.

"Ah," Tony replies. "It's a lil tough but I guess it's fair."

The Mayor nods his head in reply. His modest reply confirms the fact that something must be bothering him. "I can dig it," he says as he looks away and stares straight ahead. He can't even stand the sight of the look that he sees in Tony's eyes.

"I told you it could be done," Tony brags with a false sense of arrogance. The way that he's speaking is so unlike him. "Took me a minute but you here," he smiles. "Now for the hardest part of all... keeping you out here," he says with a solemn look on his face.

The Mayor looks over at him for a few seconds before replying. "Let me worry about that."

"Are you worried?" Tony asks sarcastically.

"Not at all. Why would I be?"

"Why would you be? Good question. You just spent over ten years of your life in prison. It can only get worse. Good enough answer for you?"

The Mayor shrugs his shoulders. "Shit happens but failure leads to success."

"Or it can lead to terminal failure. Who knows?"

"No one...I guess. But you gotta be in it to win it. After all these years in my presence I see you still don't know me huh? Don't you know I'm not afraid to lose? I play hard," he grunts. "With that being said only one of two things can happen. Either I'm going to win hard or I'm going to lose hard. I'm mentally prepared for either," he smiles arrogantly.

Tony smiles back in return. "If I didn't know any better, I

would think that you are entertaining the thought of returning back to the bullshit."

"Well, it's obvious that you don't know any better."

"You gotta be bullshitting me?"

"Have I ever bullshitted you?"

"I spent day and night for ten years trying to get you back out here and you telling me all that hard work was in vain?"

"In vain? Nah. It wasn't in vain. You got paid well to do it. You provided a service and I paid you for it. Representing and defending criminals is your job right? And I got my job. Tony, you my man. No disrespect but I don't tell you how to do your job. You tell me what has to be done and I sit back quietly while you do what you do, how you do it. I don't question anything. There have been times that I disagreed with certain moves that you made but at the end of the day, I said nothing. I just sat back and let you do your thing. All I ask is that you do the same. Let me do mines how I do it."

Tony raises his hands high in the air. "You like a lil brother to me. Pardon me for caring."

"I don't pay you to care. I pay you to defend me. You're pardoned though," he adds as he looks away.

"Come on lil bruh, just pump your brakes a little."

"Pump my brakes? I been stuck on the side of the road for over ten summers. How much pumping you want me to do?"

"A lotta shit has changed. Mufuckers ain't standing up no more. The whole fucking city telling on each other. Who you gone trust?"

"Me," he interrupts. "I never trusted anyone from the get go. In the back of my mind I already think everybody gone tell. They all got a breaking point. When a mufucker get those silver metal bracelets on his wrist and his life flashes before his eyes he gone do whatever it takes to save himself. I already know this."

"So why are you willing to even take the chance?" Tony asks.

"Cause I'm a hustler and that's what hustlers do," he says arrogantly. "Take chances. I started hustling when I was twelve years old. This is all I know. It's embedded in my heart. It's a part of my soul. I'm not addicted to this as some may think. I am this. You can put me in prison forever and it's still gone be a part of who I am. Nothing can change that."

Tony is at a loss for words. All he can do is shrug his

shoulders. Seconds pass and they both sit in silence. "I don't understand it and I don't like it...but I respect it," Tony claims.

"As you should," he says accompanied by a head nod. "Look, I'm glad to be here and I thank you for making it possible."

"Do you really?" Tony interrupts.

"Indeed I do. Listen, I know we haven't seen each other in a minute. We have a lot of catching up to do and we will catch up but just not right now. I hate to end this reunion but I'm pressed for time, feel me? I have places to go and people to see. So, if ya'll could just get me on my way I would really appreciate it. Gotta get back to bizness."

Tony looks at the Mayor with disgust. He rolls his eyes away from him. "Driver, let's go."

The driver does just as he's instructed and pulls off slowly.

"To the airport," Angelique utters.

A half a block behind

A metallic colored Impala with smoke grey tinted windows pulls off slowly.

"Careful, careful, not too close," says the Federal Agent that's known to the Mayor as Agent Dumbest.

Just as the Mayor figured, they were not too far away from each other. Never did he once think that they were on the outside waiting for him though.

From the passenger's seat, Agent Dumbest snaps away with his digital camera. He must have taken at least twenty shots already starting at the time the Mayor and Angelique stepped out of the courthouse. "That prick you just saw is the smartest, dumb motherfucker in all the land. He's gonna slip up and guess what? We're going to be right there to catch him. He may have gotten away this time but never again will that happen," he says as he looks over to his driver.

In the driver's seat there sits the newest addition to their team. The thirty year old, black male is the perfect decoy. His slick talk, cool demeanor and street knowledge make it quite easy to camouflage himself amongst any group of hustlers.

This man is in no way a Federal Agent. He's a Federal Informant. He's been working side by side with the Feds on a few cases for over two years now. In such a short time period he's been able to bring in three major crews and a host of low level street hustlers.

When he was arrested a few years ago he was offered the opportunity to prevent himself from going to prison forever. In return he had to roll over on his own connect and his co-defendants. He foolishly thought it was a one shot deal but the Feds had other plans for him. They have been using him ever since.

This man's actual government name is Lance Hall but he has been attached to three different aliases already. He's gone from Michael Stafford to Richard Jennings to Sean Barnes in which he's going by in this case. In each situation the Feds have given him a new profile and job detail but each goal has been the same. So far he has successfully infiltrated each of the target crews.

"This fucker is so smart that he's stupid. His arrogance is what will get him caught. He's always felt invincible and now after this I'm sure he will feel even more untouchable. We're going to finish his black ass off this time. You know how, Sean?" he says as he looks over to the driver who looks at him attentively.

"With you. You are just the bait that we need to reel this dumb fucker in," he says as he nods his head up and down with a smirk on his face. "His ego will cause him to fall face first into our laps. That I'm sure of."

Hours Later in Washington D.C.

Dre sits laid back in the plush velour recliner as he pays close attention to Angelique. He doesn't want to miss a single word. The moment she hit the door, he attacked her with question after question.

"Babe, please let me shower first," she whines. "I will tell you all about it. The long flight drained me," she says as she's stripping herself of her clothing.

"Ok, but what was he saying though? Was he happy to be free?"

"Babe, you know your brother. It's hard to read him. He sat there, showing no emotion just as he always does."

"But what did he say though?"

"He thanked me and that was it."

"What about Tony? What did he have to say to Tony?" Dre notices a saddened look plastering over her face. She's not able to look him in the eyes so therefore she looks away. "What did he say?"

"Babe, I was sitting in the front seat. I couldn't hear it all."

"Well, tell me what you heard," he insists.

"All I heard was…."

"Was what?"

"All I heard was him saying something about he's a hustler and nothing can change that. Then he was like, drop him off at the airport because he has places to go and people to see. It's back to business."

Dre sits there with a shocked expression on his face. "Damn, already! Stupid motherfucker. Damn. I gotta get at this nigga before it's too late. Once he get started I'm not gone be able to stop him," he says frantically.

"Dre, you know that's not a good idea. You can't go anywhere near him. It's not wise to resurface just yet. I'm sure the Feds are going to be watching his every move. It's not time yet, baby. Please, not yet," she begs. "You go near him and you take the risk of them realizing who you are."

Dre shakes his head from side to side. "I know but I gotta do something. I'm the only one that can talk some sense into his fucking head. He's not gonna listen to nobody else."

"Please, just think about the possibilities first," she says with sadness in her eyes.

"It's already thought about. I been laying back for over two years now. I have to get at him. Anyway, I can't hide down here forever. I don't know how I'm going to get to him but I have to come up with something."

Meanwhile in Watchung, N.J.

Attorney Tony Austin sits back in his favorite chair in the living room of his luxurious home. He skims over the Wall Street Journal, peeking back and forth at his wife, Mocha as she's stuffing items into the small suitcase.

She's been storming from room to room for the past hour without either of them saying a word to the other. Every time she walks past him he blows a long train of smoke in her face, from his cigar. He knows just how much she hates for him to smoke inside the house, which is the reason why he's doing it. Deep inside Tony hates the dilemma that they're going through but he's gotten quite accustomed to it. This nightmare has been their reality for some time now. There hasn't been any peace in this house for the past four months now and Tony hasn't a clue of why.

The friction initially started with petty arguments about literally nothing. Lately she's been complaining about every little thing that he does. At first he would attempt to sit her down and try to get her to tell him what the problem was. After getting no answer from her ever, his ego kicked in causing him to shut down as well. That only made matters worse. Before he knew it, they would have gone days without speaking to each other behind the smallest argument. Days eventually turned to weeks.

Today marks the fifteenth day that they have not spoken to each other. Two hours ago she complained to him about leaving the toilet seat up and all hell broke loose. They both have said some things to each other that enemies wouldn't say to each other.

Mocha snatches her suitcase from the table and starts walking toward the door. Tony watches with no emotion. Just as she gets close to him he blows yet another cloud of smoke into her face. "Stupid ass," she mumbles.

Just as she's approaching the door, Tony finally speaks. "Miss, before you step out of that door, just know that you're leaving without an option. There's no option of you ever coming back here. Outside of that door is the point of no return. We've been through it all, yet neither one of us has ever left the house. We ain't been doing it and we ain't gone start. You already know that I have a no-spending-the night- outside of the house rule. If it ain't vacation or business, we here. We deal with all ours right here in this house. At the **big table**," he adds. "You leave and you go against everything. Therefore, you will leave me with no other choice but to do what I gotta do," he says in a cocky manner.

Mocha continues on her way as if he hasn't said a word. Her mind is made up and nothing he can say can change it. Two steps away from the door, Tony speaks again. "Ok, it's your decision. Don't say I didn't warn you," he smirks in an arrogant manner.

She snatches the door open wide and steps one foot out. Tony jumps out of his seat and charges her like a raging bull. He reaches her just as she's stepping out onto the porch. He grabs her by her forearm. "Mocha, wait," he says as humble as he possibly can. "Please?" he begs.

She snatches away from him. "Get off me." He ignores her totally and he grabs her with an even tighter grip. She tries to pull away but he has her overpowered. He uses his free hand to tug away at her suitcase. "Get the fuck off me," she barks.

"Baby, please. What is this all about? Look at this. You're leaving the house. Is this what it has come down to? Six years and we can't even squabble without you threatening to leave?"

"Threatening? I ain't threatening," she says in a sassy manner.

"So, you really leaving?" he asks with pity in his eyes. "For four months we been going through this. One hundred and twenty days," he adds. "Why though?"

She looks deep into his eyes. "Tony, we got problems."

"Yeah, all married couples got problems but you don't just leave. You work them out. Please, just tell me what I can do to fix them," he says as his eyes become glassy. Mocha sees his eyes starting to water and hers become glassy as well. He embraces her tightly as she stands there as stiff as a statue. She's not being receptive at all. "What's the problem?" he whispers into her ear. "You don't love me no more?" She doesn't reply. "Huh, baby?" he asks before planting a passionate kiss on her ear. Right now he's desperate. He knows how weak she is for kisses on her ear. He's praying that it doesn't fail him. He knows that if he can get her in the bed right now and make passionate love to her everything will be alright….at least for the moment.

He plants another kiss on her ear and she pulls away from him. "You don't love me no more?" he asks once again. Still no reply from her. He slowly loosens his grip on her as he steps back. "Mocha, answer me."

Tears drip down her eyes. She looks away from him.

"I'm gone ask you again. You don't love me no more?" he asks with uncertainty in his eyes.

She looks into his eyes once again. The tears drip from her eyes so rapidly that he becomes a wet blur. She stares at him with sorrow all over her face. "I love you but I'm not in love with you."

Tony's heart drops to the pit of his belly. He can't believe what he just heard. His mouth becomes salty as he stands there in a trance. His mouth opens but no words come out. He tries again and again. "Wh, what?" he stutters with a look of confusion on his face.

"I love you but I'm not in love with you," she repeats.

"What the fuck does that supposed to mean?"

"It means, I don't feel sparks when I see you like I used to. You know, that in love feeling?"

"We been together for six years. I don't feel no fucking sparks when I see you no more either but there is no question in my mind that I fucking love you and I'm in love with you. That's some fantasy island bullshit you on! You better get with the real world. Fucking sparks," he laughs furiously. "So you just willing to blow six good years over some fucking sparks? Baby, you gotta come better than that. You can't piss on me and tell me it's raining," he barks. "What is it, another nigga?"

She shakes her head from side to side . "No. Tony, I always told you I would leave you before I cheat on you."

"Yeah and you leaving before you cheat! So it's gotta be another nigga. Listen, I ain't no fool. Ain't no way in the fucking world you gone leave all this. You got everything and you leaving it for nothing? Somebody in your fucking ear. You better ask yourself is he worth it."

"Tony, there is no other nigga. I've fallen out of love with you."

"Bullshit," he interrupts. "That's straight bullshit. I don't believe this shit. You leaving me for a nigga?" He places both hands on his head and paces a few small circles. He's now enraged at the thought of this. "Who the fuck do you think you are? Better yet who the fuck do you think I am?" His arrogance is starting to kick in as a defense mechanism for his true feelings. "I should have left your raggedy ass in that raggedy ass project building you called home," he spits with vengeance.

"Yeah, you should have," she says in defense as she starts to walk down the steps.

"Wait, baby, please. I didn't mean that. Please," he begs. "Think about what you're doing. Please don't do this to me. I love you."

She reaches the bottom of the staircase and walks toward the front of the house where six cars are parked. It takes everything for Tony to refrain from chasing behind her, falling onto her feet and holding on for dear life. Instead, he watches as the love of his life hops into the BMW 5 Series.

She starts the car up and speeds off. Tony watches through glassy eyes as the car disappears.

June 14, 2009

For the entire two weeks that the Mayor has been home he has been spending his time getting use to being back. He's basically been home, spending time with his women and enjoying his freedom. Now that he's just about gotten that out of his system, he feels like it's time to get reacquainted with the streets. It kills him to admit how out of touch he really is. He could no longer fight the urge to get out here and get a feel of what's going on.

The Mayor sits behind the steering wheel of the snow white S550 Mercedes. He looks up at the sky through the glass top. Sky is the limit, he thinks to himself as the passenger babbles on and on.

"This right here is another one of our spots. With the right food," the young man says as he points to the surrounding area. "This block is capable of moving at least fifty to sixty bricks a day. You can pull off from here," he suggests.

Although the man in the passenger's seat and the Mayor are total strangers, the Mayor interacts with him like he's known him for years. This is their very first time ever laying eyes on each other. This man here is the Mayor's ears and eyes temporarily, until he gets back into the groove. He's also the Mayor's plug into the city. He's the first cousin to the gangster Blood leader Damien Bryant, known to the streets as the Black Charles Manson.

The Black Charles Manson is extremely grateful that the Mayor hired Tony to keep him alive. The motion to give him the lethal injection was denied but free he will never be.

Even while incarcerated he controls a great portion of the Bloods in the city. His presence is greatly respected but still he's not able to move the way he would like to, which is why he has appointed his cousin here as his representative. The 'G' status he has given him gives him all the power needed to rule and control. He passes the command down to his cousin and his cousin passes it down to the organization. The command Charles Manson gave was to work hand in hand, side by side with the Mayor to take control of the city.

The Mayor can't believe the condition of the city. He can't understand how the city has destructed like this. The entire place looks deserted. When he left each and every street corner was fluttered with drug dealers in search of a dollar. Thanks to Mayor

Corey Booker, that is no longer the case. He's managed to clean the streets up. The hood Mayor plans to make that job that much harder.

"Slow down, right here," the man instructs. "See those buildings right here," he says as he points to the right. "Lotta money out here. They good for about seventy bricks a day. They going hard. When I got it good, they buy it no problem. Crips run this though."

"Crips?" the Mayor asks with confusion. "Crips buy from you? I mean, you Blood right? I thought ya'll don't see eye to eye."

"I mean, that's how it supposed to be but for that dollar we get past the color. Red and blue makes green," he smiles. "Try it. Mix red paint with blue paint and it makes green," he chuckles goofily.

"Makes sense," the Mayor smiles. "Let me keep it real with you. This gangbanging shit…I ain't with it. To me, it's the goofiest shit in the world. I can't believe I'm even considering fucking with ya'll. It's like Tabu to me but it's what's happening now. I'm like a chameleon so I have no problem adapting to the times. If it makes dollars it makes sense. Follow my lead and we gone make a lotta money. I'm gone show you how to turn wrong into right. I listened to you tell me how this block do fifty and that one does sixty a day and so forth and so on. I calculated about 600 bricks a day if it is what you say it is. I'm gone show you how to make those numbers triple. That's a lot of bread for us. I ain't no greedy nigga by far. I have no problem letting you eat off of my plate as long as you help me to prepare the food. When I eat, everybody around me eat. No soul goes hungry. The town fucked up in my eyes but I'm gone pump life back into it. One thing everybody know about me is, I'm gone get to a dollar, regardless. You heard?"

"I heard," he replies with hunger in his eyes. All you gotta do is tell me what you need us to do. You give us the mission and I will make sure every Blood in this city carries it out. I promise you we control eighty percent of this city."

"What about the other twenty percent?" the Mayor asks.

"You know, stragglers, Crips and old heads doing their own thing."

"So, you say twenty percent ain't with us, right?"

"Yeah, about that."

"Well they against us. There go your mission right there," the Mayor says as he makes the right turn. He stops short at the raggedy old Pontiac that's parked near the corner. "Now carry it out. You and your Blood homies clear the path and I'm gone show you how to get this paper."

"Enough said. Say no more," the man says as he opens the door and makes his exit.

The Mayor pulls off slowly. The only thing on his mind is the money that he's sure that he's about to make.

Tony stands in the Newark Superior Courthouse. He's already late, as usual. His tardiness is not by choice today though. For some reason he couldn't get it together this morning. Ever since Mocha left the house he has been dragging along.

His life without her has been a wreck. He lacks motivation. He's been walking around day and night in a blur. Not knowing exactly why she left makes it even worse. In no way is he buying the lame reason that she fed to him. Deep in his gut he feels like another man is somewhere in the picture.

He spends his nights just picturing her with another man. The sexual vision he pictures is enough to make him lose his mind. Just imagining her giving another man his love breaks his heart into pieces. The sound of her sexual moans play in his head over and over like a broken record.

He calls her every hour on the hour, hoping to deter her from being with another. Some calls she answers but most of the time he just gets her voicemail. He's begged her over and over to come back home but she refuses. He can hear the sound of agitation in her voice when she speaks to him but still that doesn't stop him from calling again.

The fact that she says that she's willing to work on their relationship gives him a little hope but the fact that she's said she feels that it's better to work on it away from each other scares him. He figures being away from each other will only make her fall more out of love with him.

He couldn't sleep a wink last night. He called her at least a hundred times and she didn't answer one call. He even called her mother's house where she's supposed to be staying. His last call to the house at 3 in the morning reassured him that she must have not stayed there.

He just has to call once more even though he doesn't believe that she will answer. He pulls out his phone, just as he reaches the double doors of the courtroom. His heart pounds rapidly as he dials her number. He listens with anxiety as the phone rings over and over again until he hears the sweet voices of the singing group Destiny's Child. He listens closely to the words to see what it is that Mocha may be trying to tell him. "If I don't pick up the phone like I used to, for you," singer Michelle sings. "Don't take it personal." He can't believe his ears. Kelly chimes in. "If I don't do all the things that I use to, for you. I ain't mad at you," she sings. Beyonce's voice slides in. "If you get to feeling stressed, up in your chest, thinking that you about to lose, baby it's true. And you're losing out on sleep." Michelle finishes off the verse. "Home worrying about me, ohhhhhh," she harmonizes before the beep sounds off. His heart weighs a ton after hearing this. It's as if she knows that she's broken his heart but still she's rubbing it in.

A lump fills his throat, making it hard for him to speak. "Yo, hit me," he whispers into the phone. "I been calling you all night. I'm worried about you," he claims. In all reality his only worry is her laying in the arms of another man.

He tucks his phone into the inside pocket of his suit jacket. He steps sluggishly into the courtroom. He drags along until he reaches his client. "Good morning your honor. I apologize for my tardiness."

"Yeah, yeah, yeah," the judge replies sarcastically.

Tony looks over to his client and greets him with a head nod before sitting next to him.

Nervousness covers the man's face yet he tries to look as cool and collective as he can. This man's life is on the line. He was referred to Tony two years ago after he was charged with a double homicide. Hearing and reading so much about Tony and his successful track record makes him totally confident in putting his life in Tony's hands.

Today they both will see what all the money and hard work is hitting for. Today is the last day of the two week trial. This has been the toughest trial for Tony. The situation with his wife is weighing down on his brain, making it hard for him to concentrate on his business. He knows that his home life should not interfere with his business but he just can't help it.

Hours Later

Recess is now over. The closing arguments from both sides have been made and the jury has reached their verdict. Tony hasn't been this nervous in years. His client sits on the edge of his seat with anxiety. He fumbles with his tie nervously.

The judge clears his throat, causing everyone to give him their undivided attention. He lifts the gavel into the air. "I hereby find the defendant guilty on two counts of first degree murder!" he shouts before banging the gavel.

The defendant slides off of his seat and tackles Tony like a football player. Tony is caught by total surprise. The man grabs hold of Tony's legs and lifts him high in the air before dumping him on his side.

The courtroom goes in an uproar. The bailiffs run over toward them. Tony lays on his back in shock as he looks up at the size twelve shoe coming close to his face. The bailiff gets to the man just in time and pulls him away. In seconds the man is surrounded by bailiffs, being handcuffed. Tony jumps up from the floor and rushes over toward the man with rage. He fires two power packed punches at the man, both landing on his chin. Still he feels like he hasn't gotten even with the man. He's steaming. He attempts to charge the man again, but the bailiffs manage to get the man out of his reach.

"Order in the court!" the judge shouts. "Order in the court!" A bailiff grabs Tony as well. Tony fights like hell to get away from their grip.

"You guaranteed me I was gone fucking walk!" the man shouts with fury. "Two hundred fucking thousand you took from me? I promise you, you ain't gone live your life while I'm in prison for the rest of mines!"

"Order in the court!"

"You fucked up!" the angry man shouts as he's being shoved out of the courtroom.

Tony stands there in awe at the entire situation. He plays it cool by adjusting his clothing. He hangs his head low. Never before has he been so humiliated.

"Counsel, you alright?" the judge asks.

"I'm good," he says arrogantly as he looks around the courtroom. His attention is caught by the group of at least twenty thugs that are standing in the far corner of the courtroom. These men have come here in support of the client. The anger on their faces can only mean trouble. Tony locks eyes with one man who is nodding his head up and down while mumbling something. Tony can't make out the words that he's saying. He just nods his head up and down in return. "I'm good," he sings.

"You're not good," the man says clearly.

The Next Day

The shabby shack in the backyard of the raggedy house is filled beyond capacity with about seventy Bloods. The crowd of young men spills into the backyard where another one hundred Bloods stand at full attention. Smoke, Charles Manson's cousin stands at the front of the shack on a milk crate.

His demeanor is laid back but his words are full of anger and aggression. The battery that the Mayor put in his back is fully charged and now it's his job to charge the rest of these young men up. "From here on out, nothing moves without going through us! Whoever ain't with us is against us! A bag of dope gets sold on a street corner, we want in! No more freelancing. No more stragglers! From here on out we eating off everybody plate! Whoever go against the program we mashing them out! Big bruh passed me the plug. Now we gone eat! We got enough dope on deck for all of us to get rich," he whispers. "Ain't no reason for nobody to be out here fucked up no more. We taking everything over! We gone tear this city up and rebuild it our way! Blood foundation," he says as he places both hands palm down, at his waist. "Blood in the middle," he says as he waves his hands at his eye level. "And of course, Blood on top," he says, reaching for the sky. "As we should be," he adds. "We gone turn this city into Blood Heaven. The Homies out West gone wish they had it like this!" he shouts. "We ain't got no time to waste. Time is money! The sooner we get these mufuckers out of the way, the sooner we get rich. It's time to eat. I'm hungry. Ya'll hungry right?" No one replies. "I can't hear ya'll! Ya'll hungry, right?"

"Yeah!" they all reply.

"I ain't convinced. I'm gone ask ya'll again. Ya'll hungry, right?"

"Yeah!" they shout much louder.

"Well, let's get it then! We gone rip through this city, leaving nothing standing. Remember, anybody who ain't with us, they what?" he asks.

"Against us!" they all shout in reply.

"Right," he smiles demonically. He can feel the energy charge ripping through the airwaves.

Meanwhile

The silver Impala sits in the back of the crowded parking lot. The passenger speaks. "Ok, ok, just as we figured," Agent Dumber speaks. "Knew he would be coming here to see his man sooner or later," he says as he aims his camera at the doorway. He adjusts the camera onto the Mayor who hops out of the white Mercedes Benz. The agent takes five quick pictures before the Mayor enters the building and disappears.

Sean, the informant sits in the backseat just watching the Mayor closely. Both of the two times that he's seen the Mayor, chills have run through his body. He realizes that he's dealing with a different type of dude. The other guys that he's brought in, some of them have been a little rough around the edges but not one of them were as ruthless as the Mayor. He's heard so many treacherous stories about the Mayor that he's afraid to even intertwine with him. Just knowing that one day he will have to attempt to make a move with him is enough to scare him to death.

Somehow he wishes he could get out of this one but he's sure his freedom pass will be revoked if he does. Knowing that, gives him no choice but to do what he's assigned to do.

The Mayor sits before the distraught looking Tony. On the table in front of Tony there lies the newspaper clipping with his picture on it. The reporter has reported details of yesterday's disaster. Tony has never been ridiculed like this. He's so humiliated that he's almost ashamed to show his face outside, let alone in a courtroom.

Yesterday's event is what has led the Mayor here to see Tony. "Dig this," he says. "I did the math on the young boy."

Tony looks up at the Mayor with curiosity in his eyes. "What did you find out?"

"I found out that he's a man of his word, for the most part. He does what he says he's going to do. His threat isn't to be taken lightly. True bill, he probably instructed his crew to get at you already."

"I ain't worried about them mufuckers!" Tony says with rage.

"But I am," the Mayor interrupts. "You my man and because of that I have to nip this shit in the bud before it becomes a problem for you. If it's a problem for you then it's a problem for me."

Tony knows exactly where the Mayor is thinking of taking this. "Nah, nah. Something happen to that boy and it's automatically coming back on me."

"But if something happen to you, it comes back on me. I gotta live with it. I can't afford to lose you. You not just an attorney to me. You're like my big brother. I already lost one. That was outta my control. I wasn't here. I will be got damn if I sit here, do nothing and watch you get taken from me."

Tony looks into his eyes and sees sorrow and sincerity. He figures right now would be the perfect time to tell the Mayor the truth about his brother Dre. The promise that he made to Dre and Angelique makes him keep his mouth shut. "You like a brother to me too. I don't need that type of trouble in my life. I got enough going on. Trust me, I will be alright. He was angry and was just lashing out. Please, just promise me that you're not going to do anything stupid?"

"Stupid? I never do anything stupid," he says with sarcasm.

"You know what I mean. Don't move on it. Promise me?"

The Mayor stares into Tony's eyes, with no emotion whatsoever. He doesn't utter a word.

"Promise me that, lil bruh?"

The Mayor shakes his head from side to side negatively. Tony, you my man. You know me. I never make a promise that I know I can't keep. Before I lie to you, I just won't say anything at all."

Later that Night

Three masked men stand in the darkness, outside the doorway of a small garage. Each of their hands grips a semiautomatic pistol. One man stands to the right side of the doorway, one stands to the left and the other stands in front of the door.

The man in the center feels the vibration from his phone ringing. He answers it quickly. "Yo," he whispers.

"Here I come, now," the caller on the other end informs.

"Cool," the masked gunman whispers before ending the call and tucking the phone inside his pants pocket. "Showtime," he says to his accomplices. They grip their guns tighter and prepare for the battle.

In seconds the steel door opens and a man steps out of the door. The two gunmen rush inside violently with their guns waving. The man in the center grabs hold of the man who appears to be attempting to make his exit. He shoves the man inside before him.

From the looks of it the man appears to be frightened but it's all an act. He's actually a part of what's going on. "Yo, yo," he screams, just to play it off.

"Everybody lay the fuck down!" All the men inside freeze in their positions, just staring at the doorway. Mounds and mounds of money are stacked in front of each of them. "Drop everything and lay the fuck down!" the gunman says as he shoves the man onto the floor. The other two gunmen run around the room crazily, shoving other men onto the floor. After all the men are laying in a close pile, the gunmen start their movie. "You move, you lose!" the man shouts as he waves his gun at the crowd. "Shake these mufuckers down! I swear to God ya'll better lay them pistols in a pile cause if I find one on you, I'm knocking your block off! I promise you that!"

In seconds a pile of pistols appear on the floor. One of the gunmen pulls out a duffel bag and starts dumping the guns inside. He slides the duffel bag full of guns over to the man at the door and immediately starts going through everybody's pockets. He's taking money, wallets and snatching every piece of jewelry that's visible. He drops everything in a separate duffel bag. He then makes his way around the room, grabbing the loose mounds of money that's lying around. When he's all done, he looks over to the gunman at the door and gives him a head nod.

The gunman at the door walks over to the pile of men who are all lying stiff. They're afraid to even breathe. Their hearts pump rapidly as they see the gunman coming toward them. They can only imagine what's next.

The gunman snatches a man from the center of the pile. He drags him onto his knees. The frightened man looks up to the gunman. "Come on, please," he pleads for his life.

"Please, what," the gunman replies with no compassion. "Please, what, mufucker?" he asks as he places the gun against the man's forehead. The gunman squeezes the trigger quickly. Boc! The victim's neck snaps backwards before he collapses flat on his stomach. The gunman then aims at the back of the man's head and fires. Boc! Boc! Boc! Boc! Blood gushes from three holes, as the man lies there as stiff as a board. All the other men watch with fear. All of them think that they are next. The gunman looks over to his accomplices. "Let's go!" he shouts. In seconds they're out of the garage, making their getaway.

This assignment was given from who else but the Mayor? This detail had nothing to do with his plan to take over the city. In no way was this business. It was all personal. The murder victim is the brother to Tony's client who made the threat to him in the courtroom.

The Mayor thought hard about what Tony said to him about everything falling back on him. Because he doesn't want to bring trouble to Tony, he decided to spare the man. He's sure he could have the man touched in the County Jail but he decided not to. Instead he plans to touch everybody around him. He figures if he squashes anybody that the man could get to get at Tony, Tony will be safe.

The murder victim is the younger brother to the man. After doing homework, the Mayor found out that this illegitimate gambling hall is the place that he could find him. He owns and operates the spot. This spot generates thousands and thousands every night. Two birds have been killed with one stone. The Mayor's target has been hit and his Blood hounds have been fed. One man down and at least ten more to go. The Mayor's goal of removing Tony out of harm's way is one step closer to being completed.

The Next Day

The Mayor is at one of his most favorite places in the world. He has had some of the most pleasurable times of his life here at this car dealership on Route 46, in Teterboro, New Jersey. It's like a dream come true for the Mayor to even be here again. He never thought it would be possible again. He's just grateful to be able to share yet another memorable experience.

As he stands here with his eyes fixed on the beautiful hunk of steel that sits before him he's almost ready to shed a tear. He anticipated the release of this vehicle probably more than anyone in the entire world. He just didn't believe that he would be free to witness it.

While he was incarcerated, he would dream of sitting behind the wheel of this beauty. He's fallen asleep a many of nights with pictures of it laying across his chest. Posters of this car have been plastered on the walls of his cell. He studied the Dupont Registry, Forbes Magazine and any other magazine that was blessed by this precious automobile. He can tell you the measurements and specifics of it off the top of his head.

"Damn," he sighs as he reaches his hand over to touch the car. His heart beats nervously. "I can't believe this," he says as he stares onto the eggshell white Maserati Tourismo. He gently rubs his hand over the hood and almost ejaculates on himself.

"Holy shit!" a voice shouts from behind the Mayor. His zone has been broken. "I know this isn't who I think it is."

The Mayor turns around quickly, staring directly onto the shiny bald head of the little stout man. The man grabs the Mayor and bear hugs him. "Handsome, I'm so happy to see you," he says with a deep Russian accent. "I thought you were never coming home? What happened?" he asks as he pulls away.

"What can I say, Rocco? They fucked up," he says with sarcasm.

"Look at you. You haven't aged a bit. What has it been, fifteen years?"

"Ah," he grunts. "Give or take a little," he says with a smile. "Ay man, just a long vacation for me. Now, I'm back, well rested and fully recharged."

"So, how long you been back home from vacation?" he smiles.
"Two weeks."

"Good, good. Now we have to keep you here. No more vacations, my friend."

"Indeed."

"What can I do for you? Anything, tell me?"

"You can start by giving me the keys to this joint, right here."

"One second," the man says as he rushes off.

Meanwhile in Newark

As Smoke creeps up the block in his Pontiac, he watches a group of men who are huddled along the sidewalk in the middle of the block. He pulls up a little past them and parks. "Come on," he says as he leads the way. The driver and the passenger door fly open simultaneously.

They both hop out and walk confidently toward the crowd of eight men. The men watch with baffled looks on their faces. They all are familiar with who these two men are but they're wondering why they're here. They ride through from time to time but never have they stepped foot onto the block. They have the feeling that something isn't right. The tension can be felt from many miles away. They can't believe that they have gotten caught slipping like this. Not one of them has a gun on them. Whatever these two men are up to, they are here, helpless, at their mercy.

"What up?" Smoke shouts as he reaches the crowd. No one replies. They all just keep their eyes glued onto him. They don't trust him one bit. "Damn, what up?" he smiles with arrogance. "Why ya'll all looking like that? I know ya'll like, damn, what the fuck he doing out here?" he smiles as he awaits a reply from one of them. "Ya'll looking like, ya'll wanna bust a move but ya'll thinking like...nah," he smiles. "We don't wanna do that," he chuckles. No one smiles in return. The looks in their eyes is stone cold. "Damn, lighten up. I ain't off my bullshit. That ain't why I'm here."

"Why you here for then?" one man asks in a calm demeanor. This man is known to the streets as Bills. Bills is what you call the last of a dying breed. At the young age of 38, Bills is considered to be an old head, on the streets. Outside of him there are only a couple of stand up dudes in their thirties and forties who are still around and relevant. The most of them are either cracked out, locked up in the

Feds forever or dead. The rest of them have given in to the system. In order to still move around the streets, they realize that they had no choice but to affiliate themselves with the young gangbangers in some form or fashion. If they are fortunate enough to have a few dollars, they feed the homies or supply them. If not they get up under the homies for protection.

Bills, on the other hand refuses to do any of the above. He just kind of does his own thing and always has. He operates this block, generating a dollar for himself. It's like he's here on his own little island, away from the world. The confusion and mayhem that partakes throughout the rest of the city doesn't affect him the least bit.

This block is run in an almost prehistoric manner. There are no freelancers or stragglers. There is only one Chief, who is Bills and the rest of the men are his Indians. The pitchers take their assigned shifts and they all take ten dollars off of every ten bags of dope they sell. All in all, everyone is content.

"Why am I here? It's funny that you ask. I like what you got going on out here. It's cute. Real cute," he adds. "It's like Bill's Island," he smiles. "Ya'll like away from the world, in the cut, you feel me? "Ya'll on some nineteen ninety five shit out here and by the looks of it, it's working for you. Like I said, ya'll in the cut, feel me? I just wanna bring ya'll to the forefront."

"Forefront? What you mean?" Bills asks with an agitated look on his face.

"We bringing everything together. Like everybody eating off the same plate. I wanna include ya'll in the cipher. I don't wanna leave ya'll on the outside. It's enough money out here for everybody."

"Together?" he laughs. "I'm good. I do me over here. I call the shots on this side and that shit you talking ain't even in the plans," he says with a smile.

"On the real, we off some get down or lay down type shit," he says with a stern look in his eyes.

Bills chuckles in his face as if he's a clown. "Ay man, dig this. I ain't getting down with shit ya'll got going on. I'm a man! I piss standing up. I ain't never layed down....not back in the day and not today either! Ask about me. Go home and ask your pops about me. I'm sure he heard of me. I came up with real killers...banged out with the best of them. Legends, you hear me. I ain't been around this long by accident, skating by. I been in the trenches for twenty motherfucking years. I always been respected. I will be got damn if I let some young niggas half my age dictate to me what I can and can't do!"

"Enough said...say no more," Smoke says as he turns away, giving Bills his back. He takes two slow steps before spinning around. Surprisingly, he's gripping a seventeen shot, nine millimeter. He has it aimed directly at Bills' head. Boc! Boc! Boc! Bills stumbles backwards before tumbling onto his back. The other men take off running. Smoke's accomplice takes off behind them. Bloc! Bloc! Bloc! Bloc! Bloc! Bloc! While the gunshots are sounding off rapidly, another set of shots sound off. Boc! Boc! Boc! Smoke stands over Bills and dumps three more shots into his lifeless body.

Smoke's accomplice continues to rip away until his clip is emptied. His aim is impeccable. Out of sixteen shots, only two were wasted. The other fourteen hit their marks.

Smoke and his man flee toward the Pontiac, and pull off. On the block they leave a total of three dead and four wounded. Not bad, for their first day of work.

Back in Teterboro

Rocco and the Mayor's wife, Liu Ching have finally managed to talk the Mayor out of the car. They damn near had to pry him out of the driver's seat. Now him and Liu are sitting side by side across the desk from Rocco.

"I gotta have that piece," the Mayor says with sincerity in his eyes.

"And I want you to have it," Rocco replies. "I can't think of a better man to have it. It's beautiful...has your name written all over it."

"I'm sure," the Mayor replies arrogantly. "So, what's the ticket on it?"

"Someone else...one fifty-five,"

"I ain't concerned with nobody else, never have been."

"For you...one forty after everything."

"Baby," Liu Ching whispers as she grips his hand. The look in her eyes is full of concern. "This car will only be trouble."

"Liu, please? This ain't trouble. You only talking about a hundred and fifty thousand. Any working class Joe Schmo can afford this. It ain't like it's the DropHead Coupe. That's four and a quarter.

Now, that's trouble. I'm thinking of doing that for my birthday," he smiles. "This good for now though."

"Baby, you're just getting home. You need not to buy anything. You should not be riding around here in a hundred and fifty thousand dollar car."

The owner sees what she's trying to do. She's trying to talk him out of a possible sale. He realizes he has to say something and quick. "It's a good thing you came in when you did. That baby was on her way off the lot. I have a kid from Brooklyn coming in for it today. He left a fifty thousand dollar deposit on it yesterday. He's coming back any minute now with the balance. He's going to be upset but what the hell. I will just have to sell him on something else. He wanted this Turismo so badly, though. Probably won't be another one of these around for at least six months."

"Let's start the paperwork up then before he get back," the Mayor smiles. "Hurry."

Rocco shoves a stack of paperwork over to the Mayor. "The same way?" Rocco asks.

The Mayor slides it over to Liu. "As always."

"Ok, this is the deal. Eight thousand, I'm reporting that you put down," he says as he punches the keys on his calculator. "Twenty-two hundred a month for five years. That's one thirty two. Let's say six years to cover your interest rate, gas guzzler tax and luxury tax. Six years from now...on paper, this baby is all yours. But we all know it's yours already. Bill of sales in hand when you pull off," he says with a smile.

The Mayor nods his head up and down, smiling in return. He trusts Rocco wholeheartedly. During his trial back in 2001, Rocco was brought in to testify against the Mayor for tax evasion charges but he didn't say a word. Even after threatening to give him five years for perjury, he still stood his ground. He infuriated the Feds so badly that they later offered to deduct some of the Mayor's time if he admitted that he bought cars cash money from Rocco that wasn't reported. Needless to say, they both held their ground.

"Rocco, before I take it off the lot have your men strip it down. Take those goofy ass chrome rims off. Put the factories back on."

"Why Handsome? She's beautiful just the way she is."

"Rocco, I'm almost thirty one years old. I'm off my grown man shit," he smiles. "And strip that dark ass tint off the windows.

Straight fishbowl baby. I want these mufuckers to see my face. Daddy's home!" The excitement can be seen in his eyes.

"Baby, why do you need a hundred and fifty thousand dollar car? We got three cars. Why can't you use one of those to get around in?"

"Baby, this ain't no car. This is an automobile. Anyway, they're yours. I bought them for you. You tell me what you want and I get it. No questions asked. Now I want something and you questioning me about it? I need and want a car of my own. I been gone for over ten years. I deserve a coming home present, don't I? Hand me the pocketbook, please?" he says as he grabs hold of the Gucci bag that's sitting on her lap. He unzips it and dumps the contents onto the desk.

"Baby, you know they're going to be watching you."

"Ok, now they have something nice to look at. Fill out the papers, will you?" he asks as he sifts through the stacks of money. Altogether there are 25 stacks. Each one is held together by a rubber band. Each stack consists of a hundred, one hundred dollar bills. He quickly snatches ten stacks away from the pile, before shoving the other fifteen over to Rocco.

"Wow," says Rocco. "Haven't seen these in a while, he says referring to the old hundred dollar bills. He flicks through the bills and makes notice that not only is each bill outdated, they're a dingy and greenish yellow color. The government has created new bills twice since these particular bills.

"Yeah, I'm sure you haven't. I got them all," he says with arrogance. "That's that early nineties money. Rocco, your boy got old, old money. "All those bills probably in my possession. I just may be the reason they made the new ones. I been holding them up. There are a lot more where those came from," he smiles. "Now that I'm home, I'm gone put those babies back into circulation. I'm gone spend everyone of those that I got. Then I'm gone spend the ones they made before this, the first big face joints they made in '99. Then I'm gone start spending the portrait joints from 2006 to now. Just with me circulating my old money back into the land, I'm gone change mufuckers financial situations. Corner stores, malls, car dealerships owners, they all gone thank me. I'm home baby. The recession is now officially over! With Obama on that side of the game and me on this side, shit gonna start looking up for us."

12 Midnight

Tony paces throughout his house with his ear glued to the phone. He's been calling Mocha for the past hour and a half, getting no response. Each time he hears her voicemail he gets more and more furious. He just imagines her in the company of another man, just watching his name on her screen and simply ignoring him.

He's starting to recognize her pattern. He can reach her the majority of the time throughout the day but at night he can't get her to answer his call. When he speaks to her in the morning, she always has some lame excuse for him. Either her battery died from him calling or she fell asleep early. All in all he's sick and tired of her and her excuses.

He dials once again and on the second ring the voicemail comes on. He gets the feeling that she has pressed ignore. He dials again and this time the voicemail comes on after the third ring. This enrages him. He tosses the phone onto the sofa with anger. "You stinking ass bitch," he whispers to himself.

He falls onto the recliner, grabbing hold of the remote before he lands. He aims the remote at his stereo system and in seconds music fills the air. "Damn girl, why'd you leave me like that?" singer Charlie Wilson sings in his raspy voice. "Whatever I said, I didn't mean like that. How you expect for me not to fight back, when you scream like that? Girl, I love you more than that!"

This has been Tony's theme song since Mocha left. He plays it over and over just sulking in misery. He joins Charlie Wilson in singing the next verse. "I can't forgive myself if I hurt you girl!" he shouts. "What do I do?" he whines. "I can't live without you...I can't live without you. And girl it breaks my heart if I broke your heart. What do I do?" he sings as he drops his head into the palms of his hands with pity.

Meanwhile In Newark

A group of twelve men stand crowded around the porch of the abandoned house. Bottles of Grey Goose Vodka are lined up on the porch like a bar. The men have been out here smoking weed and drinking for hours as they do every night. The little money that they have hustled up all day, they blow just to enjoy themselves at night.

Tonight they have company. A truck full of young beautiful women sit parked in front of the house with the music blasting. They scream from the window of the truck as the men entertain them. Suddenly the sound of a motorcycle can be heard in the distance. The closer the motorcycle gets to them the louder it gets. Finally the motorcycle reaches the middle of the block where the group of people stand. As the motorcycle slows down, everyone takes notice of it.

The driver of the motorcycle sits glued to the bike, gripping the handlebars tightly. The passenger on the backseat sits upright firmly. His face is covered by a red bandana. He lifts his right hand into the air. Through the darkness his chrome handgun is highly visible.

"Oh shit!" one man shouts, stealing everyone's attention. "Watch out!" the man yells before ducking low. He's seconds too late. Pop! Pop! The man fires recklessly. Pop! Pop! Glass shatters from the Yukon Denali's window. The girls begin screaming at the top of their lungs. The driver's screams are cut short as her head plunges into the already shattered windshield.

The shots continue to sound off. Pop! Pop! Pop! The young men attempt to flee but some of their luck cards have expired. Instead of getting away, they fall onto the ground. Pop! Pop! Pop! Pop! After the last shot the loud rumble of the motorcycle sounds off as the driver speeds up the block.

The block looks like a Warfield. A few men lie sprawled on the concrete while some have been fortunate enough to get away. The girl in the backseat of the Denali lifts her head up slowly only to find her two best friends both dead. Her heart pumps with fear. She tries to escape the vehicle but the bullet that's lodged into her hip makes it difficult. She whimpers with pain as she slides across the seat. She forces the door open and literally crawls out.

Minutes Later

The motorcycle zips into the garage. Both men hop off and quickly run over to the gate to close it. Their adrenaline is still racing. The driver pulls his cell phone from his pocket and starts dialing. He tries to slow down his breathing as he awaits an answer on the other end.

"Yo!" the man shouts from the other end of the phone.

"You already know," the man whispers as he tosses his helmet into the corner. He quickly ends the call and tucks the phone into his pocket.

Their mission has been completed. This was another assignment from Smoke. That particular block was run by Bloods but they are not under the same sect as Smoke. In fact they are rivals who can never seem to see eye to eye which makes Smoke quite sure that they will never cooperate with his plan. Knowing that left him no alternative but to move them out of his way. He's sure one shooting will not do it so he plans to go through there everyday until he's killed everyone or they're just to afraid to step foot out there. One way or another he has to have this block and he plans to do whatever it takes to get control of it.

3 a.m.

Tony sits on the dark block in his car. He watches closely as every car passes him. He looks at his watch and sees that he's been sitting here for two hours. His anxiety makes it seem as if the time is creeping by.

After his series of calls to Mocha he decided to drive to her mom's house. To no surprise at all there was no sign of Mocha's car on the entire block. His intentions were to drive through to see if she was there. After seeing that she wasn't he decided to stay and see just what time she does come in.

One thing for sure is she can't use the excuse that she was sleeping and didn't hear his call. She could easily be sleeping, just not here. That gives him all the reason to believe that she is and has been spending her nights sleeping with another man.

Tony sits here with his heart and mind racing. He can't shake away the crazy thoughts and visions that he's having. If only she would pull up right now his mind would be at ease. It wouldn't stop the ideas of where she could have been but it would ease his mind for the moment.

A Jeep Cherokee slows down as it nears Mocha's mom's house. Tony sits up in his seat. He can't see who is inside due to the dark tinted windows. His heart pumps with anxiety.

He grabs hold of the gun that lies in his waistband and lays it on his lap. The door opens and a female's foot dangles from the jeep. Tony pushes his door open and sticks his own leg out before he realizes that the woman isn't Mocha. The young girl hops out of the jeep and runs to the house next door.

Tony slides inside the car embarrassingly and closes the door shut. He shakes his head from side to side. He looks at the gun on his lap and wonders what he would have done if that was Mocha in the car with another man. This whole situation is driving him crazy. He can't believe that he's reacting like this. He can't believe that she has this much control over his mind.

When he left the house hours ago coming to Newark, he brought his gun along, telling himself it was for his defense just in case he accidentally ran into his client's family members. The threat that was made to him has him slightly paranoid but deep down inside he doesn't know if the gun is for his defense or if he's really planning to use it for the attack against whoever it is that is ruining his life by taking his wife from him.

Headlights appear at the corner of the block. Tony rises up in his seat once again. He watches closely as the car speeds past the house. He bangs his head against the headrest. "Damn! I gotta get myself together."

Not even twelve hours later and Smoke is in the middle of another one of his episodes. It's broad daylight and the narrow block is packed. Children are playing, running up and down the street while their parents barely supervise them from porches.

Smoke stands at the corner, peeking around attentively. His focal point is the two men who are leaning on a car a few feet away, puffing on a blunt. He's just waiting for the perfect time to make his move. "Let's go," he says to his accomplice who immediately follows his lead.

They catch the two men by total surprise. When they finally look up, Smoke is standing right in front of them. Both he and his accomplice already have their guns brandished, at their waist. The men are quite startled but try to remain calm. The last thing they want to do is to alarm the gunmen.

"Yep," Smoke whispers. "Ya'll already know. Strip." The men quickly relieve themselves of their jewelry. "I know ya'll got the word that we on a rampage. From here on out, this us out here. No more posting up. Today it's a robbery. Tomorrow it will be homicide. Smell me?"

Smoke is so busy giving his speech that he doesn't see the man creeping out of the neighboring alleyway. His gun is in hand, fully loaded and ready for action. He's just trying to get closer so that he doesn't miss. With both of the enemies strapped, he can't afford to miss a shot. He creeps up behind Smoke with light steps. Not once does the man look behind his own self but if he did he would see the man that is sneaking up behind him.

The man inches up and once he's close enough, he places the nose of the gun on the back of the man's head. The man attempts to turn around. "Ah, hah, don't move," he says as he grips the man's wrist. "What you was gone do with this?" he asks with a smile. In fear of losing his life, he lets the gun loose immediately.

Smoke turns around quickly, shocked at what he sees. It's a good thing that he was prepared for a situation like this. He instructed one of his soldiers to enter the block from the opposite end, which was the best decision that he could have made.

"Ah, look a here," Smoke says with a demonic smile. "Oh, you a brave mufucker, huh?" The fury is set deep on his face. He gives his man a head nod and without hesitation a gun shot sounds off loudly. The man falls to the ground, face first. As soon as his body lands, the gun shots start ringing consecutively. Smoke joins in automatically. Together they dump twenty shots into the man's lifeless body.

Loud screaming pierces through the air, while everyone on the block runs for cover. The two men watch nervously, knowing that they are next. They are afraid to move but they manage to muster up enough courage to make a break for it. They take off in separate directions. Three sets of gunshots follow them. Pop! Pop! Boom! Boc! Boc! Boc! Pop! Boom! Pop! Boc! Boc! Boc! Boom!

Smoke looks around at all the witnesses and reality sets in. He backpedals away, while still firing away. He feels gratification as his target stops short and drops to his knees. Smoke takes off and his soldiers follow. They flee the scene of the crime. They run as fast they can until they get to the getaway car. They all jump into the car and Smoke peels off recklessly.

Tony is a complete wreck. His spirits are at an all time low. Mocha hasn't answered his calls all yesterday. He hasn't heard from her in two days now. The last time he heard from her they had the biggest argument ever after she claimed that she spent the night at a girlfriend's house. Tony called her every bitch in the world before she got fed up and hung up on him.

In all his years of living, he never imagined hurting like this over a woman. Over the years women have come and go and he has never given them much thought. Wining and dining fine women has always been like a sport for him. He's broken the hearts of many and now he feels like it's his turn. He is starting to believe that this is his payback. Never before has he totally let a woman in, and the one he chooses breaks his heart. He questions the fact that maybe God sent her to him just for that purpose.

The fact that he's been holding onto all this, keeping it bottled up inside makes it worse. He realizes that it's best to talk to someone and just vent. Having very few friends makes that a difficult task. All in all there is only one person that he trusts enough to disclose this embarrassing information. He just prays that he will not look at him different after hearing his pain.

Tony pauses momentarily after breaking everything down to the Mayor. It feels good to actually let it all go. His burden feels somewhat relieved. Surprisingly, he let it all hang out with no shame at all.

He now sits here staring into the Mayor's eyes, awaiting a reply. The Mayor looks at him with a look of confusion on his face. He shakes his head from side to side. "I listened to your whole story from beginning to end and I don't hear another man," he says slowly. "I mean, don't get me wrong, I know a broad gone do what a broad gone do but real talk and I ain't just saying this cause you my man... but who the hell could she leave you for? By far you the smoothest cat I know. Outside of myself," he adds with a smile. Tony sits back accepting the praise. Hearing the compliment soothes his ego. "Look at you. You got it all. You're a successful attorney with crazy swag and a million dollar smile. You got a big house, big cars, what else could a chick ask for? All I'm saying is a chick gotta be a fool to leave you. You a good dude. Chicks don't leave niggas like us."

"It's gotta be a nigga," Tony blurts out. "Don't no bitch leave everything for nothing."

"Let me tell you something about chicks that I learned over the years. A chick always looking for the next best thing. You can give her everything and still she will find something else to want and desire. Think about it...you got a chick that has to have every new bag or shoe that comes out. The minute the new one comes out she no longer wants to wear the old ones cause it's now out of season. Mercedes comes out with a new model and she can no longer drive her old one. So, how do we expect a chick that gets bored with everything the minute something new or better comes along, to ever be able to be satisfied with one dude no matter what he's able to provide? They always think the one they don't have is the better one. And I'm not saying that it's a dude. I'm just telling you what I learned from observing women."

"It's a nigga in the picture. I'm telling you. I can feel it in my gut."

"Well, there it is. I move off my gut feeling and never has it steered me wrong. If your gut is telling you, it's a nigga then that's what it is. The gut don't lie. So, now what though?"

Tony sits quietly for a second. "Now, I don't know," he whispers. I'm gone keep it real with you...I'm fucked up without her. Shit crazy. Not just in my personal life but my business as well. My affairs are all over the place without her here in the office to manage them. It's crazy," he barks. "This situation got me doing shit I never ever done. Calling all day begging her to come back home. Sleeping nights in the car parked in front of her mother's house like a stalker."

"As you should," the Mayor interrupts. "That ain't no regular dame. That's your wife. You gotta do whatever it takes. You love her so it's only right that you fight for her."

Tony is quite shocked to hear those words come out of the Mayor's mouth. "This shit got me going crazy," he admits with shame. "The other night I sat in front of her mother's house with a pistol on my lap," he whispers as he looks away with embarrassment.

"A pistol? Now you bugging! Pardon my language but ain't no bitch worth that. I don't give a fuck. You just lost me with that crazy ass shit. I was with you all the way up until that," he says with disappointment in his eyes. "What was you gone do, kill her so nobody else can have her?" he asks with sarcasm.

"Nah, at the time I was thinking more like killing the motherfucker who is ruining my life."

"Kill him why? It ain't him. If it is a him," he adds. "It's her. He just doing what he supposed to do. He don't owe you shit. He not married to you, she is. She owes you loyalty...not him."

Tony becomes furious. "I can't believe this bitch!" he spits out.

The Mayor shakes his head from side to side. "Tone Capone, you my man," he sings. "I love you to death. I really don't get involved with matters of the heart but I gotta keep it real with you. A broad gone be a broad. Yours, mines and whoever else broad. They gone do whatever they wanna do and not give two fucks about how a nigga feel about it. Once her mind is made up it's a wrap. You can't stop it. You can give her the world but if she gets it in her mind that she gonna bust a move, then a move she gone bust. I ain't throwing your wife under the bus cause at this point don't neither one of us know what it is. But we both know who *she* was," he whispers.

"Feel me? Like my man Jay said, 'You was who you was before you got here. You can change your clothes but that's just the top layer," he sings. "On the real, I tried to give her the benefit of the doubt and sugar coat the shit but you my man. I ain't gone let you run around here stuck on stupid. I salute you for bringing her in out of the rain cause I believe that everyone deserves a shot. Some people are the way they are because of their circumstances. Then you have others, who even if you change their circumstances they will still be that," he says with sincerity in his eyes. "Me and you both know a dame ain't gone bounce on a nigga who got everything, just to be alone. How many dames you done dealt with in your day that will give you all the pussy in the world but wouldn't dare think of leaving their man? A smart chick will just stay there, be miserable but stable, feel me? Like you said, she told you she misses you but she confused. Confused about what? The only thing that can confuse her is another nigga. She doesn't know if she wants to stay or leave, bottom line. Her mind is telling her one thing but her heart is telling her something totally different. Which one you think she gone follow? Her heart of course.

We follow our minds and they follow their hearts. I feel your pain. You in a tough spot. Real rap, that's exactly why I don't deal with the love shit when it comes to a dame. Don't get it twisted, I love both of mine but I love me more. I don't get caught up like that.

I enjoy a chick for the moment, while I got 'em. When we together, we chill to the max. It's all good. When we're not together I flush 'em out of my mind. It's better like that. If I have no expectations of them then how can they ever disappoint me?" he asks, not waiting for an answer. "I just done over ten summers. If I didn't have that mindset I would have went crazy," he says in a squeaky voice. "I did my time without worrying what they're doing. They answered most calls but of course they missed some as well. They came to see a nigga every chance they could. What else could I ask for? Do I think they fucked somebody else while I was gone?"

Tony looks at him with his undivided attention. He can't wait to hear the answer.

"I would be a fool if I thought not," he says with no emotion.

Tony is in awe. Hearing all of this helps him to put things into proper perspective. "I hear you man. Thanks for the ear. I hope you don't look at me different."

"I could never look at you different. I seen it happen to the best of 'em. Real niggas ain't exempt. Like I said, that's your wife and by all means you should fight to save your marriage. Just don't be no fool. If she don't wanna be kept, don't try to keep her. You made her, she didn't make you. She will never find another like you...I promise you."

"Now, what am I supposed to do though?" Tony asks.

"Fight for your wife but as I said, when it's over, it's over. Just promise me, you ain't gone go out there and do nothing crazy. I need you here," he says, awaiting a reply.

"As you know about me...I don't make promises that I don't know if I can keep," he says, repeating the exact same words the Mayor said to him on a couple of occasions. "On some real shit, I know this may sound like some sucker for love shit but I put way too much into this bitch. I built everything around her so her future could be secure even if I wasn't around. You know that street mentality, where you believe something is going to happen to you and your wife will be left in the world struggling? Well, I didn't want that to be the case. To make a short story shorter...she good. In fact, she's better off than me. She could never struggle after the package I put together for her. A divorce right now will finish me off. If she thinks she gone leave me and live her life happily ever after with a motherfucker off my hard work, sweat and tears that bitch got another thing coming," he says with rage. "Not while I'm starting from scratch, struggling from day to day. I come too far, man. You know my story. I been through a lot of shit to get where I am today. I beat the odds. Just to think that I can lose everything to a cheating ass bitch, come on."

"I can dig it," the Mayor confirms. "But before I do some dumb shit over a broad and go to jail over some love shit…I would lose everything. I came into this world with nothing," he spits. "I will go to jail on any given day for getting a dollar but never for a broad. I totally understand what you're saying about losing everything," he agrees. "But me I will lose everything before I lose my freedom over a dame. I will be down Penn Station, homeless, barefoot, with no shirt on, a straw hat on my head, playing a mufuckin' guitar, for change…just hoping for a break. A dame don't mean that much to me. "You gotta get your mind right."

It's 11 p.m. and the low income housing complex is still full of people. The herds of people mostly consist of drug dealers and dope fiends, running back and forth in search of dope. Clusters of dealers stand huddled up in front of doorways pitching their work.

Smoke stands in the cut, just watching his operation. Standing close by him are a few of his men, just engaging in meaningless conversation. The ringing of his phone causes him to step away from the small crowd.

Just as he turns his back away, a huge tinted out Ford Excursion comes roaring up the driveway recklessly. The driver mashes the gas pedal as hard as he can, ripping up the center of the courts. Everyone's attention is caught by it. They're all wondering who it could be behind the dark windows. A few of the men take off instantly, thinking that it's the police swat team.

The back windows slide down on each side rapidly. Two Ak47 rifles hang from both windows. Rapid gunfire starts ringing from both guns. The gunmen aim at no particular target. They're waving the gun up and down, back and forth, while huge bullets spit in every direction. People scatter in every direction, in attempt to run for cover.

Smoke ducks down low to the ground and runs through a tight alleyway passage. He snatches his gun from his waist as he's running. He peeks around the corner of the building. From there he sees a few of his soldiers falling to the ground, just as a few innocent customers are as well. It's all playing out like a scene from a war movie right before his eyes. He wants badly to go out and start firing but he realizes how stupid that will be. There is no way in the world he can go up against two assault rifles when all he has is an eleven shot nine millimeter. He knows he will be murdered instantly. Instead of making a foolish move, he just watches with rage, trying hard to see who it could be behind the masks. He watches closely as the truck makes a wild u-turn. The shots are still ripping recklessly.

As the truck is passing the alley that Smoke is hiding in, a stack of papers are flown from the passenger's side window, blowing wildly into the air. Just as the truck passes, Smoke starts firing. Boc! Boc! Boc! His shots only tease them and makes them fire that much faster. Boc! Boc! He has no hopes of hitting anyone. He's just firing for the sake of doing so. The Excursion speeds out of the courts and disappears in seconds.

Smoke waits until they're totally out of sight before he walks out, gun in hand. He looks around at the battlefield and the sight of it makes his heart beat with fury. Loud screaming echoes in the air. He runs to the center of the court. Once he's there he bends over and grabs hold of one of the papers that was flown from the window. He wonders what the purpose of that was. As his eyes adjust to the paper, his question is answered. Bills stares up at him from the picture. The paper is his obituary.

He now realizes that the shooting is in retaliation of Bills' murder. A smile pops onto Smoke's face instantly. He nods his head up and down. "Ok, let's play."

Two Weeks Later/July 3, 2009

The Federal Agents Dumber and Dumbest stand over a desk. Dumber holds a newspaper in his hand. His face is of pure stone. "Twenty-two murders in less than a month," he says as he shakes his head from side to side. "That's an all time record," he says as he looks over to his partner. "I guess it's safe to say that he's back at it, huh? It's no coincidence that ever since he's been home the murder rate has increased. I'm willing to bet my life that he's behind all of this shit. Stupid motherfucker!" he shouts as he bangs onto the desk. "We have to get this bastard before the whole city is one big graveyard. We don't have any time to waste."

"But how?" Agent Dumbest asks.

"We can't let this bastard breathe. If he gets the smallest bit of leverage it will make it hard for us to nail him. We can't let him get his legs underneath him. We have no choice. It's time to send our informant in."

In Cedar Grove

The Mayor has just come in from his morning run. Each day he goes to Weequahic park where he runs around the lake twice which equals out to approximately seven miles. He realizes that in order to keep up with these youngsters he has to be not just mentally fit but physically fit as well.

Still drenched in sweat, he stands here reading the Newark Star Ledger that he picked up while in Newark. He receives more and more gratification after each line that he reads. In the article the reporter is ranting about the drastic increase of murders this month and labeling them all as senseless.

The Mayor begs to differ. To him the murders make all the sense in the world. Outside of the people who may have been innocent, he has no remorse whatsoever. He feels like those people are in the way and he just charges their death to the game.

Over the years while incarcerated his heart softened up. He realized the older he got the more he actually cared about things. He hardly showed that side nor expressed it to anyone but he noticed it. The moment he was released from prison he realized that he had to leave the soft part behind. He understands that caring in these streets will cost him his life. He has to be just as cold if not colder than the youngsters who run this city. He has to care less about them than they care about him. He understands that you can't think logically when you're surrounded by people who don't deal with logic. In order for him to survive he knows he has to be even more ruthless than the people know him to be.

He can't even believe that in just one month Smoke and his soldiers have erased over twenty people. The thought of it kind of blows his mind. At the first sight of Smoke, his baby face and frail frame made him appear to be harmless in the Mayor's eyes. The Mayor knows one thing for sure, you should never judge a book by the cover.

He's quite impressed with Smoke, for two reasons. The first reason is he can now say that Smoke is a man of his word. He said he would do something and he did it. The second reason is, he's impressed with the work that they have put in. He has always had the ability to press the button and have a person touched from near and far but never to this magnitude. Before this he never had the reason to have close to thirty people erased in one month.

Back before he went away it was a little easier. If everyone saw him get one guy touched for going against the rules, everyone else would follow the rules. Today is quite different. The younger generation only follow their guidelines. He could have twenty people killed for going against the rules and twenty more will still go against him. It would be a never ending cycle and he knows and understands this, which is why he has no choice but to clear anyone out of his path who may challenge him.

While incarcerated, he doubted the seriousness of the gangbanging here in this city and thought it would pass away just as every other fad does. Now that he's home, he sees it quite differently. He now sees the power that they hold.

He believes that power without brains is meaningless. He's sure that the power that they have, controlled by the brain that he has can only equal out to one thing and that's millions of dollars.

A huge smile brightens up his face at the thought of it.

Meanwhile in Washington

Dre paces back and forth throughout the spacious kitchen.

Angelique watches him closely. In his hand he holds the Newark Star Ledger, reading from the exact same article. "This is his work, I'm sure! I know him like the back of my hand. I really can't believe he's started his shit up already! What's wrong with this motherfucker? He just don't fucking get it. I gotta get at him."

"Dre, baby, I know he's your baby brother but he's a grown man. He's going to do what he wants to do. He has his own mind."

"But what the fuck am I supposed to do? Just sit back and watch him set his self up for failure? I can't do that! I'm going to Jersey!"

"Baby?" Angelique whines.

"Baby, my ass! That's it. There's no option."

"He's only going to drag you into his mess."

"Well, that's what it's gone have to be then."

The Next Day

The Mayor just arrived at the Maryland House rest stop in Baltimore Maryland. His legs are quite stiff and cramped up from the 3 and a half hour drive. Why he's here he has not a clue. He received a phone call from Angelique stating that it's urgent that they meet here. He can't imagine what could be so urgent. Unless it's something to do with his freedom, he can't think of anything that could be worth the long drive.

The water blue colored convertible BMW Z 4 Roadster sits in the far corner of the huge parking lot. Inside of the car there sits Angelique all alone. Her phone rings. "Hello?"

"Yeah, I'm here," the Mayor replies.

She shakes her head from side as she watches the Maserati rip into the parking lot. He just don't learn, she says to herself. She hits the high beams. "See me?"

"Cool," he says as he hangs up and speeds over toward her. In seconds he's side by side with her. He hops out casually.

She gets out as well. She holds his hand and gives him a phony hug. He can feel her coldness. It's not that she hates him. In fact, she loves everything about him, his confident demeanor, his character and his personality. The only thing she hates is the fact that he's the only person that she feels the man in her life loves more than her.

The Mayor notices her peeking around nervously. She's making sure no one has followed him here. "What's up?" he asks with major concern. "You alright?"

She looks him directly in the eyes. "Go inside, into the men's room," she mumbles, while barely moving her lips. "Someone is in there waiting for you."

"What?" he asks with confusion on his face. "What are you talking about?"

She peeks around more nervously. "Please, just do as I say. Trust me, you know I would never put you in any type of danger. Just go into the rest room. Someone is there waiting on you," she says, still peeking around. "Go now," she commands as she opens her car door and gets inside. She slams it shut behind her, leaving him standing there alone.

She hates the thought of all this but this idea is much better than Dre's original idea of going to Newark to meet him.

The Mayor finally makes it to the rest room. He steps cautiously inside. He's baffled at the entire situation. He walks in and sees an elderly white gentleman standing at the sink washing his hands. The Mayor stares at him, awaiting some type of signal. Who the fuck is he, he asks himself. The man stares back at him with an agitated look on his face, wondering why he's being stared at. The man rolls his eyes and exits the bathroom.

The Mayor stands there in total suspense. The creaking of the stall door sounds off from behind him. He turns around abruptly and what he sees scares him to death. His fear takes over. He stands there still, not able to move. He double takes at the sight of his brother in the stall. Dre peeks out to make sure no one is in the bathroom with them. Once he sees that the coast is clear, he walks out slowly.

The Mayor stares at his brother who stands there looking like a ghost. In fact, the Mayor believes that he's really seeing a ghost. He shakes his head, trying to shake away the sight. Since his brother's death, he has had this very vision before his eyes so many times. Sometimes he sees his brother in the dark. He's even had dreams of them holding long conversations.

"Welcome home, bruh," Dre says with a smile as the Mayor stands there with his feet glued to the floor. This particular time it feels so real unlike the dreams that he has had. He stands there with a confused look on his face. "Close that door," Dre instructs.

Without even realizing it, the Mayor has closed himself inside the bathroom with what he believes may be a ghost. He can't believe that he just actually took instructions from his brother's spirit. He's confused.

"Surprise, lil bruh. Erase that dumb look off your face. This really me. Pinch me...I'm real," Dre says as he extends his arm toward the Mayor who pulls away with nervousness. "I'm here in the flesh. You counted me out, like the rest of these mufuckers? Dead to the world? Let me help you get that stupid look off your face. It's a long story but now is not the time nor the place," he says as he grabs hold of his earlobe. He then touches the tip of his nose. The Mayor knows exactly how Dre feels about talking inside public rooms. They could easily be bugged.

The Mayor still can't believe what's going on? What the fuck is going on, he asks himself.

"Bottom line is…I'm here. Right now, that's all that matters. I'm here and you're here. Free together for the first time in what, twenty something years?" he asks with an arrogant smile.

"What's going on?" the Mayor asks with frustration.

Dre peeks around as he digs into his back pocket to retrieve his wallet. He holds it open and snatches an ID from deep inside. He places his left index finger up to his lips as he hands the ID to the Mayor with his right hand. "Shhh," he whispers.

The Mayor clearly reads the name on the ID. "Gregory Brown," he reads as he looks at the picture of his brother staring at him. "I'm confused. What the fuck?"

Dre snatches the ID from him. "Don't worry, I will fill you in," he whispers. "Let's just say, your big bruh Dre drowned in the water," he whispers. "The boy Latif drowned too," he says as he winks his eye.

The Mayor thinks back at what he's been told. If his memory serves him right, there was no mention of Latif being drowned. The paper only mentioned finding one body. "I didn't…" he manages to get out before Dre cuts him off.

"Trust me, he did," Dre says with another wink. He nods his head up and down with a smile. "I'm here…been here," he whispers.

The Mayor is happy to hear all of this but in the back of his mind he's pissed off that they actually had him believing that his big brother was dead. All the sleepless nights and all the tears that he's shed was all for nothing, he says to himself. He can't believe it. He feels like they played a trick on him. He feels like the butt of the joke. He becomes enraged. "So, everybody knew this but me? How about Tony?"

"I been with Angelique ever since," he whispers. "Only she knew. Tony just found out a few months ago."

How the fuck could he keep this away from me, The Mayor asks himself.

"Don't be mad at him. She made him promise to keep his mouth shut. I had to stay low. Nobody knows but ya'll. The bottom line is, I'm here though," he says with a smile. "Damn bruh, we together, free after 20 plus years," he says with joy. "I never thought this day would ever come," he says as he opens his arms for a hug. The Mayor hugs him in return. The Mayor gets caught up in the moment. He lets his anger with Tony and Angelique go and just appreciates the fact that his brother is here and alive.

"You home, lil bruh. They counted you out, but you got back up. Now what you gone do?" he asks.

"What you mean what am I going to do?" the Mayor asks.

"I mean, what's your plan? That's what. I know you got one," he says, knowing exactly what the Mayor's plan is.

"Yeah, I got one," the Mayor replies arrogantly. "It's back to bizness for me. You know me."

"Back to bizness?" Dre asks with a look of disgust on his face. "You gotta be kidding."

"Kidding? Not at all. Did you expect anything different?"

"Yeah," Dre says as he nods his head up and down. "I hoped you learned a lesson."

"Yeah, I did. Never to get caught," he smiles. "That's the only lesson I learned. I been on ice for over ten years, well preserved. Now I'm back. I'm sharp and full of energy," he says casually.

"Ten years and the only plan you come up with is to come back to the streets? You are a fool, huh?"

"Shit, you did it after doing sixteen years so that must make you a bigger fool than me.

"That was different," Dre blurts out. "I came home to nothing. My shit wasn't right. I was dead broke. Your story is different. You are more than alright," he whispers.

"I hope you didn't call me all the way down here for this? You could have saved me the trip. Man, I love you to death and you don't know how happy I am to find out the news. I thank you for informing me. Now I no longer have to grieve over my dead brother but as far as you talking me out of anything you can forget that."

"I'm just trying to rescue you before you jam yourself up again. I been reading the newspaper and I'm willing to bet anything that you're behind the bullshit that's going on."

"Rescue me? Who the fuck are you to rescue me? I never asked for help from nobody. Rescue me?" he repeats with sarcasm. "You can't even rescue yourself. You living like a fucking coward. How long do you think you gonna be able to lay low like this? Eventually you gone have to refuel that bank account. Then what?"

"Damn, you just don't fucking get it do you?"

"Nah, I don't. Tell me what it is to get?" Dre sits quietly. "Just as I figured. Listen bruh, I got it all figured out. I got the key to the whole city. Every Blood around is already moving at my command."

"Every Blood? Have you lost your fucking mind? You fucking with gangbangers? Tell me, you ain't involved in that shit? You a Blood now?"

"You sound retarded. No, I'm an opportunist. I see an opportunity to supply the whole city and I'm going for it. Truth be told, I'm out here all alone. Nobody to watch my back. Nobody I can trust. Yeah, I'm fucking with them gangbangers but in no way do I or will I ever trust them. If you get with me, we can bubble hardbody. We can eat like we never ate before. I trust you. You trust me. We both can put our feet up and close our eyes around each other with no worries about the other one putting a knife in our backs. Feel me? We break it all down the middle. I would love to have you as a partner. What you think? You with me?"

"Lil bruh, I think you fucked up in the game. I feel sorry for you," he says while shaking his head from side to side with pity in his eyes. "I feel guilty like it's all my fault. I introduced you to this shit. You watched me when you were a tiny kid and you were infatuated with that shit. I wish I would have known better I would have shown you something different but I didn't. I can't turn back the hands of time. All I can do is try to save you from any further trouble that you can get into."

"How you know that I want to be saved?" he asks. "You can't save a mufucker that don't want to be saved."

"Then, I'm gone have to leave you alone to self destruct." The Mayor looks into his brother's eyes and as usual he shows no sign of emotion. Dre, on the other hand, his eyes are full of sorrow. "I'm dead serious bruh. I ain't going back to prison for nobody, not even you. I got a second chance at life as a free man and I'm not about to fuck this one up. I got a few legal things in the making. Me and your boy Tony got the cigar thing rocking. We ain't getting a lot of money but I see the potential. My lady has invested a few of my chips in the stock market. And that's doing way better than alright," he says with enthusiasm in his eyes. And for the most part, I got some trap put away for a rainy day. You know I don't spend mines like that. So, until a big payday comes along, I will be ok. Even if I ain't, I'm not going back to that shit. I would rather be out here dead broke than to be in somebody prison. It's over for me. I'm forty five years old. That last bid finished me off. I can't stand another one. A mere fifty bag charge will get me ten years with my jacket. I will come home mid fifties. Fucking with you and the shit you trying to do, I will die in prison." He steps a little closer to the Mayor. "You my baby brother. You followed my lead into this wicked ass game. Now, please follow my lead out of it. I steered you wrong back then but I promise you, I will never steer you wrong again." For the first time since the Mayor was a kid, Dre sees sadness in his brother's eyes. He truly hopes that he's getting through to him.

He pauses momentarily before replying. "Big bruh, don't feel guilty about me. At the end of the day, I made my own decisions. You're feeling sorry for me and in no way do I feel sorry for myself. I never felt sorry for myself. I been ghetto rich since I was a kid. I lived in the best homes, drove the best cars and fucked some of the baddest bitches in and out of the country. What I got to feel sorry for?" He asks with hesitation as if he's actually waiting for an answer. "Big bruh, every man has to find his own way. You sound like you found yours. Sounds like you have it all figured out. If you content with living like that, then who am I to tell you different? If you like it, I love it. But please respect the fact that, that isn't my way? I gotta satisfy me."

"So, you're telling me that there is nothing I can say to make you at least try to look at it another way?"

"I'm afraid not," the Mayor replies with sincerity in his eyes.

"I feel you. I tried...whatever that counts for," he says with a sigh. "So, you leave me with no other choice. I love you but I can't do it. From here on out, we lose all contact with each other forever. Before you got here, you had me charged off as dead so it shouldn't be that hard to keep it like that. No calls, no visits, no nothing. Consider me dead. You in this thing by yourself, lil bruh. You're all alone."

"I came into this thing by myself," the Mayor replies arrogantly. "You left me by myself for sixteen years to fend for myself and I did it...all alone! No big brother to fight for me when the older kids jumped on me or when I needed someone to watch my back so I don't get jumped. It was then that I realized that I was by myself. Since then I made a vow to turn it all the way up and make the world fear being in my presence. Guess what? I did that...all alone too," he adds. "I built an empire around me and I became one of the richest and most feared men in the history of this city. And guess what?"

For the first time ever, the Mayor actually is making sense to Dre. He now understands his brother's mind frame. It breaks his heart to hear this come out of his mouth. Now he really feels guilty. "What? Dre replies with sadness plastered all over his face.

"I did it my way. That's the only way I know how to do it."

Tears creep into the corners of Dre's eyes. He nods his head up and down, causing the tears to drip down his face. "I can dig it," he whispers. "I understand that and I respect that to the utmost. Hopefully you will respect and understand my way and my decision. From here on out, I no longer exist to you. Continue to do it your way."

The Mayor nods his head in return. "I will and I do," he says as he stands there firmly. They stare into each other's eyes momentarily. Tears are dripping slowly from both of their eyes. "You done with me, here?" the Mayor asks with more arrogance than ever.

Dre shrugs his shoulders and puts his hands into the air. "I guess so."

"Well, on that note...so long," the Mayor says as he spins around and exits the bathroom. He leaves his brother standing there drowned in his own guilt.

The Mayor's words play over and over in Dre's head. 'You left me by myself for sixteen years to fend for myself and I did it. You left me by myself for sixteen years to fend for myself and I did it. You can't save a mufucker who don't want to be saved.'

Two Days Later in Paterson, N.J.

With the Mayor having no solid dope connect of his own, he's starting to get desperate. His whole operation has been shut down since the Block Party connect fell through. He's learned so much from that situation. One thing that he learned for sure is nothing lasts forever and all good things come to an end one day.

The Mayor made millions with them for over ten years straight. He's never imagined them not being there for him. He foolishly thought they would make money together, forever and ever. He did everything in his power to safeguard them from any danger, only for them to flip in the end.

One thing that he can't understand is why they never implicated him in anything. He was sure that he would be brought up on some type of charges but he wasn't. When it all first blew up, the Feds did in fact come to see him. They pretended to actually have something on him. He in no way is a stranger to Federal pressure so he knew exactly how to handle them. He said nothing at all. He found out a long time ago, the less you tell the Feds the less they actually know. Feds don't crack cases as most may believe. Niggas give themselves and others away. After a few visits and getting nothing out of him, they eventually gave up and the visits stopped.

The Mayor's biggest priority over the past year or so has been to land a prominent connect just in case he ever made it home. His nightmare has come true. He's home and doesn't know where to start in finding a connect that has the magnitude to supply him.

Since he's been home he's met with a few dudes that he was incarcerated with. In jail they ranted and raved about how big they were doing it on the street. Just as the Mayor figured though; it was all talk. He called each and every one of their bluffs. The men who supplies their supplier doesn't have the capacity to hold him.

All the guys that he's ran into buy their dope packaged already. That is something the Mayor hopes he never has to do. He likes to go to the table himself, mix it up and make all the profit. That way seems to be old fashioned and prehistoric with today's generation of hustlers. He has one last option before even considering settling for already packaged dope. If this falls through he will be very disappointed. His dreams of becoming super wealthy will be crushed.

The Mayor sits in the living room of the cozy apartment. His search for work has led him here. He's met many men who claim to be in position but this particular man, the Mayor chose because he's the closest to him. He hopes the man can do what he said he can do but if not he will have to go on a hunt. Where it will lead him, he doesn't know. Hopefully the man that sits before him will be the end of his search process.

While incarcerated, the Mayor took a liking to this man. They spent hours and hours at a time talking about everything under the sun, including business. The man would brag to the Mayor about how he went from nothing to something, overnight. His claim to fame supposedly was cutting his own dope and quadrupling his money. Supposedly, the entire city of Paterson was buying his dope from him. The Mayor hardly ever believes what a man tells him but in this case a few reputable guys have cosigned everything the man told him and even more. The Mayor just hopes what they have said is true.

The Mayor knows that this man is nowhere near on his level financially but if he can do what he says he can do he can be put to use. He claims to have a raw dope connect and he claims that he can play the chemist position as well. If what he has said is true, the Mayor is willing to handle the rest. In return for his contribution, the Mayor plans to change life for the man as he knows it.

The Mayor is in dire need of work. Each time he turns on the news and hears the results of the work that Smoke and his squad is putting in he gets stressed. He knows that they're on their job, which inspired him to hurry up and get on his. He expected the process to take longer and thought he had more time but from what he's hearing, the time is right now.

"So, you sure this the right shit?" the Mayor asks with hope.

This man has always talked to the Mayor about them linking up together but never really did he think the day would actually come. He can't believe that the opportunity has presented itself. This is like a dream come true for him. He wouldn't blow it for the world. "Listen, you know I just don't talk to hear myself talk. I'm sure of what this is!" he shouts with confidence. "Can't nothing in Paterson stand up next to mines."

"First of all, Paterson and Newark are totally different. What may be a nine, ten for ya'll may be a six, over there," he claims. "We got a different breed of fiends over there. I spoiled them with that Block Party," he brags. "You can't just give them anything now cause they won't accept it. I got a reputation. If my name is attached to it, it has to be grade A," the Mayor says clearly.

"Listen...enough of the talking shit. Take these," he says as he passes the Mayor four bricks of dope. "Pass it out to your people and let them tell you what it is. I'm done talking," he says arrogantly.

"Two hundred bags?" the Mayor asks with sarcasm. "What can I do with that? I got the whole city waiting on me. I need to pass out more than that on one block. Make it worth the while. Get me a hundred so I can get a real reading."

The man's face drops. "I can't give away a hundred bricks for samples."

"Give away? Who said anything about giving away? What's your price, one seventy, right? I got seventeen stacks for you. I pay my own way, no problem. Put it together and I will give it to my people. If it is what you say it is, we're in business. If it ain't, I will consider it a tax write off and charge it to the game," he smiles. "But we can never do business on any level ever again. Your word is everything," he says staring into the man's eyes. "Make it right. Remember, you only get one chance to make a first impression.

One Week Later

Tony is just getting home from a long and stressful day and feels quite relieved to finally be here. His bed is calling out his name. He plans to have one of his favorite cigars and crash right after.

After the conversation that he had with the Mayor, he's been doing a little better. He still calls Mocha throughout the day but not as much. He stopped all the begging and pleading as well. He's now trying to use reverse psychology on her. He figures if he acts nonchalant about it all and stops all the begging, she will think that he may have someone else and not care if she ever comes back, she may give in and come home. He knows how jealous she once was over him and he hopes to capitalize off of it.

At this point he's desperate. He's tried everything but nothing seems to work. It's already been over a month that she's been out of the house. The funny part is instead of getting use to her being away, he's actually missing her more and more each second of the day. In his mind he thought this would all pass but he's now starting to believe that it's only getting worse.

He puts the key into the hole and surprisingly the door opens before he twists it. He stands there in awe. "Damn, I know I didn't leave the damn door open," he mumbles to himself. He walks in and the sweet smell of Mocha's perfume smacks him in the face. His spirits are lifted as he entertains the thought that she has come home to him. My plan worked, he says in his mind. A bright smile pops onto his face.

He quickly erases the smile and replaces it with his normal look of arrogance. He can never allow her to think that she can come and go as she pleases and think that it will be that simple for him to accept her back. Although he's happy, he can't show it just yet.

He stomps up the steps with a false sense of anger. The sweet smell of her perfume is blessing the entire house. Tony is becoming hornier with each sniff. He can't wait to have make up sex with her. He can picture it now; him pounding away, punishing her for being a bad girl. Suddenly the thought that maybe she's been having sex with another man creeps in. That thought disgusts him terribly but at this point he's just happy to have her home.

His competitive edge comes into play. He knows that he definitely has to bring his A- game out tonight. He plans to fuck her like he hopes she's never been fucked. He has to make her forget about the man that he believes that she is now seeing. It hurts him to think like that but it is what it is.

He puts a frown onto his face before pushing the bedroom door open. At his entrance, he looks around and is shocked to find not a sign of her anywhere. The bed is still made and everything is in the exact same place that he left it this morning. He quickly walks over to her walk-in closet. The emptiness that he sees makes him heartbroken. Nothing is there but bare walls, empty shelves and a clean floor. He realizes that she's come in and taken all of her clothes and shoes.

He shakes his head in despair. It's over, he says to himself. Damn, this nigga got my baby fucked up, he mumbles to himself. "I guess she ain't confused no more," he mumbles. "She must have her mind made up."

Meanwhile

The tall slender man exits the black R500 Mercedes wagon. He walks sluggishly toward the small two family house that sits right on the corner of the block. Just as the man reaches the porch, he turns around and locks the doors on his vehicle from his remote.

Once the lights dim, he spins back around, only to be greeted by a masked gunman. The gunman stands up from behind the bushes that surround the front of the house. The man's eyes stretch wide open with fear. Bloc! Bloc! Bloc! The second shot lands right between the man's eyes, forcing him backwards until he tumbles over and lands onto his back.

The gunman leaps over the bushes, still aiming at his prey. In three giant steps he's standing directly over top of the man, staring into his half closed eyes. Bloc! Bloc! Bloc! His eyes close shut after the very first shot.

The gunman takes off. He runs a half a block until he reaches the getaway car. He snatches the door wide open and hops into the passenger's seat of the car. The car starts to roll before he can fully get seated. "Man down," he says with wrath as he slams the door shut. He pulls off his mask and looks over to the driver's seat.

The dead man was not only a supplier in the town. He was

also the cousin and henchman to Tony's client. The Mayor ordered this hit to serve both purposes. The Mayor figures this is one less man to worry about harming Tony. It's better to get him out of the way now so he can not be a problem in either regard.

"You sure you finished him?" Smoke asks from the driver's seat.

"Positive," the passenger replies.

Two Days Later

The Mayor struts gracefully throughout the Ralph Lauren store here in Short Hills Mall. Walking side by side of him is the homie, Smoke who has just linked up with him.

The Mayor's head hangs low. He's staring onto the floor at his feet as he takes each step. "So, what's the verdict?" the Mayor whispers.

"Ah," Smoke grunts. "Not too good, big bruh."

"What? It's garbage?"

"Pure-dee, garbage," Smoke barks. "Niggas don't be liking that beige dope," he claims. "A few of the shooters, said it's good but the sniffers all gave it thumbs down."

Damn, the Mayor says to himself. Just as I figured. Deep inside he figured it would be a blank but he hoped like hell that his man would prove him wrong. He stops short in the middle of the room. His mind is racing, trying to figure out what his next move will be. "How much of it you got left?"

"None. I gave it all out," he lies. Sure he gave it out but not as samples as the Mayor instructed him too. He gave it to his soldiers and he expects two hundred and twenty five dollars a brick back. He knows what the Mayor told him to do but no way in the world was he going to miss out at a chance to make some free money. That would be like expecting a starving man to throw away a steak. By the end of the day, he should have in hand, $22,500.00.

"Cool. Don't worry, lil bruh. Give me a couple of days and I'm right back at you. It's like that sometimes but we're going to get it right. I bullshit you not. I ain't even gone come back to you until I got that banger.

West Caldwell, N.J/ 2:00 A.M.

Agents Dumber and Dumbest sit in their car parked. It's extremely dark outside. The only light in the area comes from the spotlight that's shining on the mansion on the very top of the hill that they're looking at. They've been sitting here in pure envy, watching this house for the past seven hours.

This 2.5 million dollar, 9,000 square foot, surrounded by 5 acres of land, home belongs to the Mayor's girlfriend, Liu Ching. The Feds were able to track her down from the names on the Mayor's visit list. They've always had a line on her, knowing exactly where she's been all the while.

The Feds have given up on tying her into his madness long ago. Her successful nursing career and her wealthy parents, all make it easy for her to cover her tracks. Her salary coupled with the huge amounts of money that her father transfers into her bank account makes it easy for the Mayor to filter any money that he wants through her account. There's nothing in the world that he can't buy with his own drug money that can't be accounted for.

Agent Dumber speaks. "One thing you can't deny is this filthy scum bag definitely knows how to live."

"That's for sure," Dumbest says as he looks through his night vision binoculars. He pays close attention to the light that comes on near the back of the house. He assumes this must be the bathroom.

They're here trying to catch the Mayor coming home. They're just trying to do an observation of what time he comes home at night and leaves in the morning. It hasn't been easy because they've been here for two nights and still no sign of him.

Meanwhile in Long Island, N.Y

The Mayor stands in the kitchen of the beach home, here in Hampton Beach. He stares out the window, looking through the darkness at the Atlantic Shore. The calm water and huge sand castles make up a peaceful sight. As he's standing there his girl Megan grabs him from behind. She pulls his body up to hers, grinding away, while she grips his manhood.

"One more time, please?" she begs.

As much as he would love to make love to her once again, he can not. She's managed to drain every bit of sexual energy out of him. He's been here for the past three nights and she's been fucking his brains out every second that he allows her to.

He knows what all the sex is about. The two-girlfriend situation has it's disadvantages. It brings out insecurities in both of the women. It makes them extremely jealous. Both of them secretly try to outdo the other one. They both want more than the other gets. That isn't only financial. Sexually, they try to drain him before he leaves so he will be worth nothing when he gets to the other one. Luckily, he has an extremely high sex drive or else he would be a tired wreck.

He has it worked out. He has them on a three day rotation system. That's three nights with Liu Ching and three nights with Megan. It all works out perfectly. That is for him at least.

"Come on, Megan, please?" he pleads as he wiggles out of her grip. "The dick ain't going nowhere ma. Stop it. I'm here. You act like I'm not coming back to you. I have a flight to catch in a few hours. I need to rest up."

She lowers her head and starts pouting like a baby. He reaches over and grabs the bag that lies on the counter. "Here," he says as he pulls the stack of bills from inside. The hefty stack of one hundred dollar bills is her allotted monthly allowance of $20,000.00. The money puts a smile onto her face.

Back in West Caldwell

The agents continue to watch from the bottom of the hill. They're both leaned way back in their seats. "This here job takes patience, my friend, patience. I have all the patience in the world. We have nothing but time. I will sit here forever as long as we're on the clock."

Many Hours Later

The Mayor just arrived here to Detroit less than thirty minutes ago. He boarded the flight where he sat in the comfort of a First Class seat and now he's sitting cramped up in the passenger's seat of a Toyota Solara. He compares the comfort of this vehicle to the bus that commutes inmates to and from court. He can't believe that he's actually riding in this lack of luxury.

He had no clue that his man would ever disrespect him and pick him up from the airport in this. All the big time talk that Ronald Trump talked in Fort Dix Federal Prison, the Mayor expected him to pick him up in a G5 airplane. Instead, he's in a Toyota Solara with cloth seats, which he claims is his wife's car. The Mayor would never disrespect his worse chick by making her ride in this.

In Fort Dix, these two men were arch rivals. Half of the jail was on the Mayor's side while the other half was with Ronald Trump. They couldn't get along because deep inside they were similar in many ways. There wasn't enough room in that jail for the both of their egos at the same time. That's why they always bumped heads. Neither of them took the competitiveness serious. They looked at it as friendly competition.

After coming up with a blank with the man from Paterson the Mayor thought long and hard about who he could talk to next. At first he couldn't come up with anyone else. With him having no other alternative, he was forced to come here and holler at Ronald Trump. As much as he hates to do so he has no choice. He feels like coming here in search of work is like bowing down to Ronald Trump in some way. He can only imagine how much this will boost Ronald Trump's ego but the Mayor has to swallow his pride.

"So, what brings you to Detroit?" Ronald Trump asks as he cruises through the city.

"Following that rainbow...hoping to find that pot of gold. Feel me?"

"Shit. Ain't no gold here. The recession done took all that."

"Recession?" the Mayor asks with agitation. "Come on, don't tell me you letting the media brainwash you too? The rich still rich and the poor still poor. The recession ain't nothing but an excuse for a nigga to use to justify why he fucked up. Everybody screaming that recession shit but was fucked up way before. Niggas always been fucked up. Anyway, the recession don't affect us. We from the blacktop. Shit tighten up, we just go harder!"

"I hear you," he replies sadly. "If you find that pot of gold point me in the right direction."

The Mayor has never heard him talk like this. He's sure this can't mean good news. "Come on, man? I know you know something good?"

"Shit, when you called, I was hoping you had something good for me. I'm hurting like a mufucker," he admits with no shame.

"Oh no, not you, Ronald Trump." The Mayor says with sarcasm. "Mr. how much you worth in cold cash!" he shouts. "Mr. I tricked off more money than you ever made," he says with a smile. "Ain't that what you told me over and over?" he asks with sarcasm. "I know you ain't fucked up. Looks like you done tricked off more than you made as well, huh?"

"Ay man...shit happens," he says as pity darkens his face. "I came home expecting niggas to still be in position but all them fucked up like me. Man, I left niggas with hundreds of thousands and they fucked everything up!" he says with rage. "Shit, you must not be in a better situation. You down here in my face," he says, trying to defend himself.

"Nah bruh, totally different. I'm out here looking for a plug. You looking for a life support machine," he teases. "As I always told you...I got *fuck* you money as the Italians say," he says with arrogance. "I wasn't just talking, as a lot of you motherfuckers was, I see. The bottom fell out on my network. I lost my connect, not my money. I'm not here looking for a handout. I'm here in search of a plug. Nigga, we're in two total different situations." Now he's ready to go in for the kill. "How could I ever think you could help me when it's obvious that you can't even help yourself?" he asks with no compassion at all. "What is to be expected? After all you named yourself after Donald Trump," he smiles. "The man you idolize filed bankruptcy for crying out loud," he laughs. "I guess you're just following the pattern, huh?"

Ronald Trump is speechless for the very first time ever. He can't even think of a slick comeback if he had to. He's forced to humble himself. "I don't know shit. I wish like hell, I did."

The Mayor feels victorious. He can hear the sincerity and the pity in Ronald Trump's voice. He doesn't even feel sorry for him due to all the shit talking that he used to do. He realizes that he's beating a dead horse. There's no need in wasting his time here with this man. "Ay, do me a favor?" the Mayor asks.

"What's that? Anything I can help you with, I'm here bro." Ronald Trump is desperate. He's willing to do anything with hopes that the Mayor will bring him back to life.

"Bust a u-turn and get me back to the airport. Doing bad is contagious. The last thing I need is for you to pass that shit off to me."

The Next Day in East Orange New Jersey

The white Mercedes creeps down Park Avenue. As the Mayor is driving, he pays close attention to the store signs. A few feet ahead, he sees a canopy that reads 'Rock Da Boat II. He spots the green Pontiac that's parked in front. He pulls up and parks right behind it.

Smoke hops out quickly. The Mayor hops out as well and they meet right in front of the restaurant. They shake hands and take a few steps away from the entrance. "What's goodie?" Smoke asks.

"Ah," the Mayor replies. "Same shit."

Smoke called this meeting, stating that he's run into a problem. The Mayor has no clue what that could be. "What's the deal though?" he asks as he peeks around, observing his surroundings.

"I got a small problem, boss," Smoke says as he looks away.

"Talk to me. If I can solve it, consider it solved."

"This the situation. We cleaning up the city, just as I said we would. We bout...I say, fifty percent done. The problem is, I ain't got enough work to supply all the blocks. The little work I get ain't enough to spread out. The Homies starving. I can only give them a brick or two, here and there."

"That's your problem?" the Mayor asks with sarcasm.

"Yeah," Smoke replies with shame.

"That's nothing. I can fix that overnight. What you need?"

"I mean...I don't know. I never really had this much access."

"Tell me how much work you think you need to supply everybody on your roster?"

"Honestly, I can't even answer that."

"Alright, let me help you. How much work you normally get at a time?"

"On the real...I only get about fifty bricks at a time. That's all my money can buy. Every now and then a nigga give me an extra twenty, twenty five bricks on the cuff, on top of what I buy. Normally my load last me about three days. Now, that shit wide open, it don't even last me a half a day."

"That's a good problem though," the Mayor smiles. "Dig this, I ain't got no line of my own yet. Believe you, me, I'm working on that as we speak. I'm on it, hard body. Trust me, we gone be in position sooner than you can imagine. Until then, do you know somebody?"

"I know a few mufuckers but I mainly be fucking with my man. He got the Star Trek stamp. The shit always fire. I just don't have enough fetti to get enough of it to really come up."

"How much he charging you for it?"

"Two hundred and twenty five dollars a brick and he won't come down for shit."

The Mayor starts calculating in his mind quickly. "What kind of capacity he got?"

"Huh?"

"He going hard? What kind of order do you think he can cover?"

"Yeah, he go hard. He definitely like dat," he says while nodding his head up and down with certainty.

"Good enough. Tell him to put a thousand bricks together for you. You think that will hold you? That should be enough to stretch out, right?"

Hold me, Smoke repeats to himself. "I ain't never even seen a thousand bricks, real talk, homie."

"I'm gone change that for you, trust me. I'm gone show you a lot of shit, you ain't never seen," he says in a cocky manner. "You gone see more bricks then you can count before it's all over. You fucking with the right one now. Trust me, I'm just playing with this shit right now. Two hundred stacks ain't no money. Your boy go hard. I swear to G-O-D, if I don't make you a millionaire my name ain't what it is. In less than twenty four hours you gone have the two hundred cash in hand. Get with your man and make it happen. I'm sure he will bring that price down with that type of cheese. He probably ain't seen that many bricks his damn self. You handle that, meanwhile I'm gone be searching for a line for us. No more, two, twenty five a brick either. You gone have enough room to give it to your lil homies for way less than that and you still gone eat."

Smoke is dizzy from the numbers that the Mayor is throwing around in his ear. He can't even imagine playing on that level. He can't see that far but he's hoping to one day be there.

The Mayor reaches out for a handshake. "Be on the listen out for my call," he says as he walks away from Smoke, leaving him standing there wondering if the Mayor is just talking for the sake of talking.

The Mayor is a few steps away from his car when Smoke screams out. "Yo!" The Mayor turns around quickly. "You ain't bullshitting me, are you?"

An agitated look pops onto the Mayor's face. "Bullshitting you? I ain't never bullshitted anyone. I say what I mean and mean what I say. You don't know me yet, but let me tell you something bout me. My word and my reputation means everything in the world to me. It took me years to build and I will never do anything to tarnish or even blemish it…not for you or anyone else. I said I'm gone do something so consider it done. Remember this, a man who doesn't keep his word is not a man. You kept your word, right? Now watch me keep mine. All we got is trust," he says as he's getting into the car.

A block away

The silver Impala sits parked with Agents Dumber and Dumbest, sitting inside. Dumber sits in the driver's seat while Dumbest sits in the passenger's seat, flicking away with the camera. "Zoom in on the kid," Agent Dumber says. "Make sure you get a close up so we can ID him."

"Tail him?" Agent Dumber asks.

"Nah, tail the kid. Let's see what he's up to," Agent Dumbest replies. "Hopefully he will lead us to something."

The Next Morning

The Mayor has been up bright and early just as he always is. He's on a quest to make some things happen. Last night he did a great deal of thinking. At the young age of thirty one years old, he feels like an old timer. Never did he imagine ever being thirty. He can remember how he looked at the thirty years olds when he was in his early twenties and just to think that the young dudes are looking at him like that blows his mind.

The new generation has taken over. They show even less respect for their elders than the Mayor's generation did. They have their own set of rules and even their own language. Even with him having his ear to the street, knowing pretty much how everything goes, he still can barely understand what some of their slang actually means.

The Mayor's biggest beef with the young generation is their lack of morals. With him having such a strong code of honor and them having no honor, he feels like a fish out of water. He trusts not a one of them which is why he hoped that his brother would have come out of retirement. Together he feels like they could have stayed a few steps ahead of the game.

The Mayor thought long and hard about who he could link up with that he could trust. It was hard because his original crew members who he had labeled as the Goon Squad are all gone. After he left, the team just fell apart. Two were murdered before he left. Two more got murdered while he was away. One is in prison for a homicide. The last one is burned out on drugs, just as the majority of the people from his era are. After thinking hard, he could only come up with one person that he feels he can trust.

A tall, stocky built man comes walking out of the raggedy house. At the sight of the man, the Mayor gets out of his Maserati, shining like the star that he is. He diddy bops toward the man. The Mayor pays close attention to the man's snow white head and beard. The man looks nothing like the Mayor remembers. The gray hair on his head and his beard makes him look at least seventy years old. His used to be, muscular physique has been replaced with a chunky frame and a protruding belly.

The last time they actually saw each other was back in 2001, when this man was on the witness stand, where he was supposed to be testifying on the Mayor for shooting him. Surprisingly, this man didn't go through with it. That is when he won over the Mayor's heart.

The Mayor took care of him from prison, while the man served his own time. His account was always to the limit. His commissary was always stocked and his family was always fed. While on the stand he had no idea the Mayor would take care of him. That had nothing to do with his reason for not telling. The reason he didn't tell is because he's a stand up dude who hates snitches more than anything else in the world.

"My man," the man shouts with joy.

"Mike, motherfucking Mittens," the Mayor replies in return. "What's good with you?"

"Nah, what's good with you? They really let you the fuck up outta there, huh?"

"They had no choice," the Mayor smiles. "I was innocent."

"Innocent, my ass," he chuckles. "You said you was gone give all that time back and you did it. I ain't gone lie to you. I didn't believe that shit for one minute. In all my years in the penitentiary, mufuckers always screamed out that appeal shit and giving time back but I ain't yet to see it happen, till now."

"None of them had my attorney," he smiles. "Everybody counted your boy out," he says with seriousness in his eyes. "They thought I was over. American Gangster, Feds Magazine, and Don Diva Magazine...they all came to visit me on a few occasions trying to offer me money for my story. You know what I told them all?" he asks. "I told them I don't halfway do anything and if I give them the story now it will be a half ass story. Cause I'm not finished yet," he adds. "I let them know that I ain't one of them washed up kingpins who so desperate to get some exposure that I'm gone let ya'll exploit me. Anyway, I ain't got nothing to say. I'll let the streets tell my story," he says with passion. "But anyway, what's good though?" he asks, trying to change the subject. "What you up to?"

Mike Mittens shakes his head from side to side with despair. "Shit...just working."

"Working?" the Mayor barks.

"Yeah, I'm on that graveyard shift at Shoprite, stocking shelves."

"Come on, man. Say it ain't so? Is that what it has come

down to? You terrorized the streets all your life to end up working at Shoprite? What's it about?" he whispers, sounding like an old Mob boss.

Mike Mittens can't help but laugh. "It ain't bout nuffin," he barks. "I ain't terrorizing shit these days. Them days is over with. I'm just happy to still be here. I ain't gone bust a grape in a fruit fight," he smiles. I'm just staying outta these niggas way. I done squared all the way the fuck up. I'm working like eighty hours a week with my overtime."

"Stop it, please," the Mayor says sarcastically as he places his hands over his ears. "You killing me, talking that working man shit. Damn, they got you too, huh?" he laughs.

"Yeah," he replies. "In fact I'm trying to find me a part time gig to help make ends meet."

"Good to hear," the Mayor smiles. "That's what brings me here today."

"Yeah? What you got in mind?"

"I need you with me, full time. You can lose that goofy ass job you got."

"Nah, man, I ain't fucking with them streets. I'm too old for that shit. I will be fifty three years old, next Monday."

Damn, fifty-three, that's it, the Mayor asks in a joking manner as he looks at the gray on Mike's head.

"Yeah, full grey," he says as he rubs his hands over his head. "That last bid killed me. Had me stressed the fuck out. They can have that prison shit."

"Listen, the position I got for you is fool proof. Dig this, I know these niggas gone be on my back so, I'm gone have to stay out of the way. All I need you to do is represent me. I load you up with the work, then you drop it off."

"Like deliveries?"

"Nah, not at all. There's only one dude you have to see. He supplies the rest of the city. When he done he calls you to give you the money. You get with me afterwards. You will be acting mediator cause I can't be coming through the town like that. It's simple. Not on no everyday shit. We start off like once a week. Once we get used to working with each other we step up the workload, meeting twice a week. Then eventually once a month."

It's all starting to sound too good to Mike. He's actually entertaining the thought. "Who the dude, I'm gone be seeing."

"This lil Blood nigga named…"

"Oh, hell no," Mike interrupts. "I don't fuck around with them gang banger niggas and I advise you not to either. I'm surprised at you. You way too smart to deal with them."

"Yeah, I'm smart enough to know that the city is now flooded with gangbangers. In that case, why wouldn't I deal with them? It is what it is. When in Rome, do as the Romans do. These young boys got power. They're the machine that we need to get this money. We both too old to be running around. That's what we got them for. There's no other way."

"It's a way, bruh. I'm gone stay working. I been doing this shit since I came home. Been home for a year now. This is the longest I ever been home without getting into some type of trouble. I ain't even had a traffic violation. And this is the first job I ever had in my life. It ain't that bad bruh. I don't fuck with them young niggas. You can't trust them. They're stupid as hell. They murder for bullshit. Senseless fucking murders…innocent bystanders getting shot while the mufucker they want, gets away. Then after all that gangster shit, they telling on each other, the first chance they get. Man, I will keep trying my hand at this nine to five shit."

"Man, you can keep your nine to five. I just need you once or twice a month for about an hour…boom, bang," the Mayor whispers. "I will guarantee you at least twenty stacks a month. Come on, you can't beat that. You see a mufucker twice and you get twenty thousand, just for that? And the two hundred dollars a week you make at your full time," he says with sarcasm. You can add that eight hundred and you will have twenty thousand and eight hundred dollars," he says mockingly.

Mike Mittens stands there contemplating. The Mayor is starting to get to him. "Damn," he grunts. "You make it sound so simple. I know it ain't gone be easy fucking with them gangbangers running round here, stuck on stupid."

"It's what you make it. They like dogs. If they sense fear, they're going to attack. Since when you been afraid to get money?"

"Phew," he sighs. "Let me think about this?"

"Cool, get at me after you weigh out your options. Meanwhile, **Just For Men**, all them got damn grays. You gotta camouflage yourself," he smiles. "You look about eighty years old. Of course they will try to take advantage of you," he smiles. "Just think about it but not too long though. You know time waits for no one."

Short Hills Mall

The Mayor hops out of his Maserati as the people in the surrounding area watch him in admiration. He grabs the shopping bag from his passenger's seat before tossing the keys to the valet parking attendant. He walks inside of Neiman and Marcus as the attendant cruises away.

Meanwhile

Agent Dumber sits at his desk, staring at his computer while Agent Dumbest stands behind him looking over his shoulder. A beautiful middle aged black woman steps in front of the desk. She holds a yellow envelope in her hand.

"Justin Jackson, age twenty six," she says. "Aliases, Thomas Moore and Justin Jones. He's known on the street as Smoke. He's the first cousin to O.G. Blood, Damien Bryant, the Black Charles Manson who has appointed him as the lieutenant. Over twenty arrests and eight convictions. Possession of an unlawful weapon, two aggravated assaults and five drug possessions," she utters as she hands him the file. She spins around and switches away, giving them a nice glimpse of her tight little rear, squeezed into the form fitted pin striped skirt.

"Thank you, Johnson," Dumber says in a playful manner. "One day, I'm gone pay you back so big," he says in a perverted manner. She ignores him just as she always does. He quickly diverts his attention onto the mug shot of Smoke, that is staring right into his face. "Yep, this is our man," he sings. "Now it all makes sense. Remember the dumb, nigger attorney defended the kid in the lethal injection battle?"

"Yeah," Agent Dumbest replies as he puts it together in his mind.

"You wanna bet that the fucker hired him for the case? Now they're all in cahoots. My guess is he's using the Bloods to flood the city with his heroin. He must be getting stupid as he gets older. This is the all time dumbest move that he's ever made," he laughs. "This is going to be a piece of cake."

Back in Short Hills

The Mayor has picked up a total of six shopping bags in his journey throughout the mall. He leads the way as he exits the Gucci store. Smoke follows close behind. In his hand he holds the bag that the Mayor came in with.

The Mayor walks over to the railing. He turns around facing Smoke. "So, there it is," he says as he looks down onto the first floor. "Two hundred stacks," he whispers. As promised. You said he at two, twenty-five but I'm sure you got enough leverage in that bag to get him to bring that price down to two hundred. Go ahead and do what you have to do. By the time you get through those, I should have a line on something of our own,"

Smoke is speechless. Just to think that he has two hundred thousand dollars in his hand. This is like a dream come true for him. He's never seen this much money ever. "So, how much I have to give you back?"

"Two hundred thousand," the Mayor replies quickly. "That's what I gave you, right?"

Now Smoke is confused. He can't understand why he's not interested in a profit. He knows that nothing is free and wonders what he will have to do for this. He thinks that he may owe the Mayor forever for this favor. "You don't want nothing off of it?"

"Nah, I want you to get the work that you need to feed you and your homies. Do ya'll. That little bit of money ain't enough for all of us to eat off. What kind of profit is in that? Fifty dollars a brick at the most. I can't eat off of that. I have a huge appetite," he says with a serious look on his face. "Just do ya'll and bust back at me when you done. By that time, I will be up, feel me?" Smoke looks into the Mayor's eyes. He's in somewhat of a trance. "You feel me?" the Mayor asks again.

Smoke finally snaps out of it. "Y, yeah," he stutters. "I feel you," he says, while gazing into the Mayor's eyes. "Yo, you a real mufucker. Here it is, I'm in a city with niggas I knew all my life who scared to deal with me. I have to go through this nigga and that nigga to get work cause the fag ass niggas scared to even do business with me. They definitely ain't gone front me nothing cause they too scared that I ain't gone pay them back and they know they can't do shit about it if I don't. And here it is, you don't know me from Adam and you put two hundred stacks in my hand," he says with disbelief.

"For all you know, I could run off and never get back at you," he says. "Even though I would never do that," he claims. "Like, real talk, I was feeling you on the strength of big bruh, Manson at first but now this shit deeper than that. I fucks with you...no homo," he adds. "Damn, you a real mufucker. Yo, you just did something nobody ain't ever did for me. You believe in me and you taking a chance with me. I promise you, I will never do anything to fuck this up."

"Life is about chances and for the record, that's the difference between me and a lot of niggas. I ain't never feared nothing or nobody," he says in attempt to let him know that he's not the least bit worried about him not paying back. The Mayor feels like Smoke may have been trying to let him know how much people fear him, possibly trying to instill fear in him. His ego forces him to now lay down his murder game. "True bill, all gangsters don't wear red, feel me? Some don't wear no color. They're like ghosts. You feel their presence but you don't see them. As far as the cheese goes, I never give anyone anything that I can't afford to lose. The only problem is, I don't lose well. I'm a poor sport," he says staring Smoke dead in the eyes. "And I don't play fair, meaning I will do anything and everything that it takes to win. As far as me being a real mufucker, you are absolutely correct. When I'm with you, I'm with you but when I'm against you, that's a different story. Just like there is nothing that I won't do for the niggas I'm with, on the flip side of that, there is nothing I won't do to get at the nigga I'm against. It's a thin line between love and hate. Nigga with some sense would know to stay on this side," he says with a smile. "But on some other shit. That's nothing. This is only the beginning. Trust me, we gone do a lot together. We're gonna make a lot of money," he says with determination in his eyes. "A lotta fucking money."

"Listen, bitch!" Tony shouts furiously. "You crossed me for a fucking nigga after all the shit I done for you? I'm gone show you. I can't believe you! You with another man? I gave you more credit than that. You're a married woman. I didn't think you would go out like that. I was totally wrong though. Once a whore always a whore. I got you though. I hope you don't think he gone respect you. He fucked you while you was married. He's never gonna take you serious. He will always see you as a slut. I'm fucked up," he chuckles with sarcasm. "You won this one. It's all good though. I will be alright. You wasn't the first bitch that fucked on me and I'm sure you won't be the last. All bitches are the same."

The more Tony talks the angrier Mocha becomes. She's been on the phone listening for ten minutes without saying a word. Finally she begins to chuckle as well. "Laugh bitch! It's a joke now. I feel you though. I'm Bozo the clown, I guess. Keep on laughing. Laugh now cry later."

She interrupts him. "I told you this ain't about no man but you insist that I'm fucking someone. In this short conversation I been about five whores, three sluts and a million bitches but that's it. Now, I'm gone show you what a bitch is. Yeah, I'm laughing all the way to the bank," she says before hanging up on him.

"Hello? Hello?" he shouts over the dial tone.

Meanwhile

Smoke sits in the passenger's seat of the Cherokee SRT. In the driver's seat there sits his man, the Star Trek dope connect.

The man in the driver's seat presses a few buttons on his steering wheel and in seconds the dashboard pops open. In the compartment there is a duffle bag that Smoke is sure contains the thousand bricks that he placed the order for.

Smoke talked him down from $225.00 a brick to $190.00 a brick. He tried to stay firm at his price but Smoke was persistent. Once he realized that Smoke was willing to walk away from the deal, he gave in. There was no way in the world that he was about to let a $190,000.00 cash deal slip out of his hands. Even with the drastic price reduction, the man still scores a $20,000.00 profit. This deal will give Smoke an extra $20,000.00 which he considers free money.

Smoke looks at the gun that lays on the man's lap, just as it always does in every one of their meetings. Smoke always takes offense of it but he understands that it's business. He wouldn't expect it any other way, nor would he respect it any other way. He's gotten used to it. Hardly anyone wants to do business with him but the ones who do have the heart to, makes sure that he sees their weapon. They all hope that showing their weapon will make him think twice about crossing them.

The man takes the gun from his lap and tucks it underneath his leg. He leans over to reach into the compartment. Smoke speaks. "Yo, I'm gone be busting back at you in like a week," he says as he grabs hold of the duffle bag that he has on his own lap.

"Alright, cool. I'll be ready for you," he replies as he's fumbling inside the stash box. He leans back while handing Smoke the bag of work. Smoke grabs hold of the bag with his right hand and with his left hand, he reaches over and snatches the key out of the ignition. The man looks at Smoke with surprise. The sudden opening of the driver's side door snatches his attention away from Smoke. He reaches for his gun but it's already way too late. Boc! Boc! Boc! The sound of gunfire rings off from the .40 caliber that the man standing at the door holds tightly. The smell of gunfire fills the jeep.

The top half of the man's body folds as his head bangs onto the middle console. The gunman continues to fire, aiming for the back of the man's head. Boc! Boc! Boc! All three shots land in the back of his skull, killing him instantly.

Smoke grabs the gun from underneath the dead man's leg. He forces his way out of the jeep lugging the bag of work. The man standing in the street closes the door shut and they both take off, leaving the dead man in a pool of his own blood.

Smoke's initial intentions was to keep this as a clean business deal. After thinking about it over and over the scum bag in him talked him into this. A good deal has gone bad.

Days Later

    Sean, the federal informant sits inside of the sky blue Bentley GT. Coupe, parked on the secluded street. He has his cell phone up to his ear, listening patiently as the phone rings on the other end. Finally the call is picked up. "Hello?" the sweet voice of a female blesses his ear. "Hello?" she says again, not knowing who is on the other end. The blocked call strikes her curiosity. "Hello?" she says once again.

    "Lisa," he whispers.

    "Hello?"

    "Lisa," he says again. "Please don't hang up," he begs.

    "Phew," she sighs. "What?" she barks with anger. "What do you want? I asked you to stop calling my phone."

    "Please, Lisa, just hear me out? I need to talk to you."

    "What the fuck is there to talk about?"

    "Lisa, you're my wife and you have my two sons. How do you expect me to stop calling you? Why are you being like this?"

    "Why? Why? I know this motherfucker didn't just ask why," she spits out. "You really don't know why? You fucking snitched on the whole hood and you're asking why? You leave me and your sons to look in the faces of these peoples' loved ones. You say you love us but how the fuck could you do that? Everyday, we have to live with the fear of someone retaliating on us for what the fuck you did. Is that a good enough reason why? Huh?"

    "Lisa, you know I love ya'll. You had the option of moving away with me but you decided to go back."

    "Motherfucker, I ain't living in no witness protection program! You snitched. Not us! Why the hell we gotta live our lives on the run, hiding from the world?"

    This woman is his wife. After he snitched on his squad, she lost any respect that she had for him. In the beginning she tried to ride it out with him but after finding out that his job with the Feds wasn't done that was the straw that broke the camel's back. She could no longer even look him in the face.

    Her and the kids moved back to the old neighborhood and cut off all contact with him. She's lying to him about living in fear, just to make him feel bad about what he's done. In fact no one has ever threatened them because for the most part she grew up in that neighborhood and the people there love her more than they ever loved him. They all hate that it was her husband who finished off the majority of the neighborhood but they also know how she feels about the matter.

More than anything else in the world, the way his wife talks to him makes him regret what he's done but it's too late for regrets. He knows he can never gain back the respect that she's lost for him. Living without his family hurts him more than actually rolling over on his squad. He has accepted the fact that she will never forgive him and he will never be able to be a part of his sons' lives.

Even without him present in their lives they are still taken care of. In return for what he's done, the Federal Government, not only provide him with an apartment and a fifty thousand dollar a year guaranteed salary as an informant but they also provide a two thousand dollar a month check to his wife. Every month faithfully, on the first of the month her child support check is in the mail.

"Huh?" she repeats. "Just as I figured, no answer. I told you before stop calling here. You're dead to us. The day you did what you did, you said fuck us. Now it's fuck you."

"But Lisa, what about the kids? They need a father in their lives."

"Well, you should have manned the fuck up! Now I don't want you in their lives. After all, snitch ass, bitch ass niggas raise snitch ass, bitch ass babies!" she says before slamming the phone on him.

He holds the phone, listening to the dial tone. He's heartbroken. Just as he's sulking in misery, his business phone rings. He knows exactly who it is. "Yeah?"

"Get ready. Here she comes," Agent Dumber says as he pays close attention to the young girl who is leaving out of the house that they have been watching for hours. "Come on, right...now."

The young thick body woman that they're watching is Smoke's younger sister. The day they followed him, he led them directly here. After digging up his file they found out that this is his actual place of residence. They've been watching this house for a few days now. The constant running in and out of this young girl sparked their interest. They watched her and watched her as she jumped in and out of cars all day long. In the course of one day she would average at least four or five visits a day from different men.

That raised their suspicion causing them to think that maybe she has some illegal dealings going on. They investigated the matter and found that to be totally false. What they did find out is she's just the local skeezer. Finding that out helped them to put together the perfect plan.

The young stallion gallops sexily up the block, exposing all her goods in the two sizes too small clothing. She shows all the warning signs of the classical hood rat. Normally he would never look at her twice but this here is business.

He times it perfectly. Just as the young girl reaches the corner, her attention is caught by the sparkling beauty on the side of her. She continues to stroll along as if she doesn't know that $200,000.00 is cruising alongside of her.

"Shorty," he whispers in a calm but confident voice. She ignores him as if he hasn't said a word to her. "Shorty," he calls again.

She would hate to blow this once in a lifetime opportunity so she decides to give in before he gives up and pulls off. She's a firm believer in the saying, 'if you play too hard to get, you won't get got.' She can't afford to let this go by. She would feel like a fool. One thing about her is she can smell money a mile away. She can already picture herself in the passenger's seat of the beautiful car. She quickly pictures herself in the comfort of his bed. She's sure that if she plays her game right, all of her financial problems will be over.

She puts her aggravated look on her face before looking over to him. "What?" she barks. "You know me?"

"Nah, but I'm trying to get to know you," he lashes back at her in a playful manner. "One minute of your time is all I ask, please?" he begs accompanied by a charming smile.

Meanwhile

The Mayor sits in the food court here in Livingston Mall. Across from him sits Smoke, who called the Mayor asking to meet with him. Underneath the table, there sits a Footlocker bag with two hundred thousand dollars cash inside a sneaker box.

Smoke slides the bag closer to the Mayor with his foot. "There it goes Boss."

"How much is that?" the Mayor asks.

"That's all of it," the man replies. "The whole two hundred." The Mayor is shocked to hear that but he tries hard not to show it on his face. Just a few days and the man has the money ready for him. In no way was he expecting this. He was sure the amount of dope they had, would last them long enough for him to land a connect.

"So, you all done? That was fast."

"Nah, I ain't all done. I put it all out there and got most of the money back. I'm probably waiting on about ten thousand dollars," he lies.

The truth of the matter is, he's barely even put a dent in the work. He's lucky if he's retrieved ten thousand in total. He's put all the work out there but the fact of the matter is they're still getting through it. The money he's given the Mayor is actually the money the Mayor gave him. Each bill is the exact same place the Mayor gave it to him.

Robbing the Star Trek connect helped him tremendously. He's now able to give the Mayor his money right back in a timely manner, with hopes of building a strong business relationship. He hopes that the Mayor is impressed with how fast he thinks he was able to turn the money over. Robbing the connect has also put him in a much better financial situation. Just a few weeks ago, he was damn near broke with only a few pennies to his name and no hopes of ever getting out of that situation. The thousand bricks the Mayor gave him for samples gave him a little hope after scoring $22,500.00. Now after the thousand brick come up, he has the potential to score well over two hundred grand. There is no one to pay back which means all of it is profit. They are just getting started but he's sure linking up with the Mayor is the best thing that could have ever happened to him.

"I just wanted to get you yours back. Get you outta the way, feel me? Ain't no need in holding yours up."

That statement wins over the Mayor's heart. In fact that has always been his own motto. He's done the exact same thing except on a larger level. Connects in the past have fronted him a million dollars worth of dope and the very next day he would take a million dollars out of his own money to pay them, but acting as if he made the money over night. Of course that made the connect eat out of the palm of his hand. The Mayor is well aware of the game but one thing he's sure of is Smoke in no way has his own two hundred grand. So knowing that makes the Mayor believe that the man may have actually scored that money in a few days.

If that's the case, he has no time to waste. He has to get on his job. They need dope and in a few days they will be expecting him to be able to deliver. He just hopes he will be able to come through as he has promised.

Back in Newark

The agents watch with satisfaction as their plan unfolds. Federal Informant Sean has gotten out of the car. He stands there in total disguise. His bald head and thick Muslim type beard, makes him fit in with the rest of the men in the city. His eyes are hidden behind oversized aviator shades. His white v-neck t-shirt, slim fit jeans and white Chuck Taylor Converses makes him look like a Rock Star.

The young girl is smiling from ear to ear and touching on him as if she's known him for years. The level of comfort that she's showing lets them know that he's got her. Agent Dumber looks over to his partner. "Look at S-Dot in action," he says using the nickname Sean will be using for this particular case. "No doubt about it, we're in."

Days Later

The Mayor is leaving Short Hills Mall once again. Boredom usually leads him to spending money. Today both hands are filled with bags. He stands at the doorway of Neiman and Marcus, waiting for the valet attendant to bring his car to him.

He hears the loud sound of tires screeching coming from the parking garage. Seconds later, he's shocked to see the Range Rover coming out of the garage. The valet attendant sees the look that the Mayor is giving him and he slows down. The driver pulls right up to him and hops out, leaving the door open.

"Damn, playboy," the Mayor says as he hands over a crisp twenty dollar bill. "A little heavy on the foot, huh?" he asks with a smile as he's lifting the hatch of the truck. He dumps the bags inside and slams the hatch shut but it bounces back up, almost smacking him in the face. He slams it again but it bounces up again. He tries again and again before he lifts the hatch high and examines it. He assumes that the spring is bad. He plays with it but it seems to be working perfectly well. He closes it slowly and this time, just as it's about to close fully, it stops as if something is stopping it. Right in that area, he notices a small black metal box the size of a matchbox. The box seems to be attached to the body of the truck. He looks at it closely. He fumbles with it a little but he doesn't want to snatch it off because he figures it could be something that belongs on the truck.

He hops in the car and pulls off. He's never noticed that gadget before. His paranoia has his mind racing uncontrollably. "I hope that gadget belongs on this truck, he says to himself.

An Hour Later

The Mayor stands here in this crowded auto body shop here in the Bronx. The gadget on the truck is all the inspiration he needed to come over here. He drove almost twenty miles over the speed limit all the way here. He figures the box may be nothing at all but he would rather be safe than sorry.

The Mayor has known these guys here ever since he was sixteen years old. He's never used them to repair any of his cars but he has used them to install secret stash boxes in every vehicle that he has ever owned.

"Papi, what's the problem?" the stout Spanish man asks.

The Mayor lifts the hatch. "Ay Papi, look at this for me," he says as he points to the box. The man examines the gadget closely. "What is that? I was trying to close the hatch but it's getting in the way," the Mayor explains.

The man turns toward the Mayor with a frightened look on his face. He places his index finger over his lips as if to say shhh. He backpedals away from the truck, signaling for the Mayor to come with him.

Once they get into the next room the man finally speaks. "Papi, you in big trouble," he whispers while shaking his head from side to side. The Feds, they track you and follow you. Please, leave here. I don't want trouble with them, Papi."

"What?" the Mayor asks.

"That's a tracking device," he whispers. "They know your every move."

"A tracking device," he repeats. His heart pumps with fear. The only level of comfort that he has comes from the fact that he has not made a move yet. He wonders if the gadget records as well. He tries to think back about anything that he may have said in the truck. He quickly remembers that he's never had anyone in the truck with him. "Papi, that thing record too?"

"No, but if they had time to attach it without you knowing then maybe they had time to do anything else they want to do. The truck could be bugged too, Papi. Be careful. Do you know how they had time to do it? Were you arrested? Was your car towed or anything?"

"Nah," he replies. "I'm just coming home. Arrested for what? I haven't done anything."

"Well, how do you think they did it?"

The Mayor thinks hard before speaking. "I do not have a clue," he says with confusion. "I do not have a clue."

Little does he know, the night they stalked his West Caldwell home, they attached the devices on every vehicle that was present.

One Hour Later

The entire ride from New York to Jersey, the Mayor rode in fear. He was even afraid to think aloud. His paranoia led him to believe that he was being followed. He watched every car that tailed him. He can't understand how they managed to pull this off without him knowing it. He can't believe that they have been this close to him without him knowing it. Normally he can feel their presence. Fear enters the equation when he thinks of the fact that one wrong move could have finished him off. This entire ordeal has his mind boggled.

He now sits here in Tony's office. He called an emergency meeting, stating that he's run into a problem. The funny part is, he called the meeting but Tony has been doing all the talking. From the time the Mayor walked in, Tony has been babbling on and on about Mocha.

"It's all fucked up now," he says. "This bitch done crossed the line. I'm really trying not to do something to this bitch but I swear to you my pistol keep calling my name. This bitch trying to finish me off, bruh," he says while shaking his head from side to side. "I fucked up big time," he says with shame. The other night we on the phone going through it and the last statement she made before hanging up on me didn't sit too well with me. I put one and one together, figuring what she could have been saying and I will be damn if I wasn't right. I call the banks and the three accounts I had in her name are cleaned out. You hear me? Cleaned the fuck out, empty, zero balance. I had a quarter in each of them," he informs. "That was the rainy day stash, just in case things went wrong, she would be alright. Now she more than alright," he says with a disappointed grin on his face. "I'm the one who isn't alright."

"Ay man, look at it like this. You just brought her out of your life for seventy five punk ass thousand. Come on bruh, you upgraded her lifestyle. How long you think that's going to last? Three months tops?"

"Seventy five thousand? I wish that was the fucking case! I'm talking about a quarter of a million. Three fucking accounts. Seven hundred and fifty motherfucking thousand!" he says with passion.

"You serious? How the fuck you let that happen?"

"Man, how the hell was I supposed to know that she was going to run off with a mufucker and take all my money? And you said, it may not be a nigga. Only the power of the dick can make a bitch do some crazy shit like that. This bitch gone finish me bruh. I can see it. You know I got those two commercial properties in her name? I gotta get at this bitch before she do something stupid like sell them for dirt cheap. Right now she just trying to hurt me. The crazy shit is, I didn't do shit to her. She moving out on me like I cheated on her," he says with pity. As sorry as the Mayor feels for Tony he's barely listening. He can't keep his mind off of his own problem. "Right now bruh, I need you to talk me out of doing what I keep on thinking about doing. That's murder this bitch before she murders me. I just can't sit back and watch this bitch mash me out for no reason. If I got caught cheating or something, I could understand it. I would just take it on the chin, follow me? Seven hundred and fifty thousand? She probably somewhere blowing it all on that nigga! What the fuck! The bitch won't even answer my calls. She thinks it's a fucking game."

Tony pauses for one second and the Mayor jumps in. "Tone, I got a problem. Hear me out for a brief one then we can get right back at your situation. The other day, I go to close the hatch of Liu's Rover and it wouldn't close. I'm trying to figure out why. As I look closer, I see a little black box. You know me…I'm paranoid as hell. I instantly start thinking the worse. I take the truck smooth over to my Spanish boys in the Bronx. And what the hell you think I found out? It's a fucking tracking device."

"What?" Tony asks in total shock. He sits there in silence for a few seconds before speaking. "This isn't good."

"Who the fuck you telling? I go home and I search every car there. Sure enough, they got one on every car, except the Rati."

"The Rati? What Rati?" The Mayor forgot that he never spoke about the Maserati to Tony. He didn't want to hear the speech that would go with it. "You bought a fucking Maserati?" he asks. "Come on. Where is your brain?"

"Not right now, Tony. I ain't doing shit and they fucking with me already. There has to be something you can do to keep them away from me?"

Tony stands up and starts pacing back and forth around the room. "Fuck!" he shouts. "Let me make a few calls and see what's going on. I need to know if you have a federal warning or if they're just fucking with you. Meanwhile, you have to stay in the shade. Way underneath the radar," he adds. "No talking on the phone, no talking in cars and don't make, even the smallest move on the outside. Everything you do, you do behind closed doors. You follow me?"

The Mayor nods his head up and down. "I follow you."

"How do you think they got that close to you without you knowing it?"

"I don't have a clue."

"Phew," Tony sighs. "Shit! Listen...leave all the devices on the cars. You didn't take them off, I hope?"

"Nah, I didn't touch them."

"Good. That's the smartest thing you ever done. Don't...you don't want to alarm them. If you take them off, they will know that you're onto them. Drive the cars normally, except for making moves. Follow me? Take them on a wild goose chase every chance you get. Let them follow you nowhere. As long as they think that you're ignorant to the fact, we are ten steps ahead of them...I hope."

Days Later

Tony is in Club Macanudo in Manhattan, N.Y. This is his favorite smoke shop in the world. Whenever he can he comes here to puff some cigars and relieve his mind. God knows with all the stress he has he definitely needs to relieve his mind right now.

The upscale smoke shop is also a bar and restaurant. The atmosphere is a smoker's dream come true. He happens to be a member here, which gives him full access to all the amenities. The club keeps it's exclusiveness by charging a fifty thousand dollar a year membership. One of the amenities is the private locker each member gets access to for another twenty thousand dollars a year. Tony's locker is filled with all types of exotic cigars, coming from Cuba, Dominican Republic and Honduras. In total, the cigars in his locker value at close to thirty thousand dollars.

The people who frequent this spot on the regular range from the average corporate dude to celebrities of all magnitudes. There's also plenty of eye candy strolling throughout the place, from exotic Spanish women rolling and lighting cigars, to beautiful women in sexy evening gowns puffing cigars.

Tony also enjoys the networking opportunity that lies in here. Through a cigar he has the opportunity to engage in a conversation with a person that normally he could never get close to. Just tonight, Ahmad Rashad, Denzel Washington, Butch Lewis and news reporter, Brenda Blackman are all in the building at the same time.

Tony has been in here for two hours already. For one hour he sat here smoking and sipping on Merlot, alone. Shortly after that, his solo engagement was interrupted by a beautiful green eyed white woman, who invited herself to his candle lit table. Before he knew it they were indulging in harmonious conversation. The chemistry was magnetic which made him feel comfortable in talking and opening up to her. He hasn't even realized that he's poured his heart out to her. As of right now, she's been listening to him talk endlessly about his wife Mocha for the past thirty minutes.

"Wow," she says with pity in her eyes. "I look at you and I see an awesome species of a man. How could any woman leave you? If I had you in my life I would be the happiest woman in the world."

Tony gets an instant ego boost. God knows that he needs

that right now. "You think so?" he asks hoping that she will boost him even more.

"I know so," she replies with confidence. She blows a ring of smoke from her thin lips before speaking again. "Awww, I feel so sorry for you. Can I help you in any way?" she asks with a beautiful Colgate smile. Suddenly Tony feels her hand land on his knee underneath the table. The firm touch then transcends into a light stroke up his thigh. She stops at his crotch. She leans over the table close to him. The cigar breath that seeps from her mouth would turn anyone else off but to him it increases her sex appeal. He gets an instant erection. "For a thousand dollars," she whispers over a cloud of smoke. "I can take your mind off of that tramp," she says with a seductive smile.

Damn, she's working, he thinks to himself. I thought she was really feeling me. It's all business for her. Every minute of the day since Mocha left him, all he can think about is her. He would love to free his mind, even if it only lasted a few minutes. "Oh yeah?" he asks. "Could you really?"

"Yes...I'm, sure."

The Next Day

The long drive here to Connecticut was exactly what the Mayor needed. It gave him time to get his thoughts in order. Now that he knows that the Feds are on his back, he realizes he has no room to breathe. He has very little room to slip which is why he plans not to. Even with them on his heels he feels like the show must go on. The pressure only brings out the best in him.

The Mayor sits in the passenger's seat of the old body Honda Accord. The driver is his man that he met many years ago in Otisville FCI. This man is the Mayor's last resort. Every other lead he had has come up blank.

This man, Raymos, hardly ever spoke but when he did, the Mayor could sense sincerity in his words and his stories. Raymos made mention of a few things that always stayed in the Mayor's mind. He spoke of things that only a person that has been there could talk about, while others spoke in general about the game.

When Raymos was released, he gave the Mayor his number and told him to stay in touch. The Mayor is glad that he did. Two days ago, the Mayor called and here he is, in Connecticut.

Raymos pulls into the parking lot in back of the small, ran down Mexican bar. "Listen, I'm doing something that I never do," he says with a stern look on his face. He backs into the narrow parking space. "Me, I never introduce nobody to nobody. That's how I keep my name out of shit. I don't want to be implicated in nobody paperwork. I put two people together and one of them ain't right, shit goes down and it's all on me. Or even worse, the boys get in the situation and they implicate me all because I introduced them. I ain't worried about that with you though. I trust you one hundred percent."

"As you should," the Mayor replies casually.

"Listen, when we go in there, don't take it personal but these mufuckers in here are racist. Especially the two older brothers. They don't fuck with blacks at all. My man is the youngest brother. He's a good dude. He like us. He don't give a fuck about white, black, none of that. His only concern is green. His brothers always tease him calling him a nigger lover, no disrespect. He did like twelve years in the Feds and came home and took off in less than a month," he says with his eyes stretched wide open. "They real low though. If you would have brought that Maserati to this bar, that would have been a definite deal breaker. They're not into the spotlight. All they do is drink Coronas and trick off with young Mexican chicks," he says as he starts dialing numbers on his phone.

Minutes Later

The Mayor follows Raymos' lead toward the back of the bar. Raymos taps on the door and it opens instantly. The man who opens the door keeps his eyes glued onto the Mayor, watching him like a hawk. The Mayor feels the tension but he ignores it. He automatically assumes that this has to be one of the older brothers. The man closes the door behind them, still watching the Mayor. He looks him up and down before barking hastily in Spanish.

Raymos looks at the Mayor with a half a smirk on his face. The younger man who is sitting in the back of the room, barks something back with anger. The older man snatches the door open, exits the room and slams the door behind him.

The young man stands up and starts walking toward them gracefully. "Please excuse my brother. He's on his period, today," he says just as he gets to them. He looks at Raymos as if the Mayor isn't standing there.

"Eddie, this is my man that I was telling you about," Raymos says. "He's a good dude. Like a big brother to me."

"Ok," he says while staring into the Mayor's eyes. He's trying to get a reading on him. He nods his head up and down. "I don't know if Ray- Ray told you but I'm not into meeting people. The world is crazy, you know? I really don't trust no one and I probably never will. Ray-Ray told me all about you. If it wasn't for him, we wouldn't be standing here together now. This is one of the only guys that I trust. If he ever crossed me, it would break my heart into pieces," he says as he looks into Raymos' eyes. He hopes that this is a legitimate meeting and not funny business. "To make a long story short, let's get to the bottom of this. I'm not really one for long meetings. What can I do for you?"

"As far as the long meeting goes, I'm with you on that. I'm not into all that talking shit. I'm about a dollar. I let my money talk for me. I'm not standing before you looking for a handout. I'm not down. I just got a situation. I have a huge network waiting on me to come through. The problem is, I can't find a supplier that can hold me."

The man smiles with arrogance. "Is that so? You could easily be looking at the answer to your problem."

"I hope so."

"You know, I like your style. I consider myself a good judge of character. I can be around someone for two minutes and know if they're good or bad for me. With you, I'm getting a good feeling," he claims. "Where are you from again?"

"Newark," the Mayor spits with pride.

"Oh, Brick City, huh? A good friend of mines was from out there. He was murdered over ten years ago though. I'm sure you heard of him. Maybe not...he's a lot older than you. Probably before your time. He came home from jail and took right off. Just when he was about to take over Newark, his rival wiped him out. I think the streets called him the Governor or the President," he says as he tries to remember the correct name.

"The Mayor?"

"Yeah, that's it. You know him?" he asks, realizing that maybe he has said too much.

"Yeah," the Mayor smiles. "I know him personally. I am him," he says with coldness in his eyes. "Who is your good friend though?"

The man stands there with a cheesy grin on his face. He realizes that he's put his ass out there. "Donald Pierson...Cashmere they called him," he says wishing the topic could be changed.

"Before we start this, let me say this to you. Believe none of what you hear and only half of what you see. They tried to charge me for his murder but I came up clear. Cash, was like a big brother to me and I would have never murdered him or have him murdered. My reputation was the reason the streets wanted me to be responsible for his murder. Let me tell you, I have never hurt anyone that didn't deserve it. I'm not a slime ball, a thief or stool pigeon. My reputation is flawless. I owe the streets nothing. People have their views of me but at the end of the day, I am probably the realest mufucker in the world and deep down inside anyone that has had the privilege of being in my presence knows that. I ask you not to judge me according to what you may have heard. Judge me according to what you feel. If after that, you're not interested in working with me, I have no choice but to respect your decision," he says while staring deeply into the man's eyes. "And for the record, it came up a few years ago that his sons' mother's boyfriend did it. Look at that," he whispers. "And they tried to send *your boy* away for the rest of his life for something he had nothing to do with."

"Oh, wow. I didn't know that."

"Now you know the truth," the Mayor says with a smile. "It cost me a hundred grand to defend myself in a murder that I wasn't behind."

"I never got that from him. I was away at the time. I met him in Fairton and we became good friends. He was released before me, so I connected him with my brother for the ye-yo (cocaine). Somewhere down the line, they started working the heroin. That's when all hell broke loose. From what I hear," he adds.

"Yeah, that's about the size of it but not as far as people believe it went."

"I got the information from the prison. We both know how that goes."

"Yeah, well now you're getting straight from the horses' mouth," he says while showing no sign of emotion. "Again, he was like a brother. In fact, him and my real brother were like this," he says as he crosses his fingers.

"Who is your brother?" Eddie asks.

"Dre."

Eddie squints his eyes with a smile. "Dre Money?"

"Indeed," the Mayor replies.

A look of grief plasters his face. "Man, I'm sorry to hear what happened to him. A lot of people loved your brother. It seems like half of the jail was in mourning when the news hit. People seem to know him from prisons all over. I heard he was a beautiful dude. Cashmere talked real big about him. Damn," he says as his eyes light up. "You come from good stock. Damn, it's a small world."

"For sure but it's a lot of money out there in that small world," the Mayor says, in attempt to get back into their initial meeting about work. "So, you said, Cash was going through ya'll for the work?"

"Yeah," he says, nodding his head up and down. "I'm sure you're familiar with the 'Bang Man' stamp? That was ours. As a matter of fact, it's funny that we are standing here talking about this," he says grinning from ear to ear. "I just ran across that stamp a few days ago, while cleaning up."

The Mayor's mind goes back to the day he became aware of that situation. That was the first dope that actually put his Block Party to shame. He knew nothing else to do but shut the operation down before the dope shut his business down. He thinks of all the drama that stamp brought into his life. Most of the murders that he was suspected of, all came behind that stamp. Suddenly dollar signs wipe out all the bad points. "Oh yeah? Ya'll was behind that stamp?"

"Yeah, I got the recipe for it," he brags. "If it was me, I would have done it different. A little less of this and a little more of that. You know what I mean? Everybody got their own way. My brother said Cashmere would ask him to turn the volume down because he didn't want to bring too much attention to himself."

"Well, I ain't afraid of no attention. It comes with the game. I love the spotlight. For me, you can turn the volume all the way up. If you can guarantee me that you can get it right and keep it right consistently, we're in business." A stern look pops up on his face. "I'm gone tell you straight up...I ain't got time for the back and forth bullshit. Buying it and bringing it back, that ain't me. I work smart not hard. I never touch the same workload twice."

"You don't have to worry about that with me," the man interrupts. "I agree that going back and forth is a waste of time for both of us. And time is money. Anything I give you is guaranteed. I always make sure it's right before it leaves here. It will never be less than a nine, ten."

The Mayor nods his head up and down. "That makes sense," he whispers. "Now let's make dollars."

Sean a.k.a. S-Dot lays back in the bed, drained and exhausted. His sex-capade has been over for twenty minutes already and still he struggles to catch his breath. He no longer believes the statement, 'age is just a number.' At 35 years of age, he's thirteen years older than his sexual partner, or should I say, sexual challenger. The age barrier feels more like twenty years to him.

In no way was he prepared for the challenge. Two hours and six orgasms and still the young girl screamed, harder, harder, faster, faster. Instead of following her instructions, he just went slower, and softer until he collapsed on top of her.

She backed it up on him, danced on it, spit on it, licked it like a lollipop, bent over doggy style, rode it horsey style, bounced on it frog style and still she claimed she had more tricks in store. She done things to him that he never had done. For the first time in his life, he screamed a woman's name.

Here he lays drenched in sweat in the king size bed, inside of the Marriott Hotel. He's beat and all he wants to do is sleep but the young girl won't let him. He nods once again but the sound of her squeaky voice awakens him yet again. Damn, he whines to himself. Would you, please? He wonders how she's able to do it. Instead of being tired as he is, she seems to be fully charged. His job really is to get valuable information out of her. The more they indulge in sex, he figured it would be easier and it would be if he could just stay awake and listen to her.

"I swear to God that was the scariest shit I ever seen in my life. The way his eyes rolled into his head, uhmm," she grunts. "He was shivering like he was having a seizure. How you think I felt watching my brother kill my baby father?" she asks before staring off into space. "You better not tell nobody that. I never told nobody that," she adds.

He opens his eyes halfway. "Damn," he says barely conscious. He's damn near sleeping but he hears her loud and clear. Nervousness fills his gut as he thinks of how much danger he may be in.

She laughs at him. "Sleepyhead," she teases as she rubs her hand over his heavy eyelids. "You mad cool. That's why I like dealing with older men. Young niggas be mad immature," she says as she nestles closer to him. The perspiration makes their bodies stick together. "You just might be my new boo," she says seductively. "I don't know," she teases. "You like an old man though," she smiles. "You better get your Viagra stash up fucking with me."

"Is that right?" he asks with a closed eye sexy smile.

"Yep," she says before putting a wet kiss on his cheek. She runs her fingers through his thick course beard. "It's hard for a bitch like me to find a nigga. A good nigga anyway. As soon as I meet one, my family just runs him away. As soon as he finds out who I'm related to, I never hear from him again."

"Yeah, why is that?"

"Boy, my family crazy," she says before lifting her head up. "It's like the whole world scared of them. My brother, Smoke, he crazy but my cousin is the craziest. They call him the Black Charles Manson. When he was home niggas was dropping like flies. He would kill a mufucker in a minute. Niggas was happy when he got locked up. It was like they was celebrating. He ain't never coming home. He good though cause he passed everything down to my brother."

"Everything like what? He closes his eyes, pretending that he's falling asleep and barely paying attention to her.

"Everything, everything. My brother control all the Bloods. He got G Status. He can do whatever he wants to do and nobody can't go against him. If he wants someone killed he don't have to do a thing but make a call and their ass is outta here."

"Yeah right," he challenges. He's hoping to hear more. "That Blood shit really like that?" he asks as if he's clueless to it all. He has introduced himself to her as a dude from New Brunswick who makes out of state moves. He acts as if he knows very little about Newark.

"Is it like that?" she repeats. "You don't know the half. If I told you all the murders my cousins and brother behind, you wouldn't believe me. Shit," she adds. "The majority of the unsolved murders," she whispers. "Comes from them. If I called in all the anonymous tips they have rewards for, I would be rich," she laughs.

"Yeah right. I don't believe that," he challenges once again. He's hoping that his challenging will reel her in and make her tell him everything she knows.

"You better believe it," she barks.

"How you know so much?" he asks her sarcastically.

"Psst, boy you don't know me. I know everything. I'm like a mafia princess," she smiles. "They tell me everything."

"Oh yeah, he says to himself, as he hugs her tighter. She slips away from his grip and gets out of the bed. She steps away, looking over her shoulder. "You wanna leave me now?" she teases.

Bitch are you crazy, he says to himself as he watches her perversely. Her body is like a piece of art to him. Her tight ass bounces vibrantly with youthfulness. Her smooth baby skin turns him on tremendously. At times he forgets that this is business. This is by far the best assignment the Feds have given him. He's getting good sex and in the process he's doing his job. "I would never leave you," he replies. "Not in a million years."

Days Later

The Mayor cruises through the city with no set destination. The windows are down and the roof is wide open, allowing the breeze to blow in freely. He knows it's not wise to be lurking around but he can't help himself. He loves the attention. He just hopes he doesn't receive any more attention from his least favorite people in the world. While incarcerated he missed just riding and observing the view of the raggedy city. While he was away, he realized how addicted he is to these streets.

As he's cruising around in the Maserati, the onlookers staring and admiring him gives him an adrenaline rush. In his mind, he feels like he's doing it for them. He feels like them watching him shine, motivates them to strive even harder.

The deep bass pumps from his Bose speakers as he sings aloud with rapper, Jay-Z. "I mean, I gotta be the pioneer of this shit. You know I was popping that Cristal when ya'll niggas thought it was beer and shit. You know, I was wearing that platinum shit when ya'll chicks thought it was silver, bottom line," he says with passion in his voice.

He glides down Central Avenue. With just the slightest touch of the accelerator the car roars like a lion. The vibration rolls under his feet, giving him the feeling of power. The people in the cars coming in the opposite direction gawk at him as they pass each other. Heads are spinning from both sides of the busy street. All the attention just makes the Mayor more calm and cool.

He slows down as he approaches Twelfth Street. He sits there bopping to the beat as he spots a car in his side mirror squeezing alongside of him. The sports car damn near scrapes the curb. The Mayor pays close attention to the license plates, memorizing them quickly, before looking at the BMW emblem on the hood. It's a habit of his to study license plates, just in case he needs to remember them.

He notices two men in the car and he automatically assumes the driver is thriving for attention. The car pulls side by side of him, while he looks straight ahead as if they're not even sitting there.

The horn sounds off once but the Mayor keeps his eyes glued onto the road in front of him. The horn sounds of again and again and again, until the Mayor finally looks in their direction.

The driver of the 645 smiles from ear to ear. The Mayor stares hard, trying to figure out who he is and where he knows him from. He pays close attention to the big bulky, junk jewelry as he calls it, which laces his ears, neck and wrist. "Nigga, I'm loving your movie," the driver barks while hanging out of the window. "You painting the perfect picture!" the man says with mockery.

The Mayor doesn't know if he should take it as a compliment or sarcasm. He just watches the man, further trying to figure out who he is. Suddenly the man's face becomes slightly familiar. He recognizes him but doesn't quite remember actually knowing each other. He's sure that they have only seen each other in passing.

"Got damn, nigga! You brought that beat back, huh? They finally let you out, huh? Welcome the fuck home!" The Mayor shrugs his shoulders with his normal amount of arrogance but he doesn't say a word. "You don't remember me, do you?"

The Mayor stares with uncertainty. "You look familiar but I'm not good with names."

"JB," the man spits. "Used to be with your man, Shaheed."

"Shaheed, Shaheed," the Mayor mumbles. "Oh, ok, Twentieth Street," he says with a half a smile. What's happening?"

"Ay man, it's all good. I see you still at it," he says while pointing to the Mayor's car. "Cute, real cute. My man just copped one of those in black though. I ain't gone front though…I expected a little more from you. I mean…you the Mayor." The Mayor senses the attack in his words but he just accepts the wound gracefully. "You was doing Bentleys and shit back in the day. The streets are probably expecting a little bit more from you too. Don't sweat it though. I'm about to give them what they looking for. I'm about to get out of this and jump in something crazy. I fuck around and go helicopter on these pussies!"

"As you should," the Mayor replies modestly. "If your coins up, go for it."

"If my coins up? Shit changed since you left. **Your boy** got real money now!"

"One thing bout money is, it has no discretion. It goes to anybody," the Mayor says sarcastically. "But I guess it's all according to what you consider money."

"I know what money is," he replies with a tight smile. "I guess you ain't heard, me and my team up."

"Nah, I didn't get the memo, I guess. Is that your version of the story or the peoples' version?"

"Ask around," he smiles. "Ain't nobody doing it like us."

"You know one thing I learned is, just because you're doing better than the people you're around doesn't necessarily mean that you're doing good. It just means you got one dollar more than the rest of the broke mufuckers around you. Anyway, you should be rich. Ain't nothing in your way. You're only as good as your competition."

"Competition is none. Me and my team run this city."

"You bragging? Looking at the condition of this city, I would hate to have to claim it. I come home and all I see is empty blocks and a bunch of mufuckers white mouth and starving, waiting to be fed. Have no fear though. I'm home and I'm gone feed them. Don't worry I got a plate for you too. Stop while your ahead, running your mouth or I might have to put you on Ramadan. Shaheed my man, so on the strength of him I may just let you lick the gravy off of my plate. You gone hear about me sooner than you think or should I say, you gone feel my presence. I'm gone show you how you lift a city up. I'm gone breathe life back into these streets." The light changes from red to green. The Mayor looks at the man who is sitting there fuming. He's speechless. "They gone have to send the National Guards in for me." He taps the gas pedal lightly causing the engine to growl ferociously. "Ay, word to the wise…save your little money you got. That's a 06, right? They changing the body style on that next year. When I'm done you will be lucky if you can scrape up five stacks to upgrade to a 07," he says before speeding off, leaving the man sitting there inhaling the smell of burned rubber.

The Mayor is livid but he's trying hard not to show it. He would never let the man know that he's gotten under his skin. He can't believe the man had the audacity to come at him like that. "Motherfucker," he snarls. He stops short at the next light. As he sees the BMW creeping up behind him, he blasts the volume on his stereo. Jay-Z's voice echoes through the airwaves as the man sits there in rage listening to the words that are ripping through his soul.

"And now these young cats acting like they slung cats. All in their dumb raps, talking bout how their funds stacked. When I see them in the street, I don't see none of that. Damn playboy where the fuck is the hummer at? Where is all the ice with the platinum under it? Those ain't Rolex diamonds, what the fuck you done to that? Ya'll rapping ass niggas, ya'll funny to me. Selling records but still ya'll wanna be me. I guess for every buck you make it's like a hundred for me. And still you running around thinking you got something on me." After the verse, the Mayor looks over to the man, staring coldly at him as he peeks back with hatred. "Young dumb ass nigga," the Mayor whispers to himself.

The Next Morning

The Mayor didn't sleep a wink last night. He tossed and turned all night. He was out of the bed before the sun even thought about rising. He has a sour taste in his mouth from what was said to him yesterday. At this point he has something to prove.

The Mayor storms into Rocco's office here in Teterboro. In his hand he holds a black duffel bag. "Handsome!" Rocco shouts at his entrance.

"Rocco, I need to speak with you," he demands as he peeks around at the few people that are present in the room.

A look of nervousness appears on Rocco's face. He can feel the tension coming from the Mayor. "Sure, sure. Sir, excuse me," he says to the customer who sits in front of him. "Can you please give me one second?" he begs. "Donny, take this gentleman out back and show him the beautiful X5 we have back there! Selma, you go with them," he says in attempt to clear the room. He watches as everyone makes their exit. He jumps up from his seat and closes the door behind them. He turns around anxiously. "Handsome, what can I help you with?" he asks while looking into the Mayor's eyes. Agitation is evident in them. "Is there a problem?"

"Yeah, there's a problem," he replies bluntly. "You played me, Rocco."

"What?" Rocco replies with no clue of what he's talking about. "Me? How?"

"I thought we were better than that, Rocco. We got history together. You don't do friends like that. How are you going to allow me to play myself like that?"

"Like what?"

"Oh, you don't know? Them shits," he says, while pointing to the Maserati through the huge window. "Come a dime a fucking dozen. They're like skittles in the hood. Niggas got every color. You got me riding around looking like everybody else."

"Psst, Handsome, that's not true. I only know of one other person in Newark who has that same car."

"That's one too many," the Mayor interrupts. "I want out of that car. Today," he barks viciously. He slams the duffel bag onto the table. "This four hundred. I need that Drophead Coupe," he says while staring Rocco dead in the eyes. "What is she four fifty? Get rid of the Maserati and take the balance from that."

"Handsome, Handsome, come on?" he pleads.

"Come on what? I know you can get your hands on one. You the best in the business. I know if nobody can do it, you can," he says attempting to boost his ego. "I want all white, stainless steel hood, with walnut seats."

"Handsome, I can't allow you to do this to yourself. You haven't been home ninety days and you want to jump into a $450,000.00 Rolls Royce? What's it about?" he says with sadness in his eyes. "You're headed nowhere fast. Do you know the attention that you're going to get? Handsome, Handsome, Handsome," he says shaking his head from side to side. "You must stop living for the people."

"Living for the people?" the Mayor interrupts with anger. "For the people? I live for me. I sat in the cell for over ten summers," he says while tapping his chest. "Many sleepless nights. Nobody did that time with me. While in there, you know what I realized? I realized that I was bullshitting out here. Yeah I lived good but good ain't good enough. Risking your life and your freedom just to live good, that ain't bout nothing! The whole purpose of this shit is to live a life that's to dream for."

"But Handsome you've done that already. You already live a life that people dream of."

"Yeah the people dream of but those ain't my dreams. Most people dream of being rich. I been rich since I was eighteen years old. I dream of being wealthy. While I was knocked off I promised myself one thing," he says with a smile. "That is if they ever let me go, I was going to do it bigger than I ever done it. I done it all, Rocco," he smiles. "All that a young nigga on my level could do. Now I'm on my way to the next level. I feel you trying to warn me but on the real, one thing bout me is once I make up my mind ain't no changing it. While away I said I was buying the Drophead Coupe for my birthday if I ever made it home. I'm home now. My birthday ain't until a few months from now but God willing it will come," he smiles. He exhales a huge sigh of relief. "So Rocco, with all that being said... are you going to take the four hundred or do I have to go over to my man Norman over in Queens?" he asks with a threatening demeanor. "The ball is in your court."

Samirah, Smoke's younger sister sits on the edge of her broken down, full sized bed. This tiny attic apartment is a part of her mother's one family house. The stench that lurks in the air is stomach turning. It's derived from a mixture of two day old spoiled Chinese food, three day old Jamaican food and a few soiled tampons that all lie in the waste basket. Although the smell is horrific, she's quite used to the odor.

The entire room is a complete mess. Mounds and mounds of dirty clothes are piled on the floor in layers, covering every square foot of it. Clean clothes are mixed in there as well, making it hard to differentiate them. Expensive pocketbooks hang from the four walls like art. The far corner of the room is the neatest area. Her costly shoe collection sits neatly in a pile. In total there is over forty pair of shoes ranging from Gucci to Jimmy Choo.

Samirah sits up in the bed for the very first time today. It's almost four o'clock and she's just awakened a few minutes ago. The ringing of her phone disturbed her extra long beauty nap. She peels the crusty sheets back, exposing her fully nude body. She holds the phone close to her ear as she gets out of the bed. She stomps loudly with no regard for anyone who may be downstairs. She climbs over the clothes on the floor until she reaches the bathroom. In there the clothes are piled up even higher. She makes it to the toilet where she plops onto it. As she's tinkling, she looks down at her beautifully manicured toes, twirling her feet, appreciating them from every view.

She looks over to the cardboard roll and realizes that she's all out of tissue. She hops off of the toilet, coochie still dripping as she walks over to the full sized mirror. She stares into the mirror at her slob stained face. "Uhm, uhm," she finally says after listening to the girl on the other end babble on and on. She unravels the silk scarf from her head and begins fingering through her hair. Once her hair is down, she continues to tease at it. "That bitch trifling!" she shouts. "Always been," she adds. "He just as trifling as her," she says as she turns around in the mirror. She watches her naked rear in the mirror from every angle. She dances sexily, swaying her hips from side to side. She struts away sexily, practicing her walk. Her ass is her claim to fame. She learned that many years ago. This is her biggest asset and she knows it which is why she treasures it dearly. "I thought you knew that!" she shouts. "Girl, Junior and them killed him," she says. "Girl, let me tell you. Everybody think Darryl did it but he didn't. It all started behind Cassie. She was with Omar but was fucking Junior. They was living together and everything. He took care of that bitch. She didn't want for nothing. Soon as a new bag came out she was the first bitch with it. Her and Junior started creeping around and Omar found out. Girl that's when all hell broke loose. Everybody think it was a robbery but it was all over Cassie. I heard he got like $250,000.00, girl. You know that nigga was holding! Junior came up. Now that bitch ain't got neither one of them. That nigga back with his baby mother. How I know? You know I got my sources," she says with a smile.

Meanwhile Downtown Newark

Agents Dumber and Dumbest sit at a desk inside of the headquarters. Earphones are lodged into their ears. The both of them are jotting down notes as they listen closely to what they're hearing. They are careful not to miss one syllable.

The words that they hear in no way shocks them. They've been listening to Samirah's conversations for weeks now. They tapped her line through Sean's phone. They have labeled her the queen of gossip, Star Jones. The young woman on the other end of the phone is her good friend who they have given the nickname, Oprah Winfrey.

Through these two women they have learned enough to arrest and convict over half of the city already if they wanted to but at this point it would be a waste because she hasn't mentioned a word about who they would like to hear about. All the information that they have stored may one day become valuable to them but at this point there are only two names that they're really listening for and that's Smoke and the Mayor. They're quite sure that they're bound to hear something about them sooner than later.

"But keep that to yourself," she whispers. "Don't nobody else know that."

Smoke stands in the center of the court, just observing his surroundings. Packs and packs of people swarm throughout the projects. They're damn near tackling the dealers. They fear that they may run out of the dope that they've been giving away most of the morning.

Smoke watches with anger as he thinks of how much money he could have made today if he had sold the dope instead of giving it away free. Late last night the Mayor met up with him and gave him one hundred bricks. He also gave strict instructions for Smoke to give out every bag of dope that he had given him free of charge. He instructed him to give the samples away between the hours of 5 a.m. and 8 a.m. He made Smoke give him his word that he would do it. He promised him and will not revoke but he plans to sell every bag that may be left, the minute after 8.

Every heroin addict in the town must have come through here this morning. Even people who never used heroin came here and tried their first bag, after hearing the word of how good the dope is. The word has spread near and far.

Smoke can get a reading on what scale the dope is, without asking a soul. All he has to do is watch the reactions of the addicts. He's seen more nose bleeding today than he's ever seen in a heavyweight boxing match. He has had to run more junkies away from the set than he ever has as well. They've been lingering around, walking like zombies. They're bent over, nodding like they're sleepwalking. In all his years of hustling, he's never seen anything like this. The Mayor has definitely made him a believer.

Smoke stands here in awe. As he watches and appreciates what's happening before his eyes, his phone rings. His enjoyment is interrupted. He looks down at the display and the word 'Boss' is spelled out in bold letters. He answers with no further hesitation. "Yope," he whispers into the phone. "Trills," he says before ending the call

Minutes later a black Ford 500 cruises into the parking lot. Smoke spots the Mayor sitting low behind the steering wheel and starts to walk hurriedly toward the car.

Smoke lowers himself into the passenger's seat, while the Mayor leans back nonchalantly. He's staring at the sight before his eyes. This sight reminds him a tad bit of the old days. A look of satisfaction appears on his face as a few memories run through his mind. He looks over to Smoke. "Now this is what a block supposed to look like. When I'm done the whole city will look like this," he boasts. "So, what you think?"

"Hands down, they say it's a ten all over the board."

"Why wouldn't it be?" the Mayor interrupts rudely. "Did you doubt me?" Before Smoke can answer the Mayor lashes back at him. "When you look at all this, what do you see?"

"I see a bunch of fiends."

"See, that's where you're wrong. Don't look at them as fiends. Look at them as clients. When I look out there I see promise. As long as we take care of them, they will take care of us. Yeah, they're only here today for free samples but tomorrow they will all be copping. Each one will tell another and another and so forth and so on. This is only the beginning. I'm not satisfied until the entire city looks like this and it will. Trust me when I tell you. Now that we see that the work is what it is, I'm gone press the button and in three days you will have two thousand bricks in your lap." This catches Smoke's attention. He turns his head so fast that his neck almost snaps out of place. The Mayor now has his undivided attention.

"Listen closely. I know you never played on this level and it all may seem like it's happening so fast. You might feel overwhelmed but I'm here to help you breathe easy. I got you. Just follow my lead. I'm gone walk you through this thing baby step by baby step. Keep your eyes and ears open and your mouth shut and you will be alright. I got the blueprint all laid out. First of all, no more seven dollar bags. We taking this back to the days of the old...straight ten dollar money."

"Psst," Smoke sucks his teeth. "That ain't gone work, bruh. I been selling dope over half of my life and I never even heard no price like that."

"Yeah, like you said, **you** been selling dope. This dope sells itself. That's why the price is what it is."

"But these mufuckers can barely scrape up seven dollars."

"That's cause nobody ain't giving them nothing worth scraping it up for. You gotta motivate them. Listen, when you got good dope you set the tone. Trust me on this one, lil bruh. You have to train them. Show them what you got, tell them the price and leave it up to them to come up with the money. It's simple. You dictate to them. You don't let them dictate to you. You think they on dope cause they wanna be? No. They on it cause they need it. They have no choice. Always remember...a mufucker gone get whatever he need to get what he want. As I said, ten dollar money. We're gonna make it where that seven dollar dope don't even stand a chance next to ours. But if I'm not mistaken, there should be no one standing next to us because your duty was to get rid of him. Correct?" he asks with firmness in his eyes.

"Correct," Smoke confirms. "But it's a recession out here. Mufuckers ain't got no money."

"Here we go with this fucking recession shit again," the Mayor barks with frustration. "Ain't no fucking recession. That's a figment of your imagination. That shit don't affect hood mufuckers. Niggas in the ghetto always been broke long before they started screaming that recession shit. Niggas around here been starving. Ain't nothing new for us," he barks. "Now as I was saying before I was rudely interrupted. Niggas been getting that seven dollar dope off cause it's nothing good out here. Now we're going to give them something to compare that garbage to. We're going to put a lot of motherfuckers out of business," he says with confidence in his eyes. "The only niggas who gone be eating is us. We're going to raise the bar. We also gone raise the price. By raising the price we also gonna clean the game up. The broke mufuckers gone have to pack it up and do something else. All that two hundred dollar a brick shit. Anybody can come up with that. That's why everybody and their momma hustling. Erase all that outta your head. I'm gone re-program you. I know that's all you know because that's all you have ever seen. Let me school you. That seven dollar a bag shit started when I went away. That would have never taken place while I was around. That's a disrespect of the dope game. When mufuckers lowered the price they lowered the quality. By lowering the quality, you lower the value of the game. We're going to bring the value back up to speed. At first I was gone come out here and beat them at their own game but I changed my mind. I would never disrespect the game like that. Ain't nothing bout me cheap so I refuse to sell cheap, garbage dope."

"I can dig it," Smoke whispers.

"Your price," the Mayor says with hesitation. "$195 a brick. You gone front it to your team at $275 a brick. If you get some wholesale dudes spending heavy, you let them get it at $250. You still giving him room to make fifty dollars for himself. Anybody else get it at $300.00."

"Three hundred?" Smoke interrupts. "You bugging. Nobody ain't paying that."

"We make it where they don't have a choice. Anybody who goes against the plan and makes our job harder, move him outta the way. Once we make them believe that they must have this, it will be a piece of cake. Just because of the price alone, they're gonna know that it's better than anything else and they will have to have it. It will be exclusive in their eyes. Also by raising the price per brick we're forcing mufuckers to sell it at ten dollars a bag. There's no way he can sell it any cheaper and still make a profit. If by chance anyone sells it for less than ten dollars that could depreciate our value. Twenty five dollars a brick goes straight to your cousin, Manson. Without him there would be no us, feel me? That brings you up to $195.00 a brick but you got the freedom to score anywhere from fifty five dollars to one hundred and five dollars profit per brick."

Smoke immediately starts calculating in his mind but frustration kicks in when he can't figure out the numbers quite fast enough. The Mayor can see the aggravation on his face. "Let me break it down for you. In about three days you will have two thousand bricks in your possession. At the bottom number you will score one hundred and ten thousand dollars after the deal is sealed. At the max you have the ability to score two hundred and ten thousand. Now you understand?"

"Loud and clear," Smoke replies with a huge smile. "Loud and clear."

"Off this deal alone, Manson scores fifty grand. Again, we can't forget about him," the Mayor emphasizes. "Without him there is no us." The Mayor knows how evil greed is and would never want Smoke to count his cousin out.

The Mayor has figured it all out to a science. He's made it where it's lucrative for everybody. Buying the raw dope at $45.00 a gram leaves him with a $125.00 profit margin. Even after paying his chemist his fee he still has over one hundred dollars worth of flexibility per brick. He too will score over two hundred grand off of this deal. Of course, two hundred grand doesn't mean to him what it means to Smoke. To the Mayor it's a drop in the bucket but he knows the name of the game is longevity. Five deals of that magnitude will land him another million in cash.

The Mayor speaks again. "You know why the game fucked up? Cause the leaders really should be following. The blind leading the blind. There's no structure in the game. We're going to bring organization back to it. The stronger the foundation, the more money for everybody. Like I told you, I'm gone walk you through this. Watch closely. We are about to change the city as niggas know it."

Twenty Minutes Later

The Mayor sits patiently behind the steering wheel of the Ford 500 as his passenger's door is snatched wide open. He looks over as Mike Mittens plops into the seat. "What's good?" Mike Mittens asks as he slams the door shut. A smile pops onto the Mayor's face as he notices the jet black color of Mike's hair and beard. There's not a single strand of gray hair visible anywhere.

"I see you took my advice," the Mayor teases. "Looking, early thirties," he laughs. "So, I guess it's safe to assume that you're going to accept my proposition?"

Mike Mittens chuckles in reply. "How could I refuse?"

"Good," the Mayor replies. "Your promissory of employment was just about to expire," he says with a slight grin. "You couldn't have called me at a better time. Everything is in order. Tomorrow the work will be in my hands. First thing in the A. M., we are going to get you a rental so you can maneuver the V. Just for the time being," he adds. "I got my Spanish boys dropping a box in a G-ride for you as we speak. I'm gone connect you with the young boy and ya'll take it from there. The rest is history."

"Psst," Mike Mittens sighs. "Only you, boy," he mumbles. "Only you could talk me into some crazy shit like this. I vowed to never ever come back to this shit. Now look at me. About to go against everything...fucking with these young gangbangers. Un-fucking-believable."

"Have I ever steered you wrong?" Mike Mittens shakes his head negatively. "Then why are you questioning my judgement? I got this. Don't worry about it. Mike, it ain't about red or blue. It's about green. The game don't change. Only the players. You putting way too much emphasis on the color that a nigga wearing. What's a color when the same punk mufuckers are behind the color? Look at it like this, a bunch of mufuckers wearing the same color uniform like a baseball or basketball team. The color don't change what's in their heart. It doesn't change what they're made of. They only pump fear into mufuckers who respect that shit. Niggas like us, it don't work on cause we fear nothing," the Mayor says staring into Mike's eyes. He needs to make sure that Mike agrees. He thinks he knows what Mike used to be made of but he needs to find out where he is today. As he's staring into Mike's eyes, he sees fatigue which he assumes comes from being tired from the life he's lived. Behind the fatigue he still can see a spark of killer in his eyes. "We only respect what demands respect. Anything less is meaningless. Follow me?"

"Unfortunately," he replies sarcastically.

"Trust me on this. It's all gonna work out," he says as he reaches out for a handshake. "Be on the listen for my early morning call."

"I'm here," Mike replies while returning the handshake. He forces the door open with his free hand. "Later."

As Tony steps into the spacious room, the sweet smell of cedar awakes his sleeping nostrils. He sniffs the air twice, just enjoying the fragrance. He turns the lights on and the reflection from the sun bounces off of the glass showcases that cover every wall in the room. More cigars are displayed in the showcases than a small cigar store. His huge inventory exceeds hundreds of thousands of dollars. The cigars in no way are for sale. They're purely for his smoking enjoyment.

The basement of his home is his favorite room in the entire house. He's done more reconstruction to this room than he does anywhere in the house. Huge glass showcases, brass trimming, oversized mirrors and marble floors fill the room. He spent a hundred grand on his ventilation system alone. He can smoke in here all day and not a trace of smoke will be left in here or the rest of the house.

In this room he not only smokes but he also does his second most favorite thing, which is stock trading. He has the corner of the room set up like an office on Wall Street. Three huge flat screens are hung from the wall and four computers surround his desk. Years ago Tony was introduced to the stock market and he has been trading ever since.

Through the stock market he has learned to make his money work for him. He starts his morning off in this very room everyday. His morning cigar while checking up on his stock portfolio are two things that he can't go without.

He grabs a cigar from the humidor before walking over to his office area. As he powers on his computers and his screens he holds the cigar up to his nose and sniffs the wrapper. "Ah," he exhales as he seats himself. As he's lighting the cigar he listens closely to the Bloomberg Report. He can barely concentrate on what the man is saying due to the thought of Mocha that he's having.

He grabs his phone and dials her number. As usual it rings over and over until her voice mail comes on. He slams the phone down with rage. In seconds the phone begins to ring. His spirits are lifted as he hopes that it's her returning his call. "Hello?" he says without looking at the display.

"Mr. Austin," the man says. "Andy."

"Yeah?" Tony replies with evident aggravation in his voice.

"Mr. Austin, I have the deal of a lifetime for you. It's an opportunity that neither you nor I can afford to miss."

"Is it anything like the last deal of a lifetime that you had for me wherein I lost a half a million?" Tony asks with sarcasm.

"Mr. Austin, please? Just hear me out?"

"Andy, not right now," he whines.

"Mr. Austin, please trust me? There's no better time than right now. I have been calling you all morning. I can't let you miss this opportunity. If you don't get in on this you're gonna hate yourself forever."

"Andy, things ain't looking good for me right now. I've been losing tremendously since our last unfortunate situation. Right now I can't afford to lose another dime. I lose anymore and I'm going to be in the homeless shelter," he says with disgust.

"Well that's even more reason for you to get in on this. It's the perfect solution for your problems. It will remove you from the poor house," he laughs. "Tony, you gotta trust me on this one. I know I messed up big last time but please just give me a chance to redeem myself?"

"The last time?" Tony asks sarcastically. "How about the last few times?"

"Tony, I admit I have made a few wrong decisions throughout our relationship but this one my friend will make up for all of my mistakes."

His persistence has Tony quite curious. ""Let me hear it then?"

He sighs with joy. "Remember the new drug I told you about months ago? Well, it's in effect. Right now it's trading at a dollar and sixty eight cents a share. Next week predicted to be trading at six dollars."

Tony calculates in his mind. The numbers that he comes up with causes him to give his broker his full attention. "Oh yeah?"

"Yeah," he replies. "A smart man will get in right now. It's expected to go up to three dollars by the end of today. That's double your money in just one day."

Tony logs onto yahoofinance.com. He looks up the noted drug to get the quote and sees exactly what Andy just said. He carefully reads over all the information that's posted. He really hates to blow an opportunity like this but he really can't afford to lose another dime. "Hmphh," he sighs.

"Mr. Austin, trust me on this one."

Tony is now looking at his bank account online. His heart is racing and his palms are sweaty. Trading stocks is like a bad habit for him. He knows that he shouldn't but still he would hate to miss out. "What can I get for two hundred grand?" he asks. His legs are trembling right now. He takes pull after pull of his cigar trying to ease his nerves.

The man quickly calculates. "For two hundred and one thousand, six hundred, I can get you a hundred and twenty thousand shares."

Tony looks at his account again and realizes that he really can't afford to lose two hundred grand right now. "Put me in for a hundred grand."

"Mr. Austin, please? If you have two hundred grand don't be afraid to put it up. We can't lose on this one."

"A hundred grand and I'm in. No more, no less. I'm letting you know I have lost much more than I'm willing to lose with you. If this doesn't work not only will you lose me as a client but you will lose your life as well."

The stockbroker laughs. "Mr. Austin is that a threat?"

"No, Mr. Klomenski, that's a promise!"

The Mayor stands here in front of the parking lot of Hertz Car Rental in Bloomfield. "There it is," the Mayor says with joy as he points to the silver Chrysler Sebring. "Your joint should be ready in a few days. I talked to my Spanish boys earlier. Until then just move around in this. This is the beginning of our future," he says with a smile. "I put the work inside the car already. In the floor of the front seat, there's a duffel bag. In the bag there is two thousand bricks. You and my young boy gone get together and the rest is history in the making. We are on our way," he says with excitement.

"On our way, where?" Mike asks with sarcasm. "That's the question."

"Come on man. You're changing in your old age. Everything is negative with you. You over thinking. Why can't you just see things for what they are? I look at the glass as half full but you see it as half empty. Get your mind right. That working class mentality got you fucked up. Sonny was right," the Mayor says mimicking the young actor from a Bronx Tale. "The working man is a sucker." He laughs in Mike Mitten's face. "This is going to be a piece of cake. Easy as one, two, three. "Here," he says as he secretly passes two Motorola pagers over to Mike. "These are for you and the young boy. No phone conversations between ya'll. From here on out, ya'll set up a meeting place and just page each other stating the time that ya'll want to meet each other. We don't need no slip ups," he says with seriousness in his eyes.

"Absolutely not," Mike agrees.

"Come on," the Mayor instructs as he walks toward the car. He walks to the driver's side and Mike goes to the passenger's side. Once they're both seated, the Mayor peeks around cautiously before placing his hand underneath his shirt. He pulls his hand out and in his grip there lies a fully loaded handgun. He holds the gun low, out of sight as he clicks the lever on the side of the gun. Like magic the magazine drops from the bottom. The Mayor then hands the gun and the magazine over to him separately. The Mayor then pulls up a few feet, just to get away from the rental place.

Mike grips the gun in his hand, on his lap. Suddenly he gets a huge adrenaline rush. He grips the gun tighter and the rush shoots through his entire body. Suddenly his alter ego reveals its presence. His top lip curls upward while the corners of his mouth sag like a dope fiend. His eyes drop low, half closed. Mike shakes his head from side to side, trying to erase the feeling that he has. He quickly unzips the duffel bag and drops the gun and the clip inside. He grabs a sleeve of five bricks and studies it. His eyes get lost onto the magazine paper that covers each brick. "You said two thousand, right? How much he gotta give me back?" he whispers.

"Three, ninety," the Mayor replies.

Got damn, Mike thinks to himself. Never in his life has he seen that amount of money. It sounds unreal to him. In his heart he feels like the Mayor is a fool for even trusting some young Blood niggas with that amount of capital. He fears what they may be willing to do. In no way does he believe that they are worthy of having this much work, let alone paying the Mayor back. Fear pumps into his heart as he thinks of the trouble that amount of money can generate. He also fears the type of heat he could get from the law even handling this amount of work. He's sure a four hundred thousand dollar flow can get him sent away for the rest of his life if he gets caught up in the action.

He's second guessing all of this once again but he realizes it's way too late in the game to back out. He's already in too deep. He would hate to let the Mayor down. While he was incarcerated, if it wasn't for the Mayor he would have been a state baby. Because he had the Mayor in his corner he lived like a king.

Mike flips the sleeve over and sees the stamp taped across the middle of the package. It gives him a weird feeling. Bang Man, he utters to himself. Quickly his mind goes back over ten years ago but it all plays clearly as if it were yesterday. He remembers how much confusion this same stamp caused. It changed his life for the worse but he bears witness that it was all his fault.

Cashmere didn't want to bring the stamp to Newark but he begged and begged until Cashmere finally gave in. Mike thinks of all the lives that were claimed behind this stamp. He thinks back to his little man Rah Rah who was killed while trying to protect him. He also thinks of how lucky he is to still be alive. It all plays out like a movie...A bad movie at that. He often sinks into guilt mode when he thinks of how many died because of his bad decision that he made out of greediness.

It feels strange to be sitting here over ten years later holding the same dope but now the only difference is he's now on the same team as the man who ordered the hit to end his life.

"Yo," the Mayor shouts, waking Mike out of his thoughts. Mike snaps out of it and looks over to the driver's side of the car where the Mayor is now standing on the outside. "Damn, what the hell you thinking about? I'm talking to you and you not even responding. Where your head at?" he asks with a smile. "I'm out. Hit me," he says as he walks back toward his own rental that is parked a few feet away.

Mike shakes his head at the thought of all this. "What people do," he sings aloud. "For money."

Less than forty five minutes pass and here Mike Mittens is sitting parked in Target's parking lot on Route 22. He feels this is the perfect meeting spot due to the heavy volume of customers coming and going. He feels that they can make their transaction without anyone paying attention to them.

Mike has been awaiting Smoke's arrival for a little over fifteen minutes now and he's quite furious. Not only is he furious but he's nervous as well. The last thing he needs is to get knocked off his first day in business before any actual business is made. The way his luck has been in his life he could very well see that happening.

Another five minutes pass and Mike finally spots the green Pontiac creeping into the parking lot. As the car is approaching he notices a young female driver and a young male in the passenger's seat. Mike tries to get a clear view of his face. They've spoken on the phone a few times but this will be their first time meeting in person. Mike is definitely looking forward to this meeting just so he can get a feel of who it is he will be doing business with. He trusts none of the young generation and always limits his interaction with them. For the dollar bill he's putting all his feelings to the side.

The green Pontiac parks in the middle of the parking lot. Mike peeks around the lot cautiously before making his move. Finally he starts the car up and proceeds toward the Pontiac. In seconds, he's parking right next to Smoke's car on the passenger's side.

Smoke looks over and they lock eyes with each other. Mike gives him a head nod to let him know that it's him. As Smoke is getting out of the car, Mike watches him closely. In no way does he match what Mike expected him to look like. Judging by what the Mayor has told him about Smoke he expected some hideous looking, big young boy. Instead he's a frail, light skinned pretty boy.

Mike has to laugh to himself. In his day this young boy would have had a hard time. Back then you had to look up to par to be accepted as a gangster. Today it's totally different. The most harmless looking kids are the deadliest and most dangerous. He's just happy that he knows better than to judge a book by the cover.

At fifty three years old, Mike is just happy to still be here.

With all the things that he's seen in his life and been through, he knows it's a blessing to still be alive. He's seen so many gangsters come and go. He has gone against some of the most ruthless of them but with this new generation it's totally different. They have no boundaries, no perimeters. He can't figure them out which makes him leery to even deal with them. He doesn't understand their method of thinking or better yet, non thinking. As he looks at the young boy, he can't help but wonder why he's willing to put it all on the line. He quickly remembers that it's all for the almighty dollar. He's willing to do business with him to make money but *trusting him,* he will never.

As Smoke is walking around to the Sebring's passenger's side, Mike quickly grabs hold of his nine millimeter and lays it visibly on his lap. Mike can feel his negative vibe from feet away. His slow and sneaky walk and his shady eyes tell a complete story.

Smoke hops into the car and the first thing that he sees is the gun. Mike catches him looking at it and plays it off as if he doesn't want him to see it. He grabs it and tucks it down his waistband. He then reaches over, extending his hand. "Mike Mittens," he says in a strong and confident voice.

Smoke extends his hand but not once does he look Mike in the eyes. That's another bad sign to Mike. He sits there as if Mike is nothing or nobody which is making Mike more angry. Mike's huge hand swallow Smoke's hand. He squeezes it tightly until Smoke looks his way. Mike's look pierces through his young soul, making Smoke uncomfortable. He looks away from Mike once again. He squeezes his hand even tighter. "I didn't get your name," he says with sarcasm.

"Smoke," he replies with massive arrogance.

Mike grips his hand even tighter, causing Smoke to try and draw it away from him but the grip is too tight. "Excuse me. I still didn't hear you.

"Smoke," he says in a louder tone.

Mike finally lets his hand go. At this point he gets the feeling that he's done what he set out to do. He can now see underneath his false sense of armor, realizing that he's just a regular young boy. He now agrees with the Mayor. He's just a scared young nigga hiding behind his color. He hopes that he has made enough of an impact on the young boy for him to know that he means business as well. He's not quite done with him yet though.

"Young fella, I don't know you," he says while staring at Smoke, who is staring out the window in front of him. "And you don't know me. The *big boy* put us together for a reason. To get this money and that's what I plan to do. It's obvious that he thinks we can play well together. It's all about the chemistry. We ain't gotta like each other," he says while leaning closer over to Smoke. "But we gotta respect each other. Having me sitting out here for twenty five minutes, waiting on you while I got two thousand bricks of dope in my lap... that ain't respect. I wouldn't do it to you and I ain't gonna allow you to do it to me. We clear on that?"

Smoke looks over to him. "No doubt. My bad, old head. My bitch drive slow as hell."

"Nah, no need for excuses. It's just a pull up. We gotta look out for each other."

Mike Mittens reaches behind his seat where three shopping bags sit. He grabs them by the handles and pulls them toward him. He passes them over to Smoke. "Here," Mike says as he flips open the middle console. He retrieves a pager and hands it over as well. "From now on we gonna communicate through these. The *big boy* told me to give it to you. No more phone conversations. My pager number stuck on the back of that pager. Memorize it and get rid of it. When you ready to get at me, page me and put all ones in and the time you wish to meet with me. This is our meeting place right here until I tell you otherwise. If by chance I can't make it at that particular time, I will hit you back with the time that I can. Understand?"

"Trills."

"Trills?" Mike asks with agitation. "What the hell is that? I don't understand that lingo. Talk to me in plain English."

"True. I got you."

"Alright, cool. That's more like it. I guess that's about it, for the most part. Be safe, young fella."

"Ah," Smoke says while shaking his head with distress. "That *be safe* shit, I don't like it. It makes me feel like something is going to happen to me. I hate that. Just say something else like... do you. I don't know."

"Alright then, young fella. Have it your way. Do you," he says with a smirk.

For the very first time throughout this meeting a smile appears on Smoke's face. He pushes the door open and makes his exit. "You do the same, old head."

Tony is a living wreck. He's been in the house sulking in misery for days now. He hasn't showered in those days either. Nor has he eaten. This state of depression is getting the best of him. Losing his wife is stressful enough but to lose his finances as well takes the stress to another level.

As he thinks about all of this he realizes that losing her is really nothing compared to losing his money. The fear that she's going to rob him blind brings fury to his heart. She's already cleared out three bank accounts and threatened to sell his properties. To add insult to injury she made another threat to take half of everything he has left.

Tony constantly wonders how they've gotten to this point. The anger that she speaks to him with baffles him. He can't figure out what she's so angry with him about. He's done everything in his power to provide the perfect lifestyle for her. Instead of being grateful she acts as if he's crossed her some sort of way.

He can't figure out the answer to save his life but he realizes he can't continue to sit back and try to figure it out. Time is running out. He refuses to sit back and allow her to lead him to the poor house. He realizes he has to do something quick before it's too late.

He lays back sunken into the soft mattress of his king sized bed. He stares at the chandelier that's hanging from his ceiling. He shakes his head from side to side, attempting to shake away the thoughts that are running through his mind. I can't, he says to himself. That's some sucker ass shit. But if I don't, he thinks. "Fuck it," he whispers as he leans over toward the nightstand. He quickly grabs hold of the half a sheet of paper that lies next to the lamp. He stares at the phone number, debating if he should actually make the call. "I have no choice," he utters aloud as he grabs hold of his cellular phone. "I have no choice."

Two Days Later

As the Mayor cruises up Springfield Avenue there is only one thing on his mind and that is getting money. It's been a long time coming but his plan now seems to be coming together. He dreamed of being back on the streets making moves and can't believe that he's actually here.

Smoke has been calling him updating him ever so often. He just wishes he was able to hang around and see the action for himself but he knows the peril in that. He gets a rush watching transactions transpire. He has been tempted to go through there several times but he's sure that it's better to stay as far away from Smoke as he can. The last thing he needs is to be attached to Smoke and his gang banging affairs.

His love for the game makes it hard for him to stay out of the light. His passion is business. He gets enjoyment from making deals and closing them. His talent is his ability to create lucrative situations. He gets the most satisfaction changing people's lives. He looks at it like a project. He loves to take a dude who has nothing and change his life as he knows it. It makes him feel like a ventriloquist controlling his puppets.

He's driving in somewhat of a trance until his zone is interrupted by an Audi which has just pulled side by side of him. He looks over casually and happens to notice a baby faced driver and two baby faced passengers staring at him. Neither one of their faces look familiar to him.

They appear to be no older eighteen or nineteen. They're staring at him with evil eyes but the Mayor isn't taking them serious at all. He charges it to their ignorance. He automatically assumes that they're car thieves just joy riding. He turns away from them and continues on his way.

They ride side by side for a few seconds before the Audi falls behind a few feet. They tail him for a block and a half. The Mayor isn't taking them serious but he watches his mirrors just to see what type of mischief they could be up to. Their presence gives him a slight sense of discomfort.

He stops short at the red light while keeping his attention on the Audi which is creeping up on the side of him. The sudden screeching of car tires squealing snatches his attention from the Audi. He looks in front of him, where he sees a red blur cutting in front of him, slightly passing him. In seconds a hand gripping a chrome handgun appears from the back window.

The barrel is aimed straight at him. He ducks down low. Boc! Boc! Gunshots sound off loudly. The windshield of the Mayor's car shatters in his face. Boc! Boc! He leans down lower attempting to get out of the way. He mashes the gas pedal as hard as he can. He swerves hard to avoid hitting the Cherokee that has him blocked in between the Audi. Off by a few inches, he bangs into the bumper, ripping the edge off but still he manages to get away. Random gunshots sound off from the passenger's side as well. In seconds the passenger's side window caves in, so does the back window.

The Mayor floors the Ford up Springfield Avenue with confidence. His speed exceeds 90 miles an hour but the Audi is close on his bumper. Gunshots sound off from behind, inspiring him to go faster and that he does. Just as he approaches the Irvington borderline, the gun clapping stops.

The Mayor lifts up slightly to make sure that the coast is clear. He looks in his rearview mirror, only to see the Audi making a wild u-turn in the middle of the busy street.

Twenty minutes later and the Mayor has arrived at what he finds to be safety. He's enraged. Never has he been disrespected like this. The fact that the gunmen were kids makes him feel that much more disrespected. He hops out of the car, examining it carefully. With all of the damage done to this car, he has no choice but to be grateful. The golf ball sized bullet holes could have easily been in his body instead of the body of this car.

He lifts his leg up high and kicks the back of the car with all of his might. "Young, dumb motherfuckers," he snarls. "Somebody gotta pay for this!" But who, he thinks to himself.

Later that Night

The Mayor listens to the phone ring as the anxiety rips through his gut. He's pissed off like he's never been pissed off before. He can't believe that he's been disrespected like this. He replays the faces of the young boys in his head over and over again. He's one hundred percent sure that he doesn't know them. He also knows that they're too young to know him. He wonders if that was a random, malicious act or if it was purposely intended for him. He weighs the options but can't quite understand why. If it was intended for him he wonders who is behind it.

The crowd of people who are lurking around the court of the projects all run for safety. They're attempting to get out of the way of the Chevy Trailblazer that's ripping through the entrance recklessly. They assume that it must be a stolen truck. The dark tinted windows cause a great deal of mystique. They have no clue who or what is behind the darkness.

The Mayor grabs his phone from the console and starts to dial away. "Yo!" he shouts into the phone with rage. "I'm here," he barks viciously.

"Where you at?" Smoke asks while looking directly at the Trailblazer.

"Right in front of you," the Mayor says as he flicks the high beams on.

Smoke walks to the truck quickly. The sound of the Mayor's voice causes concern. Finally he gets to the truck and opens the door slowly. As he's sliding inside he looks over at the Mayor out of the corner of his eye. He's quite shocked at what he sees. The bulletproof vest that the Mayor has strapped over his white t-shirt strikes his curiosity but the Uzi with the extended clip that rests on his lap causes major concern. White latex gloves cover the Mayor's hands.

He looks up into the Mayor's eyes and sees something that he's never saw in them. The fire in his eyes speaks volumes. The Mayor snatches the skull cap off of his head and throws it onto the dashboard. He's steaming. He presses the button to lock all the doors. As they click, he pulls off, mashing the gas pedal hard.

"Big Bruh, what's up?"

The Mayor grabs hold of the Uzi as he's driving recklessly. "You tell me," he says as he lifts the gun in a threatening manner. He peeks back and forth at Smoke with anger in his eyes as he speeds through the street.

"Huh?" Smoke asks.

"Huh what?" the Mayor snaps as he stares through Smoke as if he has x-ray vision. The Mayor has been thinking long and hard. No one in the town knows that he's here let alone what he's driving but Smoke. He feels like it's a crazy coincidence that he just gave Smoke 2,000 bricks a day ago and today someone tried to murder him. Something makes him think that maybe Smoke ordered the hit hoping he could come up on 2,000 bricks of free dope.

Uneasiness fills Smoke's heart. "Big bruh, what's the deal? What is this all about?"

"What's it all about? Let me tell you what it's about. I'm cruising through the city doing me and before I know it, I'm trapped in between two cars being shot at by a bunch of young niggas with red bandanas on. Now you tell me what it's about!" he shouts as he makes a wild right turn. He lifts his gun high in the air. "I assume they were Blood and I know you Blood. If I remember correctly, you told me don't nothing go down in this city without going through you first!" He puts the gun to Smoke's head. "You did say that right?"

Smoke looks at the gun that rests on his temple and his nervousness turns to pure fear. "S, somebody shot at you? Who? Where?"

"Springfield Avenue. A silver Audi and a red Cherokee sport…all young niggas! They tried to take me out. They fired at least fifteen shots at me," he says as he floors it up the narrow block.

"Big bruh, breathe easy. Please take the gun off of my head?" he begs but the Mayor ignores his plea. "A silver Audi and a red Cherokee? Hold on," he says as he grabs his phone and presses the button on the side. Seconds later, he speaks again. "Yo!"

Chirp, chirp! A voice busts through the line. "What's goodie?"

He presses the side button again. "Yo, who got that red Cherokee and the silver Audi out there?"

Chirp, chirp! "Audi and a Sport?" the man asks.

He taps the button and holds it. "Trills."

Chirp! "I don't know. Why what's up?"

"Nah lil niggas did some fuck shit. I need to know who in

there."

Chirp! "Say no more." Chirp! "I'm on it. I'm gone bust back at you as soon as I hear something."

"Yeah, do that." He lays the phone down on his lap. "Big bruh, I will know something in a minute. I will get to the bottom of it"

"That would be your best bet," the Mayor says coldly. He slows the truck down tremendously and is now cruising at a moderate speed. "For your own sake. As of right now, don't nobody in this town know shit about me but you. With that being said, I only got one suspect."

"I know you don't think I'm behind that?" he asks with a shocked expression on his face. "What would I gain from that?"

"I don't know...two thousand bricks maybe."

Hearing this breaks Smoke's heart. "Are you serious, Big bruh? What type of slime ball do you think I am? Big bruh, you bugging right now! On my **Hood** I won't never cross you."

"Nah, I ain't bugging. Not yet," he smiles devilishly. The Mayor looks closely at Smoke and the look on his face actually makes the Mayor have second thoughts. Maybe he is innocent in this matter. "Dig this, get me some answers or I'm gonna be forced to move on what I *think* this is all about. Lil bruh, this ain't a threat. I don't make those. I only make promises and as you know...I am a man of my word. If I find out that you're behind this you're gonna have to round up every Blood in the country to team up with you and come for me. I don't give two fucks about that Blood shit. I can show you better than I can tell you," he says sternly.

Smoke isn't paying the least bit of attention to the Mayor's threat. The fact that he believes that he's behind it, actually hurts his heart. "Big bruh, I promise you I ain't got nothing to do with that shit. Not me or none of mines. I can guarantee you that. Trust me, I will find out who is behind it though. Consider this beef handled. You're the boss. You ain't got no business out here like this," he says as he points to the gun and the vest. I need you out here," he says with sincerity in his eyes. "If something happen to you out here big bruh gone have my ass on a plate. Cousin or no cousin," he adds. "Man, I don't need to hear this shit from him," he whines. "Yo man, please don't let this get back to him. I'm gonna handle this. You can just go ahead and put your feet up. I got this," he claims. Smoke's eyes bleed with pity.

The Mayor pulls over at the middle of the deserted block. "Meeting over," the Mayor says as he presses the button to unlock the doors. He gives Smoke a head nod signaling for him to get out.

Smoke does just that. He forces the door open and steps onto the asphalt. "As soon as I hear something, consider it handled. I will call you when it's done."

"Close my door," the Mayor instructs. Smoke closes the door as he's told. The Mayor peels off recklessly, leaving Smoke standing there in the middle of nowhere.

Sadness is plastered all over Smoke's face. He stands there momentarily, just reenacting the whole scene. Never before has his life been threatened like that. He had a ton of respect for the Mayor but the way he waved that gun around in his face made him lose a great amount of that respect. As he thinks of it a part of him wants to get even. He feels so violated. The more he thinks about it the angrier he gets. He paces a few circles with anger as tears of rage drip down his face.

The Next Day/August 7, 2009

The shack is filled beyond capacity. Blood gang members fill the backyard and spill over into the alleyway. All of their attention is focused on Smoke, who stands at the broken down podium inside of the shack. He speaks loud and clear so they all can hear him.

"The meeting today is called because of a situation that needs to be situated. Yesterday something happened that shouldn't have. Somebody close to me almost got touched. He was this close," he says as he holds his hand in the air with his fingers slightly parted. "To losing his life. Over fifteen shots were fired close range. It's a good thing that he still here. I just got the call an hour ago, telling me who was behind the shooting. The reason, I don't know yet but I will know soon. In the meantime we gotta handle this. Nobody is exempt...from the little mufuckers to the head. Anything under that sect is now officially on a plate. Eat away!" he says with passion. "The broad, Mother Nature passed down the command."

Everyone stands at full attention after the sound of her name. Mother Nature is a Blood leader who happens to be a woman. Just because she's a woman, in no way should she be taken lightly. She's just as treacherous as any other leader. Her countless murders and relentless tactics has earned her the label as the coldest bitch in the world.

This is one battle that none of them are looking forward to engaging in but the command has been passed down. They have no choice.

"As you all know, we can't play around with this bitch. We have to get in and finish this bitch ASAP. No room for mistakes. At the end of this meeting, you all are to get on the streets and murder everything affiliated with her. I don't care what has to be done...do it! Remember all is fair in warfare."

Meanwhile a Few Miles Away

A tall slender man paces back and forth before a small group of four people. Rage sets on his face. "Fifteen motherfucking shots and the motherfucker drove away?" he asks as he looks at the person standing at the center of the group. "Fifteen shots? What the fuck was they shooting at? Who the fuck was shooting? I told you how serious this matter was! Who the fuck did you put on the job? Must have been the goofiest mufuckers you could find. You fucked up. Now how the fuck you gonna fix it?"

The short, stout, dread headed woman stands up. Her red dreadlocks coupled with the pitch black tone of her skin makes her look demonic. She stands there accepting the chastisement. She hates the fact that he's talking to her like this but she knows that he is correct in what he's saying. The man told her how urgent the matter was and she hates that her men missed their mark. She hates to disappoint him because without him there would be no her. He supplies her with the dope to give to her underlings.

She throws her head back, unraveling her dreadlocks. She stands there momentarily before speaking. "I take full responsibility for what happened. I'll fix it though," she says with confidence. "I sent the wrong mufuckers at that time. Don't worry bout them though. They already been disciplined. Best believe that will never happen again. I got my best men on the job now. I promise you, it will be handled."

"I hope so," the man replies as he steps toward his 645 BMW. He stops short at the driver's side door, holding it wide open. "The mufucker got plans on taking over the whole city. He told me that with his own mouth. It's your job to make sure that doesn't happen." He gets into his car and starts it up. He rolls down the passenger window and shouts from it. "Do your fucking job! His plan is to stop my flow. If I don't eat, ya'll don't eat!"

Days Later

The Mayor walks up to the counter of the Post Office here on 4th Avenue. He digs deep into his pocket and pulls out a huge wad of hundred dollar bills. "Gimme twenty five, five hundred dollar money orders." The man behind the glass looks at the Mayor with pure hatred, despising the work that he has before him.

The Mayor plans to send money orders to a few of the dudes that he has befriended over the years of his incarceration. Every person that he can remember, he sends a money order to them to fill their accounts. While incarcerated he met so many good dudes that had it all while on the street but got on the inside and struggled just to get their basic necessities.

It breaks his heart to see anyone struggling, especially good people. It bothers him to know that while those guys were on the street, they took care of their loved ones but while away those same loved ones have turned their backs on them. It was then that he made the promise to himself that as long as he's alive he would do whatever it takes to make their journey less stressful. While he was on the inside he took care of a lot of guys but now that he's not there he's sure they are in fear of not having. He plans to remove that fear.

After paying the man over twelve thousand and five hundred dollars, he grabs the stack of money orders and makes his exit. He hops into the Rover and pulls off slowly. His next destination he's not sure as of yet. He's just making up things to do as he goes along.

Meanwhile Downtown Newark

Agents Dumber and Dumbest sit at their desks in front of their computers. They watch the screen carefully as the little red dot travels along a geographical sketch of the city. Their eyes have been glued to this screen for hours with hopes that the Mayor will lead them to something prominent. Little do they know that he's taken Tony's instructions of leading them nowhere. Every couple of days he takes one of the cars that he knows has the tracking device on it and travels with no set destination. He's sure that they're watching him and plans to make their jobs that much more tedious.

Smoke sits on a milk crate. From the angle that he's sitting he has a clear view of all the action that is taking place. It's been back and forth business all day long, just as it's been everyday since he released the Bang Man. Each day the volume has increased a little more. The first day his team sold an all time high of sixty- seven bricks. Today, which is the third day, he's sold eighty bricks and the day is not even over.

This is like a dream come true for him. He can't believe what's happening out here. He's still quite upset at what happened between him and the Mayor but the rapid flow of money that he's making pushes it further and further into the back of his mind.

Not only has the block sales picked up but his wholesale game has increased as well. His phone has never rang this much. He's never felt this popular. Nor did he realize how many people have his number. The Bang Man is bringing people out of the woodwork...people that he hasn't heard from in years. Everyone wants to get their hands on this stamp.

It's gotten so bad that he's started ignoring calls from numbers that he doesn't recognize. Even with him ignoring calls the people still don't give up. Their desperation forces them to call back again and again. It's the hottest stamp on the streets and everyone is willing to do whatever it takes to get hold of it.

His phone rings once again from a particular number that has been on his display at least fifty times today already. He looks at it with frustration before pressing ignore. As he's doing so he looks up at the entrance of the parking lot where he spots a tinted out white Bonneville creeping inside. Got damn, he thinks to himself. "This mufucker caught me." He quickly puts his mad face on, just to throw the man off.

The Bonneville pulls up and stops short, right before him. The window rolls down slowly. "Smoke, what's good, homie?" the man asks with agitation on his face. "I been calling you all day."

"What's good?" Smoke asks nonchalantly. He's sure that he knows exactly what the man has been calling about.

"I heard you got your hands on a smoker. I need that in my life," he says with joy on his face. "What a nigga gotta do to get his hands on it?"

Smoke gets disgusted with the man. He hasn't heard from him in months. He's what Smoke calls a switch hitter. He runs around the town chasing the hot names. He has no loyalty to anyone. Smoke has called him on many occasions trying to shake different dopes that he's had but if it isn't a name that's making noise he doesn't even want to be bothered. Also when the man gets hold of a dope that may be hard for the average person to get hold of the man capitalizes off of it by over-charging everyone. "I got it but I can't help you right now. I ain't got that much," he lies.

"I mean, whatever you got, I'll take it," he says with desperation in his eyes. "You got fifty?"

"Nah," Smoke lies once again. "On the real, I only got enough for my team...the niggas that been riding with me from day one, through thick and thin. You know?"

"Come on with that shit," the man replies in his defense.

"I ain't selling it to nobody else, right now. No wholesale. Me and my squad taking everything to the earth, brick by brick. I gotta bring my *hood* up first."

The man refuses to take no for an answer. "Come on?" he begs. "Twenty bricks then? Anything?" he pleads.

"Not right now," Smoke says with anger in his eyes.

The man pauses once he senses the fact that Smoke is getting frustrated with him. Still he's not ready to give up. "When then?"

"When I'm ready, I'll bust back at you," he says in a cocky manner. "Give me a couple of days till I get my new work."

"Hmphh," the man sighs with frustration. "Don't forget me, big bruh. I'm gone be on you," he says with a goofy smile. "I need that. I'm gone hit you if you don't hit me. Answer my call, bruh," he says as he's pulling off.

Smoke watches as the car exits the parking lot. In seconds his phone rings again. "Hmphh," he sighs. He looks down at the display with aggravation. He's shocked to see this number. He was expecting another person to be calling in search of dope. His aggravation is replaced by nervousness as soon as he recognizes the number. It's his cousin, Charles Manson. He suddenly gets the feeling that this is a phone call that he shouldn't accept. He thinks of not answering but curiosity erases that thought.

He accepts the call. "Yo!" he shouts with a false sense of joy. His heart thumps loudly like a drum.

Meanwhile in Forrest City Arizona

The Black Charles Manson lays back in his bunk. He holds his cell phone close to his ear as he keeps his eyes glued on the bars of his cell. "What's the deal?" he asks in a low whisper.

"Same shit," Smoke replies.

"Yeah?" Manson replies.

The sound of Manson's voice lets Smoke know that his assumptions are correct. What he hoped wouldn't happen has happened. He now prepares himself for whatever speech Manson has in store for him.

"Short and to the point," Manson says. "I gave you a position because I thought you were the best man for the job. You've made me second guess my decision. If you can't handle it, let me know right now before we go any further. A million motherfuckers would love to be in your place, feel me? That was a close, close call. Too close for comfort," he adds. "The homie is supposed to be bulletproof. No man in the world should be able to get that close to him. I don't give a fuck if you have to lose your life to prevent something from happening to him. His safety is your top priority."

Smoke lowers his head with shame. He has always idolized his older cousin and the last thing he would want to do is let him down. Of course, he would never want to look like a failure in his cousin's eyes but that isn't the biggest reason he wouldn't want to let him down. His biggest worry is letting his cousin down and risk the possibility of losing his life if he does so. There's one thing that Smoke knows and that is he hates to look anything less than the perfect leader that they all consider him to be. Everyone knows that he has no problem eliminating anyone who tarnishes his image, no matter who it may be, family or no family.

"As soon as you get the word on that, you are to move on it. ASAP and not a second late. Follow me?"

"I'm already on it," Smoke replies.

"As you should be," he spits out quickly. "Again that should have never happened. Furthermore, it should never ever happen again. The first time it's shame on you. The next time it's shame on me. Never , ever put me to shame. You heard?"

Meanwhile Downtown Newark

Agents Dumber and Dumbest sit in the office at Agent Dumber's desk. Earphones fill their ears. They both listen as the call between Smoke and Manson ends.

They both look at each other with smirks on their faces. They speak simultaneously. "We heard."

Three Days Later

Smoke has finally given in. The more he refuses to sell the dope to outsiders, the more calls he gets. It's like the exclusiveness of it is making everyone want it even more. Being that he understands that, he's careful of who he's selling it to. He's handpicking who he sells it to instead of just selling it to everyone who attempts to get it.

Smoke passes a shopping bag over to his passenger. His passenger in return hands him a bag which consists of fifteen thousand dollars. Smoke is shocked to find out that people are actually giving him his price for the dope. Sure they complain a little and attempt to haggle with him but at the end of the day they give him what he's asking for. The dope is so good that they just have to have it. The noise that it's making has them willing to pay any cost just to get their hands on it.

The man in the passenger's seat and Smoke have met three days already. In just three days he has bought over one hundred and fifty bricks. This is so unlike him. Normally he buys about 25 bricks at a time and that lasts him an eternity. Smoke blames his rapid return on the goodness of the 'Bang Man.' The first day he only bought his regular load of twenty five bricks. Each day his order has increased. Smoke just hopes that it continues to increase. The more he buys, the faster he can get through his own load.

"If shit go right, I'm gone need a hundred tomorrow," the man claims. "Make sure you keep a hundred to the side for me," he pleads. "I don't wanna go a day without this shit!"

"Got you, bruh," Smoke replies casually.

Meanwhile a Few Miles Away

The low income housing complex is packed with people. Young dope dealers cover every inch of the property while a few customers run back and forth, purchasing. A variety of dope stamps are for sale out here but none of them are moving. If it wasn't for the few bricks of Bang Man that was available here earlier today, there would be no action out here at all.

The stragglers, who are still coming through, have come here thinking they can fill their addiction with the infamous Bang Man. Unfortunately that isn't the case. Once they find out the dope is sold out, they leave in search of finding someplace that still has some. Only a few bricks have been obtained through a third party. They had to work a miracle just to get their hands on it and will have to work an even bigger miracle just to keep it out here consistently.

On the outside of the complex a tinted out Yukon Denali pulls up to the entrance. Inside the truck there sits four men equipped with heavy artillery. The driver peeks around at the surroundings. He picks up his phone and hits the chirp button. "It's packed like a mufucker in there," he says into the phone.

A black Pontiac Grand Prix with tinted windows bends the corner up ahead. Four men are piled up in this vehicle as well. Each of them are fully loaded with semi-automatic weapons and more than enough ammo. The driver barks into his phone. "Let's go in?" he suggests.

The driver of the Yukon pays close attention to the people who are just standing around. He's sure they're strapped as well. He can almost pick out which ones have guns on them, and by the looks of it, he thinks it's safe to assume that the majority of them do.

As the Yukon and the Grand Prix sit front bumper to front bumper, the lookout at the gate notices them. He quickly makes a loud weird sound to alert everyone. People start looking around frantically. They all stand at full attention. The focal point of all of them becomes the two vehicles in front of the complex.

The short dread headed woman peeks her head from behind the sliding board insides of the children's play area. She studies the vehicles carefully but because of the extremely dark windows she can't see who is inside of either of them. Her gut feeling tells her something isn't right. She makes a loud call and in seconds, guns are drawn. Four men surround her as if she's the president. Not only are the men around her strapped with guns but gunmen are scattered around the complex as well.

Three small children climb the monkey bars with no idea of what's going on. She rushes over to them. "Get outta here," Mother Nature shouts as she damn near snatches them off of the bars. She pushes them away with force. "Ya'll go, get in the building, hurry!" she says as she keeps her eyes glued to the entrance way. Gunmen pop up on both sides on alternate sides of the entrance, behind the gate. They have the complex guarded like Fort Knox.

After Mother Nature sees that all her soldiers are in place, she just stands there arrogantly. She doesn't know what this is all about but whatever it is she's prepared for it. She bops her head up and down with arrogance. She raises her hands high in the air, waving them to come in. "Come on in," she says with a devilish smile.

The driver of the Denali sits back furiously. As bad as he would like to go in, he knows that wouldn't be wise. He hits the chirp button on his phone. "Yo, not right now," he says into the phone. "Let's get outta here," he says before he cruises off. The Pontiac makes a u-turn in the middle of the street and follows close behind. As they get to the corner of the block, a Cherokee catches up with them as well.

They all realize how foolish it would have been to go inside but that will not stop their plans of carrying out the command that was passed down to them. One way or another they are sure they will catch up with her.

Smoke steps toward Grape Street Leader, known to the street as Baby Grape, as he leans against his four door Mercedes S550. Smoke discreetly adjusts his gun, making sure it's secure in his waistband. Baby Grape leans back on the car, twisting the tips of his long dreadlocks.

In just four days the word has traveled like lightening. The moment Baby Grape heard of the places the Bang Man stamp was being sold, he knew exactly who to get in touch with to find out where it's coming from. His goal is to get hold of the dope to distribute it to his people.

Excitement fills Baby Grape's eyes. "What's good?" he asks.

"It's all good," Smoke replies in a cocky manner. "What's up with you?" he asks. He knows damn well what this meeting is about.

"Straight to the point man, what's the story with that Bang Man? I know if nobody else know anything bout it, you do," he says with hopes of hearing something worthwhile. "Tell me, you know who got the line on it?"

Smoke gloats with arrogance. "You looking at the line."

"Yeah?" he asks with a smile. "Bingo! So, what's the ticket on it?"

Smoke's glow fades away. "Three hundred," he replies with shame.

"Three hundred? Where they do that at? That shit sound crazy!"

"I mean, I don't know what to tell you. That's the number."

"Man, fuck that. What can I do with that? That don't give me no room to do shit. I got a seven dollar spot."

"This ain't for you then," Smoke interrupts. "This ain't seven dollar dope. This ain't that bullshit. This a ten plus, all over the land. Ask around."

"I don't have to. I heard it's fire but three hundred?"

"I mean, my hands tied. If I could do better for you, I would."

"Come on man, you can't get three hundred from nobody these days. That's some back in the day shit."

"This some back in the day dope," he replies in defense. "And I been getting three hundred with no problem."

Baby Grape stands there thinking a million thoughts a minute. He's so desperate right now but just can't imagine giving up that price. He thinks carefully before opening his mouth. "What if I go in with you? Let me put mines with yours?" He knows Smoke and assumes that he will fall for this. He's never known Smoke to have real money. The only reason he has to deal with Smoke at times is because they're gang rivals and most Bloods would never do business with him. He assumes that Smoke may have one hundred bricks tops, if he's lucky. "I'm sure your peoples will give you a better number then. I don't have to know him. I will go straight through you," he lies. He knows damn well if Smoke agrees he would try and talk him into introducing him to the connect.

"Nah, I doubt it," Smoke replies. "He ain't gone budge."

"Anybody budge for that fetti. Especially at a time like this."

"I'm telling you," Smoke replies. "The nigga ain't beat for paper like that. He rich already. He just doing me a favor."

"Bullshit," Baby Grape interrupts. "Don't let nobody tell you no bullshit like that. I don't give a fuck how rich he is, everybody like money. At the end of the day he's in the business to make money. If the price is right, I got money for a thousand."

Smoke's mind starts racing. He quickly thinks of the hefty profit he could make but he then thinks of the fact that he doesn't have a thousand bricks left. He has less than five hundred bricks left. He's now waiting for the money to come back to him from his squad. "I don't even have a thousand," he says.

"What you got then? I will take them all, if the **number** right."

Smoke realizes how valuable this man is. He did plan to get with him just not as of yet. He planned to make sure all of his soldiers were good before he stepped out of the box, allowing everyone else to eat. He wanted his team to have a nice head start on the rest of the city.

He quickly thinks of how good it will look on his behalf if he finishes the huge load in such a timely manner. The only problem with that is his team won't be the only team with the dope anymore. He quickly weighs it out and in seconds he's ready to give in. He remembers the Mayor telling him not to go any lower than $250.00 a brick.

Strictly because of the fact that the man isn't Blood, he has to add some extra tax on the price. He would never sell the product to a rival gang member for the same price as he sells it to his own people for. He has to add something to the price just so his people will always stay ahead of the game. He quickly comes up with the price of $260.00 a brick.

He's sure he has at least 400 bricks left. A grand total of $104,000.00, he will score a profit of $26,000.00 off of Baby Grape. "I can get hold to four hundred of them for you, right now. Give me a couple of days and I can have whatever amount you need," Smoke says with confidence.

"Four hundred?" Baby Grape asks. "At what price though?"

"At my price, two sixty," he lies. "I'm just gone sell them to you at my price to move them faster and reel him in," he lies again. "If he sees what *we* about, maybe he will drop the number."

"Got damn," Baby Grape sighs. "That's high as hell."

"Listen, ain't nobody getting it no lower than that."

"Damn, I'm gone have to be at two eighty, to three hundred just to make a profit."

"That's the going rate. I guarantee you nobody will get it lower than three hundred. Better than that, I guarantee you, I won't deal with nobody else on your side. You can hit all of them. Whatever number you set, that's what it is. You got my word on that," he says with sincerity."

"Well if you guarantee that, we got a deal."

"That's a deal then," Smoke says as he extends his hand for a handshake.

Baby Grape extends his hand in return. "Deal."

Agents Dumber and Dumbest sit parked on the busy street. They have their eyes fixed on the traffic that's going in and out of the projects. Watching the heavy activity infuriates them to no end.

"Look at this shit," Agent Dumber says with rage. He sits slumped down in the passenger's seat. "It hasn't been a quiet second since we have been sitting out here. There's one thing for sure...the fucker knows how to get a party started. I haven't seen this much drug activity since nineteen ninety five."

"Yeah?" Agent Dumbest asks. He's clueless to what exactly the nineties looked like because he just signed on to the force a few years ago.

"Yeah. In the nineties the whole city looked like this. That was a hell of a decade. Work was plentiful," he smiles. "It was like the birth of the heroin era. Before that the city was built around the cocaine market. It was all about a bunch of young kids getting sneaker and beeper money. They considered themselves fortunate if they made enough to buy themselves a car. Not many murders. Every now and then someone caught a leg shot but nothing serious. Not until the heroin era came in and changed that. Heroin taught a poor black **nigger**," he says with rage. "From the ghetto how to be a millionaire. Then came the murders stemming from the turf wars, home invasions and kidnappings. The dumb ass **niggers** lost their minds. They were not used to the large amounts of money they then had access to. It gave them a sense of power. Power that they didn't know how to use. The end result of it all was countless murders," he says with disappointment in his eyes. "**Our man** happens to be one of the pioneers. I watched with my own eyes as he corrupted this city then and I can't believe that he's been given a second chance to do it all over again," he says with disgust. Look at this bitch," he says as he changes the subject. He points up ahead. "Now can you give me any other reason why a beautiful white woman like that would be coming out of the projects in this neighborhood? No way in the world does she belong anywhere near here," he barks. It infuriates him to see his own people being affected by the drug epidemic. He watches with fury as she climbs into her BMW X5. "Tail her," he instructs.

Agent Dumbest slams the car into drive and pulls off at a moderate speed. They follow a half a block behind until she bends the corner. As they bend the corner, Dumbest mashes the accelerator to catch up with her.

The woman is stopped by a red light. As she sits there, she has her eyes fixed on the bag of dope that she's trying hard to split open. She's being extra careful not to rip the bag and spill the goods. Finally she has it open. She buries her nose into the tiny packet and vacuums the powder like a Hoover. One sniff and it's all gone like magic. She lifts her head up only to find the Agents' car obstructing her path. "Oh my God," she cries out loud.

The two agents pop out of the car aggressively. The sight of their badges and guns almost gives her a heart attack. She sits there stiff. She thinks quickly. She purposely pops open the two top buttons on her blouse, causing her breasts to spill over. She's hoping the deep cleavage of her beautifully rounded breasts will prevent them from any trouble they have in store for her.

"Turn it off!" Agent Dumber barks as he's walking toward her side of the vehicle. Slowly she turns the key back in the ignition. Her heart pumps with fear as she watches them closely.

Agent Dumber stands at the driver's side while Dumbest stands at the passenger's side. The woman is now trembling with fear and they both can see it. "Good afternoon, maam," Dumber says with a false sense of politeness. His eyes stay glued to her eyes. Not once does he even look down at her *get out of jail free card*. She's so shocked to see that they're not even fazed by the sight of her twins. Normally police melt into her hands at the beautiful sight of them.

"Good afternoon," she says as she sneakily slides the empty dope packet underneath her leg. She desperately aims her torpedoes at him, hoping he will notice them. He pays no attention to them at all.

"Maam, is everything ok?"

"Y, yes," she stutters as she aims the twins at his face, high beaming him with her brick hard nipples. She becomes even more afraid once she realizes that none of her antics are working.

"We're just checking. We were just passing through and happened to see you running out of the projects back there. We were not sure if you were being chased or maybe you were chasing a purse snatcher. You know, no disrespect but you stick out like a sore thumb. The three of us are the only white faces around here. I know our purpose around here," he says as he points to his badge. "What's yours?"

She reads the letters, FBI and gets even more frightened. She thinks quickly. "Leaving a friend's house."

"Oh ok. What's your friend's name?"

"Huh?"

"Your friend? What's his or her name?"

She can't think of a name fast enough so she gets frustrated. "Sir, what is the problem?"

"Problem? There's no problem. Just checking on you Miss. We're here to serve and protect. Where are you headed now Miss?"

"To work," she replies in a sassy manner. "If you would be kind enough to remove your car from my path," she snaps.

"Where do you work?"

"The hospital," she replies. "The University of Medicine and Dentistry."

"Ok, nice. Your name? You have ID?"

"My name? Annette Blake. Dr. Annette Blake," she says with confidence, hoping that this will cause them to back off of her. "Yes, I have ID."

"Doctor? Ok, Dr. Blake. Your nose," he says as he touches the tip of his own nose. "You have powder on your nose. That wouldn't be dope residue would it?"

She looks in the mirror and there the evidence lies all over the tip of her nose and around the rim. Damn, she thinks to herself. Oh my God," she says to herself. She realizes the trouble that she's in.

Doctor Blake, you mind stepping out of the car please?"

"Stepping out of the car for what?" she asks in a frightened voice. "Can I call my husband, please?" she pleads. "Trooper John Blake. Maybe you know him?" she asks with desperation. "He's a sergeant."

"I'm afraid not. Step out of the car please?"

"For what, Sir?"

"Uh, maybe because we observed you running in and out of the projects which is heavily drug infested. We pull you over and residue is covering your nose, which gives us probable cause to check your vehicle. Do I need any more reason?" he smiles with sarcasm. "You can cooperate or we can make it difficult. I can call the locals to send a woman officer over to search you. If she finds drugs, you will be arrested and your job will be notified. Doctor," he adds. "I'm sure we will find something that will land you a few hours in jail and cause you a host of other problems. You'll be in and out, though. I'm sure Sergeant Blake won't let his beautiful wife spend a night in jail. Does he know about your drug problem? Does he have any idea that his precious wife is in Newark running in and out of the projects? Where do you reside, anyway?"

"Livingston," she whispers with shame.

"Ok, now tell me what I need to know. It will be easier for all of us." Tears drip down her face rapidly. "No need for tears, beautiful. Just answers. You can answer my questions with no bullshit and drive away from here or I can have you searched, arrested for possession of heroin and have you driven away from here. Unless you have a prescription for it," he says with a smile. Doctor Blake, it's your choice. Now again, what is your purpose around here?" She sits there without replying. The tears are now pouring from her eyelids. "Let me answer it for you. Your purpose here is purchasing narcotics, correct?" She slowly nods her head up and down. "Ok, turn the goods over."

She hesitantly digs underneath her thigh and retrieves the empty packet of heroin. She hands it over to him slowly. "All of it," he demands. She digs into her Burberry purse and collects three more packets. She hands them over as well. "Is that all?"

"Yes," she replies, while nodding her head up and down with embarrassment.

"You sure?"

"Positive."

"Ok, Doctor Blake. Have a good day. Don't let me catch you around here again. Ok?"

"Yes, Sir."

Agents Dumber and Dumbest walk toward their car casually. They hop in and Dumbest pulls off slowly. Agent Dumber stares at the packets. "Wow, he's giving away a lot of dope for the money," he says as he lifts the bag into the air. The packet is filled from edge to edge all around. Like a little pillow," he adds. He reads the stamp aloud. Bang Man, huh? One more piece to the puzzle."

Mike Mittens sits in Target's parking lot. He looks down at his watch and reads the time of 1:58. Suddenly his attention is grabbed by the loud sound of tires screeching. He looks up and is almost blinded by the bright yellow Chevy Camaro that's ripping into the parking lot at full speed. The sun bounces off of the chrome rims like mirrors.

Smoke spots Mike Mittens sitting in the rental car in the middle of the parking lot. He turns the car in that direction quickly, causing a loud squealing of the tires. The back of the car fishtails as he tugs at the wheel to regain control of it.

He's overly excited. He's like a kid with a new toy. All his prior cars have been used hoopties and not by his choice. He was never able to afford a brand new car. Actually he has never had a car over the price range of $2,000.00. To actually be in a position to buy the car of his choice, straight cash, he could never imagine. This 2010 Chevy Camaro before this morning was his dream car. Today his dream has come true.

He foolishly thanks God for the dope game. The dope game is teaching him to bring his dreams into reality. Never before would he believe that he could ever go to a car dealership and give them $40,000.00 cash money. Today he made himself a believer.

Mike watches as the Camaro pulls side by side of him. He watches carefully, not knowing who will get out. Nothing can be seen through the pitch black windows. The door opens wide and Smoke exits the vehicle.

Mike watches with frustration as Smoke walks toward him lugging a huge duffel bag. Mike looks around the parking lot attentively. He's worried about the attention Smoke may have drawn to them. Young dumb motherfucker, he says to himself.

Smoke hops into the passenger's seat. Pure excitement fills his eyes. His adrenaline rush is still at an all time high. "What's goodie, big bruh? Two on the dot," he smiles. Smoke places the bag onto the backseat. Mike watches him with disgust. "Three hundred and ninety cash just like the doctor ordered," he smiles goofily. Smoke is so happy to be handing over this money. He feels the most satisfaction that he has ever felt in his life. He can't believe that he's been given this much responsibility and actually held it down successfully with no problems. For the first time ever he feels like he has a purpose in life.

In such a short time period his entire life has changed. He knows that he owes it all to the Mayor. Before meeting the Mayor he was a young foolish gangbanger with more power than he knew what to do with. The Mayor has taught him how to transfer that power into currency. In less than one week he has generated $460,000.00. Never in his wildest dreams did he imagine him earning that amount of money.

"Youngin, that car don't go no slower than that?" Mike asks with sarcasm.

Smoke hasn't a clue of what Mike is getting at. "That bitch souped all the way up! Just got her two hours ago. I didn't do the whole dash yet but I promise you before the night is over, I will," he says full of energy.

Mike looks over at Smoke with pure agitation. "You speed racing through Union Township with pitch black windows, doing a hundred miles an hour, with four hundred thousand dollars in your lap," he says with disgust all over his face. "What's wrong with that picture? How stupid would you feel reading that in the newspaper as you sitting in the day room of the County Jail?" Mike gives him a second or two to reply but he doesn't. "Watch your movements," he says before rolling his eyes. "But on another note, Phil Jackson said we're on a thirty second time out."

"Huh? Phil Jackson?" Smoke asks without a clue of who or what Mike is talking about. His code talk has him confused.

"The **big boy**," Mike revises. "He said we gone be down about a day or two till the officials blow the whistle, calling the ball in play."

Mike's code talk has Smoke dizzy. He laughs. "You're crazy. I got you though. Well at least I think I got you," he smiles. "That's cool cause I got close to two hundred breezies still floating around."

"Breezies?" Mike asks. The age barrier is affecting the both of them. Their slang and code talk is like the two of them speaking in foreign languages to one another.

"Bricks," Smoke chuckles. "I got two hundred bricks left out there. I will just let them marinate until we back in position. I'm good. I got ya'll outta the way. The sixty thousand profit is mine so I ain't under no pressure. Just bust back at me as soon as you hear something." He looks up at Mike and sees the confused look on his face. "Call me when you hear something," he revises. He forces the door open. "Later Old Head!"

"Alright, Young fella, be safe," he says. Smoke looks back at him with disgust. "My bad...do you!"

Meanwhile

Tony stands in his office. His heart pounds ferociously as he stands before the tall slender Caucasian man who digs into his briefcase. Tony can't believe that he's actually gone through with this. He's quite embarrassed at this whole ordeal but he was desperate and felt as if he had no choice.

The man lays a yellow envelope onto Tony's desk. He opens it up slowly. He pulls a stack of photos from it and passes them over to Tony. "Here goes nothing," he whispers with sadness on his face.

Tony's heart skips a beat as his eyes lay on the very first picture of the stack. He can't believe what he's actually seeing. Damn, he thinks to himself. This lying bitch, he says under his breath as he stares at the photo of Mocha walking side by side with a man. Tony studies the background and quickly realizes that they're on Mocha's favorite street, which is Fifth Avenue in New York. Both she and the man have their arms filled with shopping bags. What disturbs him the most is the man that she's walking with. Not only does Tony know him but he was a one time client. Of all the people in the world, she had to fuck with somebody who knows me, he thinks to himself. The fact that she done all of this underneath his nose infuriates him to no end. He inhales a deep breath, preparing for what the next photo may be. It's Mocha and the same man sitting inside her BMW. The man is sitting in the driver's seat. The investigator caught a clear shot of them kissing.

"This here was taken in West Orange," the private investigator says.

Tony shakes his head from side to side with disbelief. "Rotten bitch, he says to himself. The next photo is of the two of them entering the W Hotel.

"That's Manhattan," the investigator informs.

"I know," Tony smiles a cheesy smile. "That's our favorite Hotel," he says as he lays the photos down onto the table. He can't stand to see another photo. He's heartbroken and disgusted.

"Hmphh," he sighs.

"There's more," the investigator says with enjoyment. Deep down inside he loves to see men's reactions when he busts their cheating wives in the act. He gets enjoyment from this. "You don't want to see the rest of them?"

"Nah, I'm good," Tony replies. "I've seen more than enough. Thanks."

"Ay, it's my job. After all knowing is better than not knowing right?"

Tony is sick right now. His mind is a blur. "If you say so."

Federal Informant Sean sits across the table from Samirah. They're sitting inside of Ruth Chris's Steakhouse in West New York. Samirah gazes out of the window at the magnificent view of the River. To travel anywhere outside of Newark makes her feel like she's actually gone somewhere. She's never been anywhere outside of Essex County.

She's ashamed to admit that she's never sat down in a restaurant and eaten outside of McDonalds.

Never before has she met a man who made her feel like this. Normally she's treated like a jump-off. The only time a man has time for her has always been after hours. They would come to her with only enough time left in the night to sex her and go to sleep. The next day they would be out by the time the sun comes up. All the many hours of sex that she would give them and she still couldn't get pamper money from them if she needed it.

With Sean, it's different. The way he makes her feel, she doesn't even have the proper vocabulary to express. He actually treats her with respect. In just the short time that they've been dealing, he has taught her so much. Something small to most, like what the second spoon and fork at the dinner table is actually for, she didn't know until tonight. He's taught her to not rest her elbows on the dinner table, talk with her mouth full, smack on her food and not to pick her teeth at the table after eating. All in all, he's taught her to appear to have some class. He's also taught her how to be a woman and have pride in herself. She's purely grateful to have him in her life.

She knows how happy he's made her in their short relationship and can only imagine how the long haul with him would be. She gazes deeply into his eyes. "Hmphh," she snickers.

"What?" he asks with a dazzling smile.

"Nothing, just thinking...that's all."

Meanwhile in Belleville

150

The Mayor sits inside of the brand spanking new, black Buick Enclave. He's parked in front of Hertz Rental Agency. He's here to trade cars with Mike and turn in the rental that Mike has been riding in.

Mike hops into the passenger's seat. "What's goodie?" he asks.

"What's goodie?" the Mayor smiles. "Them young boys rubbing off on you," he laughs. "What you think? You like her?" he asks as he waves his hands around the interior of the vehicle.

"Yeah, she alright," he mumbles.

"Good...she yours," the Mayor says with cockiness. A huge smile appears on Mike's face. "She better be more than alright. I spent damn near fifty stacks on this joint. You better love her. You smell that new car smell?" he asks before sniffing the air. "When the last time you smelled that?"

Mike Mittens shakes his head from side to side. "Never."

"Well, there's a first time for everything. But there's one thing I can guarantee you. It damn sure won't be the last time." The Mayor peeks around cautiously. "Peep this," he says as he steps on the brake and fumbles with the steering wheel. "Voila," he says mimicking a magician. He points to the dashboard as the secret compartment shelf slides open slowly. "Look at how deep *that pussy* is. She holds twenty five hundred bricks and two guns."

"Damn," Mike replies with awe.

"Don't damn me just yet. We ain't done," he says as he starts fumbling with the radio. "Ta da," he says. In seconds another compartment slides open underneath the steering wheel. "She holds fifteen hundred bricks and one gun. Do the math. That's four thousand bricks and three pistols," he says with a smirk. "Now you can damn me."

"Damn!" Mike says as he thinks of the trouble that four thousand bricks and three guns can get him.

"Here," the Mayor says as he passes over a few papers.

"What's this?" Mike asks as he grabs the documents.

"The bill of sales. Sign everything and you good to go.

Mike Mittens sits there in awe. He barely knows how to accept gifts because he's hardly ever been given anything. Everything that he's ever had in life, he's stolen from others. "Thanks."

The Mayor spent close to fifty thousand on this truck but that's a mere drop in the bucket compared to what he plans to make off of it. He just considers it a business expense. With just one fully loaded trip he can make the fifty grand back and score an additional three hundred thousand dollar profit.

The Mayor fumbles with the buttons and the compartments close slowly. "So, everything, everything?"

"Yep...three ninety cash, back there in the rental. Well, that's what the **young boy** said it is. Of course I didn't count it. I brought it straight to you."

"That's cool," the Mayor replies. He lifts up in his seat as he digs into his pants pockets. He pulls a huge stack of bills from inside. He hands the entire stack over to Mike who pays close attention to the bills. He quickly spots the old image on the dingy green hundred dollar bills.

"Damn, where the hell you had these buried at? I ain't seen these joints in years."

"Well, get used to seeing them," he says with arrogance. "I got a lot more where those came from," he boasts. "That's ten thousand, for you."

Excitement fills Mike's eyes once again. He hasn't seen ten thousand cash in over ten years. The last time he had ten thousand of his own was back in the day when he was moving around with the late Cashmere.

The Mayor sees the joy in Mike's eyes and it makes him feel good. More than anything in the world, the Mayor loves to make others happy. Anyway that he can alleviate a person's stress or make someone's dream come true he's all for doing it. "Yeah, you back, baby. Look, two short runs landed you ten grand. Just think about it...it would have took you a half a year to score that at your piece a **job** you had. Do you see the benefits in fucking with a nigga like me?"

In Newark

Sean pulls up in front of Samirah's house. She's quite sad to know that such a beautiful day is coming to an end. Still in his presence yet she's starting to miss him already. He's lied to her, telling her that he will be away on business for a few days.

Just as he's parking, the door to her house opens. Smoke

steps out of the door. "Oh boy," she mumbles.

'What?" he asks.

"Nothing, my brother. I don't want to hear his shit." Samirah has been trying her hardest to avoid Smoke from seeing him and she has done damn good up until now. She knows how overprotective he can be over her. She's afraid that Smoke may say something to run him away just as he has any other man that she's taken a liking to.

Sean looks up at the porch and just the sight of Smoke pumps fear into his heart. All the stories that she's told him have instilled a tremendous amount of fear into him. He takes a deep breath and tries hard not to show his true feelings of fear. He turns his head but he watches Smoke carefully through his peripheral.

Smoke stands on the porch with his eyes glued onto the Bentley GT. Seeing his little sister in the car sends him into a jealous frenzy. They both can feel the heat coming from him.

"I know he gone have something to say."

"Something to say about what?" he asks in a squeaky voice.

"I don't know," she replies. "Pssst, oh boy. Here he comes. Don't mind him, ok? Just ignore him."

Now Sean is frightened. He watches Smoke as he approaches them. Samirah turns to Sean and starts babbling about nothing. She's trying to act as if she doesn't see him coming toward them.

A loud banging on the window forces her to turn toward him. She rolls the window down. "Huh?" she asks with fear?"

"Yo, where the fuck was you at? I been calling you for hours."

"My battery died," she whispers.

"Come here for a minute."

Sean's entire body is trembling like a leaf. He tries hard to hide it from Samirah. "Yo, go ahead and handle your business," he whispers. "I will just see you when I get back."

"No," she whines. "S-Dot," she whines. "Please just wait. I will be right back."

"Yo, get the fuck out the car. That nigga ain't that important!" Smoke shouts, looking at him. He's hoping to get him aroused and hopefully he will say something in defense. That would give him all the reason to do what it is he really wants to do anyway. He loves to embarrass her male friends just to prove to her how cowardly they really are. He has not come across a match yet.

She forces the door open with no hesitation. "Don't leave,

please?" she begs with all of her heart. "Please?" she begs once again as she exits the car. She slams the door shut.

Sean watches as she follows Smoke up the steps. "Yo, who the fuck is that clown ass nigga?" Smoke asks as they're walking away. He hears him loud and clear yet he doesn't utter a word. "You sure know how to pick a sucker, huh?" he shouts as he looks back at Sean. The look in his eyes is of pure hatred. Sean looks away with fear.

He bears witness that this is by far the most dangerous assignment they have given him. He realizes one tiny slip up can easily cost him his life. He takes a deep breath and exhales before banging his head against the headrest.

In a matter of minutes, he watches as Samirah comes stepping out of the house. Smoke follows her by a few steps. Sean pays close attention to the shopping bag that he's carrying. It doesn't take long for him to figure out what Smoke has been calling her for. It's quite obvious that Samirah is holding his work for him in her apartment.

She gets back into the car. "Don't worry about him. He be bugging."

Sean watches closely as Smoke is getting into the car that's parked a few feet away. He studies the yellow Camaro, in search of a license plate number that he can turn over to the Feds, but there is none. All he sees is a white temporary tag that's posted in the back window. He's sure it can't be that difficult to find a bright yellow sports car.

"It's alright," he replies. He sighs with relief as he watches Smoke pull off. He can't wait until this assignment is over. The sooner this case is cracked, the better it will be for him. He just prays that he's still alive when it's all said and done. "I ain't worried," he lies. The truth of the matter is he's actually scared to death.

Broad Street is packed with shoppers from one end of the block to the next. Mother Nature and her four soldiers walk in a small cluster. Each of them has their hands filled with shopping bags. As soon as they bend the corner onto Branford Place, Mother Nature makes an abrupt stop, right at the group of vendors who stand at the very corner, huddled around a wooden stand.

"Mother Nature, what's good?" the vendor shouts as she runs over to her. They immediately start doing the signature Blood handshake. The other female vendors stand in line impatiently waiting their turn to properly greet her. Mother Nature stands there arrogantly as they salute her like the boss bitch that she is. They respect her not just because of her G-status but they also respect her for the fact that they're all members of another group; the gay society.

After they all have saluted her, Mother Nature walks off gracefully. "Ya'll hold it down, ya heard?

Mother Nature and her crew then continue on their way up Branford Place. In a matter of a few minutes, they reach another small block which they turn onto. This side street is quite empty and abandoned compared to the rest of the shopping area. They look up ahead at their vehicle which sits parked, halfway up the block.

Four men sit on the corner of Branford cramped up in a black GTO. The driver watches closely as Mother Nature and her goons walk casually. They're backs are turned. They're so heavily engaged in their meaningless conversation that they're paying no attention to their surroundings.

"Let's go," the driver says as he steps on the gas. They've been sitting here for an hour or so, waiting patiently for their prey. Purely out of coincidence, they were just cruising through the area and happened to spot Mother Nature's van here on this side block. They knew she would be returning and they planned to sit here and wait, just as they have.

The man in the passenger's seat quickly flicks the safety off of his nine millimeter. He grabs hold of the lever on the side of the seat and lifts it. He bounces in the seat to make sure that it's locked in position. He braces himself against the seat as he presses the window button. The automatic window rolls down slowly.

"Go," the driver says just as they get about five feet away from their targets. In seconds the loud sound of gunfire rips through the air, echoing throughout the entire downtown area. Boc! Boc! Boc! Boc!

The man closest to the street falls to the ground. Mother Nature turns toward the street with a shocked expression on her face. "Oh shit," she mumbles as she attempts to get out of the way. She ducks low, using the car in front of her as a shield. The man next to her pushes her to the ground as he grabs hold of his own gun. In seconds he has his gun drawn and he's firing away. Bloc! Bloc! Bloc! Another set of shots ring off from another one of Mother Nature's goons. Boc! Boc! Boc!

The man hanging out of the window ducks back in his seat but fires with a vengeance. Boc! Boc! Boc! Boc! He watches with satisfaction as one of his random shots land. Another one of Mother Nature's men has been hit. This inspires the man to continue on. Boc! Boc! Boc! The man stumbles backwards, falling onto the gate that's behind him.

"Get them mufuckers!" Mother Nature says as she kneels close to the ground. At the sound of her voice two of her soldiers run toward the car with no regard of being hit. Their only concern is to carry out her command. They both fire as they're running toward the car. Boc! Boc! Boc! Bloc! Bloc! Boc! Boc! Bloc!

The GTO speeds off, while the gunmen continue firing away. They continue firing until the car is way out of range. The sound of gunshots is replaced with the sound of police sirens. Mother Nature quickly stands to her feet, looking around nervously.

She spots one of her soldiers a few feet away from her laying on the sidewalk rolling around in pain. He looks up to her with pity in his eyes. "I'm hit," he says as he clenches his abdomen.

The look of pain on his face should make her sympathetic but instead it makes her furious. She looks to her men who are standing over him, watching without a clue of what they should do. "Get him, and let's go!" she shouts as the sirens get closer. She takes off sprinting toward her car. The other wounded man follows her closely as he's looking down at the blood that's leaking from his shirt. The blood comes from the bullet wound to his chest.

The men grab hold of the severely injured man and together they carry him to the car. They pile into the van and Mother Nature speeds off. Rage fills her heart. At this point only one thing is on her mind and that's revenge.

Mike Mittens pulls up to a small raggedy house in the middle of 20th Street. He double checks the address that's posted on the door, hoping that it's not the right house. Unfortunately it is. He peeps the scenery, paying close attention to the crowd of young men who stand around the house. Herds of people swarm the entire block.

"Hmphh," he sighs as he parks. He hits the buttons on his steering wheel and his secret compartment opens slowly. He snatches the shopping bag from it. He then snatches the gun that's in there as well. He tucks the gun into his sweat jacket pocket before forcing the door open. He gets out of the vehicle, with the shopping bag held tightly in his grip. He closes the door behind him using that same hand. With his other hand, he holds onto his gun inside his jacket.

He walks toward the house slowly. He keeps his eyes straight ahead, as if he's not paying the least bit of attention to the young boys who are all watching him. The truth of the matter is they have his full attention. If they make one false move he's prepared to fire.

He walks past the boys avoiding eye contact with them but he feels massive tension around him. He walks up the steps, still being mindful of what can possibly happen. He steps onto the porch and hits the bottom bell. He turns around facing the street so no one can sneak up on him.

The creaking of the door behind him snatches his attention toward it. A middle aged woman stands there with half of her frail body behind the door. "Yes?" she whispers.

"Miss Bryant?" he asks in his most polite voice.

"Yes. "James?" she asks.

"Yes," he says with a smile as he agrees to his alias that he's given her.

"Come in," she demands.

Mike steps inside and the woman closes the door behind him. He doesn't hesitate to hand the bag over to her. Her son, Charles Manson told her that someone would be stopping by to bring something but he didn't tell her what.

She opens the bag curiously and what she sees damn near

causes her eyes to pop out of her head. Stacks and stacks of money fill the shopping bag. "What is this for?" she questions.

"Maam, I don't have a clue," he lies. "I was just instructed to bring it over. Have a good day," he says as he opens the door and makes his exit.

The money in the bag was Manson's cut of the deal that was just sealed. Manson just scored fifty grand without moving a muscle. Manson has kept his word and now so has the Mayor. The Mayor promises Manson that every time he scores off of Smoke, so will he.

Mike Mittens let's go of his gun as he pulls away from the group of men. "Safe and sound," he says to himself. "Thank God," he says before exhaling with relief.

Meanwhile in Livingston, N.J.

The Mayor and Smoke sit parked in the Mayor's rental car. They're parked smack in the middle of the parking lot. The Mayor listens with full attention as Smoke speaks. "I got the information that I promised you I would get. You know a dude named JB?"

"JB, JB?" the Mayor repeats. The name sounds vaguely familiar.

"JB from East Orange. He got a black 645. I think he originally from Irvington but he moving around in East Orange though."

"Black 645?" Suddenly an image appears in his head. He visualizes the man in the BMW talking to him that day on Central Avenue. His face is clear in his mind. "Yeah, yeah. What about him? I don't know him, know him but I know who you talking about."

"Well, that's who ordered the hit on you. I don't know what it's about but he pressed the button."

The Mayor gets furious. He knows exactly what it's about. He's sure it has everything to do with the brief encounter they had. The hit had to be made out of embarrassment or fear of him taking over. He believes it's because of both. "I know exactly what it's about."

"What?"

"Doesn't matter. It is what it is. So, that's who it was, huh?" He never thought he would see the day that a non descript would have the heart to go up against him. The fact that the coward had the audacity to lean on a woman to do his dirty work makes it all the worse.

"Yeah, the broad Mother Nature commanded her pups to move on you."

"Mother Nature? Pups?"

"Yeah. She a fake ass G," he says downplaying her position. "I guess she affiliated with him some way. He ain't Blood, though. She ordered her pups to take you out."

A devilish smile appears on the Mayor's face. "Hmphh," he sighs with a smile. "All I need you to do is point me in their direction and I will handle it from there."

"Negative," Smoke replies. "What you think I'm here for? Put your feet up. I'm already on it. As far as the nigga JB, my man got a line on him. He gonna bring him right on in. The nigga JB be selling a bunch of garbage ass dope all over the town and my man be copping from him from time to time."

"Oh yeah? What's in it for him?"

"I mean, he fuck with me like that. No homo," he adds. "At the end of the day he happy with getting a few bricks of this Bang Man. Feel me?"

"Totally."

"As far as the bitch Mother Nature, we already on that, too. My squad busted a move on her yesterday but she got outta the hole. Two of her lil pups got hit. One critical. I heard he may not make it. Hit him all up here," he says as he rubs over his own chest. We ain't gonna stop till they all outta here. I promise you. The nigga JB, he will be outta here before the weekend. Know dat!"

One Day Later

The Mayor looks into Tony's eyes as he speaks. He can see the pain and sorrow all over his face. Tony turns away from the Mayor with shame. "Yeah, I hired the private investigator," he says with shame. "I needed to know." He shakes his head from side to side. "The worse part of it all is the garbage can ass nigga that she crossed me for. She could at least have fucked around with a nigga on my level but instead the bitch out spending my money on a broke ass nigga and he owes me fucking money!"

"He owes you money? How? You know the dude?" the Mayor asks with confusion.

"Yeah, I know the nigga. I represented him in a petty ass drug beef. He got pinched with some real lightweight shit like a couple of punk ass ounces of blow. I charged the mufucker like ten grand and he had to pay me on a payment plan. The last three thousand I never got from the mufucker. I had the bitch calling and calling for the money but I never got it. Trifling bitch probably was never asking for the money. They were probably putting all this shit together then," he says as he stares ahead in a trance. "Of all the mufuckers that have come through this door with real fucking money she chose this broke ass mufucker. I gave her more credit than that. He can't do shit for her! Her monthly hygiene bill would break his ass. Hair, nails, waxing and spa," he adds. "He can't fucking afford her. He ain't even in position!"

The Mayor shakes his head from side to side. He can surely feel Tony's pain. He hates to say this but he has to. "True bill...he doesn't need to be in position. She don't need a nigga for bread. She got her own."

"Nah, she ain't got her own! She got mines. Filthy ass bitch! Real talk, losing the bitch ain't the worse of it. I can get over that... eventually. Losing the paper hurts me the most. If the raggedy mufucker would have left without the bread...yeah it would have hurt me but I would have gotten over it. Feel me?"

"Absolutely but that ain't the case. So now what?"

"Now I really don't fucking know. I guess I got the clarity that I was looking for so now I have to move on." He shakes his head from side to side with grief. Tear drops fill the corners of his eyes.

He turns away with shame and so does the Mayor.

He can't stand to see Tony like this. His cold heart has actually been broken. "Ay man," the Mayor says as he looks down onto his own lap, trying not to look Tony in the eyes. "We really can't be mad at the nigga. He did what a sucker is supposed to do. He saw an opening and slid in. Like you said he a broke mufucker with nothing. He just trying to get something. A chick that got everything in place already. He don't have to bring nothing with him, bottom line. In all actuality it probably was never about her. The sucker was really in love with you. He respects your stature and loves your swag. He digging your ghost," he says with arrogance. "It was all about you. Somewhere in a sucker's mind they believe if they bag your dame, they're equivalent to you. It probably was never about her and always about you," he says with passion in his eyes.

He continues on. "It's really the principle of this shit though," he says with a frown on his face. The fact that he in your office and you helping this mufucker and he shit on you like that. You don't do real mufuckers like that," he says as he pauses for a few seconds. "Yo," he says before pausing once again. "The shit I'm about to say goes against my belief system but you my man and I will pretty much break any rule for you. Again, it ain't about a nigga taking your wife. It's all about the principle. It bothers me to see you like this. It hurts me to see you hurting. With that being said, all you have to do is say the word and I will have him taken care of," he says as he shakes his head from side to side. He can't believe that he just said that. He always felt like any man that will kill another man over a woman was a weak man. Tony isn't just any ordinary man though. He's his main man. "Fuck it, justify it by saying we doing it over the money he owes you," he says trying to make himself feel better. "It ain't gotta be about her," he says as he looks into Tony's eyes. Tony stands there upright with no sign of emotion on his face. "All you gotta do is give me the word and I will press the button."

7:15 A.M. The Next Morning

Mike Mittens just finished meeting with the Bang Man deliverer here in Jersey City. This is the furthest they are willing to come. This is also the latest that they are willing to drive here. They prefer to make their moves during the rush hour when everything is busy.

He peeks around nervously as he tucks the dope securely into the stash box. Once it's closed, he slams the vehicle into drive and pulls off slowly.

Meanwhile in Newark

The smoke grey late model Ford Taurus creeps up the narrow street slowly. Inside of the Taurus is one of Smoke's pups. He cruises up the block that surrounds the project buildings. He looks around and sees not a single dope fiend in sight. The time of day, has everything to do with how empty it is.

He slows down the vehicle as he approaches the entrance. He peeks inside discreetly, trying not to bring any attention to himself. He takes notice to two dudes standing in the center of the court, with two dope fiends in front of them. He feels great satisfaction in knowing that one of these young men happens to be the driver of the Audi that was involved in the shooting.

Smoke got the word that he's the one who opens up the projects each and every morning. Smoke was sure that this would be the perfect time to move on them. At this hour the projects are bare. It's less activity which means fewer weapons in their defense. That makes it easier to carry out their duty. The driver hits the chirp button on his phone before speaking. "He's out here. Just him and another dude."

Chirp. "Say no more," the man on the other end of the phone shouts.

In seconds the Taurus and the GTO pass by each other. The GTO reaches the entrance and speeds into the lot. The passenger's window is rolled down and the passenger sits on the edge of his seat with his weapon drawn.

The two young men stand there stiff as they watch the GTO

speeding toward them. They're both caught totally off guard. They want to run but it's already too late. The car is not even three feet away from them.

The two dope fiends take off in opposite directions as soon as their eyes lay on the gun which hangs from the passenger's window. Boc! Boc! Boc! He fires, just to prevent them from drawing their weapons in retaliation. He forces the door open and jumps out while firing. Boc! Boc! The smaller of the two men collapses onto his back while the other young man takes off in a sprint.

The driver slams the car into the drive position and hops out of the car, leaving the door wide open. He chases the young man down, firing aggressively behind him. Bloc! Bloc! Bloc! Bloc! After the second shot the young man tumbles over onto his belly. The gunman picks up his pace to catch up with his victim. In less than one second, he's standing over the man who is lying face down with no movement whatsoever. He fires two more shots. Bloc! Bloc! The bullets sink into the back of the young man's bald head, causing it to burst open like a bloody cantaloupe.

The gunman turns around with no hesitation. He wastes no time in getting to the getaway car. On his way there, he watches as his accomplice stands over his prey, squeezing away. Boc! Boc! Boc! Boc! Boc! "Let's go!" the driver shouts as he's getting into the car.

The driver's shout snaps the gunman out of his zone. He quickly runs to the car, hops in and slams the door shut behind him. They speed out of the projects successfully. Mission complete!

Two Hours Later

Mike Mittens sighs with relief as he watches Smoke pull out of Target's parking lot. Another successful drop off completed. The Mayor has made his job so much easier with his new vehicle. With his secret stash boxes, he feels total comfort in riding throughout the town with the enormous amounts of work. He feels good, knowing that he's now working smarter not harder.

Two Days Later/August 21, 2009

It's 1:15 in the morning and Smoke is still busy at work. He walks into Emigrante Lounge, on Ferry Street. At his entrance, he feels a great amount of tension. The opposing gang members present in here can smell that he's a rival. They can sense Blood in their presence. With him being Blood and these guys being members of the Crip gang and Grape Street gang, he understands that he's totally out of bounds being here.

He looks around at the packs of gang bangers who occupy the tiny go-go bar. Before he can get in comfortably, a beautiful petite Brazilian, half naked dancer approaches him. He looks over her shoulder as if she isn't standing there. His eyes land on the back of the room where he spots Baby Grape and his crew sitting with a table full of drinks in front of them.

Baby Grape stands up and waves Smoke over to him. The rest of the room becomes at ease as they see that someone has approved of him being in here. He approaches Smoke. "What's good?" he asks. "What you drinking on?"

Smoke looks around with caution. Although he has a certain amount of trust in Baby Grape he would never leave his life in his hands. At the end of the day they are gang rivals. He understands that anything can happen and he chooses to eliminate any problem that could derive. "Nah, I'm good. Let's just make it happen," he whispers as he spins around and walks away.

Minutes later, Smoke watches from his rearview mirror as Baby Grape creeps up from behind. In his hand he clutches a duffle bag. Smoke looks to the doorway of the bar where two of Baby Grape's men stand. He then looks to the corner where another two men are posted. Smoke is sure that they're all strapped but he feels no discomfort at all. He charges it off as business. Baby Grape is only protecting his investment.

Baby Grape steps toward the passenger's side while Smoke's passenger exits to let him in. Baby Grape slides into the vehicle slowly. Smoke's man leans against the Camaro's hood, staring directly at the two men standing on the corner. Inside his pocket, he grips a seventeen shot nine millimeter, just in case things get ugly.

"Here you go," Baby Grape utters. "Two hundred and sixty

cash," he says as he hands over the duffle bag.

Smoke hands him a duffle bag in return. In his duffle bag there lies one thousand bricks of Bang Man. "That's what it is," Smoke replies over a handshake.

Meanwhile

In Samirah's apartment, S-Dot tiptoes around quietly. The sound of running shower water sounds off loudly. While Samirah is showering, he's busy snooping around. After seeing what he saw the last time he was here, he's sure there has to be something of value in this apartment. He's not sure if she's holding Smoke's money or his dope but he's sure that she's holding something.

He quickly thinks of the places that he hid his valuables while he was in the game. He doesn't have much time so he has to make his search fast but thorough. He bends over and looks underneath the bed and finds nothing but shoes and a few dirty panties; not to mention a couple of empty condom wrappers. To his surprise, none of them are of the brand that he uses.

He quickly stands up and runs over to the dresser. Drawer by drawer, he pulls out, tossing clothes to the side. Still he finds nothing. He quickly tiptoes over to the closet and snatches the door open. The closet is a total wreck. Mounds and mounds of dirty clothes are piled up on the floor. His hustler mind set leads him to look up at the top shelf. "Bingo," he whispers to himself as his eyes land upon the large duffle bag that lies on the edge of the top shelf.

He carefully snatches it down from the shelf with care. He's not sure whether he should expect to find dope, money or guns, or maybe all of the above. His heart is pounding ferociously. He unzips the bag carefully as he listens in the next room to hear if the shower is still running and it is. He looks inside where he finds thousands and thousands of loose, little square packages. He lifts one up and reads the stamp aloud. "Bang Man." He pulls out his Blackberry and snaps a clear shot from his camera.

The sound of the shower water comes to a halt. He zips the bag and tosses it back onto the shelf. He shuffles it until it sits as it was. He steps out of the closet and slams the door shut. He runs over to the bed, where he lays on top of the covers, just in the nick of time. He closes his eyes, pretending to be asleep.

Samirah comes walking into the room, stark naked and

soaking wet. She pats herself dry with the soiled t-shirt that she wore today. "You ready for me?" she asks with sex in her eyes.

"Absolutely," he replies with a dazzling smile.

Kansas

Damien 'Charles Manson' Bryant sits at the prison table here in the mess hall in USP Leavenworth. After being in Arizona for a year and a few days, he was taken away from there and shipped here early this morning. He was flown here in style, G5 plane status.

He always had a fear of flying and had never flown until he got into the Federal Penitentiary system. They helped him to get over his fear by forcing him to fly. With the help of them he's no longer afraid to fly. He has been on three planes to date.

This has been the most he's ever traveled in his life. Before getting involved in this he never left the state. Now he has the feeling that he will get the involuntary chance to travel the country.

This is a completely new experience for him. In all his years of incarceration he's been bounced around every year or so and he's gotten accustomed to that. He's not only been able to adapt in every prison but he's also been able to control every prison that he's been in. He's been successful in recruiting new Bloods everywhere he's been.

By far this appears to be the most complex prison that he's had the opportunity to be in. The people look completely different here. The movement and procedures are different. Even the air seems different. Here he feels like a fish out of water.

He looks around at the many prison guards and sees not a black face in sight. Every guard fits the exact same description; Caucasian, over six feet tall, bald headed and built like professional wrestlers. They all stand on their posts as they watch the room with hatred in their eyes that he's never seen before.

He watches a guard that's approaching. His eyes fall onto the man's huge biceps. The size of his arm catches his attention but the tattoo that's posted on it keeps his attention. The picture of a pitch black baby with a noose wrapped tightly around his neck sends a chill up his spine. He holds his breath with a slight sense of fear as the man passes him.

His attention is then caught by a black inmate who is walking behind him. The man's thick full beard makes him assume that the man is Muslim. He watches out of the corner of his eye as the man takes the seat right next to him. Charles Manson instantly puts on

167

his ice cold demeanor.

"What's up lil bruh?" the man asks as he stares at Charles Manson. Charles Manson ignores him as if he doesn't even exist. "Lil bruh," the man says with aggression in his voice. "I said what's up." Charles Manson still doesn't reply. The man chuckles under his breath. "I can dig it. You don't have to answer me. That's on you. I'm just trying to put you up on the game. You don't have to say a word but for your own sake just listen as I educate you on something. I don't know where you just came from but wherever it was it ain't nothing like this joint. That attitude ain't gone get you nowhere out here. These crackers don't give a fuck about you *or* me out here. They will take your ass outta here in the middle of the night and nobody won't ever see you again. Have your ass hanging on a tree in the woods somewhere. Yeah, the KKK is real," he whispers. "I seen a lot of young cats like yourself come in the door with that same attitude but it takes no time at all for them to change up. If they know what's better," he adds. "These crackers will learn a mufucker."

Charles Manson continues to eat and stares onto his tray as if the man isn't speaking to him. It appears this way but truth of the matter is the man has his full attention now but his arrogance won't allow him to give in.

The man takes notice to the three teardrop tattoos that are lined up underneath his eye. He then automatically looks down to his forearm where another familiar tattoo is plastered. The tattoo of dog paws is posted boldly into his skin. "You Blood?"

Charles Manson looks over to him for the first time. He stares into the man's eyes for a second or two before turning away and looking back onto his tray.

"Let me tell you something else. These crackers especially don't give a fuck about no gangbangers. This is a whole different world out here. Again, I don't know where you came from but this ain't nothing like it. Trust me when I tell you. I done seen gangbangers come from other prisons that they ran and when they get here they tiptoe around this mufucker. See the dude in the corner over their with the Bible in front of him? Yeah, he's a good Christian here. I met him in Otisville when he was a Blood. You follow me?" he asks. "Bloods and Crips don't beef with each other out here. Out here Bloods and Crips gotta roll together. They put that shit to the side. Muslims and Christians too," he adds. "It's all of us against them," he says as he nods his head at the corner of the room. "You see that table full of Mexicans over there? And that group of them over to the left? They stick together. You beef with one of them, you beef with all of them. Them little mufuckers don't stop stabbing until you stop moving," he warns. "And them right there," he says as he nods his head at the table directly in front of them. At the table there sits twelve inmates. All of them are Caucasian, bald headed and covered with tattoos. They all have thick overlapping mustaches and raggedy beards. "The White Supremacists a.k.a. Aryan Brotherhood. Quiet is kept, the Skin Heads, they run this shit and they despise gangbangers. In the two years I been here, I can't count how many gangbangers that have been murdered by them. See the one in the middle," the man says.

For the first time Charles Manson responds. He looks up to the man who is being referred to. He's a frail, middle aged man, who's is covered with tattoos. His bald head looks like a globe with geographical sketches covering it entirely, as well as it covers his face. "He got twenty years in on a two hundred and ten year sentence," he chuckles. "Yeah," he chuckles while nodding his head up and down. "He ain't got nothing to lose. There are a lot more in here just like him."

Charles Manson is now quite intrigued in what he's hearing. He looks over to the man and stares him in the eyes once again. His arrogant demeanor is now simmering down. He doesn't say a word but his eyes tell a story.

The man reads the tattoo that's posted on Charles Manson's neck. It reads Brick City. A sense of joy rips through his heart. He feels good to see someone who is from his hometown. "You from Newark?" Charles Manson nods his head up and down. "What part?"

"South Orange Avenue," he says with strong confidence.

"Yeah?" the man asks with a bright light in his eyes. Charles Manson gazes into his eyes and gets the sense that he's in the presence of a fellow Newarker. The man extends his hand and Charles Manson returns the gesture. "El Amin Bashir," he says as he grips Charles Manson's hand. "They call me Bas on the street for short. "I'm from all over Newark," he chuckles. "What's your name?"

"Charles Manson," he replies as he stares coldly into the man's eyes. "The Black Charles Manson."

Bas smiles as he peeks around. "Don't say that too loud," he chuckles as he looks to the table of White Supremacists. "You don't want the wrong mufucker to hear that. They may take that as a disrespect. Mufuckers idolize Charles Manson. I can show you a few mufuckers that will make the real Charles Manson look like a Saint," he smiles. He looks at Charles Manson with a grin on his face. "I knew it was something special about you. I can smell Newark on a mufucker. You good in here, lil bruh. No worry."

"I ain't worried. I'm good wherever I go," he replies with defense.

'Nah, not to say it like that. I'm just letting you know that you ain't alone. It can get crazy in here. We got your back but you gotta drop the flag though for the most part. On the street you can do whatever you wanna do but in here it ain't about red or blue. It's about black. Bloods, Crips, Muslims, Christians, Hebrew Israelites and Five Percenters," he says with severity in his eyes. "It's all of us against them."

Meanwhile in Brick City

The man slouches behind the steering wheel of his car. Sitting next to him is his partner in crime. These two men are hardly ever seen without each other. Some call them inseparable.

"I only had twenty three," the driver says. "Fifteen of em is Incredible Hulk and eight of em are X Men," he says referring to the stamps that are on the dope. "I got more coming though." He gives the passenger a head nod, signaling him to give the man in the backseat the bag of work.

"Alright, that's cool," the man in the backseat replies. "So how much is that?" the man asks as he attempts to calculate in his mind.

"Take away four hundred. Give me forty six hundred."

The man in the backseat digs into his bag, shuffling through his money. He grabs the chrome plated .40 caliber from the bottom of the bag as he looks up into the rearview mirror. He sees the driver just staring out of the window while the passenger is busy texting away on his phone.

Boc! The loud gunshot sounds off from the backseat. The driver looks shocked as he watches the passenger's head drop onto his lap. Boc! Boc! Two more shots ring off before the driver's head bangs onto steering wheel. The gunman lifts up from the backseat and fires once again. Boc! The hot slug melts into the skull of the passenger. He leans over toward his left and fires once again. Boc!

This slug slams into the head of the driver.

The gunman coughs as a result of the thick gun smoke that fills the car. He clears his throat as he places the heated gun into his waistband. He peeks around nervously as he pushes the backdoor open. He exits and slams the door shut behind him and takes off like lightening.

Hours Later

The Mayor cruises while listening to the tunes of Drake featuring Trey Songs' 'Successful.' The sound system is blazing loudly, so crisp and clear as if he's actually sitting in concert with them. He makes the quick right turn into the parking lot of Tony's office building, in Union. He lowers the music from his steering wheel and presses another set of button on the steering wheel.

He dials Tony's cell phone number and listens as it rings loudly over his intercom. After a few rings Tony picks up. "What's happening?" he asks casually.

"You tell me!" the Mayor barks in a demanding but playful tone. He pulls into the parking space right next to the white convertible Bentley that sits parked. He initially bought the automobile for his brother a few years ago. The Mayor took it as a complete insult when his brother denied the gift from him but overall he was happy that Tony could make use of it.

Seeing this car makes him think of his brother. He hasn't heard from him since their meeting. He misses him and often wants to reach out to him but his pride won't allow him to. He feels like his brother made the call to end their relationship so he should make the call to fix their situation.

The Mayor looks up at Tony's office window. "Look out your window," he demands.

Tony gets up from his desk and walks over to the window. "What's up?" he asks as he looks out of the window. What lies before his eyes is of pure beauty. He has to readjust his vision just to make sure he's actually seeing correctly. His mouth drops open in awe as his eyes lay on the gleaming medallion that's posted onto the stainless steel gray hood. He recognizes the make instantly. It's the Rolls Royce Drophead Coupe. The black body and stainless steel hood looks mix and match but it all seems to blend in perfectly.

The Mayor sits behind the pitch black tinted windows arrogantly. A devious smile appears on his face. Although Tony can't see his face he's sure he knows the exact look that's displayed on his face. "Catch up sucker!" the Mayor barks in a teasing manner.

Tony stands there speechless. He has mixed emotions at this point. As happy as he is for the Mayor right now a part of him is

172

fearful. He can only imagine what type of trouble that's in store for the Mayor.

"Ay man, pack it up for the day. I got plans for us. Come on down," the Mayor demands before ending the call.

As the Mayor is waiting he shuffles through his CD collection looking for the perfect CD for Tony's entrance. In just the nick of time, Tony is walking out of the door. He drags along as he walks toward the car. He shakes his head from side to side with great disappointment.

Finally he stands before the eye candy. His heart races as he grabs hold of the passenger's door. He attempts to snatch it open but the weight of the door surprises him when it barely parts. He leans his head inside and before he can actually sit down the Mayor speaks. "Yeah," the Mayor says with a cocky demeanor.

Tony slams the door shut behind himself. He can't even look the Mayor in the eyes. "This is a beautiful automobile," he says trying to hold back what he really wants to say.

"Yeah...automobile. You said it right," he says with a smirk.

"But, what are you doing though? Tell me you didn't buy this?"

"I can't tell you that," he says as he points to the temporary tag in the back window.

"What you mean?" Tony asks. "What are you doing?"

"I'm doing me as I always do." Tony shakes his head from side to side with grief. The Mayor knows exactly where he's trying to take him. "Hold up, hold up." He stops him before he can get started. "Before you get started let me share something with you. I'm having a beautiful day and before I let you fuck it up by preaching to me about the Feds and the trouble I'm gonna cause, I will leave you right here. Please don't fuck up my moment."

Tony doesn't know what else to say right now. He thinks hard but nothing comes to mind. All he can think to say is, "I think, congratulations is in order then, huh?"

"Thank you," the Mayor replies. "That's more like it."

Tony sinks into the plush leather upholstery. A smile pops onto his face. "I can't lie...this is crrrazy." He pays special notice to the beautiful wood trimming that looks more natural than he's ever seen. "Damn," he utters.

"Yeah," the Mayor smiles. "This bitch got it all. Custom fit, just for *your boy*. Bulletproof windows," he says as he knocks on the extra thick glass. "Guess what else she got?" he asks, not giving Tony time enough to reply. He can't hold it in. "Six inch doors," he boasts with excitement. "Just like *your* President's Cadillac. A mufucker can stand right in front of me with an AK47 and the bullets won't penetrate her. Obama calls his car the ***Beast***. I call this bitch the ***Monster***. I even got the run flat tires," he brags.

"Yeah?" Tony asks with amazement.

"Yeah," he barks. "My man done it up for me," he boasts. "Some thing to think about," he whispers. "***Your*** President, Obama," he says slowly. "No disrespect to him cause I'm all for him. I agree with a few of his points," he says with sarcasm. "He gives hope to the people. A poor black kid in the hood now believes that he can be whatever he wants to be in the world. That's cool. If that's what they need, I'm all for it. Me, when I was a baby I knew I would be whoever or whatever the fuck I wanted to be in life and I am," he snarls. "I mean if he can get all Blacks together to follow him cool. I ain't following him nowhere though," he barks. "It's just crazy though...the black man who runs the whole country," he whispers as he stares into Tony's eyes. "He *rides* Cadillac. And your boy...*me*. I *ride* Rolls Royce. Something is definitely wrong with that picture," he smiles arrogantly. "The Mayor going harder than the fucking President. But just like *your* President, I provide people with hope as well. They look to me and wish they could be in my shoes. I give them something to aspire to be. Me," he adds. "Because of me they pound the streets and grind their hardest with hopes of being as successful and as prominent as *me*. Although it's a slim chance of that happening, at least they have a goal," he says as he looks into his rearview mirror and rubs his hand over his hair.

Tony sits there in confusion. He can't believe that the Mayor is actually comparing himself to the first black man to ever run the country. He always knew the Mayor was a little messed up in the head but now he's convinced that he's all out crazy.

The Mayor turns up the volume on his stereo and the crisp sound of Marvin Gaye's voice graces the automobile. "Dreamed of you this morning," he sings. "Then came the dawn and I thought you were here with me. If you could only see how much I love you. That's all, that's all, that's all." Jay-Z chimes in. "This is the shit you dream about with the homie steaming out. Back, back, backing them Beamers out. Seems as our plans to get a grant, then off to college didn't pan or even out. We need it now. We need a town.

We need a place to pitch. We need a mound." Both Tony and the Mayor fall into a deep zone in somewhat of a trance as they both utter the verses. "For now I'm just a lazy boy, big dreaming in my lazy boy. In the clouds of smoke I been playing this Marvin. Mama forgive me, I should be thinking about Harvard but that's too far away…niggas is starving. Ain't nothing wrong with my aim, just gotta switch my target." They bop their heads to the beat, eyes half closed. "I see pies every time my eyes clidd-ose. I see rides, sixes I gotta get those. Life's a bitch. I hope not to maker her a widow. American Dreaming," they both utter under their breath.

The Mayor lowers the volume for a second. "I got something for you to take your mind off the nonsense," he claims. "*Your* boy is in concert over there in Brooklyn. Let's go see what he talking about," he says as he pulls off. He quickly blasts the volume. "American Dreaming."

Later that Night

    Samirah and S-Dot lay in the bed stark naked after yet another body crashing sexual adventure. As usual he lays there half dead while attempting to listen to her run her mouth. "His life done changed since he hooked up with the Mayor," Samirah utters.

    "The Mayor?" he asks with his eyebrows raised. "Corey Booker?" he asks as if he has not a clue.

    "Psst," she giggles. "No stupid. Not the Mayor, Mayor. The Mayor of the streets. He like the biggest drug dealer we ever had in Newark," she informs. "He a old head kingpin who used to run Newark. He just came home a few months ago. He done took everything over already with the help of my cousin and my brother. All he gotta do is say the word and they do whatever he wants done. He got everybody going crazy right now as we speak. It's a war out there. A gang war," she adds. "Somebody tried to kill him not too long ago. Now everybody beefing."

    "Like Bloods and Crips?"

    "No, Bloods on Bloods," she replies.

    "How Bloods beef with Bloods?" he questions. "This shit crazy. I don't understand it."

    "Cause it ain't for you to understand," she smiles. "You a five-fifty. This ain't your world. It's called set tripping."

Meanwhile a Few Miles Away

    The young man sprints fearfully for his life. He races up the pitch dark block. He peeks behind him, over his shoulder. Behind him, he sees a gun toting bandit.

    Bloc! The gun sounds off loudly causing the young man to sprint even faster.

    The young man in flight is another one of Mother Nature's pups. This young man is the other driver of the stolen vehicle who attempted to assassinate the Mayor.

    After getting a tip on his whereabouts, Smoke ordered to have his house and his child's mother's house put under surveillance. After spotting him less than two minutes ago, coming to his child's mother's house they jumped on him. They waited for him to exit the cab that he was in before they made their move. At the sight of the car with the dark tinted windows on the side of him, he took off like a jack rabbit.

The sound of gunshots behind him causes him to flee desperately, hoping to find safety. He looks around for a get away. Bloc! Bloc! To his right he spots a house with a wide open door. Escape, comes to his mind quickly.

He takes four giant steps before grabbing hold of the railing. He pulls himself upward as he skips the entire flight of stairs. The gunman is more than ten feet away. The young man storms through the doorway.

He stands in the hallway with fear, not knowing where to go or what to do. The sight of the gunman busting through the door, forces him to take off running up the stairs. The gunman follows closely, on his heels.

The young man kicks backwards. Luckily his foot slams into the face of the gunman, forcing him backwards a few steps. This gives him enough time to take a small lead.

He makes it to the top of the staircase in no time. This time he has nowhere else to go. He's trapped. With no other option, he runs toward the door. Using all of his might he forces his body into the door, shoulder first. The door flies inward, falling off of the hinges. The young man falls into the apartment, landing onto his knees.

"Owww!" a woman screams at the top of her lungs as she grabs hold of her small child. She runs away from the door with fear. The small child cries at the sight of the stranger. The woman stops short, standing in the middle of the living room. She stands there in complete shock without a clue of what's going on. "Oww!" she screams again frantically as she watches another foreign person coming through her doorway.

The young man attempts to crawl to safety but there is none. Bloc! Bloc! Bloc! The bullets to the back of the young man's head knocks him flat on the floor. Bloc! Bloc! Bloc! The young man lies there lifelessly.

"Owwww!" the woman screams again as she watches the gunman exit her apartment. "Owwww!"

One Hour Later

    The Black Charles Manson lays on the top bunk in his cell. He's consumed with thought. Everything that the brother Bas told him has been ringing in his head over and over. In just the one day that he's been here he can already see the validity in everything that he's been told.

    Tension fills this entire prison but as he was told, most of the tension comes from the White Supremacists. While in population he's extra mindful of his surroundings and watches his movements closely. He gets the feeling that they're just waiting to make a move on him. He can tell they're looking for a justification for what they already want to do. Knowing this keeps him on high alert. When in population in this prison or any other prison that he's been in, he's always on guard and prepared for any drama that can break out. That's just the way prison is and he's gotten accustomed to it but to have to be on the same watch at night is absurd to him. Normally he has bunked with men who he has a certain amount of trust in or at least they have a mutual respect for one another. In this matter that is by far not the case. Of all the people that they could choose for him to bunk with, who did they pick? Yep, a member of the White Supremacist Brotherhood.

    He's sure that they did this purposely just to make his bid here uncomfortable; and they have definitely managed to do that. In fact he's more than uncomfortable with the entire situation. All today he's been moving around not in fear but with extreme caution.

    He really hates to be trapped in here alone with this man. He barely feels secure while awake so there's no way that he will be able to sleep around him. They haven't said one word to each other the entire day that they've been here together. The man doesn't have to say a word with his mouth because his eyes say it all. The looks that he gives Manson alone, could slaughter him. The fact that Manson doesn't back down, infuriates the man. After each stare down the man's pale white face becomes blood red.

    There's no doubt in Manson's mind that one minor slip up could turn into a major altercation. Manson doesn't underestimate the man at all. He definitely sees the cold look of murder that lies in his old and weary eyes. It's evident that the man has killed before which is why he's here in the first place. He's also sure that the man will kill again. Two mass murderers trapped in a tiny cell together can only result in one thing and that's one more murder. Manson refuses to be the murder victim.

Manson looks over to the corner of the tiny cell where his cellmate is sitting on the floor, Indian style. Across his lap there's a book in which he's been reading from for the past five hours. By the looks of the huge library he has on his side of the cell one would think that he's very studious. The only problem is all his books consist of white power and anti- black literature. He reads hatred and most importantly he practices hatred.

Manson hops off the bunk quietly. He stands still, watching the man to make sure that he isn't paying attention to him. He tiptoes toward the man cautiously. As he's doing so, he psyches himself up to do what he has to do. Truly he hates to make this move due to the repercussions that he's sure will come but he has no choice. He feels as if his back is against the wall. It's either lay in this cell alone with the man and get not a wink of sleep, in fear of what he's sure the man will eventually do, or make his move. One thing he knows for sure is, when in war it's best to make the first move and most importantly make it count.

He stands over the man for not one second before he crouches down, intertwining the man in the tightest grip that he has. One arm locks underneath his arm while the other one wraps tightly around his neck. The man squirms like a fish, desperately trying to get out of the hold but he has no success at all.

"You black motherfucker," he snarls viciously as he bangs his head into Manson's face. He rams his head consecutively. Manson becomes enraged when the taste of fresh blood fills his mouth. He tightens his grip, trying to choke the life out of him, yet and still the man continues to ram his head into Manson's face. Manson becomes dizzy. Blood pours from his nose, dripping onto the man's white t-shirt. Manson squeezes even tighter.

The man gags as he's being strangled. Instead of calming down, he gets more excited. Losing a fight to a black man is not even an option for him. The thought of that causes him to go mad. He rams his head harder and harder, causing Manson to get even dizzier. Weakness overpowers him, causing him to unloosen his grip slightly.

The man feels a small sense of victory which motivates him to ram his head even harder. Blood spills from Manson's nose, mouth and his head. The man manages to get one hand almost free. He uses that hand to gouge Manson's eye.

"Aghh," Manson grunts as the man drives his nails into his eyeball. He's blinded by the blood that fills his eyelid. This gives the man the freedom to squirm out of the hold. He reverses the hold by wrapping his arms around the back of Manson's neck. He pulls downward with all of his might. Manson's circulation is cut off by the man's shoulder blade. The harder he pulls downward, the less Manson can breathe.

The sound of the cell being unlocked can be heard over the commotion. Manson peeks upward and sees three correction officers coming to his aid. "Break it up! Break it up!" The man disregards the instructions and squeezes harder in attempt to strangle Manson to death. The officers struggle to separate the two men but the man only fights harder to keep his grip. "Aghh," Manson grunts.

Finally they're separated. Manson is peeled off of the man. The man jumps up from the floor violently. A demonic look is on his face. He snatches away from them violently. It takes a total of four men to restrain him.

Manson stands behind one officer, just watching the man who is literally throwing the officers off of him. He's like a madman right now. Two more guards come in to help in restraining him.

"Let me at that nigger," he growls satanically.

"Take him to lock up!" the guard says as he tries to catch his breath.

Manson is forced out of the cell to safety. "Phew," he exhales. All the commotion has drawn all the neighboring inmates to their gates. They stand behind the bars like animals in a zoo. The guard pushes him down the narrow corridor. "You fucked up, nigger!" one man says as Manson approaches the cell. In return Manson spits at him. Thick, white, dry saliva, plasters the man's face.

Manson disregards the racial statements coming from the men. Off to lock-up he goes. His plan is a success. He didn't necessarily plan to murder the man. His main concern was to cause a ruckus and be removed from the cell. He also wanted to make a statement to everyone that he doesn't give a fuck. He figured it all out. There's no doubt that the Skin Heads run this joint. The majority of the men here are afraid of them and don't stand up for themselves. When everyone gets the word that he moved out first they will either respect him or murder him. Manson is prepared for either but for the time being he's going to lock-up. At least there he can breathe a little. Solitary confinement will be much better living conditions for him. At least in there he can rest without worrying about being murdered in his sleep. In any other prison, lock-up is a form of punishment. In here, he views it as an amenity. If he's lucky he can spend his prescribed time here in this prison in lock up.

The smell of sweet perfume mixed with perspiration fills the air. Mocha's dark chocolate skin glistens from the sweat that covers her nude body. She's straddled over the man who lies flat on his back. The look on his face is of pure pleasure as she slides up and down slowly onto his manhood. He grabs hold of the pillow and squeezes tightly as the sensation becomes more intense. Watching him squirm with pleasure gets her more excited and wetter than Niagara Falls. Her aim is to please him like he has never been pleased.

She grabs hold of the headboard tightly to position herself. She plants her feet flat onto the soft mattress. Suddenly she bounces up like a frog, an inch into the air before falling back onto his manhood. Up and down, up and down she bounces as she stares into his eyes with passion. The noise of the headboard crashing into the wall sounds off loudly. Each bounce becomes more intense than the last one. Her insides become creamier and creamier.

Her beautiful cantaloupe shaped breasts spring up and down, jiggling like water balloons. Her nipples resemble dark chocolate chip cookies. The tiny nipple is planted in the center like a Chocolate Hershey Kiss. He watches the nipples sway from side to side until she has hypnotized him into a sexual trance. He grabs her rear, digging his fingertips into the pillow softness. He tries to slow her down because the feeling is just too much. With the sway of her hand she slaps his hands off of her. "Don't touch me," she growls. "Ain't this what you wanted?" she asks while looking into his eyes. She now punishes him by bouncing even harder. Her cheeks crash into his pelvis area fiercely. Their sweaty skin claps together loudly.

He sways his head from side to side and tightens up his abdomen muscles to prevent the eruption that he feels building up in his testicles. The head of his manhood swells up massively. The juices in his sack boil like steaming hot water heating up his entire body. It bubbles violently as it shoots up the pipeline. "I'm about to cum!" he shouts. "Here it comes," he grunts. "Ah," he roars.

Mocha bounces once more before jumping off in the nick of time. She lands at the bottom of the bed. She grabs his manhood with a gentle grip, aiming it at her wide open mouth. "My mouth," she whines. "In my mouth," she whispers. In less than a second, hot lava lands onto her tongue, melting away her taste buds. Buck shots plaster her chin as she misses a few pellets. "Uhmm," she whispers as she licks her chin dry.

Ring, ring! Ring, ring! Tony's eyes pop wide open. He looks around, not realizing where he is. He looks down at the recliner that he's sitting in and realizes that he is home. He also realizes that he's just had another one of his famous nightmares of Mocha having sex with another man. He shakes his head from side to side trying to erase the vision that still remains in his mind. Ring, ring! Tony looks up at the clock on the wall and reads the time of 9:32 A.M. He has spent yet another night here on this recliner. Ever since Mocha left him, this is where he has slept most of the nights. For the life of him, he can't fall asleep in bed without her.

Ring, ring! "Hello," he answers in a groggy voice.

"Mr Austin! This is Andy!" the stock broker shouts.

Tony snatches the phone away from his ear. "Andy, please... my eardrums," he says with agitation.

"Sorry but you, my friend, are going to love me again," he says with joy.

"Is that so?" Tony asks rather blandly.

"Yes, sir. That is most definitely so. The market my friend, has just opened up and I see that our investment has made you a wealthy man. That poor house you talked about...trade it in."

Tony is quite anxious. His curiosity is getting the best of him. "Andy, cut the shit! Talk to me!"

"Not even a couple of months and a half ago you bought in at a measly dollar and sixty eight cents a share. Today my friend, the market opened up at thirty four dollars and sixteen cents a share!"

Tony jumps out of his seat, damn near hitting the ceiling. He scurries around frantically, looking for a calculator. "Are you serious, Andy? Don't bullshit me," he says as he runs over to the coffee table and snatches the tiny calculator from it. He quickly presses in the numbers.

"As a heart attack," Andy replies.

Tony's eyes damn near pop out of his head. He can't believe the numbers that are on the display. "Holy shit," he utters.

"That's right," Andy boasts. "No, your eyes are not deceiving you. Two million, thirty three thousand and three hundred and five dollars."

Tears of joy fill Tony's eyes. I'm fucking back!" he shouts. "I'm back, bitch! You thought I was fucking finished you stinking bitch!" Andy holds the other end of the phone with not a clue of what Tony is talking about. "Andy, you're a fucking genius."

"Is that right?" he asks with sarcasm. "So I guess I'm not a dumb fucking Polock anymore?" he laughs.

"No motherfucker. You are a genius."

"Mr. Austin this stock is expected to reach fifty dollars in less than two weeks."

"Two weeks?" Tony asks in a high pitched voice. "Andy, you my man but tomorrow ain't promised to none of us. I want out, not now but right fucking now. I'm taking the money and running like the bandit that I am."

"Come on Mr. Austin, this is just the beginning."

"No Andy, it's the end. Don't you see the credits rolling? This movie is over! I can't afford any risk. With my luck it will drop to ten cents tomorrow morning."

"Tony the reward outweighs the risk. Trust me."

"Andy, I'm out! Chalk it up! Game over! Done deal! It's a wrap!"

Days Later

The Mayor slouches low as he cruises in the 'Monster' as he calls it. In the passenger's seat there sits Smoke who sits back in total awe. The stereo plays at a moderate volume as the Mayor raps along with Jeezy as he spits his 'Corporate Thugging.' "Not a day go by that I ain't high. Hit the mall everyday nigga, I stay fly. Twenty six inches, yeah I'm sitting high and I'm gone keep it hood niggas...that's no lie."

"Got damn, you snapped!" Smoke shouts with excitement.

The Mayor smiles as he accepts the praise that he's sure he deserves. "This what a half a mill feel like," he whispers. "Fucking with me, you gone get there," he smiles.

"Damn!" Smoke shouts. "This shit crazy!"

The Mayor knows he should not be driving around the town in the car but he can't help himself. To buy such a prestigious vehicle like this and not be seen it is senseless to him. "We gonna show these lame ass niggas how to play," he utters. "The city is ours. We got now. We don't give a fuck who got next!" he says with confidence in his eyes.

Meanwhile

Federal Informant Sean sits in front of the desk as Agents Dumber and Dumbest pace around him. He's babbling on and on, reporting to them as he does every few days or so. "Supposedly, Smoke just added another few murders to his resume. Right now he's in the middle of a war with a Blood chick who goes by the name of Mother Nature. She's labeled as treacherous. *Our girl* told me that two dudes from her projects were recently murdered. One of them was the driver of the vehicle full of men who attempted to gun down *your man*. A man by the name of JB is the one who ordered the hit. A few days ago JB was murdered. It may have been charged as a drug deal gone bad but there was definitely an ulterior motive. Smoke ordered his murder in retaliation for what they attempted to do to the Mayor dude."

The Agents listen with their mouths wide open. They can't believe how much this man actually knows. In all their years of working, never has their job been this easy. "Who actually murdered

185

JB?"

"I'm not sure but she mentioned something like Diddy," he says with a baffled look on his face.

"Diddy?" Agent Dumber questions as he jots down the name on his pad. "The murder victim is JB, you said, right?"

"Yep," he replies with a big smile.

"Ay kiddo...how the hell do you get all this information out of her?"

He winks with arrogance as he grabs a handful of his crotch. "I got the magic stick," he smiles. "Look what else I got," he says as he shuffles through his phone. He locates the photo that he's looking for. He hands the phone over to Agent Dumber.

"What's this?" he asks as he stares at the screen.

"The work load," he smiles. "Our girl holds it all in her tiny attic apartment."

A huge smile appears on both of the agents' faces. "About how much would you say is in there?" Dumber asks.

"Aww man, I don't know. If I had to estimate...about a couple of thousand bricks," he replies.

"Yeah?" Dumber asks.

"Yeah," he barks in reply.

Dumber smiles as he stares him in the eyes. "Good boy. Good fucking boy."

Everyone watches in amazement as the Rolls Royce cruises through the city. The dark windows cause so much mystery. They have no clue of who is behind the dark tints but they would sure love to know.

Smoke watches from behind the windows as they receive the attention. He so badly wants to roll the window down so he can be seen. Just riding in the vehicle motivates him to get back to the block and get on his grind.

"Your boy JB," Smoke whispers. "It's a wrap. Dead as a door knob."

The Mayor looks over at Smoke with no emotion on his face. "As he should be."

"And so is both of the drivers."

"What about the Blood bitch?" the Mayor questions.

"We on her," Smoke replies with disappointment. "She

slipping and sliding but we got her on the radar."

"Fuck the radar. You need to have her under the scope. Why is she so hard for ya'll to get? What...mufuckers scared to get at her?" he asks, trying to charge Smoke's battery. "That's what it sounds like to me. What ya'll need some type of incentive to make ya'll work harder?" he asks. "Ok, how bout I cut off the lifeline? I pull the plug out, so ain't nothing moving...no distractions. That way ya'll can concentrate on getting the bitch. No more Bang Man on the street until she's murdered. How about that?" the Mayor asks with rage.

"Nah, nah, nah," Smoke interrupts with fear. He can't imagine life without Bang Man. "We on that ASAP, big bruh. I promise you!"

The Next Day

Tony speeds up Route 78 West doing a hundred and thirty miles an hour in his brand new toy. He switches lanes for the hell of it just for the sake of showing off. After scoring two million dollars off of a measly hundred grand, he had no choice but to spoil himself. He figured after all the stress that he suffered from the past couple of months, he truly deserves it. The three hundred grand cash that he spent on this automobile barely put a dent in his stock earnings.

The best part of the two million dollar score is the fact that he hasn't once thought about Mocha since. The money has helped him get over her almost overnight. He looks at it as the beginning of his new life and he plans to live it like that. The lack of confidence and self-esteem that he suffered from a few days ago is no longer.

Once again he thanks God for the drug game as bad as that may sound. Almost two decades ago the success that he had in the drug game gave him the opportunity to better his life. Now here it is almost two decades later and the drug game has come to his rescue once again. This time it's the legal drug game that he invested stock into.

Tony sings along with singer Mark Morrison. "Oh, oo, o, oh," he whines. "Come on. Ooh yeah! Well I tried to tell you so. Yes I did!" he shouts. "But I guess you didn't know. As I said the story goes. Baby now I got the flow. Cause I knew it from the start. Baby when you broke my heart…that I had to come again and show you that I'm real. You lied to me," he shouts with harmony. "All those times I said that I love you. You lied to me! Yes I tried. Yes, I tried. You lied to me! Even though you know I'd die for you. You lied to me! Yes I cried, yes I cried. Return of the Mack!" he shouts with a bright smile on his face. "Return of the Mack! It is! Return of the Mack! Come on! Return of the Mack! Oh my God. Return of the Mack! With my flow," he whines. "You knew that I'll be back. Here I go! So, I'm back up on the game. Running things to keep my swing. Letting all the people know that I'm back to run the show. Cause what you did you know was wrong. And all the nasty things you've done. So baby listen carefully while I sing my come back song. You lied to me! But you did, but you did. You lied to me! All these pains you said I'd never feel. You lied to me but I do, but I do. Return of the Mack! It is! Return of the Mack!

Tony lowers the volume of his stereo and dials the Mayor's number. The phone rings over the intercom. "Yo," the Mayor whispers.

"Meet me at the valet section," Tony says with a false sense of depression in his voice as he zips off of 78 and pulls into the Short Hills Mall area. He immediately spots the Mayor's Rolls Royce parked in the valet section. Tony mashes the gas and the vehicle roars like a lion. In seconds he's parked right behind the Mayor's automobile as he calls it. He revs the engine ferociously causing the lungs on the side of the vehicle to breathe like a tired bear.

The Mayor watches the beautiful triple black Aston Martin DBS with admiration. The price tag posts in his mind immediately. He's totally familiar with this 'James Bond Edition.' He knows all the specifics of it like the back of his hand. His heart melts at the very sight of it.

Tony's passenger side window rolls down automatically. He looks at the Mayor, still singing along with the song. "Return of the Mack! It is! Return of the Mack!"

He hops out gracefully and steps toward the Mayor. "I didn't catch up sucker but I'm on your heels," he boasts arrogantly. A sparkle brightens up the Mayor's eyes. "I'm back baby. I'm fucking back!"

"As you should be."

"Motherfuckers thought I was dead! But I came back to life on their ass," he says with arrogance as he tosses the attendant the keys.

"Got damn baby," the Mayor says with respect. "You ain't bullshitting, huh?"

"Not at all," he smiles. "I couldn't have done it without you. As you say, you motivated me to get out of that bed and make it happen." The Mayor nods his head up and down with a smile. "Thanks man," Tony says with sincerity.

"For what?" the Mayor asks rather casually.

"For being you."

"I have to be me," the Mayor replies with arrogance. "Anything less would be uncivilized."

The young, small framed, dread headed man steps into Upscale Barber Shop and Beauty Salon, on South Orange Avenue. He becomes disappointed as he sees how crowded the shop is. He looks over to his stylist as he rubs his fingers through his dirty, messy dreadlocks. "How many you got?" he asks.

The stylist looks around the shop rather quickly. "Uhmm," he grunts. "You after this one," he says as he points to the man who is sitting in the chair in front of him. He twists the man's dreadlocks meticulously. "As soon as he's done at the sink, go on over," he says pointing toward the sink.

The young dread sits in the first vacant seat that he sees. He grabs a magazine from the stand and starts to skim through the pages immediately. He looks up briefly and his attention is caught by the chair in the middle. The stylist spins the person around and there they sit almost face to face. His heart skips two beats when he realizes who the man in the chair is. He's a member of Mother Nature's squad. Oh shit, he thinks to himself. He drops his eyes onto the magazine as he attempts to play it cool and calm. He peeks up discreetly as the stylist spins the man around to face the mirror. He then peeks to his right where he notices another one of Mother Nature's soldiers sitting in the very last chair. The person at the sink finally lifts his head up momentarily. Damn, the man says to himself. He's at the absolute wrong place at the absolute wrong time. He's caught dead to the rear. Here he sits in the presence of three of Mother Nature's pups and he's all alone with no weapon. He's completely petrified right now but he has to keep his composure. The last thing he wants to do is cause them alarm. He has to get out of here but how?

Meanwhile

The Mayor lays back in his California King sized bed. His eyes are glued to the 72 inch flat screen. This is something that he hardly ever does. He is totally against television watching. He calls it (tell lie vision.) His belief is that the government uses television to brainwash the people into believing what they want the people to believe. He looks at it all as a conspiracy.

He watches with hatred in his eyes as he listens to Mayor Corey Booker of Newark speak. The Documentary entitled Brick City is airing. The only reason that he's even watching is because this is his city and he wants to know what people have to say about it. He also hopes that he will learn some secrets as far as law enforcement and so forth goes.

The Mayor listens closely as Mayor Corey Booker states some statistics. He brags on and on about how the crime rate has decreased since he's been in his office. The Mayor chuckles with a sense of sarcasm. "Bullshit, Corey." The Mayor refers to him as Corey. He refuses to ever call him the Mayor. In his mind he feels that there is only one man worthy of that title and that's him.

The Mayor speaks aloud. "That's all bullshit." He looks at the huge screen, staring into Corey Booker's eyes. "I'm about to make it hard for you, *Corey*. "I'm gonna send you and all of your statistics back to Bergen County where you from, with your tail up your ass. You know nothing about *my city*. How the hell you gone be the solution when you don't even know the fucking problem? *The Mayor*, please," he snaps. "I'm gone make you work for that measly two hundred thousand a year salary. I'm gone give you a run for your money," he smiles. "Will the real *Mayor* please stand up," he says as he's getting out of the bed. He plants his feet firmly onto the hardwood floors. "You gonna have to bring all the troops out for me."

Back in the Bricks

The young dread slowly gets out of his seat. He's trying hard not to draw any attention to himself. He peeks around and takes notice that all three of Mother Nature's soldiers are still in their positions, getting worked on. He steps toward the door to make his exit.

He takes one last peek as he steps out of the shop. He quickly grabs his phone and starts dialing Smoke's number to inform him of his findings. He has no weapon on him so there's really nothing he can do but get away from them. He plans to sit back in his car and wait for Smoke to send help. Once that's done they will hopefully wipe out three more of her pups.

He listens impatiently as the phone rings and rings. "Damn," he whispers. "Pick up the phone." Finally he gets an answer. "Yo, what's goodie?" Smoke greets.

"Big bruh, I'm over here at Upscale," he says with anxiousness. "Three of the bitch, Mother Nature's peoples in there. Get over here, quick," he says as he reaches the corner. He looks behind, just to make sure no one is following him. He turns back around as he bends the corner onto 12th Street. Pop! Pop! The sound of the gunshots deafens him slightly. The bright orange glare blinds him before the ball of hot fire melts into his face. He drops the phone as he stumbles backwards. His feet tangle and he falls onto his back. He turns over in defense as he lies there in a fetal position. Pop! Another gunshot sounds off. His body cringes as the slug rips through his abdomen. "Aghh," he grunts with agony.

He peeks up through his half closed eye and notices four boots, inches away from his face. Over the sound of loud screaming in the background, he hears a female voice sound off from behind him. "Hold up, hold up. Turn that motherfucker over!" she shouts. Before he knows it, he's laying on his back staring upward through thick blood that covers his face. Through his blurry vision, he sees who else but Mother Nature herself. Terror floods his heart.

"Look at me motherfucker. Look at me!" she repeats with more aggression. "I want you to know who did this to you," she says as she aims her gun at his head. She taps the trigger and the infrared beam shines a red dot right in between in his eyes. "Mother Nature did this to you!" she shouts as she mashes the trigger. Boc! His head explodes like a melon. Flat line!

Fifteen minutes too late, the Pontiac GTO pulls up to the scene of the crime. Smoke sits in the passenger's seat. He's sure he already knows the outcome of this matter. They're obstructed by the yellow tape that surrounds the entire area. He looks at the many homicide detectives that swarm the area. Flashing lights of a camera draws his attention to the corner where his little homie lies.

A burning sensation fills Smoke's eyeballs before his eyelids well up with tears. He turns his head before a single tear drops from them. "Pull off."

The Mayor sits in the back room of the bar here in Connecticut. In front of him there sits his plug. The man listens with close attention as the Mayor speaks clearly. "At the end of the day, I'm just not satisfied. I thought you were going to be able to do better."

"You're not satisfied?" the man asks with attitude. "That material is good," he says with extreme confidence.

"See, that's the problem right there. You think I'm looking for good, when I'm really looking for great. I need better," he snaps. "It took my people close to three weeks to shake six thousand measly bricks. That doesn't add up," he says. "Not when we supposedly got the best dope in the town."

"Six thousand bricks in the last three weeks?" the man snarls. "And you are complaining? Anybody would be happy to move half of that load."

The Mayor stares directly into the man's eyes. "I'm not just anybody and I will never be satisfied with that. It's just not acceptable. I got the entire city on my back and I'm trying to push this shit to the limit. I have a quota to meet. By next month I wanna be ripping through twenty thousand bricks a month with ease."

The man looks at the Mayor like he has three heads. "Are you kidding? That's a lotta dope."

"Yeah...and there's a lotta money to be made."

"I don't know if I even got the manpower to push out twenty thousand bricks a month."

"Well hire more men."

"You're not my only customer. I have other orders to fill."

"Do the right thing and you won't have to fill other orders. Fucking with me alone you will have all the scratch you need. It's money to be made and I ain't gone stop until we've made it all. Six thousand bricks in three weeks, that's absurd. That's foreplay for me...a complete waste of time. If I can't rip through at least five thousand bricks a week I may as well stop while I'm ahead. I just spent many summers in the bing. I made history. I was never supposed to see the streets ever again. I get caught with one lousy brick in my possession and they will fuck around and give me the electric chair. Keeping that in mind, I can't be playing around with this shit. Three weeks, six thousand bricks," he whispers. "It just don't add up. It's not worth it."

The Mayor isn't as upset as he's pretending to be. He's just trying to spark the flame under the man's feet, hoping he will turn the volume up on the material. Overall he does realize that over six hundred thousand dollars profit in less than three weeks is nothing to complain about. His greed tells him it's really nothing to brag about either. He understands that he's rebuilding the city from the ground so it's going to take some time but patience is something that he's never had.

"Listen," the Mayor says as he slides the duffle bag closer to the man. "Here is four hundred and fifty thousand," he says. "That's money for ten thousand bricks. Another hundred thousand for the chemist to do what he do. And another buck fifty for you to put the pepper on the mufucker," he says with determination in his eyes. "I want it so bad that I'm willing to cut my own profit just to get the best quality that you seem to think is impossible to produce," he says with sarcasm on his face. "Altogether, right in front of you, there is seven hundred grand. I don't know what you gotta do but do it."

By giving them an additional two hundred and fifty thousand dollars he's cutting his profit margin by approximately ten percent but the work being of a higher power he's sure he will be able to move it faster. Normally a flip of this magnitude, he would expect to score a profit of approximately 1.1 million dollars. By giving them the extra two hundred and fifty thousand dollars he loses in the beginning but expects to regain that ten percent plus a few more ten percents in the long run.

The Mayor has a motto, 'greedy people starve.' A greedy man would be afraid to lose two hundred thousand dollars in profit. He would be satisfied with scoring 1.1 in one month all in one flip. The Mayor, on the other hand, realizes that the real money is all in the flip. He has no problem losing two hundred grand on the first go round. If he rips through ten thousand bricks in two weeks, sure he only scores nine hundred grand but if he's able to rip through another flip he will then be ahead seven hundred thousand dollars for the month.

"Listen man, I been sitting back thinking and planning for over ten and something years. Now it's time to bring all those thoughts and plans to life. I ain't got time to be playing around with this shit. I'm thirty one years old. By the time I get thirty-five it's over. Whatever I don't get by then I won't get. With that being said, I got four good years left. Let's make the best of them," he says with severity in his eyes. "So, how long ya'll need to make those ten thousand bricks available?"

Two Days Later

Charles Manson lays back in the pitch dark lonely cell. In the two days that he's been here, he's gotten more than enough sleep. Laying here in loneliness leaves him nothing else to do but sleep. Although he's bored to death, at least he has serenity.

Manson is hungry and dehydrated. He has barely eaten or drank anything in two days. He doesn't trust the food that has been coming to him. A letter from brother Bas yesterday made him aware that his assumptions were correct. The letter stated that he made a big mistake in the decision that he made. He told him that he has made it harder on himself. He instructed Manson to be extremely cautious with what he eats or drinks. He said that there's no telling what the 'Skin Heads' who work in the kitchen will do for pay back of his act. That statement explained the dirty brown, foul smelling rice he was given yesterday. Something told Manson that it was not meat sauce and gravy over rice.

Brother Bas also stated that he would pull some strings to get at least one feasible meal a day. Unfortunately that meal hasn't come yet, today. Manson grabs hold of his stomach to muffle the loud growling sound. The hunger pain rips through his abdomen violently.

Two seconds and not one second too early, a white officer stands at the gate, holding a tray. "Chow," the officer whispers.

Manson gets up and walks toward the gate. His stomach rumbles as he watches the food with hunger in his eyes. He looks at the officer, wondering if he can trust him or not. Brother Bas gave strict instructions for him to follow but at this point he's so hungry that he's almost willing to take his chances.

Manson looks into the man's eyes with desperation, hoping he gives him the code word which would let him know if it's ok to eat from this tray. The officer hands over the tray without uttering a word. Underneath the tray, Manson feels another envelope. The officer walks off leaving Manson hungry and quite disappointed.

After a few steps the officer peeks over his shoulder. "Club Sensations," the man whispers. Hearing this Newark landmark brings tears of joy into Manson's eyes. Brother Bas sent the tray here so it has to be Halal(permissible).

"Thank God," Manson whispers to himself. He stands in the exact same spot that the officer left him standing in. He digs into the pile of whatever with his free hand. In less than one minute he's devoured everything on the tray. What exactly he's just eaten he has not a clue. It didn't stay on the tray long enough for him to figure out what it was.

He lays the tray onto the floor before ripping the envelope open. He unfolds the yellow, lined paper and holds it up to the gate, just to be able to read it in the darkness. He's expecting another letter from Bas but instead it reads: *Dear Nigger. You may as well have committed suicide before making the foolish move that you made. You will never live to utter a word of what you done. To put your filthy nigger hands on a member of our Brotherhood is such a grave sin. You can run but you can't hide. This problem will not be resolved until you're no longer breathing. When you look up or should I say down we will be standing right there. Hanging from the bars, noose tied tightly around your nigger neck. Your nigger eyes will be carved out of your nigger head like a Halloween pumpkin, while you're alive. Your testicles will be cut out as well and put on display for the rest of the niggers to see the repercussions to your act. There's no punishment that can deter me from getting even with you. I have only one year in on a triple life sentence. I'm not going anywhere. See you sooner than you think.*

Manson crumbles the paper tightly into the palm of his hand. "What the fuck ever," he mumbles to himself. He's been sentenced to 180 days here in lock up. "I'll deal with that when that time comes."

Attorney Angelique Reed steps into Tony's office with a confident and sexy swagger. She's dressed in a form fitting, pin striped business suit and three inch stilettos.

Tony has rubbed off on her tremendously. When they first linked up she was the typical, square, Harvard graduate. She lacked confidence and could barely look a person in the eyes. Today she looks right through a person. Tony planted the cocky seed into her. He knows that he created a monster but he loves it.

She's like a female version of him. At times he looks at her and wishes she was his wife but the reality of it is it would never work because they're so much alike. Because of that reason, he just appreciates her as his partner.

"Hey Champ!" Tony shouts as he opens his arms for a hug. He plants an innocent but caring kiss on her forehead.

"Ay," she replies.

Tony releases his grip and backs away from her. He turns around and leads the way toward his desk. They both take their seats. Angelique slides the briefcase across the top of the desk to Tony. "That's two hundred and fifty," she whispers.

"Cool," Tony replies. "Let him know that I have everything under control. No need to worry."

"Worry is an understatement," she says with agitation in her voice. "I have been hearing this shit for over two years now. I just want it to be over with. I can't take another day of it. He feels so badly about the entire situation."

"Tell him to stop worrying. She's good. I spoke with her earlier this morning. Her spirits were up as usual. Honestly, I never heard pity in her voice. Not in one single conversation. She sounds like she's taking it on the chin."

The person that they're referring to is Lil Mama, Dre's former transporter. Dre hired Tony to defend her after she was nabbed with his load of heroin. After hearing the news of Dre's tragic death she assumed that her life was all over. She figured she was in this all alone but little did she know that Dre had her back all the while.

When Tony came to visit her in the correctional facility she felt a little bit of ease. She felt like she at least had a shot. After

198

almost two years of sitting she was finally called before the judge. She was willing to take the plea bargain of twenty years, thinking that was the best that she could possibly get. Tony refused the plea and told the judge arrogantly that they were willing to take it all the way. In a few days the both of them will find out if that was a mistake or not.

"She's better than me," Angelique smiles. "I would have told everything I knew."

"She knew nothing though. Those that know won't tell. Those that tell don't know," he sings. "Keep that to yourself," he smiles. "I respect you as a stand up person. Don't tarnish the perception I have of you. I would hate to believe that my partner in crime is a stool pigeon."

Angelique smiles dazzlingly. "Whatever."

Meanwhile

Mike Mittens parks in front of 'Coney Island Halal Restaurant on Orange Street. All eyes are on the beautiful Rolls Royce. The car looks completely out of place, even being on this raggedy block. All the people on the block watch with awe, wondering who is about to get out of the car.

Mike Mittens hops out of the driver's seat with modesty while the Mayor climbs out of the passenger's seat with his normal amount of arrogance. The Mayor leads the way toward the restaurant. He sways from side to side freely as Mike Mittens walks with a semi-tense swagger. Mike watches his surroundings closely. The pack of young thugs standing in front of the store causes him discomfort. He grips his gun tightly inside his jacket pocket. He's prepared to bust if need be.

A dirty, shabby looking man appears out of thin air. He steps directly in front of the Mayor, blocking his path. "That's a beautiful ride ya'll got there, young brothers. Can I wipe down the rims?" he asks. Mike Mittens steps in between the man and the Mayor. He stares coldly into the man's weary eyes. Mike's look says **_murder_**. The man backs away with fear. "Sorry...I'm just trying to earn a few dollars. I'm starving," he whispers with shame.

The Mayor looks at the man with sympathy. Hearing a man admit that breaks his heart. "You hungry? Come on," he says as he waves the man along.

Mike Mittens looks at the small crowd of thugs who are blocking the doorway. He's surprised to see that they're opening up their crowd to allow them to step into the restaurant. "Alright, alright," the Mayor says as the three of them step into the crowded restaurant. All the attention is on their entrance and the Mayor loves it.

"Ay Brother!" the owner greets in a Middle Eastern accent.

The Mayor smiles in reply. "The usual for me...and?" he says as he looks at Mike Mittens.

"Pancakes, double beef bacon and home fries," Mike shouts.

The Mayor then looks at the other man who stands close by him. He nods his head signaling the man to order. "Waffles, turkey sausage, beef bacon, home fries, cheese eggs and let me get a small order of French toast," he says as he looks at the Mayor for his approval.

The man behind the counter looks at the Mayor with disgust in his eyes. The sight of the man pisses him off. The Mayor shrugs his shoulders. "Ay...he's hungry. Feed him," he smiles. "My mother always told me to never eat alone."

The three of them sit at the counter. Normally the man wouldn't be allowed to even sit in the restaurant but because he's the Mayor's guest he's being treated like royalty.

One Hour Later

The Mayor stands up after finishing his hearty meal. He's been so focused on his food that he hasn't paid the least bit of attention to how much more crowded the restaurant has gotten. Maybe he hasn't but Mike Mittens definitely has. Mike peeks back and forth around the spot, watching the people who are watching them. The whispering that they're doing amongst each other gives Mike the feeling that they may have a problem or two in store.

The Mayor walks to the rear of the counter, where the owner is standing. He digs into his hood sweater's pocket and retrieves a plastic bag. He secretly passes the bag over to the owner. Through the clearness of the bag, mounds and mounds of scattered loose bills can be seen. All the customers' attention are now on that bag.

The Mayor hates to have dollar bills in his stash. He despises them and will do almost anything to get them out of his possession. Having a bunch of singles makes it even harder for him to hide his money. Every few days he brings a bag full of them here to the owner. He's been doing this many years before he went away. He isn't looking for any particular thing in return.

He's been doing this since the restaurant opened. When it first opened, the Mayor and the owner developed a friendship. He took a strong liking to the man and respected his determination to build his business. The Mayor offered to help but the man refused.

The Mayor has helped more than he can possibly imagine. He doesn't have a clue of how many dollar bills that he has contributed to the man's business. Each time he drops his singles off here there are no less than a thousand of them in the bag. In a month he dumps at least ten thousand, dollar bills here. Multiply that by the seven years that he ate here before he went away. He's contributed enough here to be a partner but instead he wants nothing but a few free meals in return.

All eyes are glued on them as they strut to the door. Everyone wonders who this mystery man is. The shabby man holds the door wide open for Mike and the Mayor to exit. Once they're outside he runs over to the Rolls Royce and snatches the passenger's side door open. He holds it open for the Mayor to get inside.

"You full now?" the Mayor asks as he's sitting down.

"As a Bull," the man replies with a smirk on his face. "Thanks," he says gratefully.

"No problem," the Mayor says as he digs into his pocket and pulls out a thick wad of singles. The entire stack consists of approximately two hundred singles. The Mayor hands the man the entire stack. "Here. That should hold you till the next time I see you. Stay up," he says as he slouches in the seat.

"Thanks," the man replies as he stares at the wad of money. He closes the door carefully.

Mike Mittens hops into the driver's seat and cruises off slowly. "Boy, you ain't gone be happy until you get me a hundred years, huh?" Mike asks. "Psst."

"Huh?" the Mayor questions.

"You pulling out all that money in front of them hungry wolves, pulling up in a Rolls Royce and shit. The only thing that's gone happen is somebody gone step out of pocket and make me murder a mufucker or a few mufuckers," he says as he imagines the whole sight. "You can't keep flashing like that. Did you see the look in them niggas eyes? Straight hate and hunger," he adds.

"That's the look that you saw?" the Mayor asks. "I didn't get that. The look I saw in their eyes was motivation. I motivate them to work harder."

"Nah," Mike denies. You gotta stop doing that shit. You never know who is watching."

"Mike, you know me. I don't give two fucks who watching."

"I hear you but you gone force a mufucker hand. Fuck around and motivate them to do something stupid and lose their lives."

The Mayor shrugs his shoulders nonchalantly. "Well, if that's how the ball bounce, then bounce the mufucker then."

In the restaurant

The group of four people gets up from the table after finishing their breakfast. The female dread head leads the pack as the other three men follow her. A rowdy young man steps into the restaurant. "Mother Nature what's good!" the man shouts with happiness.

"What's up, nigga," she shouts as she stands in front of the counter. "How much?" she asks as she digs into her pocket.

"Nothing, sister," the owner replies. "The meal was free. All compliments of the Mayor."

"The Mayor?" Mother Nature repeats under her breath as she plays back the face of the man who gave the owner the bag of bills. Suddenly it all comes together. The whole time that she's been sitting here she was wondering where she knew him from but she couldn't place his face. Even when she ordered his murder, she really didn't know his face. She really only knew the rental car that he was driving. Mother Nature looks to the man that stands on her right side. A devilish smirk pops on her face. "The Mayor. Hmphhh," she sighs. "The motherfucking Mayor." She quickly thinks of her people that he's responsible for their murders, including JB. She gets furious at the very thought of it. "That fucking close to getting payback and we let him slip away," she says as she shakes her head with frustration. "At least I got his face down now. I'm sure there will be another time.

Samirah is on the second floor, inside her mother's apartment. She's washing the dishes that are left over from the scrumptious brunch that she made for her and the love of her life. This gives S-Dot all the time he needs to pry as he always does when she leaves the room.

He stands in front of the broken down dresser drawer. He reads from the paper that lies face up. After skimming a few lines he realizes exactly what this paper is. It's a lease for an apartment. He looks to the top of the paper where the address is posted. "Maple Gardens," he reads aloud, trying to register the address into his memory base. He then looks to the bottom where he finds the name Samirah Bryant signed. He's sure that she isn't moving because she hasn't said a word to him about it. This could only mean that she's gotten an apartment for someone else. He's so busy pondering in thought that he doesn't even realize that Samirah is standing behind him in the doorway.

"Uhmm, uhmm," Samirah clears her throat loudly. He turns around abruptly. He's been caught dead to the rear. The look in his eyes gives him away. "Nosey, nosey, nosey," she teases as she walks toward him.

He quickly grabs hold of the pile of postcards that are stacked up on the dresser. He tries to play it off as best as he can. "What's this about?" he asks with a cheesy look on his face.

"Psst. Them fliers for my brother's birthday party," she says as she snatches the post cards from him. "It's gonna be crazy! He doing it real big! Everybody who somebody gone be there....all the big time hustlers!" she shouts with delight in her eyes. "You wanna come with me?"

Yeah, and I will be the only rat in the building, he thinks to himself. They will smell me a mile away. "Nah, I ain't with that party shit. Anyway, I probably be out of town," he says as he looks at the date. "You know me, I'm in and out."

"Please? Pretty please?" she begs. "Come with me please?"

He looks into her big doll baby eyes and practically melts away. He hates to tell her no because he would hate it if she ever told him no. "I don't know ma," he whispers. "Maple Gardens," he says to himself, trying hard not to forget the name of the housing complex. He wonders who and what this address will lead them to.

The projects is swarming with customers who are all in search of Bang Man. It's packed out here like Times Square. Instead of bright lights and tourists, there are shattered windows covered by plywood and dope fiends running back and forth. The only camera flashing comes from the camera that is being aimed from behind the dark tinted windows of the black Dodge Caravan that Agents Dumber and Dumbest are sitting in a mile and half a way.

They have been sitting out here for over two hours now just watching the activity. This has been routine for them for the past week. They sit here just connecting the dots. They attach vehicles to dealers. They jot down the license plates to obtain addresses. This is all just routine work for them, quite boring. Today something different happened, adding a little bit of excitement and breaking the monotony of their normal surveillance.

Dumbest sits in the driver's seat as Dumber sits in the passenger's seat. Dumbest flicks away with the wide lens camera. He aims the nose of the camera high into the sky. His focal point is the rooftop of the building that sits in the middle of all the action. There on the top of the building stands Smoke and who else but the Mayor. "Just look at these two motherfuckers." He snaps away with the camera as the Mayor moves around quite animated.

The Mayor plants his foot on the ledge of the building as he stares at the ground level at all the commotion that's going on. He watches the activity with great appreciation.

"Bang man, Bang man!" a young dealer shouts at the top of his lungs.

"You hear that?" the Mayor says as he cups his hand close to his ear. "Music to my ears," he says with a smile. "Look at this shit," the Mayor whispers. "Just look at it. Have you ever seen anything so beautiful?"

Smoke looks down briefly. He skims the entire area before lowering his eyes onto the Black and Mild that he twists in between his fingers.

This is like the Motherland," the Mayor says. "Look what we've done in just one fucking month. And to think you didn't have faith in *your boy*," he says with arrogance. "I told you it could be done. All ten dollar money at that. We got these niggas buying three hundred dollar bricks. Who would ever think those days could come back? Me...that's who," he boasts. That cheap shit can't even sell in this town no more. We raised the fucking bar! It all started right here. This right here," he says as he points to the ground. "Is the central nervous system to the city. The heart of the city. Just like the heart, this projects pumps life or should I say *blood* throughout the rest of the city. It's impossible to live without a heart. Nobody can breathe without *us.* Knowing that, we have to take care of this. Keep it clean and healthy and the *heart* will operate smoothly for a long, long time. Follow me?"

"True," Smoke replies as he stares directly into the Mayor's eyes.

"*You* have to make sure that everything is on the up and up, around here. No bullshit," he adds. "You can operate from here forever as long as you run the most legitimate business that you can. Of course you're going to have police activity. Hell, they got a job to do," he says casually. "A few dudes catch a few cases here and there but that's the normal. That's occupational hazard. The real heat comes when the murder game comes into play. I don't give a fuck if you have to murder a mufucker, just don't do it here. Don't let them mufuckers find his body here. If there is no other option then bust his ass and drag him many miles away from this mufucker," he says as he points to the surrounding area. Feel me?"

"Indeed," Smoke replies as he intakes the valuable information.

The look on the Mayor's face changes to stone cold. Not a trace of his smile is visible. "You may look at all this and think that we have arrived but I look at it like just the beginning. We're just getting started. Trust me, this is only the very beginning. We got a lotta money to make. We just wet up the surface. The best is yet to come. In about two days I have a load of ten thousand bricks coming. All ten thousand of them, for you. Here is where we make our mark. Now is when we turn it all the way up," he says as he looks into Smoke's eyes. "It took you almost three weeks to shake those six thousand bricks. I'm not impressed. Not the least bit. I expect more. I have total faith in you. In fact, I probably believe in you more than you believe in yourself," he says while nodding his head up and down. "I know you can get through this new batch in about two weeks flat. Our goal is to move at least five thousand bricks a week. That's the potential to score a profit margin of two hundred thousand to a half a million dollars a week." Smoke listens in awe. He can't believe the Mayor is throwing these numbers around lightly as he is. "Lil Bruh, you're my new project. Do you know what my plan with you is?"

Smoke shakes his head from side to side with a baffled look on his face. "Nah," he replies.

"Let me tell you. My plan is to make you a multi-millionaire. That goal isn't as far fetched as you may believe. Numbers don't lie, men do...remember that. As I always tell you, I'm gone walk you through this shit. All you have to do is keep your mouth shut and your eyes and ears wide open. As we speak, I got my peoples at the table putting that fire together. I instructed them to turn the volume up past twenty," he says with passion in his eyes. "When we get this new shit in our hands we're going to take the city by storm. Ain't nobody gone be able to stop us...nobody."

Agent Dumber snaps another series of shots before freezing the camera in one spot. "Come on asshole...smile for the camera. Smile for the fucking camera. Say cheese."

Days Later/September 8, 2009

Attorney, Tony Austin steps into the Federal Courtroom with a swagger that is quite abnormal for him. His traditional cocky demeanor isn't present at all. Instead he carries himself with a more professional aura. He's dressed in tailor fitted slacks, traditional blue business shirt, bow tie and suspenders. He looks more like a Harvard Law student than the seasoned attorney that he really is. His square framed Tom Ford lenses add to his already preppy look.

For the first time in years, he's present before the judge. All of this is a part of his new beginning. He's taking his career back to the essence and plans to rebuild his identity.

He steps toward his client, Ayanna Simmons aka Lil Mama who sits there dressed in a crispy pressed prison jumper. The look on her face is cool and calm but her body language reveals how nervous she really is.

"Good morning," Tony says accompanied with a comforting smile. "How you feeling?"

"Nervous," she admits. She tries to hide her feelings by applying a fake smile to her face.

"Don't worry. We're good. I'm more than sure that we will be ok," he says with confidence. "We already discussed what the absolute worse case scenario will be."

She smiles once again. "That's what you say," she replies with sarcasm. "At the end of the day it's all on him," she says as she points to the judge who is now stepping into the courtroom.

"All rise!"

Meanwhile in Irvington

Here at Maple Gardens, the black Dodge Caravan sits in the far corner of the parking lot. The apartment lease S-Dot found, led the agents here. Bright and early this morning they arrived here. After cruising through the parking lot their attention was drawn to the bright yellow Camaro that's parked in the middle of the lot. They have not taken their eyes off of the car since.

"Oh, I almost forgot about this," S-Dot," says from the back seat of the van. He hands the postcard over to Agent Dumber who sits in the passenger's seat.

"What's this?" he asks as he skims over the post card.

"That's for the boy Smoke's birthday party in a few weeks. *Our girl* says everybody who somebody will be there."

"Oh yeah?" he questions as his mind wanders quickly. "So, I guess we have no choice but to be there. I mean, we are somebody right?"

Back in the Federal Courtroom

The judge looks over the courtroom with scowling eyes before speaking. His silence has Lil Mama on the edge of her seat. She's now more nervous than she's ever been. This is the moment of truth. Her life is on the line. She's been dreading this moment. Today is the day that could end her young life.

Tony's sense of ease gives her a little comfort but not enough to calm her nerves. She looks at the judge, trying hard to read his mind. His eyes nor his body language tells her anything. All she can do is wait to hear the words that are about to come out of his mouth.

"I hereby sentence the defendant to one hundred—" Holy shit, Lil Mama thinks to herself as she finishes his sentence for him. One hundred years, she thinks as her eyes well up with tears, "and twenty months in federal prison." One hundred and twenty months she says as her tears of stress are replaced with tears of joy. "She will be eligible for parole after serving eighty five percent of that sentence. I'm granting her time served of twenty four months."

Tony exhales with relief. He looks to Lil Mama with a smile. She smiles back in return as she calculates her time. Eighty five percent of ten years is approximately eight and a half years. Deducting her two years time served leaves her with a term of six and a half years. She sighs with relief as well. She's shocked to hear this. This is better than Tony's prescribed best case scenario. She quickly thanks God for Tony.

Back in Irvington

Agent Dumber zooms in on the entrance of the apartment building as Smoke makes his exit. The camera starts clicking. "Just as we figured," Dumber says. "His new found success has taken him out of his mother's house. I guess he figures he's moving up in the world. It's our job to bring him back down. Little does he know that we already have a cell with his name and Federal Inmate number attached to it." Click, click! He snaps away with the camera as Smoke gets into his car. Click, click!

Edison New Jersey
The Next Day

Tony hops out of the passenger's side of the golf cart, stepping onto the beautiful, spacious golf course of 'Fiddlers Elbow.' He's looking smooth and debonair as usual. With his stunning attire, he could actually be a Men's Golf Magazine model.

His soft pink dress shirt peeks out from the bottom, the neck and the sleeves of his sky blue Brooks Brothers argyle sweater. His oversized applejack hat is broken down just right, covering his right eye. He breaks the boredom of his attire with dark blue True Religion jeans, which are sagging an inch or two, too short for a man of his caliber. For the most part he always looks professional but today his 'hood' side is screaming to get out.

The caddy hops off of the cart and snatches Tony's bags from the backseat. He straps them onto his shoulders and follows Tony's lead, as he should. In a matter of a minute or two they reach the clubhouse where a medium height, medium built, middle aged white man stands. He's accompanied by his caddy who stands glued to his side.

Tony extends his right hand for a handshake. Judge O'Donovan," he says with a smirk. "Good morning. How are you?"

"Late for court, late for golf," he smiles. "Are you ever on time for anything?"

"Better late than never," Tony replies.

The judge ignores his reply. "You ready? Let's get this game started?" he says with an extremely competitive edge.

Meanwhile

Mike Mittens sits behind the steering wheel of his SUV, while the Bang Man deliveryman sits in the passenger's seat. Mike Mittens holds two medium sized duffle bags on his lap while the Spanish man holds a gigantic bag on his own lap.

Mike Mittens is sweating bullets. He's petrified right now.

He's peeking around nervously. The Spanish man slides the bag onto the seat as he's getting out of the vehicle. He steps onto the asphalt. "Ok Papi, be safe," he says before slamming the door shut.

Aww hell, Mike Mittens thinks to himself. Of all the things to say, he thinks, referring back to Smoke's statement about that phrase. Mike stares at the bags with fear. In his vehicle he holds the potential end to his life. In these three bags there is enough heroin to get forever in prison. Shit, he says to himself as he starts fumbling clumsily with the steering wheel. In seconds his stash box slides open. He slams one of the medium sized bags into the box and hits the buttons to close the box. It seems as if it just won't close fast enough for him. Finally he presses the magic buttons and the other compartment slides open. He slams the other bag into the box and closes that one as well.

That's four thousand bricks completely out of sight but that's only half the battle. The bag of six thousand bricks that lies on the passenger's seat, in the wide open is his primary concern. There's not a place in this vehicle that can hide them.

He's riding on pure hope right now; hope that he can successfully get this dope to Smoke without getting caught and losing his freedom forever. He slams the gear into the drive position and pulls off slowly. "God, please get me through this, please," he prays aloud.

Back at Fiddlers Elbow

Three hours have passed and Tony and his competitor have finished up their game. Tony is quite satisfied in being the winner. His competitor is fuming right now. He has pleaded with Tony to play just one more game. They stand face to face. "Great game," Tony says, further rubbing the victory in his face. "We must do this again."

"We will," the judge replies with a look of defeat in his eyes.

Tony reaches over to his caddy and carefully snatches one of the golf bags from his shoulder. "Excuse me for one minute," he says to the caddy who steps off immediately. Tony hands the bag over to the judge. "Again, Judge O'Donovan, thanks for everything. "As you already know, any help that I can ever be to you don't hesitate to call on me."

The judge winks at Tony. "I sure will," he says as he reaches over to hand the bag to his caddy. The caddy steps away, lugging the bag without having a clue of what's actually inside the bag. Sure a golf club or two is in the bag but there's actually something of more value inside that he doesn't know. Piled up in the bag is one hundred and fifty thousand dollars in cold cash.

This money was given to the judge in exchange for the light sentence that he gave Lil Mama. Such a high profile case should have easily ruined her life forever but thanks to Tony and his connections she will get a second chance to live after only six and a half years.

Normally Tony would have been worried with a case of this magnitude but once he found out what judge was assigned to the case he had no fear. Him and Judge O'Donovan have been golfing at the same club for over ten years. He was quite sure that their personal relationship would help out in this situation. In total it cost Dre $250,000.00 to save Lil Mama. One hundred thousand went to Tony to defend her while the other hundred and fifty thousand went to Judge O'Donovan for saving her life. In the end it all adds up.

Tony walks toward the golf cart. "Politics as usual," he sings to himself. "Fair exchange is no robbery."

The backyard of the run down house is bleeding with approximately one hundred and fifty Bloods. They're engaging in another one of their weekly meetings. This isn't their normal meeting place. After getting a strange feeling the other day that he was being followed, Smoke decided to switch a few things up. He's changed up a few of his movements, including his weekly meeting spot as well as the designated meeting spot where him and Mike meet to make their transactions.

He would rather be safe than sorry. He got the feeling that he was being followed but he kind of wants to blame it all on his paranoia. Little does he know that his feeling was one hundred and ten percent correct. Not only was Agent Dumber and Dumbest following him that particular day, they've followed him a few other days as well.

Smoke stands on top of a broken down, hand crafted grill so he can oversee the entire crowd. Silence fills the air as they all watch him with their full attention. "This the situation," Smoke says before pausing for a few seconds. "Shit lovely right now! We got the town on smash. Everybody eating. We up! I promised ya'll that we all was gone eat, right? A few of ya'll out there still fucking up and can't get right though," he says with disgust in his eyes. "With all the dope that we got access to, ain't nobody to blame no more. It's all on you. If you still dropping the pot, blame it on yourself! You are officially a fuck up," he says with no compassion. "Shit was already good but yesterday it just got better. My peoples turned the volume all the way up on the work. This new shit like some shit mufuckers ain't never had. This shit better than that Blue Magic shit Frank Lucas had. And I got access to double of what I already had access to." He squints his eyes tightly.

"Ya'll ever ask for something, then when you get it, you don't know what the fuck to do with it?" he asks. "Well, that's where I'm at right now. I got more fucking dope than I know what the fuck to do with! Good dope at that," he adds. "Anybody out there know what I should do with it?" he asks as he looks into the crowd waiting for someone to reply. "I'm gone tell ya'll what I'm gone do with it. I'm gone bring my motherfucking team up. That's what the fuck I'm gone do. That's more dope for my squad. Ya'll know me. I'm all about *my people*. I love *my people*! When we had garbage ya'll was there. Ya'll didn't jump ship. We rode it out together. We busted our ass together selling that garbage. We ain't got garbage no more," he smiles. "I'm eating right now!" he shouts. "And when I eat everybody fucking eat. From here on out whatever amount you was already getting, I'm dropping double that on you. You twenty five brick mufuckers," he says with disgust. "Ya'll getting fifty now. All my hundred, two hundred, three hundred brick niggas…I'm doubling that too. Two, three, six hundred bricks!" he shouts. "All on the cuff as usual. I ain't got no problem dumping the work on ya'll. I just need ya'll to get through it," he shouts.

"We got one problem though," he says as his face turns solemn. "That bitch Mother Nature. She in the way. She should have been outta the picture. Normally we would have handled her already but my mind been on getting this money. The bitch gotta go though. I don't wanna be meeting bout this same old shit next week. Let's finish that bitch so we can all concentrate on getting this money. If we don't handle this soon I'm gonna be forced to put everybody on Ramadan until she finished," he says in a threatening manner. "Twenty two South Twelfth Street is where she lives. On Munn, across from Bradley Courts is where her mother lives. Twenty eight Eppirt Street in East Orange is where her grandmother lives. Erase that bitch!" he says with fury. "But for right now," he says with a grin on his face. "Let's break bread," he says to his main man who is standing to the right of him.

The man takes off up the small flight of stairs. He runs in and out of the house in a matter of seconds. In his hand he holds the same duffle bag that Mike gave Smoke. The man hands the bag over to Smoke.

"Come on," Smoke demands. The men of lower status line up one after another while the men of higher rank surrounds him. Smoke digs his hand into the huge bag as his partner holds it for him. He grabs a big handful of sleeves and counts them quickly. In total he holds thirty sleeves in his hands. "That's three hundred," he whispers as he tosses them into a shopping bag. He digs in and grabs a handful more. That's two hundred more…five hundred," he says as he dumps these as well. He passes the bag over to the man who walks away with joy. Another man stands awaiting his load. Smoke digs into the bag and pulls out ten sleeves. He drops them into another bag before digging into the duffle bag again. This time he comes up with fifteen sleeves. "That's two fifty," he says as he drops them into the man's bag.

After all the higher ranked men are fed their work the duffle bag is 1,450 bricks lighter. Smoke then hands the other hundred and forty three men their load. Each of them is responsible for fifty bricks. He serves each of them one by one.

It's all said and done. Everyone has been served. The duffle bag has been emptied, all except for two thousand bricks. In less than twenty five minutes 8,000 bricks have been distributed. He just hopes he can retrieve all the money in a timely fashion. The last 2,000 bricks, he will save for his outside connections.

7:30 A.M.

It's bright and early and Smoke is up and at it already. At six this morning his phone started ringing off the hook. All his people have gotten the word that he's reloaded. After a couple of days with no Bang Man, everyone is desperate to get back to business.

Smoke sits in the driver's seat of his rental car while Baby Grape sits in the passenger's seat. They're parked in front of the huge parking lot which sits directly across from Newark Penn Station. This is the perfect meeting place at this time of the morning. With the heavy overload of people going to work, makes it easy for them to make a deal without anyone paying attention to them.

Smoke hands Baby Grape a brown Bloomingdales bag which is filled with one hundred sleeves (1,000) bricks. Baby Grape passes him a bag in return which is filled with two hundred and sixty thousand dollars cash.

"That's what it is," Baby Grape says before forcing the door open and making his exit. "One!"

7:35 A.M.

Mother Nature sits behind the steering wheel of her van as she listens to the young boy in her passenger's seat run off at the mouth. "Son was like you supposed to been outta here but his mind been on getting money."

Mother Nature cracks a devious smile. "Yeah? Is that right?"

"Like Son made the call to get you ASAP or he threatened to put us all on Ramadan. Niggas like fuck that, they eating now and they ain't gone let shit stop right now. Like Son got everybody on your heels as we speak. He gave everybody your address, your mother address and even your grandmother address."

She looks at the young boy with complete shock on her face. "Oh yeah? That's how he wanna play? He wanna bring mothers into Blood business."

"Nah, Son ain't order the hit on your family. He just put it out there, like just in case you be hitting either one of them spots up. Feel me?"

Mother Nature nods her head and up and down. "I feel you,"

she replies. She's steaming with fury right now. "Enough of that clown ass nigga. You got something for me?" she asks.

"Yeah," he replies. "Son doubled up this time," he says as he pulls a plastic bag from underneath his bubble vest. "Like he had a duffle bag full of more bricks then I ever seen. Son came up! I don't know who he connected with but he hot right now." Mother Nature gets a glimpse of the Mayor's face in her head. "He got like more dope than God," he says foolishly. He holds the bag open for her to view the bricks of dope that are inside.

"How many he gave you?" she questions.

"Fifty," he replies quickly.

"How many of them are for me?" she asks. "Real rap, I could move all that ASAP. You might as well give all them shits to me," she says with greed. "That will only make you look better in his eyes," she says just trying to talk him out of his dope.

The young boy sits back pondering in thought. Her mind game is working on him. He believes that the more dope he moves the more Smoke will respect him. He may even get promoted from a foot soldier and gain some real status. "Alright," he says giving in to her. "Take like thirty five. I'll just keep the fifteen," he says as he breaks the sleeves down and takes his out of the bag.

"Alright but I'm telling you, I could move all these shits in like one day," she says, further mind fucking him. "Imagine how much he would respect you if you move fifty in one day. He fuck around and give you that three star you want."

She just touched his heart. Having Three Star General Status is his dream. "Alright, take another five. I need this ten money for something. I got shit to do."

"Alright, trills," she says while laughing at him on the inside. "I will be done with these shits in no time," she claims. "As soon as I'm done I will get the fetti right to you."

"Alright cool," the young boy says as he's getting out of the van.

This young boy is from Mother Nature's neighborhood but he isn't under her sect. She watched him grow up around the area but he became Blood on another side of town which is how he ended up under Smoke's sect. Smoke is his leader and he fears him but his real love is with Mother Nature and the people that he actually grew up with. Mother Nature knows this, which is why she capitalizes off of his loyalty to her. It's because of him that she knows of things that

Smoke only tells his squad.

Mother Nature sits back just absorbing the valuable information that she just received. She nods her head up and down. "So this mufucker wanna start fucking with people's loved ones who ain't got nothing to do with this," she says aloud. "Ok, I got something for his ass. Everybody love somebody."

7:43 A.M.

Smoke sits in the parking lot of IHOP on Bergen Street. He's parked facing the entrance of the restaurant. His back is against the busy street. His eyes lay upon his older cousin who comes stepping out of the doorway. In his hands he holds his take out order. His cousin walks toward the black Cadillac truck that's parked next to Smoke's car but facing the opposite direction.

Smoke's cousin winks at him but never turns his head toward Smoke. He doesn't want to draw any attention to them. He hits the remote opener and all the Cadillac's locks pop open. He opens the back door and drops his food onto the backseat. He steps away, leaving the door wide open. He squeezes in between the open door and Smoke's car to get to his front driver's seat. He snatches that door wide open as well.

There he stands in between two wide open doors. No one can see him from the front view or the back. He leans inside of his truck and grabs a duffle bag from behind the front seat. He peeks around cautiously before spinning around and handing the bag over to Smoke through his open window. Smoke quickly hands a duffle bag to him in return.

Smoke's cousin slams the back door shut before hopping into his driver's seat. As his cousin is pulling off, Smoke pulls out of the parking space. The fact that this man is his first cousin on his father's side will not get him a better price. He's not an opposing gang member. In fact he's not a gang banger at all but because he's not Blood he has to pay tax.

A six hundred brick sale which is equivalent to one hundred and fifty-six thousand dollars in cash has been made in less than a minute. Now that's big business.

7:48

Smoke pulls up to the McDonalds parking lot on Bergen Street and West Market. He looks around for a parking space but there are hardly any available. The parking lot is congested due to the busy breakfast traffic. He scans the entire lot and at the back, in the cut he spots the car that he's in search of. Luckily there's an empty space right next to it.

As he's pulling into the spot, the driver of the Ford hops out. He snatches Smoke's door open and gets inside. He leaves the door wide open. He hands a plastic bag over to Smoke who in return hands him a bag. The man speaks. "Twenty eight, five," he utters. Smoke charges him $285.00 a brick. "I'll hit you," he says as he gets out. He slams the door shut and hops back into his car. Before he can even pull off, another man comes walking toward Smoke's car from the opposite side of the lot.

Instead of getting inside of Smoke's car he leans half of his body into the passenger's side window. "What's good, nigga?" the man asks as he drops a bag onto the passenger's seat.

Smoke hands him a plastic bag in return. This particular bag is the smallest of them all, yet Smoke has no problem with it. Normally he's all for the underdog but the problem he has with this sale is the actual person that he's serving.

He absolutely hates dealing with this man but his persistence makes him do so. He calls and chases Smoke around just to get his hands on the material. He may be persistent but he lacks loyalty. He's only with Smoke for the ride. If the work wasn't good Smoke would never hear from him. Because Smoke knows this he refuses to let him go for one single dollar.

"Yo bruh, you gone have to do something with that price," he whines. "I get fifty bricks from you everyday. That's like." He stops talking to figure out the numbers but his lack of mathematical skills makes it difficult for him. "That's like mad bricks a week," he says with frustration. "I know you can come down a little?"

"Nope," Smoke says bluntly as he stares straight ahead. "Three hundred it is."

"Come on homie. I know niggas you charging less. Why you doing me like that?"

"Ay bruh, the business I do with other mufuckers ain't your business. Got nothing to do with you."

"I mean, true but if you just let me hold a few on the cuff it would all balance out. Like I buy fifty and you front me fifty? I just need a little room to breathe."

Smoke stares straight ahead coldly. "Negative."

"Psst," the man sighs with frustration.

"Yo, you want the fifty or not?" The man backs out of the car and walks away carrying the bag of bricks in clear view. Get the fuck outta here, Smoke thinks to himself. Smoke gloats at the thought that he just made almost a half a million dollars before most hustlers are even out of bed. A smile appears on his face. "The early bird gets the worm."

8:02 A.M.

Mike Mittens stands in the hallway of the three family house. In front of him stands Manson's mother. She stands here with a look of skepticism on her face as he hands over the brown shopping bag which is filled to the top with money. In the bag there is a hundred thousand in total. The money is from the last flip of four thousand bricks.

"Sir, what is this all about?" she asks. "What reason are you bringing this money here? What am I supposed to do with all this money? I'm afraid to keep it here," she whispers. "I don't understand it."

"Maam, I can't answer any of those questions. My only job is to bring it here."

"But what am I supposed to do with it? I'm afraid someone is going to come in here to get it. Whatever ya'll have going on, I don't want anything to do with it. Whatever it is I'm sure it's illegal. Isn't it?"

"Maam, again I have no idea what it's about," he lies as he backs out of the door. He leaves her standing there with the bag of dirty money.

8:10 A.M.

Three loud knocks awaken informant S-Dot out of his deep sleep. He pops up wide eyed. He sits still with nervousness. Three more loud knocks sound off causing the door to damn near bounce off of the hinges. He looks over to the sleeping Samirah. He nudges her lightly with his elbow.

"Unghh," she whines as she turns over on her side, giving him full view of her beautiful naked behind. He grabs her by her tiny waist and shoves her strong and hard. She pops up with frustration. Anger is plastered onto her face. She's definitely not a morning person and hates to be awaken out of her sleep. With her eyes half closed, she speaks, "What?"

"The door," he whispers before two loud knocks sound off. Samirah hops up and walks over toward the door in a trance like manner. He lays back with fear. He wonders who could be behind the door.

Samirah peeks through the tiny peephole. "Hold up," she says before turning around to S-Dot. "That's my brother," she whispers.

Holy shit, he says to himself. The last thing he wants is to be caught in her bed. He pulls the covers over his head and pretends to be asleep.

He peeks through one eye as Samirah grabs hold of his shirt and pulls it over her head. "One minute," she says.

"Open the fucking door!" Smoke shouts from behind the door. Finally she cracks the door open and hides behind it. "What the fuck took you so fucking long? I been out here banging on the fucking door for twenty fucking minutes," he lies.

"Sorry. I was sleep," she replies in a groggy but innocent voice.

"If you take your fucking ass to sleep at night instead of on that fucking phone gossiping all fucking night!" he barks. "Here."

S-Dot watches closely as a duffle bag hangs at the door. Samirah grabs hold of it and closes the door immediately. He closes his eyes and acts as if he's not watching but he is watching the duffle bag closely. Samirah sleep walks toward the closet. She opens the closet door where she drops the bag right in the front of the closet. She takes three steps before collapsing onto the bed next to him.

He counts the seconds before her snoring sounds off. Now it's time to see what she has in the bag. He gets up lightly and tiptoes to the closet. He peeks back to make sure she's still asleep while he carefully opens the door. He steps inside, kneels down and unzips the bag. His eyes pop wide open once they fix onto close to a half a million in cash. "Got damn."

8:30 A.M.

Smoke pulls up to the booth of his apartment building. He

waits impatiently as the arm raises up slowly. As soon as it's raised enough for his car to clear, he zooms into the parking lot. He slows down as he approaches his Camaro which is parked in the very middle of the lot. He parks the rental car right next to it.

All his business for the day has been handled and now it's time for him to catch up on his sleep. The early morning activity is getting quite tiresome to him but in no way is he complaining. Before he started his day at twelve in the afternoon but he could barely make a living for himself. He wouldn't trade those hours in for the world.

He gets out and slams the door behind him. He struts casually toward the building. In the far corner of the parking lot there sits a tinted out black Impala in which Agents Dumber and Dumbest sit inside. They arrived here at 8:00 on the dot expecting to catch him leaving out. Little did they know he was already an hour and a half ahead of them.

"Ain't this a mufucker," Agent Dumber says. "He has switched up on us. Oh he must think he's one of those smart niggers, huh? Get a picture of that car. Make sure you get a clear shot of the license plates."

Days Later/September15, 2009

Samirah steps out of the house on her way to her best friend's house which is a few blocks away. She makes her way down the stairs, skipping one or two as she goes along. When she makes her way to the bottom, she turns to her right and heads toward the corner.

As she's walking along she coincidentally cuts her eye to the left. What she sees causes her to double take. She's completely familiar with the raggedy van that's parked on the opposite side of the street. Behind the tinted windows, she can see the silhouettes of at least three heads inside. She turns away quickly, hoping not to let Mother Nature know that she's spotted her. Samirah's heart beats like a drum. She watches the van through her peripheral. She's so frightened that the trembling of her legs is making it hard for her to walk.

As she makes it to the corner, she's not sure if she should go in the store for safety or to keep moving on her way to her girlfriend's house. She really doesn't think that Mother Nature is actually here to harm her but she can't take the risk. She peeks over her shoulder once again before sidestepping into the store.

She walks up to the counter and stands there in a nervous frenzy. "She peeks over the man's shoulder looking through the glass behind him. She clumsily pulls out her cell phone and dials her brother's number. She listens to the ringing until the voicemail comes on. "Come on," she whispers as she keeps her eyes glued to the van. She dials again and the voicemail comes on once again.

Meanwhile In Paterson, N.J.

Smoke stands in the far corner of the bar, trying to blend in with the crowd but it's evident to anyone that he's not from around here. He stands next to his man Sizzie. Smoke may be a nice distance away from home but still he's quite comfortable. Smoke can move around freely anywhere that Manson has soldiers because of the status that he has been appointed. Everyone that was under Manson's sect now has to fall in line under Smoke no matter where they may be from. Because of his status he feels completely safe here on one of Paterson's most dangerous intersections; 10th Avenue and 27th Street which is also known as Murder Ave.

Sizzie stares straight ahead as he passes the bag filled with fifty thousand cash over to Smoke. Smoke looks to his right as he grabs hold of the bag. "Later," he says as they engage in their signature handshake. He steps away from Sizzie, leaving a bag of two hundred bricks on the floor right by his feet. Smoke shakes a few hands on his way out of the bar. He makes it from the bar area into the liquor store area in seconds. He quickly exits.

Smoke hops into his Camaro and starts up the engine immediately. He wants to get out of here as fast as he can. The last thing he needs is a Bergen County beef. As he's turning the corner, he bends over and reaches underneath the seat for his cell phone. He peeks at the display while driving. He notices seventeen missed calls. "Got damn," he utters as he presses the button to see who the calls are from. To his surprise it's Samirah. His heart skips a beat as he wonders what could be so important that she's called him so many times. He automatically thinks of the worse possible circumstances. He dials her number back and she picks up on the very first ring.

"Hello," she says in a very distraught voice. "Where the fuck you at?"

"In Paterson making a move. Why what's up?"

"I called you a hundred fucking times!" she shouts as she paces down the aisle. Her eyes are still on the van. "Mother Nature," she whispers. "Is sitting parked outside the house."

"What?" he shouts, not believing his ears. "Where you at?"

"In the corner store," she replies. "I didn't notice the van until I was walking by it. I been in here for the longest. I just hope she don't come up in here for me."

Smoke plays that picture in his mind and he gets even more frightened for his little sister. "Listen don't go back out there. Stay your ass right there! I'm on my way in less than twenty minutes," he says as he mashes the gas pedal with excessive force.

"Twenty minutes?" she asks frantically.

"Don't worry. I'm about to make a few calls. Back up is on the way!"

Meanwhile a Block Away

Agent Dumber and Dumbest sit inside their van in silence.

Agent Dumbest sits behind the steering wheel, looking through binoculars. His focal point is Mother Nature's van. They've been sitting out here watching the house longer than Mother Nature has been sitting out here.

Agent Dumber sits in the passenger's seat with earphones lodged into his ear. Through the earphones he hears every word that Smoke and Samirah are saying. Not only do they listen on Smoke and Samirah's conversations but they listen to every call either of them makes. Smoke foolishly thinks that he's doing something smart by changing phones every couple of days but what he doesn't realize is that he's calling the same people with the same numbers as he did with his old phone. What he doesn't know is that him and his team have already been *Tagged*. They're *It*.

Agent Dumber snatches the earphones out of his ears. He looks over to Agent Dumbest with a smile. "Don't worry Smoke," he sings. "Back up is already here," he chuckles. "We know you're out in *P, town* making a move. We'll watch the house for you," he says with sarcasm. "We got you covered."

After hearing the details of the call, the Feds are expecting an action packed situation to take place any minute now. Agent Dumber ponders in thought for a few seconds before picking up his walkie talkie. "Yes, Federal Agent Schneider on the line. I'm here on Camden Street and," he says as he looks around. "And Fourteenth Avenue. Suspicious activity going on. I need a radio car here to patrol the area."

In less than three minutes two radio cars meet at the intersection. The Federal Agents watch as the two police cars creep up the block slowly. Samirah watches out of the store window as Mother Nature's van cruises off almost unnoticeably.

Agent Dumber would have loved to sit back and watch the episode unfold but there was a huge risk at stake. At this point they can't afford to lose *their girl* Samirah. She's gotten them way too far and they have plans of her getting them much further. He watches as Samirah sneaks out of the corner store, peeking around nervously. Once she sees that the coast is clear, she trots toward her house.

"Don't worry baby," Agent Dumber says sarcastically as he looks over to his partner. "I got your back. I would never let anything happen to *our girl*," he says with a smile. "At least not just yet."

1:18 A.M.

The tall slender man hops out of the black Chevy SS Trail Blazer slowly. As soon as his feet touch the ground he begins to wobble back and forth until he regains his balance. He lifts his leg high before taking his first step. He stumbles like the drunkard that he is.

This is how the majority of his nights end. At ten o'clock on the dot, he shuts down business and starts up on the Grey Goose. By eleven o' clock, he's already drunk out of his mind but still he continues to drink until 1:00 A.M.

After many minutes of wobbling and stumbling, the man finally makes it to the bottom of his porch. He grabs hold of the railing for assistance. As soon as he lifts his leg up to take his first step, he stumbles backwards once again. He grabs the railing tightly, holding on for dear life. He swings around wildly as he tries to pull himself up.

Directly next to the man's house is a small four car garage. From the roof of the garage two people watch the man with amusement. The both of them stand on the very edge of the rooftop just waiting for the right second to jump down on him and make their move. "Now," Mother Nature whispers to her accomplice before she jumps off of the small roof like a suicide victim jumping off of the Empire State Building. The only difference is she's not even one story up in the air.

She lands on her feet in less than two seconds. One second later, there lands her accomplice. The sound of their landing causes the drunken man to turn toward their direction. He sees the image of two gun toting people but the alcohol makes him think there are actually four of them. Instead of trying to get away he just stands there wobbling back and forth.

Mother Nature runs up to the man, while aiming at his head just in case he makes a move. The drunken man wants to take off but his reaction time is many minutes behind. She grabs him by the collar, dragging him onto the concrete steps. He sits on the step looking up at her with fear. They lock eyes. "Never fuck around with Mother Nature," she says before the gunshot rings off. Boc! His neck snaps backwards until the loud noise of his head banging onto the concrete sounds off. The man lays there in the same position with no movement at all. His eyes and mouth are still wide open with a shocked expression on his dead face. Boc! Boc! Boc! All three shots land in the man's face just a few inches apart. Mother Nature backs away before turning around and taking off.

When they make it to the corner, her van is sitting there with the doors wide open awaiting their entrance. They hop in and slam the doors shut. "Go," she instructs the driver. The driver mashes the gas pedal and the raggedy van zips through the street as fast as the raggedy van can go.

After hearing that Smoke made a threat on her mother and grandmother she realized that she has no time to play with them. One by one she plans to get them all. She has no particular order in mind. She plans to get them as they fall into her hands. Whether it be the easier ones first or the harder ones first, it doesn't matter to her just as long as she gets them.

She knows that this last murder will definitely get their attention. The first one she murdered was a Three Star General. He meant something to Smoke but nowhere near as much as this last victim does, being that he's Five Star General status. Thanks to lil Razz, her double agent, she's getting all the information that she needs to make this war go in her favor.

She looks over to Razz who is in the driver's seat, maneuvering the van like a professional racecar driver. "Slow down lil nigga. We good now."

Lil Razz does just as he's instructed. He breaks the speed down until they're cruising at a moderate speed. He looks over to her hoping for her approval. She winks her eye with a devilish smirk on her face. She holds her hand in the air for a high five. Clap! "Good job lil nigga," she says. "Good job."

September 15, 2009

The smell of new leather fills the air inside of the Aston Martin. In the driver seat sits the Mayor. No, this isn't Tony's automobile but Tony's automobile inspired the Mayor to make this purchase. Although this Vantage Edition is only half the price of Tony's DBS, the prestige is nearly the same.

In the passenger's seat there sits the Mayor's apprentice. Smoke sits there quietly with his mouth wide open just listening to his mentor. "I'm just giving you the game as I wish it was given to me. If I would have somebody in my ear showing me the way, I would be on another level," he claims. "Instead, I had to learn my own way." Whenever the Mayor speaks, Smoke is careful not to miss one single syllable.

The Mayor takes a breather for a few seconds and Smoke gets caught up in the beauty of the vehicle. The smoke grey body, caramel colored gut combination blends together perfectly. The Mayor's goal has been accomplished successfully. Allowing Smoke to ride in back to back luxury from the Rolls Royce to the Aston Martin makes him totally unsatisfied with his Chevy Camaro. Just to think a short time ago the Camaro was his dream car and now he feels like it's beneath him to even drive it. Just as the Mayor wished, Smoke has been motivated and his battery is charged.

"Look at this," the Mayor says with a look of appreciation on his face. He points at the corner store where a group of young thugs wrap around the corner. In total there are about eight of them. Each one of the young men watch the Aston Martin with amazement as it cruises past slowly. The Mayor gets to the next corner and is stopped by the red light. He points to the corner that is diagonal from them. "Look," he says referring to the group of young men who occupy this particular corner. The young men stare back at the Mayor and Smoke with no shame.

The light changes and the Mayor mashes the gas pedal. "Got damn," one of the men says loud enough for his boys to hear. The Mayor reads his lips. The young man raises both of his thumbs in the air, giving them the thumbs up. The Mayor gives him an arrogant head nod in return before hitting the horn twice. The sound of the European horn gives the Mayor an instant hard on.

In seconds they make it to the next corner where another group of men stand huddled around a mailbox. "Look over there," the Mayor instructs. "We have cruised through the whole city. Have you noticed anything different?" Smoke shrugs his shoulders without a clue of what the Mayor is referring to. "Let me tell you... every fucking street corner is filled with mufuckers who trying to get to a dollar. As they should be," he adds. "When I first touched, the street corners were bare. The blocks were empty like suburban blocks. Now look...not a bare spot in the city. The city is now breathing again. Thanks to the heart," he says with a smile. "Do you know whose work all of this is?"

Smoke looks at the Mayor, while shrugging his shoulders once again. "Yours," he whispers.

"Nah, baby boy," the Mayor denies. "I can't take all the credit. This is just as much your work as it is mines. I couldn't have done it without you. All I really did is build your confidence and make you believe in yourself. I knew you could do it. I just had to make you believe that you could do it. Just think, two weeks ago I gave you ten thousand bricks and in twelve days you gave me the money for eighty five hundred of them. One million and six hundred thousand dollars passed through your hands in twelve days. Do you know the magnitude of that? That's some shit niggas will never be able to say. Trust me, it's only going to get better. As you say...I promise you," he says mocking Smoke.

They ride in complete silence for about twenty minutes as the Mayor graces the city with his presence. Everyone watches with admiration as the sparkling beauty races through the streets of downtown Newark.

Smoke sits back in the seat just appreciating the attention that they're receiving. He feels like a big celebrity. Just to think a few months ago he was just the typical broke gang banger. Today he feels like a successful businessman. He turns toward the Mayor and looks at him in total admiration. In just a short time Smoke looks at the Mayor like the big brother he never had. Although Smoke and Charles Manson are rather close he's never felt this closeness with Manson. Manson has always had a way of downplaying Smoke and making him feel like a total nobody. The Mayor makes him feel like a man.

"Yo, big bruh, did you decide if you gonna come out to my party next week or not? It would mean a lot to me if you just peek your head in. You don't have to stay. Just one glass of champagne with me. A toast to you changing my life."

The Mayor squirms in his seat. "Ah, I would love to but…the party scene ain't really my twist. It never has been actually. I don't drink and I don't dance. Even back when I was in my prime I stayed away from that scene. I'm gone have to fall back on this one. I will be there with you in spirit though. It's your day. Go there and shine like the star that you are."

Twenty minutes later, the Mayor is speeding along Broad Street as if he's on a freeway. He makes the illegal left turn onto Central Avenue and floors it all the way up the hill. The reckless way that he's driving makes peoples' heads turn with confusion. They assume that it must be a stolen car.

"Got damn, this shit got kick," Smoke says.

"Why wouldn't it have kick?" You think she a buck fifty for nothing?" he asks as he zooms right through the yellow light on Central Avenue and Eighth Street. In seconds he's on Twelfth Street. Instead of stopping at the red light before him, he creeps into the intersection. The first break he gets, he takes it. He cuts off the oncoming traffic with no regard. He stops short just past the corner. He slams the gear into the park position. "You wanna feel it?"

Smoke looks at him with wide eyes. "Y, yeah," he stutters. The Mayor hops out and they trade seats. Smoke looks around enjoying the view from this seat. He instantly gets a feeling of power and dominance that he's never felt. To his surprise the car looks totally different from the driver's seat. He cruises off just enjoying the smoothness of the ride underneath his feet.

"Man, you driving this motherfucker like a Cadillac," the Mayor says with disgust. "Step on that bitch!"

Smoke does just as he's told. He mashes the gas pedal as hard as he can, throwing both of them against their seats. The Aston Martin floats up the wide open block. They reach South Orange Avenue in a mere matter of seconds. "Got damn," Smoke says.

"You like her?" the Mayor asks.

"I love her," Smoke replies.

"Well, marry the bitch then. I now pronounce ya'll man and wife," he says with a solemn look on his face. "She's yours. Happy Birthday."

"Huh?" Smoke says with disbelief.

"Happy Birthday. It's yours," the Mayor repeats.

"Stop playing. You bullshitting me."

A cold look pops onto the Mayor's face. "Have I ever bullshitted you? It's yours. I didn't buy this for me. I couldn't think of anything to get you for your birthday. For days I tried to figure it out. Finally I came up with a new *automobile*. I went to the dealer and this bitch was screaming your name. She looks good on you."

Smoke cruises up South Orange Avenue in complete shock. This has to be the biggest highlight of his life. He's hardly ever been given anything in his life. To receive a gift of this magnitude from a man he hardly knows, really hits a soft spot in his cold heart. "Damn," he utters. "I don't even know what to say."

"No need to say anything. Just do what you do. You're supposed to ride like this. It's the minimum. All the dope in this town comes through your hands first. Why would you drive anything less than this? You're the new poster boy. You gotta market yourself. From here on out, the world is watching you. Look at yourself as a walking billboard. The clothes you wear, the vehicle you drive, the way you walk, the way you talk…they're taking notice of. Mufuckers will emulate your swag. You're now a brand…like McDonalds. Whenever a mufucker see those golden arches they automatically crave a Big Mac and fries. When a mufucker see you, he should automatically get the motivation to get up off of his ass and try and do better for himself. He knows how you came up and that will make him want to be a part of you, hoping that he can come up the same way. Everybody gonna want to be a part of you and what you doing. Always remember… everybody loves a star. Your life is going to change at this point. Some will love you more and others will hate you more. You may even become an even bigger target. Mufuckers are gonna come for your head, hoping to take your place. Yeah, they know you go hard but the hate in their hearts will give them the courage to come at you. It's natural. It's the game. That's what I got these for," he says as he knocks on the window. "Yeah, bulletproof windows for the haters. They may want to end your life but it won't happen while you're in here," he smiles. "They can fire as many shots as they want and none of them will penetrate. You're like the Teflon Don. Completely hater-proof."

"Yeah?" Smoke asks. "Thanks, big bruh."

No need for thanks, the Mayor says to himself. He totally ignores Smoke's statement of gratitude. "At this very moment things have just changed. It's your world. I'm passing you the torch. I'm fading to black. It's your turn. Now do you and make me proud."

Tony struts gracefully across the ramp in Newark International Airport. He's dressed in a black custom fit Zegna suit with a black, thin pinstriped custom fit shirt. His Ray Ban 'Blues Brother's' shades gives him a sense of mystique. His aura demands attention. Everyone who sees him can't help but wonder where the man traveling with no luggage is actually going. In his hands he holds not a single bag or briefcase, just a leather binder and a newspaper.

He boards the plane and finds his seat, right in the First Class Section. He studies the few passengers that are seated in the First Class section. His attention is drawn to the middle aged man that sits along the same row as him. Seeing this man makes Tony feel a sense of safety. Although the man is pretending to be a normal passenger, Tony is quite sure that he's an undercover Air Marshall. As normal as he may come across, Tony can smell a Fed a mile away.

Ever since the 911 situation Tony has developed a fear of flying so when he does have to fly, he's sure to get a seat in the First Class Section of the plane to be near the Air Marshall. He exhales a sigh of relief, feeling a sense of safety. He opens up his Wall Street Journal and awaits the plane's departure.

Meanwhile

A string of vehicles line up at the corner of the block. The driver of the Suburban which leads the line hangs his arm out of the window and waves to the cars behind him. He steps on the gas and pulls off with a normal amount of speed. The cars behind him follow closely. The passengers of every single vehicle grip their weapons tightly in their hands. All the windows are rolled down and the passengers are ready to fire at will.

The driver of the Suburban steers the truck into the entrance of Mother Nature's project building. The vehicles behind him follow bumper to bumper. People are spread out all over the courts. Some are just hanging out while others are distributing dope to the few fiends that are present.

The sound of squealing tires draws everyone's attention

to the entrance but it's already too late. The element of surprise has overtaken them. The vehicles are speeding in with gun toting passengers hanging from the windows. At the sight of the gunmen, everyone disperses in an attempt to get to safety. The passenger of the Suburban hangs from the window, gripping the AK47. He braces himself as he fires recklessly, with no particular target. The driver of the Suburban races the truck through the courts. His destination is the end of the courts.

The Cherokee behind the Suburban steers to the left, while the Pontiac steers to the right. Gunmen hang from those windows as well. Everyone is in a nervous frenzy. They run back and forth trying to get away but the cars have them trapped off. A few manage to slip through the cracks but the majority of them are not that fortunate.

Smoke gave strict instructions to shut the projects down. He said no one is exempt. Anybody that is present is fair game. The first member of his camp that was murdered touched his heart but he charged it off to the game. Losing his good friend the other day had a much greater impact on him. One issue outweighed the both of those together though. The fact that Mother Nature was that close to touching his sister the other day scared the life out of him.

Although he rarely shows it, his baby sister means the world to him. She's his only sibling. To lose her would ruin him and his mother's life. He's sure she would never forgive him. With that in mind, he plans to get Mother Nature out of the way just for the thought of what she could have done.

No movement is left in the area. The people who were fortunate got away without being wounded but many lie here sprawled out on the asphalt. The entire area resembles a battle zone.

The Suburban backs out of the court while gunmen in both of the other vehicles continue to fire. No one has been left standing but still they fire just in case someone pops out of nowhere. Once the Suburban is out safely, the Cherokee busts a wild u- turn the middle of the court and speeds out uncontrollably. The Pontiac follows seconds behind. They all race up the block at top speed.

In Miami Four Hours Later

Tony Austin stands at the front door of Miami Dades Federal Detention Center as Miranda Benderas exits, dressed in her prison jumper. A huge smile pops onto her face the moment she sees him.

By the time she gets to him her face is full of tears. He opens his arms wide for a hug. She slides into his arms, burying her face into his chest. She keeps her head there for minutes before backing away.

"Mr. Austin, I thank you for everything."

"No need for thanks. It's my job," he says with his normal amount of arrogance. In just a matter of days he's already back to his own self again. As much as he's told himself he wouldn't be like this he can't help himself. It's deeply embedded in him. His self esteem and confidence was shot down but slowly and surely it's managing to rebuild second by second.

He grabs hold of her hand and leads her to the black Lincoln that awaits them. Once he gets to the car he snatches the back door open for her and holds it. She gets into the backseat. She bangs her head onto the headrest. With her dripping eyes closed, she speaks under her breath. "Thank you God."

Tony hops into the backseat on the other side and slams the door. "To the airport!" he shouts. He looks over to her. "I told you I would get you out of that mess, didn't I?" he brags.

"Yes, you did," she cries.

"The hardest part is over but still we have more to go. Now you go there and get yourself together. You got something that most will die for...a second chance at life," he says. "You should live it accordingly. I'm sure you've learned from your mistakes," he says as he looks into her watery eyes. "The nightmare you lived for the past five years is now over. Now the dreams that you've had can now be lived out. Make the most of it." Miranda sits back just absorbing his words of wisdom.

For the duration of the time they ride in silence. Miranda can't believe that this is really happening. She's dreamed of this day for over five years. As Tony stated, it's now over. It's now time to start her life over. She can't go back to Philadelphia due to the trouble that she's left behind. Because of that trouble she's forced to start over in foreign land.

She doesn't have a clue of where or even how to begin. She's never worked a real job in her life and doesn't have the skills that are needed to land a decent one. Her dreams of being a supermodel have vanished due to the fact that she feels like the prime of her life is over. This leaves her no other alternative but to face the fact that she will have to start her life over from the bottom. Her father once told her, he would rather pump gas at a service station for two dollars an hour than to get involved in the things or the people he was involved with in his past life. She now understands exactly what he meant and she concurs.

They reach Miami International Airport where they exit the car. As they enter the airport Tony hands Miranda a sheet of paper. He points to the top of the paper. This is the halfway house that she will spend the next eighteen months in. "Charlotte, North Carolina. They're expecting you in four hours. Call me the minute you land."

"Will do," she replies. Miranda has heard so many stories of how Charlotte is the new Atlanta and how it's on the up rise for black people. She hopes she can use that opportunity to her advantage to rebuild her life.

Tony hugs her once again. She doesn't want to let him go. Fear settles deeply in her heart. The fact that she's about to step into foreign land frightens her. Tony backs away, looking into her beautiful eyes; melting in them. "I got something for you," he says as he digs into his front pocket. "This is a head start from me to you," he says as he hands her a stack of hundred dollar bills. "That's three grand. Get outta that jumpsuit and get yourself some clothes. Make sure you get some business attire for job interviews," he says as he looks her up and down. "And this is from your father," he says as he hands her a check for ten thousand dollars. The truth of the matter is the check didn't come from her father directly. It came from the Mayor who has given it to her on his behalf. "That should help you get yourself situated." He pauses before speaking. He points to the left of them. "Gate A…the plane departs in one hour."

"Again, thank you," she says with watery eyes. She then walks away into her future.

Tony watches her in a totally unprofessional manner. The way her jumpsuit fits her makes him totally forget that she's a client. For the first time ever he looks at her as a *woman*. "Miranda!" he calls out. She turns around abruptly. He pauses before speaking. The look in his eyes takes her for a loop. They stare into each other's eyes as she awaits the words to come out of his mouth. Finally he opens his mouth to speak. "Live your life!"

Newark's Bureau of Robbery and Homicide

Two detectives stare closely at the flat screen that's before them. They're careful not to miss a beat. "Try and lighten the screen a little," the black detective suggests.

"Nope," the Hispanic detective replies. "This is about the best we're going to get." They watch the videotape that has captured the activity on a dark Newark street. This new system has made their jobs of tracking down criminals so much easier. Cameras have been installed at the intersections of many of the streets of Newark.

"Hold up," the black detective says. "Play that back," the man says with anxiousness. "Right there...slow it down. Pause it right there. Zoom in on the face. Ok now, move on, slowly. Ok, now zoom in on his face. Ok, let it go. Oops, right there. Zoom in on the plates. "E, B, S," he reads. "372. Got 'em" he says with complete satisfaction.

Meanwhile

Agents Dumber and Dumbest sit parked in the back of Wendy's parking lot here on West Market Street. The wire tapping of Smoke's cell phone conversation brought them here. Agent Dumber watches across the parking lot from behind the pitch dark tinted windows of the Chevy Suburban. They arrived here five minutes before Smoke who is sitting in the rented Chrysler 300M.

Suddenly a black Cadillac Escalade pulls right next to Smoke. The driver, Smoke's cousin, gets out and walks around to the passenger's side of Smoke's car. In his hand he lugs a huge duffle bag, which he holds close to his thigh.

"Ok," Agent Dumber says. "Here goes our man," he says as he adjusts the camera onto the man. He snaps a full body shot. He snaps another shot, being careful to get a clean shot of the duffle bag. He then zooms in on the man's face and snaps another shot. He then watches as the man gets into Smoke's car and seats himself. The agent quickly snaps a shot of them sitting together. Smoke leans back into the backseat. The agent then snaps a shot of Smoke handing a duffle bag over to his passenger. They shake hands and the man quickly exits the vehicle. Agent Dumber snaps two shots of the man with a different colored bag in his hand. "Transaction complete," he whispers. He quickly snaps a shot of the Cadillac's license plates.

Smoke zips out of the parking lot with no hesitation. The man exits from the opposite end of the lot. Agent Dumber backs out of the parking space and follows the Cadillac from approximately ten cars behind. "Get the locals on the phone," he says to his partner.

Agent Dumbest presses the button on his walkie talkie. In less than two seconds he gets a response. "Ah, Federal Agent Ferino," he utters. "Narcotic activity in process. We're in pursuit of suspect in a black Cadillac Escalade going South on Bergen Street....license plate number F, D, C, 4, 6, 7. Right now we're one block away from Twelfth Avenue."

Agent Dumber tails the Cadillac for three blocks before he spots a Newark radio car at the intersection of Springfield Avenue and Bergen Street. The Cadillac truck cruises through the intersection and the police car turns right behind him. They make it to Avon and Bergen before an unmarked car is spotted. That car tails behind as well.

They ride for a few more blocks before they reach Clinton Avenue. Another unmarked car's nose peeks out. In seconds that car makes a wild U-turn, cutting off the Cadillac's path. Agent Dumber pulls over to the curb and watches as it all unfolds before his eyes.

He would have loved to make this bust but he sacrificed it just so he wouldn't draw attention to them and blow their cover. He charges the huge bust off as charity for now but he's sure he will reap the benefits sooner than later.

Ten minutes later the Cadillac truck is surrounded by a total of fifteen police cars. The driver of the Cadillac lays sprawled out on the sidewalk with his hands cuffed behind his back. Police search every inch of his truck for minutes before one holds the duffle bag high in the air. The others clap with gratitude.

Agent Dumber pulls out of the parking space and drives right past the scene of the crime without anyone even noticing their Suburban creep by. "Mission complete," he says with satisfaction. "Mission fucking complete."

Days Later/12:50 A.M.

Tonight is the big night. The night of Smoke's highly anticipated birthday party has finally come. Federal Informant S-Dot pulls into the parking lot behind the Key Club downtown Newark. He pulls up to the parking attendant and him and Samirah exit the sparkling Bentley GT.

He had no plans of attending the party but Agent Dumber demanded that he attend. He looks over to his escort who is looking more stunning than ever. Tonight she's in no way looking anything like the ghetto hood rat that he knows her to be. She actually looks like a video queen. She looks like eye candy, dressed in extremely tight designer jeans, a form fitted leather jacket and five inch stilettos. The oversized Dior shades makes it hard for her to see in the dark but it compliments her outfit. The highlight of her outfit is the oversized Chanel pocketbook that she wears over her shoulder. The $2,500.00 bag was bought by S-Dot but it didn't actually cost him a dime. He charged it off as an expense for the Federal Government.

As they're walking through the parking lot he feels a slight sense of comfort as he notices the huge Chevy Suburban parked on the one way block. Samirah doesn't know it but he is well aware that Agents Dumber and Dumbest are sitting behind the tinted windows.

Minutes later the moment that he feared has arrived. Samirah leads him to the front of the long line as everyone's eyes zoom in on them. She's fashionably late as she planned to be. She wanted to get there after everyone else so she could make a grand appearance.

They cross the velvet rope like celebrities. The female security guard looks through Samirah's bag as a huge bouncer quickly runs over to S-Dot. The bouncer frisks him starting at his ankles. As he stands up he looks into S-Dot's eyes. He pats his waistband. "Sean, I got you covered," the bouncer whispers into his ear. At this point, he realizes that the bouncer is one of them. He's a Federal Agent as well.

Samirah grabs his hand tightly as she leads him through the doorway. His heart pounds rapidly. What lies before him, he has not a clue. He's nervous but he understands that he can't show it.

He quickly turns his swag on and starts diddy bopping. He struts elegantly up the runway. It's all eyes on them as everyone wonders who the unknown man is that is accompanying 'Dirty Samirah.' The attention makes Samirah pull him closer to her, stating her claim.

The women in the club watch with envy, wondering how she's managed to land such a handsome man. With the reputation that she has, they all assume that he must not be from Newark or he would know better than to be caught dead in public with her.

Singer Trey Songz' 'Say Ah' busts through the speakers as everyone dances their hearts away. "What you drinking?" S-Dot asks as he steps over to the bar. A male bartender comes rushing from the end of the bar and steps face to face with him from over the counter. The winking of the bartender's eye lets him know that he's a Fed as well. He feels more reassurance now, knowing that he's not completely alone in here with a club full of gangbangers. "Three bottles of Rose," he whispers, not even caring about the price. He will just charge the amount off as another expense.

Even more attention is on them as three golden colored buckets of Champagne are laid out in front of them. Samirah grabs a bucket as S-Dot grabs the other two. They then step toward the back of the bar toward the VIP section. It's extremely crowded in the back but they manage to slip and slide through the cracks of the people.

Smoke pops out of nowhere, cutting them off. He wraps her in a tight bear hug. "Lil Sis, what it do?"

"Happy Birthday, baby," she whispers as they separate.

"What's that for?" he asks as he points to the bucket. "We got bottles lined up for days," he says as he points to the table behind him. On that table a total of at least fifty bottles are lined up.

Smoke stares at S-Dot with disgust. The look in his eyes sends chills up S-Dot's spine. Samirah feels the tension and decides that now may be the perfect time to formally introduce them. "Smoke, this is my friend, S-Dot," she says with nervousness.

S-Dot extends his hand with fear. "Happy Birthday," he utters. Smoke leaves his hand dangling in mid air. He looks him up and down before turning his back on him and walking away. S-Dot pulls his hand away with embarrassment.

"Don't mind him," Samirah says. "He off his bullshit. He gets like that when he off the Grey Goose. That's just him," she adds. "Come on," she says as she leads him over to the table.

1:10 A.M.

Two detectives stand on the porch of a shabby three family house in Newark. The door opens and a middle aged woman dressed in a robe and a head scarf wrapped around her head, peeks her head from behind the door. Her eyes are half shut. She's been awakened out of her sleep. "Yes?" she asks in a groggy voice. She becomes nervous once she realizes that they're the police. Her eyes pop wide open.

"Miss Jackson?" the black detective asks politely.

"Yes?" she replies. "Can I help you?" she asks with a baffled look on her weary looking face.

"Hello Miss Jackson. We are sorry to wake you. I am Detective Morgan and this is my partner Detective Martinez. Hopefully you can," he replies with a smile. We are from Newark's Robbery and Homicide Bureau. We're here for your daughter Melissa."

The only thing that sticks out in her tired mind is homicide and Melissa. She automatically thinks that her daughter has been murdered. Fear freezes her heart. "Melissa?" she cries.

"Yes," he replies as he shows her Mother Nature's mug shot. "We have reason to believe that she's in connection to a homicide."

The woman sighs with relief but quickly gets nervous all over again. "A homicide?"

"Yes," he replies. "We just want to talk to her," he lies. "She's wanted for questioning," he lies once again. They're actually here for her arrest. They have all the evidence that they need to charge and convict her. The video they watched caught the entire murder all the way to the getaway in her van.

"Melissa ain't in here. I haven't seen her in months," she lies.

"You mind if we come in and look around?"

"Only if you have a search warrant."

Detective Martinez lifts the sheet of paper high into the air as he steps around her. Detective Morgan follows behind him, leaving her standing at the door.

1:30 A.M.

Everyone rushes to the back of the bar just as rapper, Chaos the Realest, hops onto the stage. Tonight he's performing his single off of the 'Back to Bizness' Soundtrack. He stands at the center of the stage while his entourage stands there guarding him like the President. The entire stage is sealed off by close to twenty men. Taliban scarves cover their heads and the greater portion of their faces. Through the opening of the scarves the only thing that can be seen are their huge beards and dark scuff marks on their foreheads.

Chaos grabs the microphone and steps to the front of the stage. He doesn't say a word for close to a minute yet the crowd is going wild. Finally the noise simmers down as they wait for him to speak. "Baghdad, Frontline, True 2 Life, 202, we up! We don't give a fuck who got next!" he shouts. "Let's get it!" he barks with vengeance before the beat rips through the speakers.

At the front of the bar S-Dot and Samirah are next in line to take pictures. The group of men before them finally step aside after their twenty minute photo shoot. "Bout fucking time," Samirah says with attitude.

"What?" one man barks as he looks her up and down with hatred.

"You heard me," she says as she stands face to face with him.

S-Dot's heart thumps in his chest. He grabs her by the hand, pulling her over to the back drop. The last thing he needs is trouble with this group of men over a ten dollar picture. As soon as Samirah turns her head S-Dot looks at the man and shakes his head from side to side. The apologetic look in his eyes is accompanied by a low whisper. "Ain't nothing," he says just loud enough for the man to hear him.

Samirah poses for the camera. She stands in front of him with her butt planted onto his crotch. He wraps his arms around her waist. "Ready," the photographer asks as he aims the camera at them. S-Dot's eyes sink to the bulge that rests on the photographer's hip. He's sure that the man has a gun on his side. Click! The photographer snaps the photo. He slowly removes the camera from his face. A sly wink of the eye from the photographer explains to Sean what the gun is all about. The photographer is a Federal Agent as well.

As Samirah and S-Dot are standing there waiting for the photo, Smoke and a group of his men bum rush the photo area. They totally disregard the man and woman who stand posted up; ready to get their photo taken. "Hold the fuck up!" the little feisty woman shouts. "Wait ya'll fucking turn!"

"Shut the fuck up, bitch!" Smoke's man shouts from the center of the crowd. He nudges her and the man to the side. The man becomes enraged but he remains silent. The crowd of twenty men now has him and his woman surrounded.

"Yo, take this fucking picture," she snaps at the photographer. "Fuck that." The photographer snaps the shot and they walk away from the backdrop.

Smoke's crew gets into their gangster poses while Smoke stands there allowing the man and woman to pass him. He pays no attention to the man at all because his eyes are glued onto the woman. He's quite saucy off of the Grey Goose yet he's still sober enough to know right from wrong. He grabs the woman by the hand and pulls her over to him. "Calm down, Shorty. We don't want no trouble," he says with a charming smile. "Come take a picture with me. It's my birthday," he says as he looks over to the man and stares coldly into his eyes.

"Hmphh," the man sighs with sarcasm as he snatches her away from Smoke.

"Hmphh, what?" Smoke asks with a satanic look in his drunken eyes. "You don't like something I just said?" he asks as he steps closer to the man. The man shoves his woman to the side and steps closer to Smoke. In seconds Smoke's crew has surrounded the man. Another group of five men come to the man's aid. Bouncers notice the commotion and run over. Before they can get there Smoke makes his move. He pushes the man in the chest. "What, you hoe ass nigga!"

The bouncers step in between them as the man attempts to get at Smoke. He realizes that it's impossible so he stops short and just stands his ground. A huge smile pops onto his face as he nods his head up and down. "I'll see you," the man utters.

"Yeah, you will," Smoke says before spinning around and walking over to the backdrop. His crew follows. They immediately start posing for the camera. Gang signs are being thrown from every direction. Some throw them up high in the air for everyone to see while others hide them inconspicuously. Regardless of how they're thrown up, they're in clear view for the camera.

"There we go dummies," the photographer mumbles to himself. "Smile for the camera." Click! Click! Click! They switch position after position yet he snaps away without one complaint. The more photos he takes the better.

2:00 A.M.

Robbery and Homicide Detectives Morgan and Martinez sit parked in their unmarked car, a half a block away from Mother Nature's house. They're hoping to catch her coming in tonight but they do realize that the chances of that are slim. They're quite sure her mother and grandmother have already warned her. If she has any sense she will know that they're bound to be at her house next. They may not catch up with her tonight but one thing they are certain of is, they will catch up with her eventually.

2:52 A.M.

The party is over and the club has emptied out except for a few stragglers who are not ready to call it a night. Instead of leaving, they're just dragging along. On the outside of the club, S-Dot clutches Samirah's hand as he leads her up the block, headed to the parking lot. Suddenly his attention is snatched by the sound of footsteps that are approaching from behind. He spins around nervously only to see Smoke and his goons running at full speed toward him. Paralysis takes over his body as he sees the chrome handgun that dangles in Smoke's hand. He stands still as Smoke and his crew run right past them. "Phew," he sighs to himself.

Smoke and his squad stop short about three cars away where a man is holding open the passenger's door of a BMW, while a woman gets into the car. S-Dot immediately recognizes the couple. This is the man that Smoke had the altercation with inside of the club. S-Dot tries to walk away from the scene to get out of harms way but Samirah holds him there as she watches the situation with nosiness.

The man turns around with total surprise. He slams the door shut behind his woman. Smoke walks up close to the man, aiming his gun at the man's face. His goons are right behind him. "You said you gone see me right?" Smoke asks with fury. The man raises his hands in the air as he tries to explain himself. Smoke ignores him totally. "You see me, right? Huh? You see me?" he asks even louder. He puts the gun onto the man's forehead. Bloc! In less than a second the man drops to his knees lifelessly. Everyone on the block scatters except Samirah and S-Dot, who wants to but she has a tight grip on him. Bloc! Bloc! Smoke empties his gun into the already dead man's back. Bloc! Bloc! Bloc! Bloc! "Now you can't see me mufucker!" Bloc! Bloc! Bloc! Bloc! Bloc!

Smoke and his goons take off running. The sound of police sirens are coming from every direction. Smoke runs right past the Chevy Suburban that's parked two cars away from his Aston Martin. As he's getting into the driver's seat, his smoking gun is still in his hand in clear view.

Agent Dumber snaps a picture from behind the dark tinted windows. "The murder weapon still in his hand," he says with a smile. He takes another shot and another. "How is that for evidence?"

The Next Day

Smoke's cousin sits in the tiny room inside of the County Jail. The room is cold and eerie feeling. It's completely bare except for two chairs and the small table that he sits in front of. The moment he was escorted here he knew he was doomed.

Agent Dumber sits on the edge of the table only inches away from him. Agent Dumbest pacing back and forth behind him makes the situation even more tense. The stone cold look on Agent Dumber's face and the rage that lies in his eyes makes him nervous. "So, Mr. Roberts, I'm not going to bullshit you. It's not looking good for you. Six hundred bricks of heroin is trouble enough. The gun you had well...that's a host of trouble on its own. This will make your third gun conviction. I'm sure you know what that means?" he says as he nods his head up and down. "That's trigger lock. You're familiar with that term, I'm sure. Right?"

The man sits there with a blank look on his face. He tries to act as if he's not bothered by them but the trembling of his legs banging onto the table is a dead give away to them. Just being in the room with these agents gives him a feeling of fear that he never knew existed.

"That's a minimum of ten years. If you're lucky," he adds. "The heroin, I'm sure will get the average man with no prior convictions at least ten years. You on the other hand have an endless record with multiple convictions. You could easily be looking at thirty years. You got yourself in this mess and only you can get yourself out of it. I'm well aware of the stop snitching campaign out there on the street but me and you both know that's bullshit," he smiles. "Every man that gets in the room with us capitalizes off of the opportunity to help himself. Don't let them fool you. It's every man for himself. Dog eat dog. The next man is going to come right behind you and tell everything that he knows. You will be a fool not to. When that cell closes it's just you. All the people out there screaming don't snitch, they already have. I know it may go against everything you believe and you will be frowned upon amongst your peers but just know, your *peers* don't give a fuck about you. This is your problem. This is your decision. Trust me, I know it's a big decision to make with such a short notice. That's why I'm not going to put any pressure on you today. Take a few days to weigh your options. I don't need an answer today." He gets up and steps away from the table. Agent Dumbest gets up and follows right behind him. Agent Dumber pulls the door open. "Sleep on it. But don't oversleep. We have a Federal hold on you. Even if you post bail, you will not be able to leave the building without *our* permission," he says as he steps out of the door and slams it shut.

Agent Dumber looks to his partner. "We got him where we want him," he whispers. "He's ready to talk right now. I saw it in his eyes. After thinking about it for a few days he will be ready to tell everything he knows. The witness stand already has his name on it. A thirty year sentence will make him testify on his mother, let alone a cousin."

Meanwhile

The Mayor walks side by side Smoke as they strut through Short Hills Mall. Their meeting is about nothing in particular, just an update.

"Ay man, shit moving lovely just as you said it would. My phone stay ringing off the hook. Mufuckers from everywhere hitting me. This shit making noise all over. Mufuckers in Paterson on down to my Homies in Trenton. We done started a fire," he says with cheer in his eyes.

The Mayor shakes his head from side to side. "Be careful of them out of town niggas. Personally I don't fuck with out of towners. I don't trust them. I need to know their history. Where you come from? How long you been off the porch? What stock you come from? Was your daddy a snitch? Cause if he was most likely you are as well. It's in your genes. I seen a lot of good guys fucked up behind out of town niggas. They have no love for you. They use you up until they think they don't need you anymore. Then they ruin you. They get their money up off of you and then if they close enough to you they'll put a bullet in the back of your head...just when you start trusting them. Deep down inside they hate you and fear that you will take over their town. Niggas in the town hate them because they're fucking with you. On the flip side if they get jammed up they have no problem telling on you cause for one they don't know you. They don't have love for you or even like you. The relationship is built on money. When the money is no longer in the equation ya'll have nothing. No memories of elementary school or playing in the sandbox...nothing! No love, no history makes it easy for him to finish you off. No one will even know or even care cause you really ain't one of them. For some, telling on an out of towner, really ain't telling. That's their way of justifying their cowardly act," he says with disgust on his face. "Me, I only fuck with motherfuckers that I can monitor. I need to know what's going on in his life. If he catches a case I need to know so I know how to move from there. For every action there's a reaction. Always remember that."

Days Later/September 22, 2009

The black Chrysler Sebring sits parked on the quiet dead end block. Mother Nature sits behind the steering wheel while Lil Razz sits in the passenger's seat. The minute he gets seated he pulls out his bag of goodies. "How much he gave you? You asked for the hundred?" she asks.

"Yeah, he gave it to me with no problem," he boasts.

Smoke was so impressed with Razz's turn around time that he had no problem granting him his request of one hundred bricks.

"So, how many for me?" Mother Nature asks with greed in her eyes. "The whole hundred?" she asks with a smile. She's hoping that he's foolish enough to give her all of them.

Razz smiles back in return. "Nah, take eighty and I'll keep twenty," he says as he breaks his away from the rest.

"Alright bet! Good looking. I'll bust back at you in like two days. Your big bruh gone be on your top when he see how fast you shaking these breezies," she says as she tries to hype him up even more. "Let me get outta here though," she says as she peeks around nervously.

Meanwhile

Federal Agent Dumbest and S-Dot sit on the edge of the desk while Agent Dumber stands directly in front of a chalkboard on the wall. They watch as he draws the family tree onto the chalkboard. From the wire tapped conversations, the information that Samirah has unknowingly given and the photos the photographer took at the party, he has all the information he needs to be able to break down the structure of their crime family. "The tip of the Iceberg," Agent Dumber says as he points to the top of his diagram where a photo is posted. "The Black Charles Manson. "Directly under him is, Smoke, who has Baby G-status. These three are of the next most important," he says as he places their pictures on that line. He then posts the next set of photos onto the board. "This is the immediate family," he says before posting some photos around the diagram. "Daniel Brown from Camden. Joshua Jones from Paterson. Michael Dorsey from Perth Amboy. This will be the biggest heroin ring in Newark's history. The Mayor will be the star of the show. Also we have Bloods and Crips together. We have multiple murders. We have a man willing to testify on the purchase of six hundred bricks. We're only missing one important piece to this puzzle," he says.

"At this point we all know that the Mayor is behind all of this but we need proof. We don't even have a photo of a transaction with him in it," he says with disappointment. "We don't have his voice on one phone conversation. To the naked eye he's clear," he says as he shakes his head from side to side. "I will figure it out but for the meantime we have an easier task before us," he says as he looks at the both of them. He points at S-Dot. "We need a buy. We need you to talk Smoke into serving you."

"Impossible," he utters with no hesitation. "For crying out loud, he won't even speak to me. How the hell am I going to get him to serve me? I won't be able to get close enough to him."

"You're a man of intelligence. You will figure it out."

Mother Nature hops onto the ramp of the New Jersey Turnpike. She's headed South bound. As bad as she wants to stay here and settle her beef with Smoke and his goons, she realizes it isn't the best decision for her at this time.

The Homicide detectives have been to her mother and grandmother's house over three times apiece. She's even crept past them sitting in front of her own house a few times. They've also been to her aunt's house and her older sister's house. It's impossible for her to get a good night sleep anywhere without worrying about them kicking the door in. She feels as if the walls are closing in on her.

Her lack of funds gives her limited movement. She's in a tough spot. Not only will she not be able to afford an attorney to defend her, she doesn't even have money to post bail if she's caught. With all the odds stacked against her she realizes that the best option is to take off and never look back.

She has family in Norfolk Virginia. She plans to go there and make some things happen. She has five thousand dollars cash to her name and the eighty bricks that she just got hold of. She has no plans whatsoever of paying Razz the money back. She's sure this will cause a world of trouble for him but at this point she doesn't care the least bit. Her only concern is herself.

When it's all said and done she figures she will have over forty thousand dollars. She's sure she will be able to find dope in Virginia. She plans to build her money up so if they do ever catch up with her she will have enough money to get herself out of the hole that she's dug herself into.

One Week Later

    The Mayor sits comfortably on the huge leather bean bag as he removes stacks of money from a duffle bag that sits in between his feet. He piles the money onto the glass coffee table. In no way is he about to attempt to count through 1.1 million dollars. Well at least that is what it's supposed to be, according to Smoke. At this time he will just have to take Smoke's word for it. Up until now he hasn't been off by a single dollar. Right now he will just take his word for it but later he will run the bills through his money machine just to double check his count.

    This is money from the last batch of ten thousand bricks in which he just gave Smoke about eleven days ago. The Mayor feels good in knowing that his 20,000 bricks in thirty days quota has been fulfilled. Actually it only took Smoke approximately twenty three days making it all the better.

    The Mayor slides a few piles of money away from the rest of the stacks. The bulk that's left, he tosses back into the original duffle bag that they came in. Assuming that Smoke's count is up to par, there should be a million dollars even, in there. He snatches another bag from behind the bean bag. That bag, he drops the loose money into. The loose money which is a hundred thousand, added to the money that's already inside will make a total of three hundred and fifty thousand dollars.

    The Mayor gets up and grabs hold of both bags. He steps over to the huge walk in closet. He drops the million dollar bag next to two other bags of the same value. The lower value bag he drops in a corner all by itself. The Mayor stares at the bags with great satisfaction. In just four flips he has grossed a grand total of close to three and a half million.

    He walks over to the huge window and stares over the East River into New Jersey. He absolutely loves the beautiful view. In fact, he loves everything about this building. The Trump Tower here in the Soho section of Manhattan has it all. It has a private spa, a health club, a restaurant and a wine cellar. It has all the amenities that one needs to live comfortably.

    The five thousand dollar a month apartment would be the dream apartment for most but for the Mayor it's just a mere stash house to keep his money safe. He learned his lesson many years ago about keeping evidence away from where he rests his head. The last thing he wants to do is get the women in his life involved in his madness, in the unfortunate case that anything goes wrong. He had done enough of that when he caught his case years ago.

Watching his girl Megan go through what she went through, when she had to fight for her freedom, broke his heart. He feels that it's best to just keep it all away from them. He trusts the both of them wholeheartedly but he figures the less they actually know the easier it will be for them to say they don't know anything. At the end of the day they won't be lying.

The Mayor has no one else in his life that he trusts with his money so he figured this would be the perfect place for it. He's sure he can give it to Tony but he feels he's brought him enough trouble as well. The building is under watch 24 hours a day by the concierge, which means no one can break into the apartment. The apartment can't be linked to him in any way because he leased it under his alias. He feels this apartment is the best situation all over the board.

He walks to the kitchen area and snatches the phone from the wall. "Sir, this is Bahande," he says. "From suite thirty two, C." The alias that he's using is of the side that he never actually considered himself; the Filipino side. The name fits him perfectly. It means, Treasure.

He figures by using that name he will attract less attention to himself. "Yes, can you have my Rolls Royce brought out front? Thank you. I'm on my way down now." This apartment building is also the hiding place for his car. After finding out about the tracking devices on his cars, many months ago, he doesn't feel comfortable leaving this one anywhere; especially outside of his homes that he's sure the Feds know all about.

Meanwhile

Federal Informant S-Dot lays back in Samirah's bed as she lays curled up against his bare chest. They're both completely naked except for the watch that he sports on his wrist. The stainless steel band, diamond bezzled, pink face Presidential Rolex is a gift to him from the Federal Government. To the naked eye one may think the watch is worth well over fifteen grand but it's really not. The true value of the watch is about fifteen dollars. It's nothing but a high quality replica. The most valuable part of the bootleg watch is the tape recorder that has been installed inside of the watch. Now the agents can listen to his every conversation anywhere that he goes, without anyone ever seeing a trace of a wire. The purpose of the watch is for the buy from Smoke that they hope he gets.

"Babe, you wanna hear something crazy?" he asks.

"What?"

"I'm all the way down in New Brunswick, in my hood and niggas down there screaming about that Bang Man. That shit the talk of the city. I didn't say nothing. I just sat back with my mouth closed. I acted like I didn't know nothing. They know I be moving around here in the Bricks so they were hoping I could get my hands on some of it. I didn't really want to tell them that I knew who actually had it cause if they knew that they will fuck around and put the bullshit dope I got on hold. I'm sure they would figure that way they could force me to get the Bang Man shit. I heard that shit fire!"

"Wow," Samirah utters. "All the way down there?" she asks with great surprise.

"Yep. That's all I would need to shut the city down! This bullshit is killing me. My peoples on some bullshit. I ain't had no good dope in months. I'm bleeding," he whines. "That Bang Man shit will put a nigga right back where I need to be. The shit I got now is alright but it ain't shutting shit down. Feel me?"

Samirah's mind races rapidly as she puts together a plan. She loves him so much and is willing to do anything to make his life easier. She figures this will not only help him but her brother could benefit as well. "I'm gone talk to my brother and see if I can link ya'll up."

"Yeah? You think he would be with that? He don't even speak to me. He don't even like me."

"He ain't gotta like you cause he loves me," she says with a boastful smile. "He will do anything for his baby sister. Let me put this together and see how I can bring ya'll together. I'm sure I can get ya'll face to face. Once you there it's all up to you to reel him in."

"That's all I need," he says with a huge smile. "The rest is history." Yep...history, he thinks to himself.

Smoke gets out of his car and walks toward the black Yukon Denali that sits parked in front of his car. The bag that Smoke is carrying is filled with money instead of his infamous Bang Man. In the bag there's a total of sixty grand. The man in the Yukon has two kilos of cocaine waiting for Smoke.

Smoke has never really taken the cocaine game serious because he's never had any real success with it in the past. He would buy ten or fifteen grams every now and then whenever he saw an open market for it. Up until last night, he looked at the cocaine game as a complete waste of time. He sees it differently after talking to one of his soldiers who sells cocaine along with the dope that Smoke fronts him.

The man bragged to Smoke about how much the market has increased since the birth of Bang Man. Wherever good dope is every other drug flourishes because of the fact it brings life to the entire area. He says before Bang Man he would struggle to score seventeen or eighteen hundred dollars a day. He says now he averages at least fifteen thousand a day with his tiny nickel bottles. He claims that he's ripping through a kilo every other day.

While he was talking, Smoke's wheels were turning. After calculating his gross worth at about a hundred and fifty grand a week he wanted in. It was then that he decided that being that he's the sole controller of his projects he should be controlling all movements that come through there.

Smoke in no way is a selfish guy so he would never take it all over. Besides he doesn't even know enough about the game to do that. He just wants a piece of the action. His man informed him that he pays almost forty dollars a gram. By letting Smoke take over the operation it will benefit him more. Smoke knows of a connection that he can get the cocaine at thirty thousand dollars a kilo. He will then front it to his man at thirty five a gram. The man scores an extra five thousand a kilo and so does Smoke. In this case everybody wins.

Smoke hops into the passenger's seat of the Yukon. "Rock, what's good?"

"Same shit," the man whispers as he digs underneath his

seat. He grabs hold of a plastic bag. He opens up the bag and shows Smoke two sealed bricks of cocaine. "Here it is," he says as he hands them over to Smoke. Smoke flips the bricks around, examining the wrappers. This is actually his first time ever seeing or even touching a kilo. Before this he's only seen them on television.

While Smoke is purposely stalling the transaction and trying to keep the man's attention on him, the GTO pulls up and parks behind Smoke's Camaro. Purely out of habit the man peeks up and looks through his driver's side mirror. What he sees alarms him. He notices the man getting out of the GTO and walking toward his truck on his side. An uneasy feeling fills his gut. "Ho," he says nervously as he looks back at Smoke. He quickly looks back into the mirror and notices that the man is now only a few feet away. Something doesn't feel right to him. His senses tell him that a robbery is in progress. He's trapped with nowhere to go.

Smoke places his hand underneath his shirt. As soon as he grips his gun, he speaks. "You know what it is."

Terror kicks in along with desperation. He forces the door open and hops clumsily out of the truck. The man is standing right at the door with his gun already drawn. He pushes the man out of the way and takes off running in the opposite direction. In less than a second a single gunshot sounds off. Boc! Another one sounds off less than a second later. Boc! The man continues to sprint up the block for his life. Boc! Boc! The gunshots that he hears behind him force him to run even faster. The gunman squeezes again and again as he chases behind the man. Boc! Boc! It's almost impossible to catch the man because he already has a half a block lead and he's still gaining yardage.

Smoke hops out of the truck. "Yo!" he calls out. The gunman turns around with a baffled look on his face. "Fuck him," Smoke says as he raises the bag in the air. "Let him go." They watch as the man runs for his life scared and fast.

Although Smoke has more than enough money to buy the work, he refuses to do so. He can't even imagine giving a man who he knows is undoubtedly afraid of him, sixty grand. He has no sympathy for the weak and feels that they have no business in the game. Because of that he takes advantage of them every chance he gets.

Smoke hops into his truck while his partner hops into his car. Simultaneously they speed off, leaving the Yukon Denali parked with the engine still running.

Less than an Hour Later

Samirah and her lover, S-Dot pulls up to her house after a delightful dinner engagement at Sushi Samba in Manhattan, New York. Coincidentally Smoke is pulling up at the exact same time. Samirah's mind immediately starts working. She looks over to S-Dot. "You ready?" she asks.

"For what?" he asks with confusion.

"The big meeting," she says with a huge smile.

He automatically becomes nervous. Although he's been instructed to do this he's still not ready to actually go through with it. "Nah, nah," he rebukes.

"Why not?"

He thinks hard to come up with a good reason. "The time ain't right."

"It's the perfect time. It's now or never," she says as she busts the door open. "Brother!" she yells out.

S-Dot sits there with a terror filled heart as he fidgets in his seat. Smoke turns around and the moment he sets his eyes on the Bentley his face goes sour. "What?" he barks as he continues to step along. The bag that he holds in his hand contains the two kilos he just took. He can't afford to stand here and by chance the police pull up and catch him with the work.

"Hold up? Come here for a second? Please?" she pleads.

Once he gets onto the steps he stops short. The aura he displays is of tension. Samirah walks over to him, leaving the door wide open. Smoke's eyes are glued onto S-Dot. The look in his eyes is of pure hatred. She finally stands right before him. "My friend wants to talk to you about something."

"What?" he asks as he looks back to the car. "Talk to me about what? I don't know that motherfucker and he don't know me. What the fuck he got to talk to me about?" he asks with rage. He rudely turns around, giving Samirah his back. He looks over his shoulder at her. "The fuck outta here!"

Meanwhile

A group of twelve men stand huddled up in front of a small townhouse in Hillside, New Jersey. A man faces them with his back to the street. Everyone is listening carefully as he's telling his story. "I gets in the car with the nigga, hit the nigga with the bag and then I just happen to look in my mirror," he says with uneasiness. "I see a mufucker creeping up on my truck. I turn back around and the nigga in the car drew down on me, talking about you know what it is."

Everyone switches their attention from that man to a tall dread head man who is standing in the middle of the crowd. They're all curious to see what he has to say about all of this. He stands there with no emotion on his face as he keeps his head hung low with his eyes locked onto the ground. He lifts his head slowly. "So, what you do?"

The man looks away with embarrassment. "I busted the door open and broke out," he says with shame. "The mufucker was standing right at the door. I had to push him out of the way and take off past him. He was ripping at me crazy."

The dread headed man becomes enraged. "So, they got away with the work?" he asks as he stares into the man's eyes, burning his soul. A smirk covers his face. "Do you realize that you the only one that has these types of problems? Only you," he adds. "Don't nobody else go through the shit that you go through. Mufuckers done been to your house to rob your ass not once but three times. You done moved three times and still you keep bringing the same raggedy ass bitches to your spot. What is it, you retarded or just a sucker for love? Now we got you in the middle of this bullshit," he barks. "Do you understand that you are the weakest link?" he says with great disgust. "You make all of us look bad with that bullshit. Nigga,we the Federation! Shit like that don't happen to us. These motherfuckers got you pegged like you some type of bitch or something. It's obvious that they don't see a man when they look at you or they wouldn't do the shit that they do to you."

"Come on, Moe," he pleads with sorrow.

"Come on, Moe, my ass!" he barks. "I'm tired of this shit with you," he says as he starts to walk away. " From here on out, either you gone stand the fuck up or lay down forever!" he adds. "Sal!" he calls out and his right hand man follows close behind him. From this point on, either you gone stand the fuck up and be a man or lay the fuck down!" he says with rage. "Load up and let's go!" he says as he steps toward three triple black customized conversion vans that are lined up behind each other. He walks to the very first one and hops into the passenger's seat while his right hand man climbs into the driver's seat. The rest of the men pile up in the other two vans. In seconds all three vans burn out.

Although the man is a grown man and should be able to stand up for himself, he doesn't. The boss wants so bad to let him get what he deserves out here if he's not willing to defend himself but at the end of the day he knows that the man is a reflection of their squad. With that being said, anyone that violates a member of the Federation, male or female will be disciplined as if they violated the entire Federation.

Philadelphia, Pennsylvania

Tony sits inside of Ms. Tootsie's Soul Food Restaurant on South Street. He watches and appreciates from the window, the beautiful side view of his Aston Martin. Not only does he appreciate the automobile the people who pass by do as well. He sits there as modest as he possibly can as a group of men stand against the car taking photos.

On the opposite side of the table there sits another gorgeous sight. The caramel complexioned, light brown, almond shaped eyed beauty sits there caught up in Tony. She's blushing from ear to ear as she's been doing ever since they first met up here. A simple smile from him makes her wet.

Tony knows how weak the woman is for him which makes him pour even more charm on her. "Damn," he blurts out. "You look beautiful as usual," he says. She looks away bashfully as she twirls a lock of her long thick hair. Tony leans closer to her over the table. He grabs her by the face letting her chin fall onto the palm of his hand as he kisses her on the cheek. While his lips are pressed against the softness of her skin, his tongue slides out of his mouth and slips into her deeply indented dimple. He twirls the tip of his tongue around before planting another wet kiss on her face.

This melts her away. As she gazes into his eyes sadness plasters her face. "So, you ready to hear what I called you here for?" she asks with pity in her eyes.

"I thought I already knew what you called me here for," he says with a dazzling smile. "The whole ride here I was thinking to myself like, she's there waiting for me to get there so she can rip my clothes off and make passionate love to me," he says looking into her eyes for a response.

"That's a given," she whispers through her full lips. She bites down onto her bottom lip seductively. "You know I been wanting to do that for years but the respect I have for you and your marriage causes me to refrain from doing so. You heard what I said right, the respect for *you* and your marriage," she says with a smile. "Fuck your wife."

"I concur," he agrees. "There's no longer a need for you to refrain," he says with charm. "So, now you ready to rip my clothes off and make passionate love to me?"

She smiles from ear to ear as she looks away. "Let's just say that some things are better done than said," she says as she grabs a sheet of paper from the table. She peeks around with caution. "You're lucky I'm so in love with you because if not I wouldn't do this. I'm putting everything on the line, my job, my pension, everything. If I get fired are you going to take care of me?"

"You don't have to get fired for me to take care of you. I will do that just because. All you gotta do is give me the word."

"Whatever," she smiles. "Here's the deal. It's not looking good. They know everything. They have wiretaps so they say. They have witnesses, photos, everything. They have all that they need to take **your boy** down for the rest of his life. For the life of me I can't understand why he chose to do business with gangbangers. He's way too smart for that."

Tony shakes his head from side to side. "Damn. He just won't fucking listen to me."

This woman is a Federal Agent from the Newark Headquarters. She's decided to meet him here in Philly because it would be too much of a risk for them to get caught out together in New Jersey. She works side by side in the office with Agents Dumber and Dumbest but she's not assigned to the Mayor's case.

Yesterday she just happened to hear them speaking about the Mayor and her antennas were raised. She ear hustled all the information they spat out. The moment their meeting was over she made the call to Tony.

Tony met her years ago in law school. From the very first time that they laid eyes on each other, chemistry sparked. It was love at first sight. The timing was all wrong though because at that time she was married. Many years later she divorced but by that time Tony was married. Although their careers went in different directions after law school, their love and respect for each other has always been the common ground.

"Babe, they have it in for you. They're still trying to tie you into his mess," she says with sorrow. "You need to be very careful. They so badly want to put you in prison right next to him."

"Be careful why? I'm sparkling clean." She looks at him and as much as she wants to believe his innocence she can't. She would never admit it to him but at times she questions his innocence. "These bastards won't let a nigga live. They insist on dirtying up my name," he says with rage. She hands him the sheet of paper that she holds in her hand. He stares at the mug shot of the unknown man. "Who the fuck is this?"

"That's the informant they have on the case. How he's tied into them, I have not gotten the details as of yet but I will. One thing that I do know is that he's already on the inside. He's already given them enough to finish off the organization."

Tony's heart drops as he wonders if the Mayor has any contact with this man without knowing it. The thought of that makes him lose the erection that he held for her ever since they first sat at the table. Fear shrivels his manhood as well as his spirits. "Man, I pray that my man hasn't made a move with this nigga."

"Apparently he got arrested in a huge drug bust a few years ago and he's been working with us ever since."

"Fucking stool pigeon," he says as he grits his teeth.

"Tony, baby, please keep this to yourself. I will lose everything if they find out I leaked the information to you. Please promise me?"

"Tina," he says as he stares into her eyes. "Baby, you know I can't keep this away from my man."

"No, Tony I only told you this to give you the heads up and stay out of harms way. I don't give two shits about your man."

"But I give more than two shits about him."

"Phew," she sighs. "All I ask is that you don't get me caught up in this mess?"

"Tina, you know me," he says with sincerity in his eyes. "That, I would never do. I would never put you in harms way. Just trust me on this one. Ok?"

The Next Morning

Tony could barely sleep last night, thinking of the valuable information he was told. The endless thoughts and worrying affected his sexual performance drastically. On a scale of one to ten, he bombed out. He's sure that she failed him on her mental report card. It hurts him that after all these years of them waiting for each other and just when it was finally about to happen it doesn't happen. He apologized to her all night but still he knows that deep down inside she will never forgive him.

He so badly wanted to leave her there as soon as he heard the news but he didn't want her to believe that he used her for the information and bounced on her. He then thought about calling the Mayor but he feared the fact that his line could easily be tapped.

Tony cruises along Stuyvesant Avenue in Union. He looks up the block in search of the Mayor's car. He called the Mayor before he left Philly, telling him to meet him here. He doesn't want the Mayor to come to his office just in case the Feds are tailing him.

He spots the Mayor's Rolls Royce parked directly in front of Smoker's Delight. Tony parks across the street from him. As Tony is getting out of his car, he gives the Mayor a head nod, signaling for him to go inside the smoke shop. Tony walks right past the Mayor's car and steps inside of the store. He goes straight to the back humidor and grabs the cigar of his choice. When he turns back around he sees the Mayor sitting in the front lounge area of the shop.

Tony takes a seat in the plush leather, high back chair which sits across from the Mayor. Tony has a distraught look on his face as he shakes his head. "It's not looking good for the home team."

"Huh? What's wrong?"

"Straight to the point," he says. "I got the word from my source that the **fuck boys** are on you."

"No shit, Sherlock," the Mayor teases. "So, is that what those tracking devices on my cars was all about?" he asks with a goofy look on his face.

"This ain't a laughing matter."

"Ay man, fuck them," he says. "They got a job to do and so do I."

Tony looks at him with the disgust. "You got two ears and one mouth, that means you should hush up and do more listening," he says with a serious look on his face. "Now listen, they're closer than you may believe. They got wire tapped conversations and informants."

"I'm not worrying about none of that because for one I haven't talked on the phone not once since I been home. Only one person has my number. The other one contacts me by my pager," he says as he holds his Motorola pager into the air.

"All that is fine and well but what about your people? How do you know that they're being as cautious as you?"

"People?" the Mayor asks with sarcasm. "I only deal with one person. Everything goes through him. Nobody else even knows me. As long as *my guy* stands up, I'm good."

"What if he doesn't?"

"Then I'm fucked," he says with a grave look. "But I will just charge it to the game. Any decision I make I stick by it however it goes. Motherfuckers wanna ride around in Rolls Royces and live in multimillion dollar homes? Then that's the other side of the game. When I stepped foot in this game again, I knew what I was up against. I ain't one of those niggas who start crying the blues if the shit fall down. I take it on the chin. Shit…wasn't crying while things were up."

"Here," Tony says as he hands the mug shot of the informant over to the Mayor. The Mayor studies it carefully. "You ever seen him before?"

"Nah, not a day in my life."

"Phew," Tony sighs. "Good for you. This is the informant that they have on the case. Apparently he's in. I don't know how or who he's linked up with but he knows everything."

The Mayor takes the photo and studies it even more carefully. "Let me hold onto this. I will find out who he is."

Tina's plea of keeping her out of the mix, pops into his mind. Trust me, he remembers saying clearly. He debates back and forth whether he should allow the Mayor to take the paper or not. After all, this could put her career on the line. "Ah, I can't let you take it," Tony whispers.

"Huh?" the Mayor asks with a look of confusion on his face. "You can't let me take it? An informant is out there on the loose in search of information to put me away for the rest of my life and you can't let me take it? What type shit you off?"

Tony exhales slowly. "Take it, take it," he insists. "But please don't let it leave your hands? Please?"

Ten Minutes Later

As Tony is pulling into the parking lot of his office building his phone rings. He picks up on the first ring. "Hello. Tony Austin speaking. I just pulled up to my office. Where?" he asks as he looks around the parking lot. "Ok, I see you," he says before ending the call. His thoughts are racing. He wonders why this man is here at his office without calling him. The look on the man's face gives Tony an even more uncomfortable feeling. Tony parks right next to the man's Maserati. Tony hops out casually; trying hard not to show the man how uncomfortable he is in his presence. "Slow Moe, what's up?"

"Listen man, I'm gone tell you straight like this. **Your boy**, that so called Mayor motherfucker," he says staring Tony directly in the eyes. "I got a problem with him. I just got the word that him and all his little Bloods are behind a situation with a member of my Federation. He passed down the command and the order was filled."

"What?' Tony asks without a clue of what Maurice is talking about. "Him and his Bloods? He ain't Blood."

"Bullshit," he rebukes.

"I'm sure he ain't Blood, Moe."

"Well, I ain't here to change your mind. I'm here to warn you to stay clear of him. You're a good dude. I respect the hell out of you. Just stay clear if you don't want to be mixed up in it," he says as he walks away and hops into his car. He peels off like a madman.

Tony stands there with a puzzled look on his face. "What the fuck?"

One Hour Later

The Pontiac GTO sits at the red light waiting the changing of the light. He holds the Black and Mild in his mouth as he looks downward onto his lap. He texts away on his phone, not paying any attention to his surroundings. That's a shame because if he was paying attention he would know that the black customized van behind him has been tailing him for two blocks now. Suddenly a second identical van pulls up directly behind that one.

The light changes and the GTO speeds off. The driver continues as he peeks back and forth from the road to his phone, trying to read the incoming text that he just received. He slows down as he approaches the next corner, trying to get caught by the light so he can reply to the text. He stops a few feet away from the corner with his eyes glued onto the phone. The second black van zips around the right of him and makes an abrupt turn in front of him, blocking his path. The first van zips around on the right and pulls up side by side of the small car.

The man looks up and is shocked to see that he's trapped by the two vans. He becomes startled, figuring that they may be police until he sees a man hanging out of the passenger's window with a gun in his hand. Boc! Boc! Boc! Boc! Glass shatters inward before four back to back slugs rip through his face. The van in the front speeds off just in time before the man in the GTO drops over onto the passenger's seat. With his foot released from the brake pedal, the car sails up the block with no guidance from him. The car doesn't stop until it rams into the building on the corner. A four car accident takes place as the driver of a Toyota attempts to get out of the way. Both vans speed away, leaving the driver of the GTO as dead as a dead can be.

Sal leans back in the passenger's seat and drops the heated gun onto his lap. Maurice stares coldly ahead. "One down and a million more of them dirty motherfuckers to go."

Meanwhile

265

The Mayor sits in the driver's seat of the Rolls Royce as his man Smoke gets into the passenger's seat. The Mayor wastes not a second. "We got a problem, lil bruh."

Smoke looks at him with concern. "What's up?"

The Mayor hands him the mug shot. "You know him?"

Smoke looks at the picture, studying the face carefully. The man looks familiar but he can't place his face. "Nah," he replies with hesitation.

"Look closer," the Mayor demands. "I just got the word that he's infiltrated the circle. He's a Federal Informant. Apparently somebody is doing business with him. Everybody's phone is tapped and they have pictures of all ya'll. All through this man. You sure you never busted a move with him?"

"Nah, I never made a move with him. I'm sure. I only do business with mufuckers I know and I don't know him from Adam." All of a sudden the face becomes a bit more familiar to him but he doesn't know why. Smoke squints his eyes and studies the features of the man's face. Suddenly he visualizes the man's bald face with a dark beard on it. His heart rips through his chest the very moment that he realizes who the man is.

The Mayor senses the change of his body language. "You sure you don't know him?" Smoke thinks quickly. The last thing he wants to tell the Mayor is that the man got in through his sister. He can't believe it. The Mayor senses his uneasiness. "You sure?" the Mayor repeats.

"Nah, I never seen him before," he lies.

"Well, somebody dealing with him. It's your job to find out who is dealing with him. When you do find out you are to murder him and the informant." Smoke's heart sinks into his belly. "You got me?" the Mayor asks.

Smoke nods his head up and down. "I got you big bruh," he whispers as he tries to speak over the lump in his throat. "I got you."

Minutes Later

Smoke speeds up the busy street recklessly. He zips in and out of traffic like a madman. He picks up his phone and starts dialing his man before he realizes that this isn't the right phone. He slams the phone down and grabs hold of his clean phone line. He dials the number hurriedly. The man answers the phone on the first ring.

"Yo!" Smoke shouts. "The fag motherfucker that my sister fucking with!" he shouts. "Yeah, with the Bentley," he replies. "The one who came to my party with her...yeah. That motherfucker a Federal Informant!" he barks. "I'm gone hit you in about an hour so I can give you all the details."

Meanwhile

Agent Dumber and Dumbest sit in the headquarters with earphones lodged into their ears listening to Smoke's phone conversation. They look at each other with surprise. Both of their faces turn as pale as ghosts. In seconds fury turns Agent Dumber's face blood red.

"Our cover has been blown. How the fuck!" he shouts with rage. "There's a leak somewhere," he says as he peeks around the crowded office. "Get him on the line. We have no choice but to go in immediately."

Ten Minutes Later

Smoke busts through the door of Samirah's apartment while she lays back on her bed. She's on the phone engaging in ghetto gossip as she always does. She gets startled at his entrance. He rushes her like a raging bull. She attempts to roll over onto the other side of the bed in attempt to get away from him.

"Dumb ass bitch," he says as he grabs her by her hair and snatches her closer to him. A painful blow crashes into her face. "You dumb ass bitch. Your whore ass done brought the Feds to me!" he shouts. "Stupid ass bitch! Where he at?" he asks before he punches her in the face once again. "Where the fuck he at?"

"Who?" she cries. "Who?"

He pimp slaps her. "Your fag ass boyfriend, bitch! Where he at?" he asks again before he slaps her again. She screams at the top of her lungs. "The mufucker used you to get at me!" he shouts before punching her again. The blow is so painful that she can't even cry. It leaves her entire face throbbing. The impact snatches her breath away. He drags her off of the bed and flings her onto the floor. He stomps her brutally. "Where the fuck he at?"

"I don't know," she cries as she rolls into a fetal position to protect herself from the blows. "I don't know."

"Bitch, tell me everything you know!" he says as he kicks her again. "Where the fuck he live at?"

"I don't know."

"You don't know?" he asks as he kneels down and punches her in the ribs with all of his might. She screams as the impact cracks her ribs. "You fucking with a nigga and you don't even know where he live" He becomes more enraged. "You dumb ass whore," he says before he throws a series of punches which all land on top of her aching head. He beats her like a slave for a half a minute before he finally lets up.

He gets up and runs to the closet. He grabs the duffle bag of heroin and jogs out of the apartment, leaving Samirah lying on the floor rolling around in agony.

1:00 A.M.

Smoke stands in the dark backyard on his podium. His crowd of soldiers all watch on curiously to find out what the emergency meeting is about. They know it has to be something serious because the look that's displayed on his face they have never seen before. The pitiful look alarms them all. The death of his lieutenant has broken his heart.

Right now he's overwhelmed. He's never been under this much pressure in his life. There's just way too much going on at one time. Losing his man is enough but to add the Fed scare into the equation makes it all the worse.

"I know ya'll probably wondering why I called a meeting this late at night," he says with sorrow in his eyes. "First thing first, I'm sure ya'll already got the word that Qua ain't with us no more? He was murdered earlier today. So, of course ya'll know that we are at war. His murderers are some motherfuckers who go by the name of the Federation. Right now they're moving around in three black Conversion Vans. I'm ordering murder on sight on all of them," he says with demand. "That situation is a serious situation but believe it or not, we have an even bigger one on our hands. An informant has infiltrated our organization." They all look around in complete shock. They each look at the man who is standing next to them to see who the informant could possibly be. "He supposedly knows all about our movements. Our phones have been tapped so be careful what you say on the joint," he warns. "They got pictures of all of us," he adds. Fear covers all of their faces. "We have no choice but to get him out of the way. No informant, no case," he whispers. "He gotta go." Smoke lifts a stack of papers high into the air. He's made copies of the informant's mug shot. "Everybody come up here," he demands. "I got a photo of him for all of ya'll." All of the men rush to the front anxiously to find out who the informant is. They each hope that they're not the one who has been serving him. "He's moving around in a sky blue Bentley GT. Wherever you find him at, make that Bentley his casket!"

4:47 A.M

Samirah lays curled up in a fetal position as she whimpers like a baby. Her face sinks into the drenched pillow. She's been crying for hours now, ever since her brother left. She hasn't been able to sleep a wink. For the life of her she doesn't want to believe that what Smoke told her has truth to it.

She loves S-Dot dearly and feels as if he loves her equally if not more. She would hate to believe that what she thought was true love was just a scheme to get on the inside, as Smoke claims that it is. As much as she hates to believe it, the fact that he's ignoring her phone calls forces her to take it as the truth.

Samirah dials his number once again just to give him the benefit of the doubt. Her heart pounds furiously in her breast. She hopes and prays that he picks up just to prove her right and her brother wrong. Surprisingly, after the second ring something different happens. All night she's been calling and listening to his voice mail come on. This particular time an automated voice states that the number is no longer in service.

Hearing this breaks her heart into smaller pieces. The tears now pour from her swollen eyes. At this point she realizes that she's been had. Their love affair was but a mere game to him. She buries her face into the pillow, almost suffocating herself.

Meanwhile

Smoke stands in the packed elevator. He's surrounded by a total of ten FBI Agents all dressed in Swat gear and strapped with assault rifles. A uniformed agent stands to the right of him while another one stands behind him.

After the informative meeting, Smoke and his crew combed the streets for two hours in search of Maurice and his Federation as well as the informant. At 3:30 he made the order to call the search off for the night. He instructed them all to go home and rest up so they could get back on it bright and early.

Smoke wasn't in the house for twenty minutes before the door came crashing down. He had the feeling that they were on his heels but never did he imagine it happening this soon.

The elevator doors open and the agent behind Smoke forces him out, holding him by the handcuffs. The agent to his right carries one duffle bag full of Bang Man in one hand and four duffle bags full of money in the other hand. As Smoke is pushed through the doorway, his attention is caught by the huge flat bed tow truck that's parked in the middle of the parking lot. The rental car and the Camaro are already on the top level as the Aston Martin is being backed onto the bottom level.

Never before has he seen a scene like this. Yellow tape surrounds the building as suit and tie agents as well as Swat team agents stand around in huddles. He can't believe that all this is for him.

A Few Miles Away

Federal Agents ransack Manson's mother's home. They search the house from the basement on up to the attic while she sits back on the couch in fear. She cries aloud but prays to God silently. She doesn't believe that all this is happening. She hopes that it's a dream and can't wait until she awakens from it.

Many years ago her home was raided by the Sheriff's Department in search of her son but this by far is a total different experience. Those policemen were extremely polite to her unlike these guys who have been rude and impolite to her ever since they knocked on the door. She can't understand why they're treating her like a criminal. What she doesn't understand is the phone conversations between Smoke and Manson have incriminated her as well.

An agent walks into the living room area holding three large duffle bags. The woman stares at the bags which she knows to be filled with close to four hundred thousand dollars and she damn near falls into pieces. "Miss Bryant, you have three minutes to slip something on."

"Huh?" she asks, not believing her ears.

"You have to come with us."

In Newark

Federal Agents literally tear the bedroom apart as a young

man lies face down on the floor. On the top of his broken down bed there lies a total of twelve handguns, three assault rifles, ammunition and several bullet proof vests. Although this is enough evidence to finish the man off for the rest of his life, they still continue on with their search for more.

Several Miles away

Samirah dozed off twenty minutes ago after finally crying herself to sleep. Suddenly her sleep is awakened by the loud sound of the door being knocked off of the hinges. She pops up, sleepy eyed and startled. What lies before her eyes proves to her that Smoke was absolutely correct in what he said.

"Freeze!" the agent shouts as he aims his gun for her head. "Hands in the air, slowly!" he shouts as four more agents run past him. All of their guns are drawn as well. They immediately start flipping furniture over and looking through the tiny apartment.

The agent walks over to her cautiously. He grabs hold of her arms bending them behind her back. He places the handcuffs tightly around her tiny wrists. She looks back into his eyes with pity. "Samirah, you are hereby under arrest."

"Arrest?" she asks with total surprise. "For what?"

The Next Day

Smoke sits in the interrogation room listening closely to every word that Agent Dumber is saying to him. He's heard of the mind games that the Feds are known to play and he refuses to allow them to get into his head and play on his intelligence. He's heard stories of how they will flip your words around so he decides to say nothing at all. He's heard of how crafty they can be and how they have a way of making you admit to things that you haven't done. Keeping all this in mind, he's careful to listen more than he speaks.

He figures whatever they already have against him is all they will have against him. At this point he's totally clueless to what they exactly know. He doesn't think that it can be that bad because as far as he can remember, any phone conversation that he's had has never been on his monthly phone which is in his name. He's done all his talking on his minute phones in which he changed up every couple of days. He also takes pride in the fact that he never said a single word to the informant let alone engage in the business deal that he tried to bait him into. He always had a bad feeling about him and now he understands what the feeling was all about.

At the worst case scenario he feels they have nothing on him but basic, general information and hearsay. He's sure the money and dope that he was caught with will stick but for the most part he believes that he will not be finished off. His only hope is that the Mayor is not caught up in any of this. At least that way he will have a fighting chance. The Mayor always bragged to him about how money can get you out of any situation. Now is the time to see if there's any truth behind his statement.

"Smoke, Smoke, Smoke," Agent Dumber sings. "The infamous gangster Blood leader, Smoke…here in the flesh," he says with sarcasm. "It's a pleasure to finally, formally meet you," he says as he extends his hand for a handshake. "It's just too bad that we have to meet for the first time under these circumstances," he says as his hand dangles in the air. Smoke turns his head, totally ignoring the gesture for the handshake. Agent Dumber finally snatches his hand away. "I commend you. Just a few months ago you were a mere local gangbanger. Today you're a wealthy, powerful businessman. The Bang Man project was by far the best business venture that you could have ever been a part of. Unfortunately it's a gift and a curse. You've built many lives with the stamp but you've destroyed many more. "You're a famous man. Tell me how it feels," he says with a smile.

Agent Dumber continues on. "Is having fame anything like you imagined? Did you ever imagine being here?" he asks with a cheesy grin. "You've managed to flood the entire city with your product. Your business sense helped you to disregard the color barrier and network with gang rivalries. At the end of the day, red and blue makes green, right? If it makes dollars it makes sense," he says with even more sarcasm. "That was extremely smart how you put Baby Grape as the representative for that side."

Smoke swallows the small lump in his throat. Hearing key words lets him know that his problem is bigger than he thought.

"Yeah, Baby Grape and a few of his acquaintances are in line waiting to get into that very seat that you're sitting in. They're waiting to get the opportunity to help themselves out of the mess that you've dragged them into. In this very room the color barrier will reconstruct. If you think they will spare a Blood, you my friend are sadly mistaken. In fact, a few of your own men are waiting to get in here as well. Everybody has a story to tell and they will," he says. "Once they're given the opportunity. Because you're the leader, we decided to give you the first shot at it. Well, the second shot...that is. Your cousin Mel," he says with a smile. "He already told what he thought would save him but I'm quite sure there's more to tell. The sale of the six hundred bricks you made to him in McDonald's parking lot, we witnessed the entire transaction. You need proof?" he asks as he pulls the stack of photos from a binder. He lays the first photo, face up so Smoke can view it. "Smoke, we're not going to bullshit you any further. If there's any doubt about what we know, let me clear the doubt up for you. We know absolutely everything!" he shouts. "Everything from the amount of dope that you sold to everyone, to the murders that were committed. Also the exact parties involved in every murder. From the seven young men who were murdered behind the Mother Nature beef to the murder that *you* committed on the night of your birthday party at the Key Club," he says as he shoves a photo in Smoke's face. The photo shows Smoke standing in front of the man with the gun in his hand. He slaps another photo onto the table. This photo shows Smoke standing over the man, aiming his gun at him. He slams another photo onto the table, in which Smoke is getting into his car with the murder weapon still in his hand.

Smoke's heart skips a beat. He now realizes that they really do know everything. Although he really doesn't want to hear it, his curiosity makes him want to know what else they know.

"Smoke, this is the bottom line. This is the biggest drug ring in the history of Newark. Right now, we have a total of twelve Crips and over sixty Bloods in custody. And the investigation isn't even over," he claims. "That's seventy-something people that we have in custody. Early this morning we rounded up close to eighty people. That's just your Newark connections. That doesn't even include your Paterson and your Trenton connections. We have all of them in custody as well. As I said before, we have your cousin. We also have your baby sister and your aunt."

Smoke's face finally shows a sign of emotion. In no way was he expecting to hear that his sister and aunt have been dragged into this.

"Yeah, lil sis and auntie," he says, nodding his head up and down. "You've dragged them into this mess as well. Your innocent little sister. All she's guilty of is holding millions of dollars worth of *your* dope in *her* home. How innocent is she, really? It's all your fault though because as your younger sister, you know she idolizes her big brother. She worships the ground that you walk on. She would never tell you no, no matter how wrong she knows it is. It's a pure shame that something as simple as doing a favor for her big brother can possibly land her fifteen to twenty years in Federal Prison.

The guilt trip that they're taking Smoke on is working. For the first time ever he realizes how stupid and selfish it was to get her involved in this.

"Now Auntie Betty...a good clean religious woman," he says with a sad look on his face. "She's always lived her life the *right way*. She has always been against the lifestyle that you and her son, the Black Charles Manson, lived. I'm sure that she's prayed for you and prayed for you. When we got there and took her into custody she prayed the entire ride to the headquarters. I'm sure that she's still praying," he says with sarcasm. "Now here she is all in the middle of this mess. The only thing that she's guilty of, is accepting over three hundred thousand dollars worth of drug money. I guess that would make her a drug dealer in a sense, huh?" he asks. She's sixty three years old now. Fifteen years of prison and she will come home at about seventy eight. Maybe all her Bible studying will pay off. Maybe she will become a preacher or a jail house Evangelist? That's how I see it. There's really no way out for her. Even God can't save her from this. That's right, not even God can save her but you can."

Smoke's heart sinks into his belly. Hearing all of this breaks his heart. All of his life he frowned upon dudes who have snitched. He can't believe that for the first time ever, he's actually considering it. He wonders how he will be looked at if he snitches under these circumstances. He wonders if it will still be considered snitching if he does it to free his sister and his aunt. He's quite sure that Manson would want him to do it for the sake of his mother. He's afraid that if he doesn't Manson will have him killed.

"Smoke, I'm gonna be totally honest with you. This beef has nothing to do with you. You just got yourself in the way of it. This beef is between us and our man, the Mayor. It's no longer business. It's personal. It started almost fifteen years ago when you were a small child not even thinking of gangbanging or drug dealing. The Mayor was well aware of this beef but still he dragged you into it. He didn't even warn you, for crying out loud. How selfish of him is that? He cared nothing about you or your well being. He only cared about himself which is why he filtered everything through you and kept his hands clean. He's a very intelligent man, I must admit. He's so intelligent that we have absolutely nothing on him. At the present time, he is about to walk away into the sunset while you, your homies, your sister and your Aunt Betty will spend the rest of your lives in prison. We have nothing on him but everything on you all. That is unless you're willing to give us a helping hand. Again, I will not bullshit you," he claims.

A pitiful look plasters the agent's face. "This beef is so personal that I'm willing to free your sister and your aunt as well as discard of all of the photos I have. I will also destroy the majority of the wire tapped conversations that I have. Of course, some of them have to be turned in. I'm not going to lie to you. I can't erase everything but I can make sure that the murder charges are wiped out and the drug charges are downgraded from Federal to State charges. I'm a man of my word," he says with sincerity in his eyes. "I will not play tug of war with you. You have one chance to fix this situation and one chance only. Giving up one man can save two innocent women, a few opposing gangbangers who if you don't save them, they will tell everything they know about you. You can prevent close to seventy of your Blood homies from going to jail forever. One thing that I know for sure is that Blood rules over **everything** to you. That's the oath that you took right? I'm sure you won't let your Blood brothers destruct because of a man who isn't even Blood. He's nothing but a selfish, *five-fifty*, who doesn't give two fucks about you or your Blood homies," he says with rage.

"It's all up to you. The ball is in your court. You have a decision to make and ten seconds to make it. Starting now," he says. "One Mississippi, two Mississippi, three Mississippi, four Mississippi, five Mississippi," he counts. "Five seconds left and not one more after that. Six Mississippi, seven Mississippi. "What are you going to do, **Blood**?"

The Next Day/October 3, 2009

Smoke cruises up Park Avenue. His mind races a mile a minute. Never before has he felt this much pressure. It was all good just a few days ago, now this. This is a part of the game that he never thought he would ever play out.

He looks up ahead where he sees the Mayor's Rolls Royce parked. He shakes his head with disgust as he thinks of what is about to take place. He's in a tough situation. His back is against the wall. He has a tremendous amount of love and respect for the Mayor and he hates to go through with this but his hands have been forced. There's too much at stake for him not to go through with it. If it was only gangbangers and criminals involved he wouldn't even consider this but the fact that his aunt and his sister are involved makes it an entirely different situation.

He's thought over and over about the proposition he was offered. He hoped for an alternative but there was none given. This is the only way that he can free them.

Smoke parks behind the Mayor's car. As he snatches the keys from the ignition, the Mayor walks out of 'Rock tha Boat.' Smoke takes a deep breath at the sight of the Mayor. He exhales. "Here goes nothing," he says as he forces the door open slowly.

He quickly erases the pitiful look off of his face and replaces it with a phony grin. The Mayor sits back on the hood of his car as he stuffs his mouth with his fish sandwich. Smoke walks over to him with his heart pounding through his chest. "What's good, lil bruh?" the Mayor mumbles with a mouthful of food.

"Shit," Smoke replies as he peeks around sneakily.

In Union New Jersey

Tony paces back and forth around his office while anxiousness rips through his gut. He holds his phone close to his ear as the Mayor's phone rings over and over again. This is his fourth time calling and getting no answer. He ends the call and quickly presses redial. He looks over to Federal Agent Tina who sits on the edge of the couch.

Just twenty five minutes ago she got the word that Smoke had been released to reel the Mayor in. It was then that she raced here to warn Tony. She cares nothing about the Mayor but she knows how much love Tony has for him. She wouldn't be able to live with herself if she lets this happen without at least letting him know. She could never put her loyalty for him on the line like that.

"This motherfucker won't even answer the phone!" he shouts before ending the call and dialing once again. "What the fuck is he doing that he can't answer the fucking phone for me?"

"Shit crazy," Smoke admits as the Mayor keeps his eyes glued onto his food. The constant ringing of the Mayor's phone draws the Mayor's eyes onto the passenger's seat where the phone is. He slides across the hood and leans in the open window. Just as he grabs hold of the phone, he peeks back over his shoulder. To his surprise he's staring into the dark barrel of Smoke's .40 caliber. The pitch black hole is suddenly brightened up by a bright red glare. Boc! The Mayor raises his forearm into the air, attempting to use it as a shield. He slides to his left to get out of the way. The hot ball of fire melts into his forehead. His head flings backwards due to the impact. The Mayor takes a clumsy step away from the car before another gunshot sounds off. Boc! The slug rips into the back of his skull, forcing him to tumble forward. He falls in between the car and the curb.

Mike Mittens hears the gunshots from inside of the restaurant. His heart thumps with fear. All he can envision is the Mayor being shot down. He runs to the doorway, snatching his gun from his waist along the way. When he gets to the door, he sees what he hoped not to see. There Smoke stands over the Mayor.

Mike aims his gun at Smoke who coincidentally sees him through his peripheral. His quick reflex causes him to spin around, facing Mike. He aims at his head and fires three shots. Boc! Boc! Boc! Mike fires two shots back at him. Boom! Boom! A slug crashes into Mike's face and another rips into his chest. He stumbles backwards three steps. His gun releases and bullets spray into the air randomly. Boom! Boom! Boom! Mike falls onto his back where he lies with no motion.

Smoke looks back onto the Mayor who is staring into his eyes. Blood covers his entire face. He appears to be dead because he's not moving but the glow in his eyes tells Smoke that he's very much alive. Smoke stands there heartbroken. He can't even look the

Mayor in the eyes. He quickly looks away and immediately starts to finish the job that he came here to do. Boc! Boc! Boc! The Mayor squirms and wiggles like a worm as he stares straight into the sky. Blood gushes from his mouth violently. Suddenly his squirming stops.

Two Blocks Away

Agents Dumber and Dumbest sit back in the black Suburban behind the dark tinted windows. They watch with appreciation as their plan unfolds. They watch as Smoke hops into his car and speeds off. With no evidence against the Mayor, they feared he would get away from them once again. They refused to let all their hard work be in vain. Now with the Mayor out of the picture, all their long hours of investigation seems worth every minute of it.

Agent Dumber watches the Mayor through his binoculars. Satisfaction fills his heart when he realizes that the Mayor is no longer moving.

Fifteen Minutes Later

Yellow tape surrounds the crime scene. Homicide cops as well as uniformed cops swarm the block from corner to corner. Spectators watch with nosiness. Mike Mittens lies dead in the doorway of the restaurant, with his gun still in his hand. Three detectives stand over him, watching with no compassion at all.

Miles Away

The Ambulance races through the emergency entrance of UMDNJ's hospital. The driver pulls up to the door, where a doctor and two nurses await them. The driver rushes out of the driver's seat and runs to the back of the vehicle. He snatches the door open. Inside of the Ambulance the paramedic is doing her best to keep the Mayor alive. She's already lost him twice but miraculously managed to bring him back to life.

Together they snatch the stretcher from the truck and push him hurriedly to the entrance. The Mayor lies on the stretcher as stiff as a board. He's drenched in blood from head to toe. His eyes are still wide open, staring into the sky. The doctor leads the way through the emergency room. He runs side by side his nurses as the paramedics push the stretcher behind them.

The Mayor's eyes close slowly. He fights to keep them open but they're getting heavier and heavier. "Come on," the paramedic pleads. "Not now. We've come too far. Come on, baby. We're here. Don't die on me, please?" she begs. "Please?"

Finally they get him into the room, where the doctor immediately starts to go to work on him. The paramedics exit the room immediately. The doctor hooks the Mayor up to the first machine and the Mayor's eyes light up with a burst of life. Still he needs more juice just to stay alive. As the doctor prepares to hook him up to the next one he hears footsteps coming into the room. He peeks over his shoulder where he sees Agent Dumber and Dumbest. Agent Dumber closes the door behind them and locks it.

The Mayor lies on the stretcher struggling to stay alive. He fights to take every breath that he takes. Although his eyes are open, he doesn't see anything. It's completely dark to him. The voices and the sound of the machine can be heard faintly.

Agent Dumber flashes his badge. "FBI," he whispers. "Step away from him," he says with a threatening demeanor.

"Huh?" the doctor asks with a confused look on his face. The nurses stand there clueless.

Agent Dumber gives the doctor a head nod, signaling him to back away. "I said back up."

The agents stand over the Mayor with great appreciation. Their mission has been accomplished. The Mayor stares upward in a trance for seconds before his left eye closes. The loud beeping of the machine sounds off, alerting them that they're losing him. The doctor and the nurses watch with sympathy. They want to save him but they fear what will happen if they do so. The machine sounds off louder and louder until the Mayor's right eye finally closes. The lines on the screen level out. Beep! Beep! Beep! Flatline.

Smiles pop onto both of the agents' faces as they watch the Mayor lie there with a peaceful look on his face. Agent Dumber walks over to the doctor who stands there with a long saddened face.

"Uh, doctor?" he asks. "What's your name?"

"Doctor Desota," he whispers with pity.

"Doctor Desota, you did all you can do. You couldn't save him. You understand?" he asks while staring coldly into the man's eyes. "We've never had this conversation," he says as he looks at the nurses. "In fact, we were never here," he says with massive threat in his eyes. "Remember, ya'll did everything ya'll could do," he says as he turns around and exits the room. Agent Dumbest follows closely behind him.

The doctor and the nurses exit shortly after. They leave the Mayor's stiffened body all alone on the stretcher to rest in peace.

At this very moment not only has the Mayor died but the game has died as well.

R.I.P The Mayor 1978- 2009

ACKNOWLEDGEMENTS

First and foremost I thank God for bestowing his mercy and blessings upon me and granting me the endurance to fight this journey. We all know that the closer you attempt to get to your Lord, the harder the shaytan fights against you. I'm sure that a lot of ya'll view my so called success in the book game and think that it's all good. Believe me it has been good but for every joint that I have dropped I have a story to tell of the different circumstances and conditions that I have been under while actually writing that particular joint. My enemies have been up against me throughout this entire journey but thanks to God, my immediate family, and you, my True 2 Life family I've managed to weather every storm and still be here.

Thanks to all of ya'll, a local street kid who rarely left his block in Newark has been able to represent his city, from state to state and even some Islands. The game is the same in every city, just different lingo. Through my joints I hoped for the reader to get a glimpse of how things are done here. Hopefully, I've done that.

Secondly, I have to thank my corner men (my loved ones.) They say you're only as strong as the people in your corner. A few times throughout this journey, I've been knocked down on the canvas to one knee. The referee even gave me a few standing eight counts but I always knew if I could just make it back to my corner I would be alright. Ya'll would patch up my wounds, grease my face up and say just the right words to recharge my battery, to go back out and fight my fight. Without ya'll, I might have given up a few times.

Thanks to my True 2 Life reader base. Without ya'll, there would be no me. I thank each and everyone of you for your consistent support. Special thanks to my niggaz behind that wall. No bullsh**, I do this for ya'll. From page one until the end, I got ya'll in mind. I been through the trenches which makes me understand how blessed I am to be on this side of the game. I honor the support that ya'll have shown me. I feel like ya'll elected me as the ghetto spokesperson. I've been saying what real niggaz have been wanting to say but have not had the platform to say it, or they've been forced to remain quiet in their graves. Each word that I write or syllable that I speak is on behalf of real niggaz that have lost their voices, by losing their lives or their freedom behind this dirty wicked game that I write about. I vow to keep it True 2 Life or I will never utter another word as long as I live. Some of you have short bids and others are never coming home. Through my books, I hope to ease your minds for a few hours and take you out of that lonely cell, making you temporarily forget the circumstances that you may be under. Just know, for whatever it's worth, I represent Us!

You don't know what the letters you send to me actually mean to me. It's been times that I was ready to give it all up and then I get a letter from one of ya'll that makes me go back into the lab. For eight years ya'll have been holding me down and giving me the inspiration to keep it moving, now let me give ya'll something back; this book symbolizes the death of the game. It's over! There's no more loyalty, no more honor. No one is to be trusted. The game is now filled with a bunch of tattle tale stool pigeons all trying to be the first to tell on the other stool pigeon. We all cheered for the Mayor because he represented the essence of the game. He represented the real niggaz from all over the world. He's one of the last of a dying breed. Before you step back into the world, be mindful of what you're up against; a bunch of sucker, tattle tale, studio gangsters. It's more of them than it is Us, so it's impossible for you to win. Be clear. Duck the ducks and stay sucker free. Shot out to Lil Bruh Reek (Baghdad.) One love my nigga. Stay up! Stay focused and keep the pen blazing. Before you know it, all this will be just a memory. Always remember, we never lose. We learn! As Salaamu Alaikum!

To my Lil Mama, I thank Allah much for you. You give me the inspiration to stay on my legal path. The thought of leaving you for a period of time gives me the chills. That's all the ammunition I need to stay away from those streets. God forbid if everything was taken away from me today, I still wouldn't go back to that lifestyle. I would rather live in a cardboard box just as long as I could crawl out of that box everyday at 2:45 in time to pick you up from school and see the smile on your face. Fajr, As Salaamu Alaikum! O Allah I beg you to bestow your mercy and blessings upon her. I beg you to guide her to the right way. I beg you to raise her to be a devout and obedient servant to you. O Allah please protect her. Any trials and tribulations that you have in store for her, drop them on me and let me bear the burden, Ameen!

In closing, I say in the words of my nigga, Big Has, R.I.P. "True 2 Fucking Life!" Nigga you stayed repping that logo, even harder than me. Everywhere we went, you screaming out, True 2 Fucking Life! I remember that True 2 Life t-shirt I gave you. You wore that joint everyday for a whole year, no bullsh**. In the winter you wore that joint like a coat, over your coat. Lol The neck was stretched out and holes were everywhere. Big Nigga every time I slid through the block, you had yo big ass sitting on that tiny ass crate. You would scream out "Yo Al, you made it! Don't leave me!" I would always bark back, "I didn't make it yet but when I do I'm coming back to get you! I swear to God I ain't gone leave you!" Wallahi on my life, lil bruh and I always talked about that. We discussed how as soon as we popped off, we were coming back to get you. It's fucked up that you left here before we could really make it. One thing for certain though, when we do make it, We gonna burn it down for your birthday every year. May Allah forgive us? Big nigga, I love you! You were born True 2 Life and you died True 2 Life, so forever you will remain, True 2 Fucking Life!

Jailhouse Muslim

I was born on the Fitrah: Muslim raised hoodlum. Shaytan shook em but his
faith was never tooken.
Because of his disobedience he faces booking. Am I a *Jailhouse Muslim*?
Inside, his faith increases. Outside it decreases. No Taqwa although Allah is
forever looking.
Too many stains hardens his culb(heart); haram women, money, drinks, drugs,
(wow)!! The muslims cooking!
A seal is placed on his faculties, so consistently on his soul he puts a whooping.
Direct or indirect he understands not, who's a *Jailhouse Muslim*? What is a
Jailhouse Muslim?
Do you know or wanna know?
One whom when faced with adversity cries and begs for Allah's mercy.
Incarceration really hurts me, because I forgot the one who truly birth me.
He whom favored me and guided me to his perfect deen. Yeah he commands
only five principles, not to live it extreme.
An incarcerated Muslim I am but my mind is never barred.
So I use my tool, turn jail into Islamic school; study long and study hard.
Those whom when blessed with Allah's grace, the Masjid never sees their face.
Never dhikr until it's too late. Ran until they crashed and caught another case
Loss the race. Knew better, had elm but what a waste.
Neglected the Sunnah. Neglected the Fard. Enjoin the Haram but won't eat
the lard.
Hard on the deen when back behind bars. A *Jailhouse Muslim*, I'm guilty as
charged.
Away from the sirat-tal-mustaqeen is where ingratitude took him.
That's my definition of a *Jailhouse Muslim*? Are we *Jailhouse Muslims*? Are
we *Jailhouse Muslims*?

Note

Answer: We are not jailhouse Muslims. Allah says in his Kitab, he named us
Muslim. With no title in front of it. We are fasiqun: Rebellious and disobedient
to Allah. We are Mujrimun; sinners and criminals. Because of our actions,
speech and deeds we give people ammunition to put a title in front of the word
Muslim.

Remember the best Dawah is Character!!!!

by *Abdul Shahid*
3/6/08

True 2 Life Publications
ORDER FORM

P.O. BOX 8722
Newark, N.J. 07108

www.True2LifeProductions.com

Also by the Author:

No Exit
ISBN # 0-974-0610-0-X	$13.95
Sales Tax (6% NJ)	.83
Total	$18.63

Caught 'Em Slippin'
ISBN # 0-974-0610-3-4	$14.95
Sales Tax (6% NJ)	.89
Total	$19.69

Block Party
ISBN # 0-974-0610-1-8	$14.95
Sales Tax (6% NJ)	.89
Total	$19.69

Block Party 2: The Afterparty
ISBN # 0-974-0610-4-2	$14.95
Sales Tax (6% NJ)	.89
Total	$19.69

Sincerely Yours
ISBN # 0-974-0610-2-6	$13.95
Sales Tax (6% NJ)	.83
Total	$18.63

Block Party 3: Brick City Massacre
ISBN: 0-974-0610-5-0	$14.95
Sales Tax (6% NJ)	.89
Total	$19.69

Strapped
ISBN: 0-974-0610-5-8	$14.95
Sales Tax (6% NJ)	.89
Total	$19.69

Back 2 Bizness:
The Return of the Mayor
ISBN: 0-974-0610-5-8	$14.95
Sales Tax (6% NJ)	.89
Total	$19.69

Shipping/ Handling for 1-3 books
Via U.S. Priority Mail $ 3.85

Each additional book is $1.00

Buy 6 or More Books and Shipping is Free.

True 2 Life Publications

ORDER FORM

P.O. BOX 8722
Newark, N.J. 07108

www.True2LifeProductions.com

PURCHASER INFORMATION:

Name: _____

Address: _____

City: _____

State: _____

Zip Code: _____

QUANTITY:

_____ ❏ No Exit:

_____ ❏ Block Party:

_____ ❏ Sincerely Yours:

_____ ❏ Caught 'Em Slippin':

_____ ❏ Block Party 2 - The Afterparty:

_____ ❏ Block Party 3 - Brick City Massacre:

_____ ❏ Strapped

❏ Back 2 Bizness: Return of the Mayor

. . . .

_____ **TOTAL BOOKS ORDERED**

Please make check or money order payable to:
True 2 Life Publications